THE SEVEN DEADLY KINS SERIES

Presents:

BOOK 1 – The Top Dog

Part 1

Written by Tiana Laveen

Edited by Natalie Guillaumier
Cover Layout and design by Travis Pennington

A Romantic Suspense Series

THE SEVEN DEADLY KINS SERIES

Blood and Rhinestone Cowboy Productions Presents:

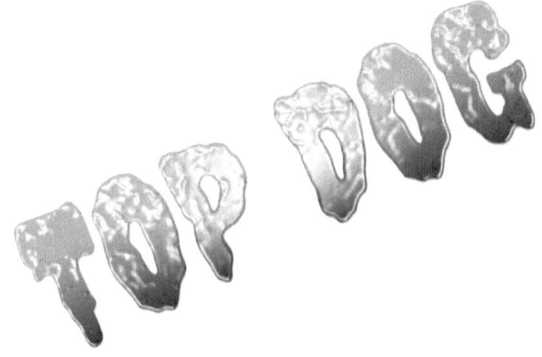

In the heart of Texas, the Wilde family dynasty conceals a dark secret society. Ruled by money, debauchery, and the iron fist of their patriarch, seven rebellious grandsons refuse to bow to their powerful grandfather's will, bringing dishonor upon the family name. As each cousin grapples with their own demons and desires, their journey of defiance leads them on a path of revenge, self-discovery, and unexpected love. From the shadows of power to the depths of passion, join the Seven Deadly Kins as they challenge tradition and forge their own destinies.

This is Top Dog's story.

Beware. You've entered the kennel...

BLURB

His bite is as deadly as his bark...

BOOK 1 and PART 1 of the 7 Deadly Kins Series:

Lennox Wilde is protective, loyal, and everyone's friend. Or so it appears... Lennox is known in different circles, to be ruthless when threatened, and revenge-seeking when crossed. By day, he's a personal trainer; by night, a bouncer at a dance club. Despite his wealthy background, he's rejected his family's fortune to prove his independence and be his own man.

Nadia 'Velvet' Deere, an exceptionally bright and talented exotic dancer, has aspirations of completing her law degree. Her goals are thwarted by a potentially deadly admirer, resentment, hurt, and unwavering ghosts from her past.

A chance encounter with Lennox, an old friend, rekindles a deep connection. But Nadia, afraid to fully open herself up to conceivable disappointment, resists his advances. Lennox is not one to take no for an answer, and the two journey on an adventure of discovery and love. However, their voyage takes a fatal turn. As their world's collide, things become dangerously unstable and treacherous.

From USA Today bestselling author Tiana Laveen, comes Book one of the 7 Deadly Kins series. Come along for a dark love story packed with suspense, revenge and passion. 'The Top Dog – Lust' is an exciting friends to lovers, second chance, destined for love, possessive alpha hero, bad boy, Southern contemporary romance. It's the first installment in the series, but can be read as a standalone novel. It has no cliffhanger, and has a HEA (Happily-ever-after). This book includes mature themes and content that may not be suitable for all audiences; reader discretion is advised. Please look inside under the 'Trigger Warnings' for possible topics that may be deemed personally objectionable.

It's a dog-eat-dog world, and I'm never full.
I love the hunt as much as the kill.
This is my nature. Survival runs in the family.
We were born to be Wilde...

COPYRIGHT

ISBN: (eBook) BOOK 1/Part 1: 978-1-962451-02-4
ISBN: (paperback) BOOK 1/Part 1: 978-1-962451-04-8

TRIGGER WARNINGS

Please do not skip this section if you have any specific triggers.

If it doesn't apply, let it fly. What may not be offensive or upsetting to you or me may be so for someone else. This warning is simply to ensure the comfort of <u>all</u> readers. Thank you for your understanding.

This book is intended for mature readers only.

This novel includes:

1. *Profuse profanity.*
2. *Discussions about domestic violence.*
3. *Heavy alcohol consumption.*
4. *Graphic sexual discussions between characters, and graphic sexual activity.*
5. *Explicit descriptions of violent crimes and murder.*

Oh, one more thing: For those unfamiliar with my work, I purposefully write 'goddamn' as 'gotdamn.' It's an intentional spelling error—just personal preference.

Let's continue…

<u>Please note:</u> This book contains a guest appearance from a Tiana Laveen fan favorite. He is the hero from the 'Saint Series', Dr. Saint Aknaten. If you are unfamiliar with the 'Saint Series' and this particular character, then prepare to be shocked! Dr. Saint Aknaten's character portrays that of a licensed clinical psychotherapist, sex therapist, and psychologist who specializes in human sexuality, family counseling, and romantic relationships. He is also a psychic and empathic healer, but doesn't advertise that. He uses unorthodox methods to assist his clients. This can include crude, profane language, sexually charged statements, and unconventional therapeutic practices.

Dedication

This book is dedicated to a beautiful woman named Natalie Guillaumier. She is my editor, and my friend. Her strength, intelligence, love for humanity, and humor are her armor. We've been through a lot together, things that go beyond grammatical errors, plot holes and misspelled words. One thing is for certain, she's an exceptional and good person, through and through. Natalie, I wish you nothing less than the vibrant moon in all of its phases, and all of the stars that have ever been born and sparkle bright each and every night. May all of your hopes and dreams come true from this day forward, and always remember that no matter what, in darkness and in light, in my eyes, you're ALWAYS more than enough.

TABLE OF CONTENTS

PROLOGUE

WELCOME, FOLKS. MY name is Anderson Wilde, and I'm seventeen years old. Today, I'm at my grandfather's house. I figured I'd take you on a tour and explain what you're gonna see today. It's amazing, isn't it? huge, too. Like a big museum. This isn't his only house though. My grandfather owns a lot of houses. A lot of land. A lot of buildings. A lot of businesses. And a lot of people…

He's a bit of a collector of people, too. Hell, he's been married five times. They say his second wife, I think she was common-law, was Ms. Tina, was the love of his life. According to my mom, she was the one that got away, but I have a hard time imagining that Grandpa really ever loved *any* woman in that sort of way. I mean, yeah, I'm just a kid my parents say, but I'm not stupid. I might even be wrong. I don't know just yet. Rumor has it, she just up and disappeared. Some believe she's dead. Others said she's hiding. Hiding from who? I think you know…

Anyway, I come from a large family. Larger than most, I imagine. Grandpa had a bunch of kids. He's got nine living sons and three daughters from those five marriages of his. Oh, and one son from an affair that nobody talks much about. Another son of his is adopted: his third wife's child from a previous marriage, my Uncle Danny. He has more grandchildren and great grandchildren than I can count—including me, of course.

I have so many cousins spread all over the state of Texas, and only get to see all of them under one roof on Thanksgivin' and Christmas. The holidays are always nice around here. That's when we all get together and have a great time. Aunts talk about how big so and so is getting, who's pregnant, who got promoted, and who looks just like their daddy. That seems to be a common theme. Kinda silly if you ask me, but, to be honest, some of us do favor. People say me and my dad have my grandfather's eyes, for instance. A lot of us do, I imagine. That's funny considering all of Grandpa's different wives. He must have strong genes. You may be wondering now what Grandpa looks like since I brought it up? Whatever you think he looks like, you're more than likely wrong.

My grandpa looks like a fit, tanned Santa Claus. It sounds funny, don't it? But it's true. Head full of silky white and silver hair that goes down his back, a matching mustache and beard. He's a handsome old man, for sure, and pulls women half his age with no issue. I've seen 'em sneaking in at night, and leavin' bright and early in the morning. He's strong, even in his seventies. He's seventy-three to be exact, but doesn't look a day over sixty. Takes good care of himself.

He wields a gold cane, one of many in his collection, but doesn't need it. I think he just likes how it looks. Style and fashion. He wears two signature bulky diamond rings, one of them a gold bull with diamonds for eyes. A long-horn, like his nickname. Grandpa says he's an animal, and all the best men in his family are animals. Animals belong in the zoo. I'm not really sure what that means. Anyway, he wears dark tailored business suits and hand sewn silk ties. Grandpa always says a man should look sharp from the time he steps out of his bedroom to the moment his head hits the pillow, even if that pillow is in a casket. He has an entire room full of nothin' but high-priced cowboy boots and big, beautiful cowboy hats. Yeah, he's rich as all outdoors, but he shares.

He gives many toys away on Christmas Eve to needy families. Turkeys with all the fixin's. Oodles of expensive dolls to the girls, puzzles for the brainy kids, the latest electronics like iPads, cellphones, you name it. He even gives away brand new cars.

His house turns into a winter wonderland covered in millions of lights that twinkle to the beat of cheerful Christmas songs. On Christmas day, the downstairs rooms are filled with hot homemade pies, soft cakes and buttery cookies from top notch Texan bakers that cater his shindigs. There's always warm cozy fires lit, roaring in almost every room of his big mansion on fourteen acres of private land. The Christmas trees inside the house, all with different themes, have a crapload of presents beneath them, all for his smaller great-grandchildren. Dad says Grandpa picks out all the presents himself. Despite all of this, please don't misunderstand. He's not jolly, and he ain't Santa by a long shot.

He's one of the most feared men in all of Houston. Hell, all of Texas. Possibly the entire country.

My grandfather, Cyrus 'Longhorn' Wilde, is the head of the Wilde Empire. Some call it the Wilde, Wilde West. Some call him, 'Bull in the China Shop.' That's because he walks into a place, strikes fear, and destroys men's egos and pride within seconds, if he sees fit.

When you work for Mr. Longhorn, The Bull, he expects complete devotion.

He doesn't care if you are blood, or a stranger on the street—if you cross him, you will pay, but not with money. No, he wants to eat your heart and soul.

When you're born into the Wilde family, you are expected to answer your calling, fulfill your destiny. That means helping run the family business. Grandpa is generous with both pleasure and pain. Some try to toe the line. As soon as he feels like we'd make a good addition to the family business, we're under contract.

Everyone's contract is different, and rarely is it available for negotiation. Grandpa revises it as we age and mature. Mine is probably being revised as we speak. Like I said, I'm only seventeen—too young to have seen it just yet.

Speaking of contracts, right now all hell is about to break loose. I'm watching some of my older male cousins arriving at Grandpa's compound in big black trucks. I imagine it's to review their agreements. Matter of fact, I'm pretty certain of it. These particular cousins have been, I guess you could say, problems…

They've been resistant. Causing difficulties. They're rebellious and have suffered for it, but it appears that Grandpa has called a meeting, and wants them to come to some sort of agreement. I only know this because I listen in on discussions that I'm not supposed to, and have done so for years. I know what closets and rooms have the best acoustics for hearing conversations throughout the house, if you figure out just where to stand. I know what rooms have landline phones that are bugged, and which have hidden cameras. I am also familiar with my grandfather's routine, and I'm aware he will change it on a dime, anytime he sees fit. Since I was a little child, people have whispered about my grandfather. Some see him as an angel. Others, well, the opposite.

I've heard people curse his name, then never see that person again. I have pressed my ear close to vents in this enormous palace and overheard crying, screaming, and pleas for mercy. I have been held in his arms as a baby, felt him kiss me on my forehead, then he'd tuck in my bed, only to hear screams of agony from another chamber in his house moments later, followed by his calm, muffled voice. As if nothing had happened. Now, if you look out this window over here, you can see my uncles stepping out of the black trucks. Seven of them.

Yeah, that's them. Now, the guy with the gun is Jasper. He's one of my grandfather's bodyguards…The head bodyguard, actually, and friend of the family. Yeah, he's pattin' them down before they come inside. That's routine for anyone who comes in. Oh, you don't have to be afraid.

Just stay out of everyone's way. Everything is set up and ready to go. The half-naked maids have already poured alcoholic potions in fancy white and black wine glasses for a luncheon Grandpa is having after this meeting. They also laid out impressive appetizers that Grandpa's personal chef made, and provided expensive, gold-wrapped cigars on a silver tray. I doubt the food is for my cousins. Maybe the cigars. Grandpa asked Alexa to turn on some Crystal Gayle's, 'Don't It Make My Brown Eyes Blue.' I heard him do it, and it's been playing on repeat for over an hour. One of his favorite songs.

Grandpa is waiting in his study right now. I saw him go in there earlier. As I stand here with you hiding behind a column with a bag of Cheetos and a thumping heart, I know he's full of fury. Waiting for his prey. His office has two big ivory pillars outside of it, like somethin' you'd see at a gallery in Washington D.C. There's a big stone lion, a bear, and a bull statue by the tall double gold and white doors. You can't see them from here, so I'm just filling you in is all. You can feel Grandpa's presence without even looking into his cold blue eyes.

You may wonder why I'm slipping and sliding around, risking being caught instead of outside in the pool swimming, playing on the home basketball court, in the game room with every video game and gaming system a kid could want, or working out in Grandpa's big gym? Hell, you may wonder why I'm here at all.

Well, he told my parents he wanted me to stay with him for the summer. In fact, Grandpa has sent for me many times during my life. He's taken an interest in me since I was a baby. Nobody told me exactly why, and when I asked, I was given a bullshit, absurd answer that I barely remember. Regardless, though he'll never admit it, he sometimes gets lonely and wants a hunting partner. I'm a pretty good shooter, if I say so myself.

Here's my theory on why I'm here: Grandpa only trusts family to run the business and be around him on a consistent basis, so here I am. I'm sure there's more to it than that, but this explains at least a part of it. He always asks me about my grades in the private school I'll be graduating from next year, and wants to know all about my football practices. He sends me presents every month, and calls me on the phone just to see how I'm doing. Sounds nice, right?

Sounds like a great old man... the perfect grandpa. I'm young, but I know I'm not here because he loves me. There I go again with that love stuff. I mean, he *might* love me, but that's not the biggest motivation, ya know? Grandpa has to run the chess board. He is a big observer. A people watcher. He's persistent, too. Just when you think he's forgotten something... Boom. He'll get his revenge. I think I'm sort of like that, too. I'm perceptive. Patient. He wants to see how my mind works before he hires me on. Maybe for a very special job? He wants to see what alterations need to be made to my contract when the time comes, and what better way to find out then to have your grandson spend time with you?

My mother, while drunk one night and probably high on too many of her damn anxiety pills, said that Grandpa thinks he's God. Daddy disagreed. He said,

"No, he doesn't think he's God, honey. He thinks he's the devil, and he's right. That's why he'll never die. Evil lives forever…"

CHAPTER ONE

In the Dog House

TOP DOG – *top dog /ˌtäp ˈdôg,ˌtäp ˈdäg/ noun IN-FORMAL a person who is successful or dominant in their field.*

"PLEASE, ALL OF you enter in single file," Jasper ordered. Dressed in camouflage with two handguns hanging off his holster belt, the tall, middle-aged man who worked for his grandfather tossed his weight around.

Lennox stood at the front of the line, his arms crossed over his chest as Grandpa's lap dog patted him down once again. He grunted when the man got close to his groin, fighting the urge to slam his fist into the asshole's jaw.

"Look, Lennox." The beady-eyed bastard glared up at him. "I don't like this anymore than you, boy, but you know how your grandfather feels about weapons in his chambers. You fellows can be slick."

He refrained from responding out loud. *Maybe if dear ol' Grandad wasn't such a piece of shit, he wouldn't have to worry about us trying to take him out.*

After Jasper had gone down the line and frisked them all, seemingly good and satisfied, Lennox and his cousins marched into the old man's study that smelled of the familiarity he'd grown used to: pungent cigar smoke and Moroccan amber. The room was bright and open with its wall-to-wall rows of windows and shades of cream and white, while the old man sitting in the lofty ivory-colored chair embellished with silver studs appeared dark and looming.

Grandpa sat there knuckling the brass lion claws of his chair arms, his face faintly directed towards his desk. Smoke eddied from his lips. A snow-white cowboy hat graced the top of his head, and a thick, wavy silver lock of hair drooped over one of his icy blue eyes. The old man slowly looked up, meeting his gaze with a crooked grin. He pointed to the seven white chairs all lined up in front of his long gold and ivory desk.

"Have a seat, boys."

Each of them got situated, sitting down in the same order that they'd entered the room. He shot a glance at the huge tank behind the old man, which housed a large black and yellow serpent. A rear-fanged Mangrove. Off to the right was a wall of rifles, mostly AR-15s. Lennox shifted his weight in his chair as silence became a close companion. Not a mutter or whisper swept the room. The quiet was broken when one of the double doors opened, followed by the clicking of high heels.

Grandpa had one of the maids he was undoubtedly fucking pass out cigars to him and his cousins. After all, Grandpa was a horny old bastard. In fact, Grandpa fucked anything that was female, pretty, and worked for him in some capacity. That's all that was required. It simply came with the territory.

Lennox didn't recognize this maid, though. She must've been new on the block. The thirtyish-year-old looking woman with long straight blond hair, dressed in a short, traditional maid's uniform stood in front of them, bending down as she offered them fancy cigars on a silver tray and certainly showing her bare ass to Grandpa in the process.

Lennox caught sight of his reflection in the shiny surface of the tray and was filled with disgust.

I shouldn't even be here.

But he had no choice. Grandpa had sent several of his henchmen to retrieve him against his wishes. It was a complete ambush, a well thought out plan to surprise him as he was leaving his home. Supposedly, the visit would be worth their while. He somehow doubted that, but his curiosity was piqued all the same.

After everyone had taken a cigar off the platter, the nameless maid passed by again, this time with a red snake-shaped lighter. A flicker of heat pulsed from the open snake's mouth with each strike of her thumb. Once that task was complete, she put several ashtrays along Grandpa's desk for them to utilize, along with small glasses of brandy. With a big fake smile, the maid then nodded at Grandpa and exited the office. Several of his cousins roughly extinguished the cigars in the ashtrays. His cousin Kage tossed his in the glass of brandy. Lennox held onto his—it might be useful to put out on Jasper's forehead.

An old 1970's song started to play: Crystal Gayle's, 'Don't It Make My Brown Eyes Blue.' Lennox recalled Grandpa shoving his infamous elephant tusk cane down some bastard's throat to this tune until the poor guy choked to death on his own vomit. He also recalled the same old man laughing in a jolly way while passing out birthday gifts to one of his great-granddaughters at her party on his estate to the exact same tune, too.

"Boys, thank you for comin'," he began, clearing his croaky throat. "Glad I didn't have to retrieve you personally. You've made it easier on yourselves."

"Can you just get to it? I'm going to be late for work." Lennox glanced at his watch. "I don't have all day."

"Lennox, I'm aware of your schedule. I'll be finished as soon as possible. I don't waste time." Grandpa stared at him as if the words had double meaning.

"You don't waste time? You sure as hell are wasting mine!" Kage barked, jerking Lennox out of his gawking contest with the old man. Kage was the oldest and possibly most dogmatic cousin of them all. They all turned towards the man who sat with his leg extended, chewing on his lower lip. "Fuck you, you ancient piece of shit." Anger poured off of him, flooding the damn room. Kage's bushy black and silver beard caught the light just so as he landed arctic blue eyes on Grandpa, daring him. The air seemed to get colder at that moment. Grandpa's face flushed in deep shades of red, but oddly enough, he didn't immediately respond to Kage's words.

"Got damn it!" Kage yelled after Jasper crept up behind him and slapped the back of his head with the butt of a rifle.

"Show some respect!" Jasper yelled.

"Respect is earned, not given, and I'll shove that up your ass and pull the trigger, you son of a bitch! TRY THAT SHIT AGAIN!" Kage jumped up from his chair, almost toppling it over. The barrel of the gun was a mere few inches from his upper lip, but Kage paid it no mind. As he swayed back and forth, Lennox could see the tiny tip of a razor blade tucked in the man's belt that Jasper obviously missed. A grin crept across his face at the sight of it.

"Kage, you degenerate bastard, calm down." Grandpa smirked as he tried to restore order. "Sit back down in your chair, or the deal I'm about to propose to you will be off the table."

"I don't want any of your fuckin' deals, Grandpa."

The old man shrugged. "I'll take the offers away from your other cousins, too. If I do, you'll be responsible for it, and they can blame you personally, when I apply that pressure." Kage swallowed, his eyes darkening as he faced Grandpa. "Now, I suggest you settle the hell down. We can do this the easy way or the hard way, bat-shit crazy boy. The hard way is one direction, and that's six feet deep. You decide."

Kage's tattooed hands curled into fists as he slumped back down in his chair.

"Jasper, everything is fine." Grandpa waved the help away. Jasper sauntered off, going to stand in the corner, eyeing them all from a short distance. "Now, I want to first tell each and every one of you that my disappointment in you is immeasurable." He leaned forward and clasped his hands. "I have an impeccable bloodline. I have sons and daughters, and other adult grandchildren who've understood what was expected, were properly trained, and do as they are supposed to do. Everyone needs a purpose in this life. You all decided to go your own way, and you've made messes of your lives because of it.

"The seven of you are wild animals. You're uncouth. Untamed. Primitive. Corrupt sons of bitches. I wish your fathers had shot you into the bitches' asses that birthed you, or your mothers had swallowed you. You're ungrateful ingrates. The whole lot of ya." Grandpa had a way of saying vile things with a placid tone, making it all more unnerving.

He surveyed them, his gaze scanning back and forth. No one seemed to bat an eye. No one moved. Perhaps none of them cared. They just wanted to get through it and return to life as it was. This entire stunt was part of being in the family clan. The Wilde's went way back in Texas. Grandpa was the one to break the spell of perpetual poverty, and struck it rich. It was more than evident that it cost him his soul to do so, and he had no qualms about dancing with the devil. If you didn't walk the straight line for Grandpa, he would find ways to abuse you, and no form of punishment was off the table.

Lennox kept his eyes trained on the old man. Watching him, just like he was watching them. Eye contact was important. Never back down.

"Now, I wanna start with you, Lennox." Grandpa

stroked his beard.

Lennox leaned back in his chair and crossed his ankles.

"As you know, I have a small faction, a sub-organization, within my business called, 'The Zoo.' The Zoo is run by family, but only certain members are eligible. The muscle. It could be mental prowess, or physical. In most cases, it's a combination of both. I wanted you to be in charge of it after Dom got sick and had to step down. You knew that. You were provided for and trained to do so. All of the karate lessons. The boxing lessons. Sports of all sorts. I ensured you had every supplement you desired. Your own home gym. Paid for you to fly all over the country to see professional prize fighters and MMA combatants. It was obvious when you hit puberty that you were a physical powerhouse, Lennox. Most of the Wilde men are tall and a bit on the thin side. You were a damn brick wall. Your father took up with that Lebanese whore, your mother, but she did *one* thing right—she produced a human tank.

"Fucking A-rab. Armenian... Whatever the hell she is. Regardless, she has kept quiet and out of my way, so I allowed her peace."

He lifted his chin, meeting Grandpa's gaze straight on. "My mother isn't a whore. Don't talk about her that way."

"Hey," Grandpa said with a black grin as he lifted his hands in the air, "I just call it like I see it, I know her background. I made it clear to her that if she ever cheated on my son, she'd pay the ultimate price. No worries. I accepted her as my daughter-in-law. After all, I don't have any interests in choosing my children's spouses." He shrugged. "I don't have to like my children's husbands or wives. I only get involved if that spouse interferes in what we've got going on, or decides on stickin' their nose in our business. Do that? Then they have to go, one way or another."

Lennox brought the cigar to his mouth, then exhaled. Smokey loops purled, then vanished in thin air.

"As I was saying… She and your father, with my funds, had you trained by some of the best marksmen in Texas. You really excelled in Boxing and weight lifting. But when the time came, what did you do? You betrayed me."

"I didn't betray you. I *never* told you that I wanted to work for you." He leaned forward and crushed his cigar in the ashtray.

Grandpa's eyes turned to dark slits. "You told me that you wanted to go your own way. I stopped the automatic deposits to your account as soon as you said that. Took back the cars and motorcycles I gave you."

"You can't buy me. You can't buy loyalty, either."

"You never knew what was good for you. Stubborn for no reason. Just to defy me. Your father tried to talk sense into you, and you all but spat in his face. You're a disgrace. A Mama's boy. What do you do now? Make peanuts at some fucking dance club?" He smirked, shaking his head as if disgusted.

"I'm a personal trainer and bouncer."

"You were destined for more."

"I already *am* more…"

"What a pity and a waste." Grandpa placed his cigar in a large black ashtray, then opened one of his desk drawers.

He pulled out an old, worn dirt brown Bible and flipped through it. "The fifth commandment declares, 'Honor your father and your mother, that your days may be long in the land that the Lord your God is giving you.' That's from Exodus 20:12. This commandment is repeated throughout the old and new testaments, boy." He closed the Bible and set it aside. "Your father told you what was expected, and you disobeyed. *All* of you did!" He slammed his fist against the desk.

"I have over forty, living grandchildren. Some of them are not eligible to work for me, mostly because they're inept or deficient in some capacity. Several have passed away, others are still in their teen years which makes them disqualified. You seven were hand-selected by me, but have decided to challenge your lot in life. You are the trouble-makers of this brood. Not your brothers or sisters. Just YOU. Lennox, your stubbornness ends today. I'm the only bull in this corral. You were going to be my right hand. My top dog. I nicknamed you top dog when you were a little boy, and it stuck. I expect you to live up to that strong name. Jasper, hand this boy his offer. A deal of a lifetime."

Jasper walked to a shelf and removed a large white envelope. He handed it to Lennox, then returned to where he'd been standing. Lennox looked at the envelope, but didn't open it. Instead, he slid it under his chair.

Grandpa turned his attention to his cousin sitting next to him.

"Roman, you're the black sheep of this family. Nothin' like any of us. A disgrace. You showed no interest in getting dirty. Doing the heavy lifting. You're an ex-Marine, and a sorry one at that. You think you're too damn pretty to play ball." Roman sat in his chair and leisurely ran his long fingers through his jet black, perfectly coiffed tresses. The smirk on his face was growing bigger. "Look at you... You're an arrogant, obnoxious, silly know-it-all with an affinity for getting under my fuckin' skin. Fucking clown."

"Really? I didn't cause the wrinkles and liver spots. I promise."

Grandpa ignored him and continued. "I had no idea what to do with you initially, but realized that your charisma, sharp wit, deviousness, and physical attractiveness that gets the ladies' attention could work well in my negotiations team. Instead, you used that charm and those GQ good looks to get one over on high rollers and take people for a ride, just for the pure fun of it! You're slick, and you're only in love with yourself, and money. You like to play with people...hurt them for fun. Well, playtime is over, pretty boy. It's time for you to be court martialed."

Grandpa snapped his fingers and Jasper was soon handing Roman his own envelope. Roman didn't open his, either. Grandpa then set his eyes on Kage...

"And now, I come to the biggest gotdamn thorn in my side. My first-born grandson. I had such high hopes for you, Kage, but after all of your shenanigans, you moved clear across the state when it was time for you to join me. You hid away so that no one could even find you. You should *never* hide from family."

"I wasn't hidin' from family, old man. I was hidin' from *you*." Kage spit on the floor and crossed his long arms.

"Is that so? Nobody can hide from me, Kage. Not even

you, you strange, demented fucker."

"You ain't no kin to me. I disowned you long ago." Kage boldly met Grandpa's eyes.

"What you did all of those years ago was against nature, and you know it. It was befitting I suppose, seeing as you're a natural outdoorsman. I should have shot you right between the eyes when I was told that you'd come to murder me in my sleep when you were only thirteen! You're a mentally disturbed bastard!"

"And proud of it."

"You should have been ineligible, but damn if you didn't have so much potential! Nobody shoots like you... You too were destined to the Zoo department. Instead, you dodged me like my first name was Draft. You're the lone wolf who sneaks about and slips around like the slimeball you are. I used to call you a wolf as a boy. You were always on the prowl. Hunting. Peering around corners. Watching. Looking for your next prey. I hate you, but damn if I don't like some of your foul ways. You're a wild beast. It's in your blood. You can't help yourself. Wilde wolves roam free."

Kage smirked, then laughed. That laugh turned into an echoing cackle.

"I told you already—you ain't family, old man. Just blood. There's a difference," Kage said in indignation. "I work alone. If I'm a wolf, then I'm a lone wolf. These men on either side of me are my cousins. *They're* family. I'm more like a big brother to them than a cousin. It was me that told 'em they ain't have to listen to you."

"Yes, I know. You poisoned the well..."

"The well was poisoned as soon as you were in charge.

From my understanding, our ancestors were poor, but they were honorable and happy before the likes of you. Ain't nothing wrong with wealth, but I don't want it if I have to deal with you. These men beside me are the true soldiers. We're all different, but we all saw through your bullshit. We stood up to you. Had a backbone. I've only made one mistake when it comes to you, Grandpa."

"And what's that?"

"I shouldn't've told that weak son of a bitch my plans that night. He warned you I was comin'. If I'd been able to blow your miserable brains out when I was a child all of them years ago, we'd all be free of you right now, and none of this would be happening. Just one shot." He held up one finger and grinned. "That's all I needed. As you said, I'm a great marksman. Satan saved your ass that day."

"You too have been demonstrating arrogance as of late. Been around Roman too much I see. Because of me, you're still alive." Grandpa pointed at himself. "Because of me, you can also be dead, Kage. There's no expiration date for a much-needed murder. Your mother's pleas be damned. Don't you ever forget it. Jasper! Give this slippery snot ball his deal, please."

Grandpa shifted in his seat and glared at Phoenix.

"Phoenix, Phoenix, Phoenix." His cousin Phoenix sat up straight and clasped his hands. He was tall, slender, but muscular about the arms. Phoenix's dark brown feathered hair framed his face and rested in layers along his shoulders. His thick beard was perfectly trimmed. The man's almond shaped, light golden-brown gaze seized Grandpa's, and his lips curled into a wicked smile. "Boy, your pride is what you got you in trouble. You and I were workin' out just fine, and then I asked you to do something that you believed beneath you. Before I knew it, you'd jumped ship. You, like Roman, are charismatic, but you've got an ego problem, boy. You tried to confront me. Challenge me. Somehow believing you should be in charge. Just like Lucifer with God. There can only be one master, and you ain't it."

"I cast myself out of hell, 'cause it damn sure wasn't heaven. I think you've gotten us mixed up, Grandpa, because you damn *sure* are Lucifer." Phoenix's teeth showed ever so slightly, as if he was preparing to take a big bite out of something begging to be devoured.

Grandpa grabbed his Bible once again, and flipped through it. "Luke 10:18, from the King James Version... 'And he said unto them, I beheld Satan as lightning fall from heaven!' Phoenix, you fell from grace. I only want you back because you *owe* me. You were part of my surveillance crew in the Zoo, but it's me that needs to watch you with both eyes open. Jasper, take care of him. Hand him his envelope." He closed the Bible, then turned to the next cousin in line.

"Maddock. You, like Lennox, were to be a head honcho in the Zoo. Physical muscle. Instead, you chose the fast life. Heavy booze. Drugs. Tawdry, cheap women. Everything with you is in excess! Flashy, flashy, flashy!" Maddock was still wearing his infamous dark shades, which made it a bit hard to read what he may have been thinking at that moment. "I know that you and Roman like to hang out and get into vile, grotesque activities together. Two charlatans painting the town, so to speak. You could have been somethin'… as big as you are. You've always been fuckin' big! Not strapping like Lennox, but just… huge! You moved too slow though, but did well on the wrestling team. Football. You were wayward. Unfocused. Bad grades in school. Nonchalant and lazy attitude. You're a glutton! Now I hear you're some big time DJ. How embarrassing. A grandson of mine makin' horrible music for people high on drugs to tap a foot to! What is that shit called? Rap music? Hip Hop? It's God awful!"

"You don't have to listen to it, Grandpa." Maddock yawned.

"Oh… so the elephant finally speaks? That's right, another Zoo member that defected from duty. You're the fucking elephant in the room, but right here, right now, I'm definitely talking about you, you son of a bitch!" Maddock sighed, but nothing more. "All of those tattoos," Grandpa hissed in disgust. "You look like a fucking comic book. Don't you have anything to say for yourself? You're probably high right now as we speak. What about your son? What kinda example are you setting for him?"

Maddock leaned forward and extinguished his cigar. Grandpa sucked his teeth, then had Jasper hand him his packet, ending the one-sided conversation.

"And now, we come to Journey. My marathon runner. A pro athlete! Tall and fit as a fiddle, you fly high, like an eagle. You've always been fast! I used to call you my little eagle scout."

Journey lived part of his time out of state, but still had a home in Houston. Lennox figured he was the hardest one to find and get a hold of, then forced to attend this little meeting. After all, he was a celebrity and had people around him at all times. Journey had wild blonde hair that was tapered on the sides and nape, an angular face, and hard jawline. But what stood out most about him were his piercing peridot green eyes.

"You decided you wanted to engage in professional sports instead of taking your rightful place by my side, with the finances. I even offered to let you do both."

"I didn't want to do both. I told you since I was a kid, Grandpa, that I had no desire to work for you. I have my own life and—"

"You excelled in collections, as I recall it. You have a good eye for numbers. A brilliant mind. You know how to make money and spot financial opportunities a mile away... ol' eagle eye. One day, your body will tire out, boy. Running will get you nowhere."

"The whole point of running is to get somewhere, Grandpa. It's called a finish line for a reason."

"Smart ass, like your cousin Roman. You won't be able to compete with the young blood entering the sport of professional running much longer. You're gettin' long in the tooth. Then, where will you be?"

"Grandpa, when that time comes, I'll be happy and retired."

"Just like you should be, minus the happy part," Kage blurted out.

"Ahhh, yes. My first-born grandson that ran away to live in the woods, like some wolf in a fairytale book, has to add his two cents. Only there's no Little Red Riding Hood with a basket of goodies, is there, boy?" He waved over to

Jasper to hand Journey his envelope.

"…But there's a grandparent in that story all right. Oh, Grandpa!" Kage squealed in a high-pitched voice. "What big fuckin' nerve you have!"

"Kage, stop performing for your cousins. We're not amused. I was speakin' to Journey, not you. I think you're hardly in any position to be giving advice on one's future, seeing as how you're a recluse."

"This isn't a performance. This is how I really feel about you." Kage waved his long finger at Grandpa's face. "If Jasper hadn't taken our weapons away when we came in here, and you hadn't had us kidnapped in the first place by those hoodlums this morning that are now parked outside these office doors like the National Guard, you'd be in the morgue right now, all on account of the seven of us!" Kage yelled. "You're a Bible quotin' yet sin totin' fossil-faced fucker! I hope you die tonight while gettin' pegged in your rusty, ancient ass with one of these ignited cigars that little blonde number handed us today. Burn, baby burn!"

Roman could be heard laughing behind a balled fist pressed hard against his quivering lips. Grandpa shot Roman a menacing glare and he stopped laughing so blatantly although his body still shook with mirth. Jasper was now standing behind Kage once again, his gun pointed towards the back of his head. Kage didn't appear phased.

"Kage, this is what you do, isn't it? This is what a lone wolf does. Pitiful as you are," Grandpa stated mildly, an ill-fitted, strange kindness behind his eyes. "It's in your nature to distract, so you can hide your true self in plain sight."

"I'm not hiding anything. I think it's clear where I

stand."

"You're a coward. You banished yourself from the family so you couldn't be examined up close. But I know you, boy. I know the *real* you. You're scared." Grandpa brandished a nasty grin. "Scared of the *real* you being exposed. The only reason why I let you still draw breath and get away with this sordid horse and pony show you've been engaging in today is 'cause of my daughter. Your mama. She begged me not to have you put down when you came to harm me. She said you weren't in your right mind. That you were only a child. I let her have her way, 'cause Sarah has been a good daughter to me. Otherwise, you would've been sucking on some bullet lollipops that night, my boy."

"I'm no coward. Isn't that rich? A coward is a guy who has to bully his family members into being employees of his corrupt empire. I couldn't be no damn coward because I'm a reflection of what you'll *never* be. Now you tell your little errand boy standin' behind me to get that fuckin' gun off the back of my skull, or I'm gonna kill him before sunset. And that's a gotdamn promise."

He and Grandpa had a long stare down.

"Jasper, you know that Kage is crazy and unpredictable." The old man chuckled. "Just like an angry rash. Please back up a little before he spreads."

Jasper took a few steps back, but kept the gun trained on Kage.

"Now, onto my second eldest grandson, and the last in this line of rejects. Ryder."

Ryder had been looking down in silence at his black

cowboy boots most of the time. A trail of smoke eddied from his lips as he slowly raised his head and adjusted his black cowboy hat just so.

"Ryder Levi Wilde, I'm *most* disappointed in you out of everyone here. It was *you* who I was planning to run my empire upon my death. "I needed someone young, but mature, and had tasted life. Younger than your father who's fallen ill. You know business. You know the way this works. You're smart! So, so smart. You have the right brain. The correct mindset. The look, too. You're the total package. A cowboy, a gentleman, and a gangster all in one. The brawn and self-control, too. Nobody knows by just looking at you how incredible you are. You seem so laid back. Slow to anger." A sinister smirk spread across Grandpa's face. "And that's what endears me most to you. We're alike. The way you can walk into the room and have so many at ease, and yet, they don't know an entire human tornado is in their midst.

"You're vengeful. You're wrath in the flesh. Focused. Determined. The dark horse of this stable. The Zoo needs you. Trottin' about, proud as can be, but you have no clue as to where the hell you're going. Instead of following my lead so that one day you could hold the reins to a life full of riches, you stay on a farm shoveling shit. Messin' with horses, chickens, and cows. What was the point of you not taking your rightful place? You've got a dead wife and daughter. No immediate family. Time is of the essence. I need to show you all that I know, *now*. One day I'll be gone. I'm not going to live forever, son."

"And I can't wait until that time comes," Kage mur-

THE TOP DOG (PART 1)

mured. "Ding! Dong! The witch is dead. Oh fuckin' happy day, like the Gospel says."

"Shut the fuck up, Kage, and I mean it!" Jasper barked.

"Ryder, the offer still stands, but this dynasty of mine will go on with or without you. I just prefer it *with* you."

"Get someone else. Not interested."

"I don't trust no outsiders 'cept for Jasper. We keep it in the family, and you know that. You've put me in a precarious situation, Ryder. You will have to accept this deal, or else."

Ryder raised his cigar to his lips, took a puff, then rested it in the nearest ashtray on Grandpa's desk. He took his time answering.

"Grandpa, I understand that you wanted to discuss with us our future with your company, as you call it. It was implied that the threatening phone calls, the men you send to follow us around and make life difficult at times over the years would stop, if we came to speak to you this fine day, and not put up a fight."

Grandpa leaned forward and rested his arm on his desk as if he were really interested in what Ryder had to say.

"'Round two this mornin', an armored truck came to my farm. A bunch of men jumped out. Faces covered. Guns drawn. My dogs were barking. The horses going crazy. I already had my gun ready, but then the door burst open, and I saw all those men, two of 'em holding Bruce, my new German Shepherd. He was dead. I figured some of the others were too since the barking had stopped. I was taken out at gunpoint and shoved in the back of one of those vehicles that were apparently bulletproof. I know because I tried to shoot my way out." Ryder gave an easygoing chuckle, grabbed his cigar and dragged on it before placing it back down.

"I have no plans or desire to work for you, and killin' some of my dogs definitely didn't swing things in your favor. You don't kill a man's dog, and expect thangs to go hunky dory. I know that almost everyone born in this family is expected to help the family dynasty, in one way or another, but my soul ain't for sale. I've told you once. I've told you twice. I'm not interested in what you're sellin', but you are my grandfather. My blood. And you have expectations."

"Indeed I do, Ryder."

"Well, ya see, Grandpa, I have expectations, too... Now, you can pull out all the stops. You can kill my livestock. My dogs. My favorite horses, too. You can make my life miserable, day in and day out. It could never be more miserable than it already is because ain't no greater hurt than losin' your wife and your baby, old man. I loved them, and that's an emotion you know little about. Ain't nothin' you can do to me that'll hurt me worse than the day my lady and my baby girl drowned in the river, so you go right on ahead and have Jasper here hand me that paper," Ryder threw up his hands and smiled, "...but I promise you that nothin' written on it, unless you have a way to bring my family back from the grave, will make me bow down to you. Not now, not never, and that's a promise I plan to keep."

The room became icier than ever. Jasper went on about his way and placed a folder onto Ryder's lap.

My heart is thumping in my body and I'm sore with rage.

Grandpa slowly stood from his desk, and with a wave of his hand, dismissed them all.

Lennox walked out of there feeling like he was being crushed under a million pounds. The weight of the world was on his shoulders, his blood burning as it flowed fast and free within his veins. When the cousins made it to the front lawn, they were told their weapons would be sent to their residences, just in case one of them got the grand idea to pop off before their departure.

Lennox noticed that no one opened their folder even while outside. This time, it wasn't armored trucks but seven black limousines that pulled up. They were instructed which ones to get into, and with only a few parting words and waves, they went separate ways.

Lennox was quiet all the way home. He didn't touch the champagne in the pail, nor the food. He simply sat there, with that unopened envelope beside him. Plotting his revenge…

CHAPTER TWO

A Trip Down Memory Lane

MOM WAS A great distance away, but I saw her clearly. She'd been reaching out to me, her hand stretching in my direction. She was about to speak, but the words died on her tongue. A deep black hole appeared where she stood and swallowed her. She was gone as quickly as she'd appeared standing there. If I'd blinked, I'd have missed the entire spectacle.

A fear like I'd never known wrapped itself around me and squeezed me like a serpent does its prey. I didn't go to try and save her. I was a child, frozen in fear, unable to move forward or take a step back. My heart banged inside of me—a severe flutter of pumping vessels and clasping muscles—and a cold sweat coated me from my scalp down to my toes. Liquid warmth trickled down my face, and my father's muffled screams echoed in the distance. His shrieks were bouncing off the walls, carrying like disembodied wails.

'Mommy! Daddy!' I called out, but no one answered. I was all alone. The odor of something sickeningly sweet filled the air. Like dead flowers.

Suddenly, it was quiet. Too quiet. The rhythmic clomping of hooves against the ground could be heard in the empty space, breaking the calm like shattered glass smashing against concrete. It sounded like a horse.

Out of the hole that swallowed Mom up burst a gigantic muddy brown bull with twisted red horns. Huge as an elephant, he was charging at me, gaining momentum. I was still frozen, as if a heavy weight were pushing me down, keeping me in place for the pending painful death. As the beast drew closer, I realized the reddish color on the horns was wet, dripping blood. Shreds of fabric clung to the jagged pointy tips of the gnarled horns. The orange-eyed beast snarled and gained traction. Moments later, I was screaming, too. Mom held me, rocking me against her bosom. She kissed the top of my head and said, 'Lenny, baby, it was just a bad dream...'

Children are afraid of the dark-eyed ghosts hiding in the closet, the smelly monsters under the bed, and the creepy shadow thing that shows up in the corner of the room in the middle of the night. So was I, but then I grew up. Something within me no longer allowed fear to be either companion or adversary. It was nothing to me, just another crack in the sidewalk. Another cloud in the sky. Another blade of grass in the lawn. I looked the ghost, monster and shadow thing in the eye, and told it, "No. I'm not scared of you." He promised me that next time I would be, and there'd be no one to wake me from the bad dream, for it would be my reality...

Yuna's, 'Strawberry Letter 23' was playing in Club Obsidian in Houston, Texas. After fixing the collar of his leather jacket, Lennox snatched a driver's license out of a young woman's hand. He peered at it, then at her. Without a word, he handed it back to her, took her thirty-dollar club entry fee, and did the same thing with the next person in the long line.

It was a rainy Saturday night. Just a miserable drizzle, but enough to make the streets slick and the air smell earthy. Lennox finished his stint by the front door as the clock struck midnight, changing positions with Todd, another bouncer in the club. They slapped hands as they passed one another in a thick crowd of hot, sweaty bodies. Reaching inside his dark brown leather jacket trimmed with white fur around the hood, he pulled out a pouch filled with five, ten, and twenty-dollar bills. Money from patrons who'd shown up for an evening of loud music, socializing, drinking, and possibly getting laid.

He sidled up at the bar and handed the pouch to one of the bartenders, Dale, then ordered a beer. He had exactly ten minutes before he needed to head across the room and start manning the place. Breaks on Saturday nights were scarce. The establishment was just too busy, and too much ruckus happened if one got too comfortable and let their guard down. He drank half the pint, pitched the rest down the sink behind the bar, then made a pit stop to the restroom. Piss-soaked tissue was scattered on the painted green floor, and he kicked a wad of it out of the way as he approached a urinal.

When he was finished relieving himself, he washed his hands and dried them with a paper towel, which he tossed in the overflowing trashcan on the way out to the dance-floor area. He scanned the room and saw two other bouncers making their rounds, guns on their hips and chins up. Slipping his phone out of his pocket, he checked the time, then headed toward the VIP tables. It wasn't long before another fight broke out, and he and another bouncer escorted three drunk men out the front door, tossing them like garbage onto the sidewalk. Curse words and the all too familiar, "Do you know who I am?!" was hurled in their direction as they turned their backs on the riffraff.

As he came back inside after the altercation, ready to head over to the dancefloor, he noticed a woman sitting at the bar staring down into a glass of red wine. Thick dark brown hair flowed down, obscuring part of her face until she tucked it behind her ear to reveal a sparkling gold and diamond rose-shaped earring. Her lips were glossy and tulip-shaped with a defined Cupid's bow, and her eyes were large with heavy lids. She was a rich umber complexion, and almost appeared in a trance.

And then, she smiled, revealing a row of snow-white teeth.

The expression was odd. Picturesque. Wretched. She reminded him of the lyrics to a sad love song, words wrapped around a slow beat, clinging to a lulling rhythm. Her smile broke out from the darkness though, like a rainbow after a storm.

His body warmed at the sight.

Where did this woman come from? I don't remember letting her in here.

Her body was encased in a long, plain black dress, the fabric clinging to curves and lengthy limbs. She nervously swung one of her crossed legs back and forth, her feet clad in white sneakers. Perhaps she'd just gotten off from working somewhere and wanted to kick up her feet for a bit. She appeared to be alone. No one was engaging in conversation with her, and she was singularly focused on her drink. It didn't seem that she was familiar with the two men chatting to her right, nor the lady on the other side of her who was texting on her phone. This woman with the expressive warm eyes was by herself.

This wasn't exceptionally strange. Sometimes people arrived solo, possibly after a bad date, or it could be, their friends decided to leave early. But something about her made him want to draw closer, see her from a better vantage point. Something about the way her body bowed forward, and the way her hand gripped the stem of the glass... reminded him of something familiar. When he was about four feet away, he couldn't believe his eyes. Had his intuition been right? *No, it couldn't be her...*

He leaned against the bar and stared at her for a few seconds. *Same features...*

"...Nadia?"

"Yeah? Who wants to know?" The woman slowly looked up from her wine glass, and their eyes locked like the intertwined fingers of lovers.

She cocked her head to the side, and her lips pursed as if to say, *'Not another shitty man trying to hit on me.'* And then, her eyes widened, and her full lips parted.

"Ain't no way... Oh my God!" She cackled. The wrinkles in her forehead smoothed right before his eyes. "Lennox? Is that *really* you?"

"Yeah, it's me. Damn, it's been a long time, lady! Come 'ere." Without a moment of hesitation, he wrapped his arms around her and squeezed tight. Her strong yet lovely perfume filled his nostrils, and the sweet scent of her hair as it brushed against his nose and lips put him in mind of strawberries and cream. They slowly pulled away from one another, and silence ensued. In this noisy place, for just a second, a mere wink of time, there was nothing but the two of them.

"I thought you lived in Atlanta now. What brings you back here?" he said after clearing his throat.

"Atlanta. Atlanta. Atlanta." She rolled her eyes and slumped back down onto the barstool. "Nah, that place didn't work out." She turned away and took a sip of her wine.

"I see. Well, so, uh, how long have you been back?"

"'Bout a year. Hey, have you talked to Abby or Marchella?"

"Names that are blasts from the past." He gleamed. "Nah, not since I stopped working in Greater Heights. They got jobs over in that same area after the Red Rooster shut down."

She nodded in understanding.

"You look good." He raked her with a slow gaze.

"So do you."

He focused on her lips.

"You work here?" she asked.

"Yeah. Bouncer. I have a few jobs, actually. Personal trainer, fitness instructor at the gym, amongst other things."

"You always did have a bunch of jobs. You're like a Jamaican," she teased, making him laugh. "One time I think you had, like, four jobs. Always had a strong work ethic."

He looked at her fingers, noticing there was no ring, much to his happiness.

She's been here a whole fucking year and didn't bother to try 'nd look me up? Weird.

"I'm on the clock, so I'm not going to keep you." He glanced at his watch. "Let's catch up. Exchange numbers. Is that cool with you?" He pulled out his phone from his pocket.

"Okay, yeah, that's fine."

So exchange numbers they did. Before he left, he leaned close to her ear.

"You're even more beautiful than when I last saw you all those years ago. I'll be in touch." With that, he waved goodbye …

…The next day

NADIA LAY IN her bed, the sound of Jack Harlow's, 'Lovin' On Me' serenading her as she clutched an old Polaroid photo of her and Lennox. It was yellowed around the edges, and a red scratch was etched along the top. There the two of them stood, arms crossed in B-Boy stances with silly expressions on their faces. She wasn't sure of the occasion, her memory shorted out regarding that detail, but she remembered distinctly how she'd felt when the photo was taken. Happiness. Elation. A sense of safety. Perhaps the picture depicted just another day in their life and not a special occasion.

Right then, her stomach rumbled. She tossed the photo to the side and her mouth watered as ancient memories emerged and flooded her heart. Bacon and egg sandwiches reminded her of him—with salsa on the side.

That's what Lennox would offer her, along with a fresh cup of coffee when they worked at the restaurant together so long ago. They'd come in early, before everyone else. The first time it happened, she thought she was alone, and she cried. He didn't ask her what was wrong when he discovered her in the back pantry crouched down next to the large bags of flour. Instead, he reached past her, as if he didn't see her, and grabbed a big container of onion powder. As he walked out, he turned around and told her to come eat 'fore George, the shift manager, got in. She got to her feet and watched as the sizzle of the griddles merged with the music from a jukebox. She kept her eyes trained on this big young man wearing a grease-stained apron as he fixed her breakfast.

And that's how they continued, day after day. She'd check inventory in the mornings, making sure they had enough grits and sliced lemons, and then set up the tables for customers. Salt and pepper shakers. Tabasco sauce. Before the sun rose and The Red Rooster was officially open for business, he'd pack her a little bag to take home. Bacon or sausage sandwiches on a fluffy, buttery biscuit with packs of strawberry jam. Sometimes he'd add an apple or banana, too.

He was one of three cooks at the Red Rooster, a decent chef but an even better friend. As time wore on, she found herself pouring all of her troubles at his feet. Lennox had that way about him. He was easy to talk to—maybe even too easy. He'd listen to her intently, then give her great advice and pep talks. Like a psychologist she didn't have to pay.

She'd learned a few things about him, too. Such as the fact that he was close to his mother, but didn't trust his father. He was protective of his sister. She realized soon after they'd begun confiding in one another that he was a gym rat but loved to stuff his face, too, and had a weakness for apple cobbler. She baked the best one he'd ever had. Or at least that's what he said.

He enjoyed reading travel brochures and planning trips, but what always struck her as peculiar was how down to earth and humble he was. Fact was, Lennox was an attractive man. *Extremely* attractive. Guys like him typically were full of themselves, at least in her experience. She'd had her share of handsome boys, and rarely did they come across as modest.

More strikingly, there was an intensity about his electric gray gaze, although not alarmingly so. Lennox radiated an invisible golden light one couldn't see but feel. Even the way he looked at a person when just walking past would make them turn to putty. He had thick eyebrows, broad shoulders, and an impressive height. He was muscular. Naturally tan. Gorgeous ebony hair covered his head, tapered on the sides and at the nape. When she saw him last night at the club, he had a beard, which made him look more mature. When they were younger, he was clean shaven and had a cleft chin.

She used to tease him about the vein that ran in the middle of his forehead, which pulsed when he was laughing, or his temper flared. Lennox didn't seem to notice how many women's heads he turned. How ladies flocked to him, attracted to all of his brawn and God-given swag. He wasn't a player. Or at least, he never presented himself as such.

They'd had many candid conversations over the two years they'd worked together at The Red Rooster. Sometimes he'd drive her home when her car was acting up. Sometimes she'd bring him medicine when he was fighting a cold and refused to take proper care of himself. She opened up to him in ways she never imagined she would, and to her knowledge, he'd never told a soul her secrets. There was no gossip spreading around town about her on account of her confiding in him, and she kept his personal information close to her heart, too. Things he told her before she left for Georgia. Things that stuck to her heart like glue.

They just *got* each other. What was understood didn't need to be explained. He had a wisdom about him, and when she found out the fucker was wealthy but working in dives and holes in the wall, she angrily confronted him. Yet, instead of being pissed off that she could blow his cover, he simply said, *"Nadia, not all money is good money. Little boys run to shiny things. I run to what's real... I'm a man. A REAL man. Shiny shit don't impress me."* And that was that. Rufus' (Chaka Khan) sang, 'Stay,' on her favorite oldies playlist, coloring her memories in sepia and honey love.

Her phone suddenly shrilled, the old-fashioned ringtone snatching her away from her thoughts. She answered it without even looking at the I.D.

"Hello?"

"Nadia, good mornin'. It's Lennox. I hope you're fully awake and sober because we need to talk..."

LENNOX'S MIND WANDERED as he waited for his special guest. That day at Grandpa's had been far from a friendly visit, and it didn't take long for old man Longhorn to get revenge for what he perceived as disrespect from his seven disobedient grandsons. Each of them was sent a warning of sorts… Country Mafia style. Grandpa didn't take too kindly to the laughter, interruptions, and questioning of his authority. Perhaps it was bad enough that they'd already told him by their actions to take that job and shove it where the sun doesn't shine.

Lennox got in trouble with the old man, too. All because he had decided to stick up for his mother, and would do it again if necessary. That put him on the target list right along with the rest of his cousins. He'd gone into work at the gym that week and been notified that a man had robbed the register. That within itself was bad enough, but the guy dropped something on his way out: Lennox's I.D. How in the hell did that show up? He figured Jasper had probably taken it during one of the pat downs. Grandpa was always thinking ahead…

The fuzzy cameras at the gym only showed a hooded guy about his same build, and sure as shit, his license was missing. Thankfully, Viola, one of the clerks, vouched for him stating that she'd just spoken to Lennox, and saw him with her own eyes as they FaceTimed. He'd been in a bookstore about thirty minutes away, picking up some materials for a client. She knew exactly where the bookstore was, for she frequented it often, and could see the books in the background during their video conversation.

There was no way he could have gotten to the gym that fast unless he was a cheetah. His other cousins had also received "special treats" from Grandpa. Some were mailed rather disgusting materials along with a threat, while others had been impersonated making obscene phone calls and what not to important folks. Not all of them had proof to exonerate themselves, or were believed. The damage was done. To ensure that they knew the old fucker was behind it, soon thereafter, a text message appeared on all of their phones from an unknown number that simply stated: KEEP FUCKING AROUND AND FINDING OUT.

You just don't talk to Grandpa any ol' kinda way, and that was that. To Grandpa, blood was thicker than water, even if that blood was black as coal, and poisonous as a venomous snake. Grandpa *made* the tricks, but he was far from a kid. If you listened to grandpa well, and paid close attention, in many ways he was rather predictable. He knew before he left that they were all up shit's creek. Lennox thought it awfully odd that the old man barely flinched while his cousins berated him. Grandpa had sat there during that meeting cold as ice. Unfazed. That wasn't Grandpa's nature at all. He was typically jovial and psychopathic. A true blue nutjob with a constant axe to grind. He knew the man had to be up to something because he'd killed men for lesser offenses, and though family was important to his grandfather for all of the wrong reasons, he was rumored to have "removed" a few relatives, too.

Lennox knew right then and there that he was correct about all of his suspicions. He'd been watching Grandpa closely during that entire meeting, and figured something was going to happen. He could smell it on the geezer. Grandpa had been collecting evidence of all of their misdeeds like stamps, while planning to return that shit to 'sender.' Sure enough, he made the punishment match the crime. At least in his own mind. Lennox's transgression had been pretty low key, so his punishment wasn't as extreme. No life taken. There would be a special gift, so to speak, for dear ol' Kage though—the one who'd spoken his mind and given it to Grandpa with no Vaseline. He had to be at the top of the old man's hitlist. Kage, the wily wolf that he was, had crossed the bull's line, and boy did he pay the price. In fact, all of their surprises from Grandpa paled in comparison and were walks in the park compared to the specially crafted retribution for Kage.

Kage let everyone know, from the comfort of his hospital room, that some motherfucker had set his garage on fire, blowing it up like a grenade had been thrown inside. The fire quickly spread, but most of the house was salvaged. A clear ominous cautioning. He'd endured smoke inhalation and some nasty scratches from flying glass and debris yet got out in the nick of time, luckily otherwise unscathed. The icing on the cake was, he was then chased into the woods by only God knew what. Kage claimed the thing appeared fast and inhuman. Maybe a rabid dog. No one was sure if that was Grandpa's doing, too. Hell, maybe it was a cruel joke and the old bull of a man had let loose a demented wolf to hunt his most hated grandson. Needless to say, it had been a rough night for his cousin, and Grandpa also left him a special text message which Kage thought too funny not to share:

DID YOU HUFF AND PUFF AND BLOW YOUR OWN HOUSE UP?

All of these messages disappeared somehow before anything could be done. It would have been their word against his, and besides, running to the police about a crime lord who ran Houston's underbelly was not only a snitch move, but a useless one, too. The police knew who the hell Grandpa was, and the last cop to try and be a hero ended up with fifty-eight holes in him, stuffed in a barrel, and floating down the river. There was no one worse than Grandpa. And there was nothing worse than a vengeful, power-hungry old man who knew his way around guns, the Bible, explosives, and technology. Amen.

CHAPTER THREE

A day late and a dollar short

W HAT LENNOX NEEDED to say, he preferred to not share over the phone. This sort of thing required looking a woman straight in the eye. Besides, he didn't believe in coincidences. He'd run into Nadia for a reason. He was going to do this right the *first* time.

Running his thumb along his lower lip, he crossed his hands over the folded Greasy Spoon Soul food Bistro menu, the place where he'd invited Nadia to meet him for dinner. He hadn't been here in a long while, but it was one of his favorite spots.

It seemed their easygoing chemistry the evening before was all but forgotten once he informed her that he didn't want to chit-chat over the phone, or do the light and fluffy stuff. He'd made it clear that right then, he was contacting her about business. That's when things went left field.

Nadia became rather serious, and started acting strange-ly, with an attitude, asking what this was all about. When that didn't work, she began to shut down, refusing to allow him to pick her up and insisting she'd meet him at the restaurant instead. She'd hung up abruptly, leaving him a bit confused but not completely surprised. She'd always been one to need to control the trajectory of things, including something as simple as a conversation—and he knew why. He'd thought her curiosity must be too great to completely blow him off, but of course, there was a first for everything. Time was ticking.

He glanced at his watch as the minutes passed. The waitress refreshed his water and he drank it down fast, then checked the time again. Nadia was seventeen minutes late—not a huge deal, but annoying all the same. She never so much as sent a text to let him know she was on her way.

As soon as he began to toy with the idea of leaving, the front door opened, and in she walked, clad in a long, furry white vest, tight dark jeans, and her hair slicked back into a ponytail. She spoke briefly with the hostess at the counter, then both of them turned and Nadia pointed at him. Her black velvet boots clicked on the floor as she approached, firmly gripping her purse straps. With knitted brows and tight lips, she slipped into the booth across from him.

"Hi," she stated dryly, barely making eye contact with him as she snatched the second menu off the table and began flipping through it. "Did you order?"

"Nope." He leaned back in the booth seat and stared at her a good long while as she kept her eye on the menu. "I thought the history we had would prevent you from being like this with *me*, of all people. But I see we're startin' from scratch."

"Like a pie? Is this about me being late? Don't be dramatic." Her lazy gaze met his, and she offered a watered-down smile before setting her eyes upon the menu again.

"The late part isn't what I'm referring to. You were a hard nut to crack when we first met, you know that? Wouldn't talk. The madder you were, the more tightlipped you got."

"Well, that was in the past," she said dismissively, her jaw moving as if she were suppressing a yawn.

"You're doing it again. Something has happened since the night I saw you at the club. Is it something I said on the phone when I called?" He knew damn well it was, but he wanted her to own it. "You won't tell me what it is though, and I don't like playing guessing games."

"I'm not playing games, and the past has nothing to do with *now*."

"Yes it does because time passes, but the nature of people stays the same. I deserve to be told what's wrong without having to pull it out of you. This shit is weird."

"Please." She sucked her teeth. "That was ten years ago. I don't know you like that, Lennox. We were much younger and—"

"I don't care if it was ten seconds ago or ten thousand years ago. People don't change. They can grow, but that's a choice, and one that is seldom made. You know, this little defensive wall of yours I've seen a thousand times. You've got something on your mind. We can't talk, Nadia, until you tell me what's wrong."

She rolled her eyes in response and gripped the menu tighter.

"I didn't do shit to you," he added.

"I didn't say you did." She sucked her teeth.

"Then why are you being rude?" He snatched the menu out of her grip and tossed it on the table. "You know what? The hell with this." He grabbed his jacket to slide it back on. "I don't need this shit, and I don't—"

"Because I'm afraid you're going to say something to make me feel bad!" She held the bridge of her nose between her fingers and shut her eyes. "You cut me off when we were talking, saying you needed to speak to me about business. I thought... I thought you were interested in getting reacquainted or maybe build our friendship back. But I was wrong. You made that clear." Her hands trembled slightly, and her complexion deepened.

Damn. She's scared.

"I think you've misunderstood, or maybe I didn't explain it well. That's not what's going on, Nadia." He tossed his jacket aside and settled back in his seat. *Damn... I think she missed me as much as I missed her.*

She didn't speak for a long while, just sat there looking out of the window. The waitress came and took their orders. After the lady departed, Nadia finally locked eyes with him.

"I'm sorry, Lennox. I was just, uh, so surprised, and a little excited to see you last night. When you called this morning and said you needed to speak to me about something serious, I got... I got nervous. I wanted to talk to you about your life, you know? About how you're doing and all the good things that have happened. When you said that to me, mentioned speakin' about business, it kind of ruined the mood, ya know? Made me feel like you were angry with me for somethin' I may have said or done in the past. Or maybe something has happened, and you think I'm to blame. I don't know… we haven't spoken to one another in so long. You were one of the few men in my life who was true blue. When I left to go to school in Atlanta, you were so supportive. I never forgot that."

He couldn't help but stare at her. She was just so damn beautiful, and now so vulnerable, too.

"Nadia, you know what? You have a way of reading people. Sometimes you read too deeply."

"Me?" She pointed at herself, sporting a sad smile. "I saw you the same way. Like you can see through me."

"How are you feeling? Seeing me after all of this time?" He grabbed his water and took a sip.

"Honestly, I have mixed feelings. You know I don't talk to people about how I feel… well, you don't know that because it's been a long time and things change… but," she swallowed and looked down at her fingers, picking at the cuticles, "I was excited to see you last night. Then everything came rushing back and I wanted to forget I ran into you altogether."

He ran his fingers down his closed menu. "I have no intention of saying something to purposefully make you feel bad, Nadia. I'm a straight shooter, but I'd never be cruel to you. Everything is going to be fine. Just relax." He reached for her hand and ran his touch along it. She looked down at their fingers.

It looked like the entire world was bottled up inside of her. He'd popped the cork by his mere presence, and all the fizz burst loose.

"You're a beautiful person, Nadia. Still today."

"I hear that a lot." She swallowed hard. Their food arrived, and the conversation became soft and less solemn.

"What I wanted to talk to you about is something I should've said before you left for Atlanta, but it wasn't the right time. I didn't want you to think that I—"

"I'm a stripper," she said around a mouthful of collard greens, cutting him off. "I'm very good at what I do, too. My stage name is Velvet."

"Velvet. Like velvet red cake."

"That's not why it's my nickname, but I'll keep the conversation light." Her voice was distant, as if she were falling asleep mid-sentence. "So, what do you think of that?"

"Think of what?" He rolled his napkin back and forth.

"Of me being a stripper? People judge me, I've lost a lot of friends because of it, but I can't afford to care." She grabbed her glass of cola and gulped down some of it.

"You care or you wouldn't have told me so fast – like you're trying to get in front of anything I might hear about you." Her wide-eyed faux virtuousness was merely a smoke screen.

"Maybe I did. I don't know." She shrugged.

"Are you good at it?" He questioned while inspecting his silverware.

"I can dance my ass off and make a gay man cum if I put my mind to it." He smirked at that. "My preacher daddy of course hit the roof when he first found out about my activities." She laughed mirthlessly. "That mothafucka wasn't even in the picture, Lennox, for the majority of my life. He was in prison as you might recall for a year or two, too, but had the audacity to pass judgment on me." Her long nails clicked against the table as she drummed them along the glossy white surface. "Came up there waving his Bible in my face, talking about I was going to hell. He should know since I'm certain his boarding pass has already been printed and his attendance confirmed. He's dead now. I imagine he's already settled in. Life is hard, then you die." She shrugged. "My bills aren't going to pay themselves. It is what it is."

"What happened to your classes? You left to go to college, or were you doing both? Dancing and taking classes?"

"Initially I was doing both. I finished undergrad and started law school, but uh, some stuff... some stuff happened. Things got complicated," she said in a tone that discouraged further inquiry. "So if there's anything serious you want to discuss with me after that brief summary of what my life has been like since we last saw each other, just keep it in mind."

"You come with a warning now?"

"I sure do." She stabbed her sweet potatoes. "Most guys see strippers as whores, anyway." She sighed. "I'm in the business of libidos. I peddle lust, as they say."

"Lust, huh?"

"Yeah. It's in the ten commandments. My daddy made sure I knew about it."

"Adultery is actually one of the ten commandments. Lust is part of the seven deadly sins, which was originally eight."

"I never took you for being religious." She placed her

fork gingerly down, and her hands tensed along the table.

"I wouldn't say I'm super religious. I believe in God, I pray, and I have faith."

"Tell me about these seven, well, eight deadly sins."

"It came about because a monk named Evagrius Ponticus wrote what's identified as the "eight evil thoughts." They are, pride, lust, gluttony, greed, spiritual apathy, rage, vanity, and uh… sloth. Nowadays, we give 'em different names, and people mostly talk about the top seven. Leaving the spiritual apathy one behind."

"You big brained?" She chuckled. "I like that. You were always smart. Not a show-off about it though. I always liked that about you. Smart people like being around other smart people. The confident ones, that is."

"I agree with that wholeheartedly. You had a good head on your shoulders. Real good with numbers."

"Yeah, I know how to make money, and make lots of it. It's easy because men can't control themselves." She gave a fretful cough. "Everything centers around control and bustin' a nut, for y'all. Y'all want a woman to be a prude and a prostitute, all at the same time. You want 'er to be traditional, but carry at least 50% of the load, all while birthin' y'alls kids, cleaning the house, cooking and smiling in your face when you're dead wrong, so that we don't bruise y'all little fragile ass egos. Remember, all of that is going on while we're raising those kids of y'alls that we popped out. Meanwhile, you bastards are outside laughing with Joel and Andy, getting white boy wasted on the golf course, or in some club making it rain."

"That's not true of all men. Many? Probably. But not

all."

"I don't care about the 'Not all men,' excuse." She rolled her eyes. "If the majority of women were brain-eating zombies, would you care about me telling you about the 2% one hundred miles away that won't eat your brains? No you would not."

"I'm in the not all categories, and I can only speak about myself. I don't represent, look like, or act like, the zombies, so to speak, so what you call an excuse, I call logic. You want me to denounce or vouch for individuals that I don't even know personally. Think of us as a monolithic group. I can't do that. I'm me, and that's all I can be."

"Smart motherfucker sitting across from me, tossing my word salad." They both burst out laughing. "As wonderful as you were, and maybe still are, Lennox, you're *still* a man. Men have egos. Could you handle being friends with a stripper? I imagine you disapprove. Takin' off my clothes and dancing real slow under dim lights would ruffle your feathers."

Lennox leaned back in his seat and placed his arm along the back of the booth.

"Did I ever tell you that before my parents got married, my mother was an escort?"

Her chewing slowed and her eyes narrowed. "Hell no... I would have remembered that."

He nodded, leaned forward, and picked with his macaroni and cheese. "According to the rumor mill, she was great at it, too. Made a lotta money. My mother had some challenges in life. She wasn't perfect. None of us are, but she was a good person. A great person even, and even in

52

death, she's a great mother to me. One of my best friends. She stopped escorting, when she met my father."

"I do remember you speakin' about her a lot... in a good way. About how nice and loving she was."

He nodded then scooped a spoonful of yams onto his spoon.

"I hope you're not offended by this question, but was your father one of her tricks?"

"Nope. Met 'er at a grocery store. He said it was love at first sight. Said she was the most beautiful woman he'd ever seen." They were quiet for a bit as 'Strawberry Fields,' by the Beetles serenaded them. "Nadia, you mentioned that men have egos. You're right. So do women, but having something doesn't mean we have to let it rule and control us. Now that you've presented your warning label," he chuckled as he popped the spoon inside his mouth and chewed the food. "You must know deep down what I might be getting ready to say, right? I mean, you immediately started tellin' me all of your so-called flaws and defects. You understand what this is all about, don't you?"

She slathered butter on her cornbread, avoiding his gaze. "I don't want to guess wrong, so humor me."

"This second time around, I don't want to be *just* your friend, Nadia. I want to get to know you on a different level. A more *intimate* level. That's what I meant by I wanted to speak to you about business."

She finished buttering her cornbread, cool as a cucumber. No expression registered on her face.

"This isn't what I expected." Her voice shook, betraying she was more affected by his words than she made it seem.

"I had no idea you liked me like that. You'd be great at poker. This is... wow."

He polished off his water then dabbed a napkin on his lips. "I had a bit of a crush on you back then, Nadia. It was more than a crush, actually. The only reason I didn't say anything is because you were going through a lot, and then you were off to college. It would've been wrong for me to bring that up and possibly confuse you. When you love someone, even if it's just as a friend, you want what's best for them. You needed to leave Texas at the time and pursue your education. To better yourself. When I saw you last night, the first thing that crossed my mind was, 'Holy shit. This is my second chance.'"

A soft gasp escaped her mouth. She stared at him. "I'm... surprised. Uh, I don't even know what to say..." She placed her knife down and sat straighter. "You know what, Lennox? If you're anything like how you were back in the day, and it sounds like you are, you're amazing, but, I gotta be straight with you. I don't have time for a relationship right now. I just had—"

"Like you, I'm not trying to hear any excuses. Also, it wasn't a question or request. I'm not askin'." He shook his head, then waved the waitress over, quickly letting her know that he was ready for the bill. "I'm tellin' you that this is what I want. This is what *we* need. And this is what you're going to get. ME. It's time." He stood and slipped his jacket on. "I may be a day late and a dollar short, but I caught the next train, and I paid off the invoice. With interest."

A mixture of anger and astonishment now showed on her face.

"Sir, that's not how relationships work. I think you need to—"

"I've got a lotta shit going on in my life right now, Nadia. Good and bad." He zipped up. "I have faith though. I'm a praying man. Just like I told you. I asked God to show me a sign regarding somethin' I'm dealing with. The next day, you were sitting at the bar drinking a glass of red wine. Hadn't seen you in over ten years. God knew how I felt about you… that every now and again, I thought about you, and I ached. He sat your pretty ass right down in front of me. May as well put a bow on your head. That's all the answer I needed." The waitress came over, and he handed her his credit card. "I have to get going. I said what I needed to say. Enjoy the rest of your day."

"You are unbelievable! You were always blunt, a little cocky at times, too, but this takes the cake!" The waitress handed him back his card, and he quickly signed the receipt. "Here I was, worried you didn't want to be friends again, or that you planned to tell me off for some transgression, but come to find out, it was the exact opposite—and not in a good way."

"Like I told you, you read too much into shit. Men are simple creatures."

"And like I told *you*, I am not interested in no damn boyfriend right now. Hell, I don't even know you the same way anymore! You could be some psychopath!" She laughed, but it was obvious she didn't find this the least bit funny.

"I'll see you in a couple of days," he whispered, leaning close to her ear. "Fuck a friend. I got enough friends… you were *always* supposed to be mine. I gave you time to get your shit together. Now, it's game on. Oh, and one more thing. I was never auditioning to be your boyfriend. Not back then. Not now. My resume is better suited for the role of husband." He kissed the top of her head.

And with that, he walked out.

CHAPTER FOUR

It Take Two to Tango

N ADIA SAT BACK in her black Ford Fusion at the red
light, anxiety sputtering through her like a lawn
sprinkler on the fritz. She couldn't stop thinking about the
dinner. About him. About everything.

The black, tree-shaped ice-scented car air freshener
waved about as she punched the air in frustration, hitting it
in the process. She shook her head and stared out of the
driver's side window. Just the other day, she'd seen a man
who'd occupied her heart and mind for years walk away
from her, get into his big silver Chevrolet Silverado, and
drive off without a word. He didn't give her an ultimatum.
Rather, Lennox had told her what the future would be. She
hadn't spoken to him since that night at the soul food
restaurant, but she knew that this wasn't the end of it. Not
by a long shot.

When he said he was going to do something, he did it,
even way back when they were in their early twenties. When

the light turned green, she pressed her foot on the gas. She turned up the radio in the car and bobbed her head to the sounds of Tanner Adell's, 'Buckle Bunny.' Rapping the lyrics, she found herself smiling from ear to ear as the music proved to be a perfect distraction. When the song was over, she seized the half-crumpled bottle of water from the cup holder, twisted the cap, and took a deep swallow of the warm liquid. Now it was all empty.

She checked the time, then her fuel gauge. Minutes later, she was at the filling station, in need of some gas, an ice-cold Pepsi and a packet of hot Cheetos before heading to Sweet Soiree, the gentlemen's club where she worked.

After filling up and grabbing her goodies, her phone rang the moment mehro's, 'K3TAMINE' started to play. She looked at the Caller-Id and her stomach clenched.

"What do you want?" she blurted as she turned the radio down. It was her ex-boyfriend. A terrible relationship she wished she could forget.

"I want my fucking money. You been dodging my calls for months."

"Boy, I don't owe you any money, and the judge already ruled on this! Is this the best you can come up with? I knew I shouldn't have answered this phone." She made a left, gripping the steering wheel tighter.

"That shit wasn't fair, and you know it."

"Life isn't fair. Being with you wasn't fair. The judgment though was definitely fair."

"You lied to the judge. Eight thousand, not includin' interest, is what you owe me, and I'm gonna keep my foot on yo' neck until you give me my mothafuckin' money,

Nadia. I don't give a damn what the courts say."

"For the hundredth time, I didn't ask you for that money. You *offered* it, LeRon. I used it for my rent, some bills, and to pay toward my student loan, just like I said. I even brought that documentation to court, despite it not being required."

"It wasn't no gift. What man you know give a bitch eight thousand that ain't his wife?!"

"You. That's who," She threw the words at him like stones. "I thought you did it because you cared, but of course, like most men, you had ulterior motives. If anyone should be talking about someone owing money, it should be you to me. Not once did I ask you for the money back for all of those car rentals, the trips, and your harebrained business ideas. When we first got together, I didn't have much, but as I stacked my money, I was more than generous with you. Instead of you callin' it even, you decided to take me to court. Funny how that happened right after I broke up with you."

"It ain't have nothin' to do with that."

"Bull! Get yo' own shit. Ain't nothing more pathetic than a grown ass, able-bodied man beggin' a woman for cash, or wanting to be kept. I see you're standin' on business in your feminine energy era. You want a soft life, don't you? Like Janet Jackson said in 'For Colored Girls,' *'Oh, so you was doin' the bendin'?'* Hobosexual ass."

"That's what's wrong with you Black females. When we set yo' ass straight, you try 'nd say we gay. We just sick of y'all shit, and that's why I'm red pill, and a Passport bro, now. Fuck y'all Black bitches. Most of y'all never support your man, but always have your hands out."

She burst out laughing and shook her head. "King Gas-lighter strikes again. Man, you ain't nothin' but a disgruntled, bitchy ass degenerate. I never accused you of being gay – I'm just highlightin' your feminine ways. Besides, most gay men I know have far more masculinity in them than you have in your baby toe, and they ain't waiting on a woman to take care of their needs. Now just admit it: You were trying to buy me, but I can't be bought, and when I had the nerve to leave yo' ass after all the mess you did to me, you were salty."

"You crazy! Ain't nobody had—"

"You thought that money would make me owe you for life. Put up with your nonsense indefinitely. Like my whole existence is only worth eight racks. Boy, please!" She cackled as she slowed to a red light. She turned up her music, and 'Interior Crocodile Alligator' by Chip Tha Ripper almost drowned out his noise.

"I *need* that money, and you're going to give it to me. I don't care if you have to sell yo' ass to the highest bidder, or what the judge said. That money belongs to me. Besides, I know you're good for it."

"You don't know what I'm good for because my financial status is no longer your concern. Now, do you have something worth discussing? Because some of us know how to make our *own* money, and do it twenty-four-seven. Take notes."

"Yeah, I got something worth discussing. I heard about yo' ass on Only Fans now. They say you hittin' six figures just for playin' with yourself."

"What I'm doin' or not doin' is none of your damn business. You don't need to be pocket watchin' people—mind the business that pays you."

"Yeah, it was *definitely* you. I know what your titties and ass look like. Egyptian tattoo…They ain't call you Nadia thee Stallion for nothin'. You got a video called, 'Cookie Monster.' Stuffin' Oreos in your pussy. Nasty ass bitch." In fact the particular video he was referring to wasn't her, but several people had told her about this doppelganger model several times in said viral video. The woman was originally an IG model. When she Googled her, she noted the resemblance. They definitely could be sisters, but that was neither here nor there.

"I don't care what you believe, and I don't have anything to prove to you. Now I bid you goodnight."

"Just pay back six thousand, and we can call it even. I still love you, by the way… I miss your crazy ass, too, you know that?" He chuckled. Forcing it – spinning into another whirlwind of twisted psychological maneuvering.

"In ten minutes, you went from demanding money and calling me a bitch to trying to strike a deal and declaring your feelings. If life was fair, I'd be filing charges on *you*. If there was a court that was truly just, I could file a lawsuit for habitual cheating. Habitual lying. Habitual love bombing and mental abuse. You don't know what love is, LeRon. Your entire identity is built on mind games, misery making, and manipulation. If I could sue you for emotional trauma, I'd be a millionaire."

"Hey, save that attorney and therapist shit for the professionals. You ain't no lawyer. You dropped out, remember?" He chuckled nastily. She was breathless with rage.

"Go to hell. I block your number, you call from a new one. Around and around we go. Don't you have a new girlfriend to harass? What the psychologists call new supply?" She caught her face in the rearview mirror. Her eyes had turned almost pitch black with sheer anger.

"I'm done playin' with you, Nadia. Don't make me come to Houston and drag my money out of you. You know I will." The aggressive version of him returned just like that... the mask slipping so damn fast.

"Oh, really? Bring yo' silly ass on down here then, LeRon, since you big and bad! But I promise you it'll be the *last* thing you do. I'm packin', and I ain't talking about no penis size, or for no road trip, either. I'll shoot you in the ass and ram some Oreo cookies in *both* holes. How's *that* for Only Fans, bitch?!" With that, she abruptly ended the call, her nerves on fire like freshly lit torches.

Ol' narcissistic ass. I wish I'd never met him. She was so pissed that by the time she reached the club, she barely recalled making the twists and turns down the various streets to get there. She sat in the parking lot for a few minutes, chugging her Pepsi and smacking on the Cheetos until there was nothing left but orange dust. Once she calmed down, she blocked his latest number, slipped her phone into her purse, and grabbed her gray and purple duffle bag from the back seat.

When she entered the establishment, the beat of 'Buttons,' by the Pussycat Dolls, made her body pulse. The odor of cigarette and cigar smoke filled the area, while dizzying red lights spun along the ceiling, walls, and floors as she made her way to the dressing room. Zigzagging past early patrons and waitresses still setting up tables for the evening, she found herself below soft yellow ceiling lights and the smell of various intermingling fragrances. She greeted a few other dancers who were milling about, then entered her small private area. Her sanctuary.

She jerked the thick black curtain that served as a door closed, then plopped down on the black leather stool and wiped her hands with an alcohol pad, removing the Cheeto stains from her fingertips. And then, she just sat there... regrouping. The music from the dance area throbbed within her, getting her into the right state of mind after her disturbing conversation with her ex-boyfriend.

Every now and again, LeRon would pop up out of the blue. She could tell he'd been drinking, so she didn't lay into him the way she really wanted to. He was draining, and though she was no stranger to ex-boyfriends trying to rekindle relationships that were in no way desirable for her to return to, he was on a whole different level. He was attractive to most of his prey, and out of his mind. Crazy, selfish, and controlling.

Shoving thoughts of him away, she focused on herself. On her job. On love that she knew didn't really exist...

She closed her eyes and thought about sexy things like black and white silk, long kisses with men that made her heart thump, sex in a hot tub with incense and candles burning, and the romantic embraces she'd longed for, but never received. Her pulse raced as she replayed Lennox's words that he'd whispered in her ear. '...*Invoice paid in full with interest.'* Her stomach fluttered, but she couldn't entertain that thought. She'd been down this road before—it never ended well.

She opened her eyes and checked herself out in the mirror. *I'm going around and around and not getting anywhere.* Her tired eyes would soon be covered by globs of concealer and red eyeshadow. Black eyeliner. False lashes.

Shoving her wayward thoughts aside, she got to her feet and slipped into her outfit: A neon black and red catsuit that glowed in the dark, with the cleavage, stomach, and ass cut out. Though it had cost a pretty penny, it made her feel sexy all over and helped to earn her big tips.

High ballers came into this club, and she was determined to drain their pockets dry. Only the best girls worked here, the ones that could really dance and not just twerk. Besides, the managers and security were top of the line. She'd worked a lot of clubs in Atlanta, dealt with crappy promoters, dudes that wanted to get some pussy before hiring or take big cuts of her pay. It was a complete circus—an arena full of monkeys, clowns and piranhas parading as humans. Ring leaders of bullshit. She was a veteran at this point and in this line of work, that wasn't a plus. Clients wanted young flesh, something to make them feel youthful. Some were naïve and too trusting. But she was book smart… street smart… life smart.

She was thankful that she looked significantly younger than her actual age as that helped her buy some time. She was black sand in an hourglass, and time was running out. She sat back down to do her makeup, then her hair to the tune of 'Contact,' by Kelela. She took her time prettying herself up, ensuring that everything was just right. Last but not least was her perfume. She went for one of her favorite scents: Mugler Alien Goddess Eau de Parfum. She sprayed it behind her knees, ears, neck, collarbones, breasts and a spritz above the navel. Then, a final pump between the thighs before slipping her perfectly pedicured feet into six-inch black heels, the bottoms bright red...

She bobbed her head to song after song as she waited for her turn to go up on the stage. Some of the beautiful dancers were high on cocaine, speed, and uppers. Others were drunk. Many were sober. The majority of them were addicted to trauma. If they weren't before they took the job, they definitely got there afterwards. Sometimes, the dancing came easy. Other times, it took two cocktails for her to make her way out there. It was easy to be intoxicated in a place like this.

This club was known not only for its premium adult entertainment and acoustics, but the top shelf liquor which they offered the dancers at a deep discount. She sipped on a rum and coke from a short cocktail straw, not needing much coercion tonight. She loved to perform, to make a man feel ten feet tall... like she only had eyes for him. Not because she gave a shit about him and his feelings, but because it felt incredible to pretend to be someone else. She also loved to make money, way more than she ever made at any other job. Besides, she didn't feel shame or embarrassment when she danced. Rather, she felt free...

"Now, comin' to the stage is the one... the only... the long-legged, and good head givin', Veeeeeeel-veeeeet!" The crowd began to applaud as she stayed out of view and handed her drink to one of the bouncers. She adjusted her attire, making sure it looked just right, and braced herself as the song, 'Snatched,' by Big Boss Vette began to play. Catching her reflection in a full-length mirror, she smiled. The glitter on her skin made her look as if she'd been rolled in crushed red ruby dust and dipped in broken diamonds. Head held high, she emerged gyrating from behind the curtain, the crowd now hyped. She fast danced, popped and shimmied until the song slipped into another tune: 'Pussy Poppin',' by Ludacris.

Slow spinning purple lights flashed across the stage as she flirted with the pole, then did the splits on the floor, bouncing up and down, making the men melt. She got up, her abs and hips bucking, her skimpy attire glowing under the orbing lights. The raucous crowd full of horny men and lesbians roared and cheered when she jumped quickly on the pole and climbed up it, then slid down fast ... and slowly, her long tongue curling out of her mouth as she hugged the pole like a long-lost lover. She slowly undid a strap across her chest, exposing more of her breasts, then swung around and around the pole, her acrobatics something she'd practiced to perfect for years.

Long, curly dark brown hair whipped around from each movement she made. Cool, wet strands stuck to her skin as she worked up a well-deserved sweat. She slipped down the pole in reverse, her body winding like a snake as men cat-called to her, clapped and lost their shit. Slipping her finger into her mouth, she sucked it like she would a thrusting dick, driving them crazy.

At last, she crashed hard on the floor and rode it like a

man she pretended to love. Crawling across the hard surface like a tiger, she paused then fell onto her back, waving her long legs in the air and bringing them back by her ears. Gripping her ankles tight. The hoarse male yells of lust were deafening. Some of these motherfuckers were there strictly for her. She was the best dancer in that club, and she knew it. Hands down. She didn't have to be the prettiest. All she needed to know was how to entertain her ass off, move like a seductress, and play her part.

The rhythm of 'Blow the Whistle,' by Too Short, filled the room. She made her way back to the pole. Slipping and sliding, grinding and fucking the long, silver stick in slow motion, she fixed her gaze on the sea of men before her, becoming their imaginary lover. She looked for a sucker to lick—a man who was more than willing to shove hundred-dollar bills into one of the sparse slits of her attire simply to be near her. She hung like a bat from the pole, looking into the warped, upside-down faces of screaming men tossing cash in her direction. Her eyes focused on a figure in front. Her mouth went suddenly dry, and her stomach clenched.

Upside down. Right-side up. Left to right. She'd recognize those vibrant gray eyes from anywhere. Standing up. Front and center. She rotated until she was vertical. There the bold bastard stood—leaning slightly forward sporting a black wife beater, dark jeans, a gold chain with a dog head medallion, and a smug smirk. Lennox.

She continued to dance, a part of her fueled with anger, and another part with hot desire. She rocked her hips harder and harder until she had to be nothing short of a blur.

He pulled out his wallet as he stood like a beacon in front of the crowd, then placed a large wad of cash onto the stage. Facing away from him, she bent down and shook her butt in his face, showing off her nice, round ass, gyrating and shaking it faster and faster as she held her ankles and stared at him from between her legs.

After a while, she stood straight and walked right to the edge of the stage where he stood. Their eyes locked. She turned away and began twerking. He lunged forward, grabbed her roughly around the waist, and she shivered at the touch of his large, warm hand sliding down the crack of her ass. Her voice caught in her throat as her pussy pulsed.

The all-too-familiar feel of cold, hard cash against her flesh followed. Even through the pounding base of the music and the yells from the inebriated crowd, she heard his voice drift to her ear like ice against her soul. She kept dancing as he leaned in close, his breath minty with a trace of beer…

"I told you I'd be back, beautiful. Keep dancing. Dance all fuckin' night if you want to, Velvet. Dance your heart out."

When she snapped around, her mind whirling, he'd already stepped back and sat down. He picked up his bottle of beer, winked and smiled at her. A genuine smile. She wondered how he'd found out where she worked because she'd never told him the club name. And why had he decided to come tonight? So many questions churned in her head. More money was thrown at her by other customers, and when she was done with her show, the final song over, she collected her scattered earnings from the floor, waved to the crowd, and left the stage, a little weak at the knees.

Some of the other strippers smiled and tried to get her attention. She heard them talking about the big spender, the sexy stranger up front that had given her a wad of cash and extra on top, like whipped cream on mounds of ice-cream. She forced a smile in response, and finally made it back to her dressing room. When she sat down, her head was pounding. It felt like the whole damn place was closing in on her. The walls. Ceiling. Floors. Everything felt smaller. Tighter. The air thinner.

She freshened up in the restroom with a bar of soap and loofah, deodorant and powder. Hair in a ponytail. Dark brown Puma jogging suit on. Duffle bag packed. She moved fast out of there, as if her life depended on it.

Memories washed over her: flashes of rich, buttery eggs swallowed after a burst of salty tears. Lying against a hard, warm chest in a cold pantry. In his big arms. Being held. Being loved—and that man not wanting a damn thing in return but to be her peace.

She made her way out to her car, cutting out early and hoping she could just disappear, but it seemed this son of a gun understood her a little too well. She found Lennox waiting for her, leaning against her car, arms crossed and a smirk on his face.

"Security is lax tonight, I see." She simpered as she pushed the button on her fob. "Excuse me. Move. You're in my way."

"You're leaving so soon?" he sneered, his lips curling in a devilish grin, the words followed by a mischievous chuckle.

"I suppose you're here to talk to me about how this isn't a place for me, or how you think you can save me from myself?"

"Nope. You've never needed saving. Just a listening ear. I remember." He tapped his temple. "You've been taking care of yourself for a long time, and I'm not your daddy." She now stood right next to him, facing the driver's side door as he leaned his back against her car. She took a deep breath and hung her head.

"Lennox, what do you want from me?" She boldly met his gaze then.

"I already answered that question. It sure as hell isn't to talk to you about your car warranty."

"You're not going to leave me alone, are you?"

"If you really wanted me to leave you alone, you wouldn't be still standing here talking to me." The words were a stab at her heart. Out bled the truth.

"Follow me to my apartment. Let's talk."

He nodded, and she watched him walk away. Getting in her car, she started up the engine, then slowly pulled out of the parking space. Moments later, his big truck's lights lit up the area. His window was rolled down, and his arm jetted out from it. Garth Brooks' 'That Summer' could be heard coming from his vehicle.

She took her foot off the break and drove, the lyrics of a familiar country tune about a man loving a woman drifting in the wind…

CHAPTER FIVE

A Candid Heart to Heart

VANILLA MUSK CANDLES flickered, casting streams of broken light across the cantaloupe-colored walls. Grey Goose Vodka and Ocean Spray cranberry juice was poured and served in frosted glasses. 'Until the End of Time,' by Justin Timberlake played just loud enough for one to hear the lyrics, but not at a volume that drowned out conversation or sidetracked from the outstanding vibe.

Shoes kicked off, Lennox watched Nadia stretch and yawn. She'd changed into something a bit more comfortable. Extending her long, shapely legs across her dark gray couch, she crossed her ankles and wiggled her dark blue painted toenails, halfheartedly looking at her diamond toe ring that sparkled under the small chandelier lights. Reaching over, she began to massage her soles.

Her small feet looked soft and smooth, as if she'd never danced, stripped, or even walked a day in her life. He sat across from her, slouched down on the matching gray loveseat, taking her all in. The lighting in the area did amazing things to her expressive dark eyes. Her skin glowed. Her aura shined.

The lavender globs of bopping paraffin wax floating slowly up and down a rocket-shaped lava lamp tossed reflections against her body and the entire room. Portions of the wall put him in mind of being poolside as the liquid and light merged, tossing abstract reflections here and there.

The aroma of a stick of Japanese cherry incense transported a sweet, smoky scent throughout the room. Time ticked by, dragging its feet. Taking a sip of his beverage, Lennox gathered his bountiful thoughts. There was a lot to say, but they hadn't communicated much since they'd arrived at her apartment. Truth be told, words weren't always needed to have a full conversation.

"I thought about you often." She broke the silence like a tiny crack in a block of ice, still looking down at her feet as if understanding his reticence loud and clear. *She's a runner… Feet walk away.*

"Then why did you leave from here and never talk to me again? I called you several times before I finally took the hint." He brought the glass to his lips.

She slowly released her feet and turned to face him, her eyes flashing like gleaming volcanic rock.

"Because you were my greatest distraction."

He took a slow sip from his drink and set it down.

"From *what?* School?" he asked, clasping his hands.

"From life. Tonight, you want me to be honest, right? We're just going to be frank? Let it all out?"

He shrugged. "Why would I make all of this effort to have a phony conversation? I can be lied to without all the effort. Besides, I know of no other way to be. What it do?"

Her lips crimped in a tilted smirk. "I'll keep it one hundred with you, Len," he hadn't been called Len in years. "I had feelings for you that a friend shouldn't have for another friend. Things got uncomfortable. That's it. That's all."

"Don't. Just don't." He waved her off and picked up his drink from the table, taking a meager taste. Held the alcohol in his mouth for a moment, dragging out the flavor.

"Don't what? Tell you the truth? You said you were ready, willing and able for that fried and piping hot honesty platter with three sides of certainty." The fringe of her lashes cast shadows onto her high cheekbones.

"You can serve me whatever as long as you don't sugar-coat what really went down. I'm hungry for answers, but not starvin'. Not any ol' bone tossed my way will do. Don't play games. You know what I'm talking about."

"I'm not playing games. I'm being for real. I didn't want our relationship ruined, Lennox, and yeah, I also needed to concentrate on my classes instead of being boy crazy—well, young man crazy." She rolled her eyes dramatically. "But I didn't even know what I was feeling completely at that time. It was new to me, that whole catchin' feelings for a friend. It felt wrong. And before you say it, I had no idea you liked me, too. I didn't know what to do. It was a mess."

"My issue is, we could've remained friends. People have crushes on their friends all the time, but don't act on it. I felt like I lost a friend. A real good one."

Willow Smith's, 'Symptom of Life' started to play, coloring the mood in shades of intangible discomfort and forlorn beauty.

"I was a complex person. I was young, too… didn't know how to process this sort of thing. My emotions misfired. I cut off what I perceived was the problem." He nodded in understanding. "One minute, you're like the White brother I never had, and the next, I am feeling things for you that I shouldn't. I didn't want the friendship ruined, and I couldn't trust myself to not say anything to you. Besides, let's say everything might have turned out great after I confessed my feelings—it would have been a long-distance thing, and I may have done something stupid like not go away to school like I'd planned, or worse, been lousy to you. You know I'm fucked up." She swallowed hard then confidently met his gaze.

"I would have never let that happen. The whole, you not finishing school. I'm one of the people who encouraged you to go on to college in the first place. You told me a million times that you wanted to be a lawyer. I fully supported that because I knew you'd be good at it, and you needed to find yourself."

"Yeah, I found myself. I just didn't like what I discovered." A glimmer of what appeared to be dread appeared in her eyes.

"After talking about your dreams for so long, finally, you decided to go forward with that particular one. Make it come true. You said your mother wasn't completely supportive, and most of your friends weren't, either. But I said, *Do that. Don't listen to them.*'"

"I know you want to know if I finished law school, and

the answer is no—not that that would be a big surprise, considering my current occupation, Though in all honesty, I make more money dancin' and doing online gigs than I ever would have as an attorney. Regardless, I didn't finish because money ran out, I got distracted with other shit, and my demons came back to collect their due."

"There's always going to be a past. Scars. Naysayers and evil. That's no excuse to run from your destiny. The people with the most to say have the least to offer, too."

"I can't argue with that." Her eyes glistened even more. "I also recall you giving me money for my books to cover the first semester of undergrad." Her cheeks darkened, and her lips curled while she looked away… as if the rush of emotions from yesteryear had returned and poked her in the heart.

"Yeah, but my main objective at the time was to do everything I could do as a friend to you, Nadia," He placed his hand over his chest. "And just be a decent human being."

"You were always good. Always decent. You're rare." She reached for a tissue from a golden box and blew her nose.

"I wasn't always a decent person." He chuckled mirthlessly. "But when dealing with you? Yeah, I was civilized." *You reminded me of my mama.* "You had so much to offer. Your potential was too big for that place. You needed to be outside of that restaurant. Bein' a waitress. Don't get me wrong, waitressing is honest work, but I knew you wanted somethin' else. You weren't happy there. You were… no, you *are* intelligent, and you wanted to help society in a different way. By going into family law."

"Yeah. I can't believe you remember the specific type of legal practice I was goin' to school for after all of these years. I did want to be somebody, didn't I?" She smiled sadly, then tossed up her hands. "It wasn't meant to be, and I didn't want to take up your time, either, Lennox. You deserved someone who wasn't... wasn't like me." *Now, the truth is finally out.* "You wanted to have your own gym. I remember *your* dreams, too. How's that working out?"

"I'm still trying to get there, Nadia... still tryna get there." He cracked his knuckles and looked down at his sock covered feet. "You wouldn't have been taking up my time, and I wouldn't have been taking up yours, but it doesn't matter now anymore." His eyes met hers. "We've spent ten minutes talking about why you never called me, and no answer you've given I find good enough." She swallowed. "I know it made sense to you at the time though. I understand. All I wanted to do was make sure you were okay. That you were good. For you to check in with me every now and again. I'm not trying to make you feel bad, but just to let you know I was a little hurt by that... actually, a lot hurt."

She looked up through lidded eyes, then her expression turned sheepish. "You stopped calling. I'm not all to blame."

"Like hell you aren't. After I left the third or fourth voicemail for you, Nadia, I had to take a step back. I'm not someone who has ever had to force myself on anyone, and regardless of how much I cared about you, you weren't going to be the first."

"What haven't I explained to you that you still wonder about?"

"What makes you think that I still wonder about any-thing?"

"Because of how you're looking at me. You used to look that same way at me so long ago, when you knew I was hiding something. Avoiding a conversation."

"Just say it." His body heated as a strange anger and sadness merged within him. Until now, he hadn't slowed down enough to process how truly upset he'd been back then about her vanishing into thin air. He hadn't sat in the feelings, stewing until they were hot and boiling. Now though, he could feel the full force of his disappointment. It repeated like hot sauce crawling up his throat from a bad burrito, and burned more than an August afternoon in Texas.

"Because I loved you, Lennox. It wasn't just a crush, or a mere need to have sex with you. You know what it was." Her fingers fluttered against her neck. "...I didn't think I was good enough to have somebody like you. Didn't matter how pretty people said I was. Or how smart. Or how funny. You were on another level. I know now that isn't true, but I had to work on me first. I wasn't fit to be with anyone, especially not a person with your sense of self, and your level of esteem. You're a lot... in a good way."

He leaned forward, clasped his hands, and nodded in understanding. He got it now. It was sinking in.

"I was broken, Lennox. Broken people look for others to put them together again. Trauma bondin'. I wanted to pretend with you, ya know? Act like I could handle the pressure I was under, but a part of me wanted you to glue me back together after I fell off my mental wall. Humpty Dumpty. That never works. Nobody can fix a broken soul but that person and God."

"True."

"You know what?" she said with a smile.

"What?"

"I was so busy back then dumping all of my problems on you, that I rarely asked about how you were doing. Your own life and feelings. That was selfish when I think back on it," she stated contemplatively. "I'm sorry about that."

"I preferred it that way." With a sigh, he flopped back against the couch and closed his eyes for a brief spell.

"You know what blew my mind about you? When I found out that you came from a rich family. I was pissed you didn't tell me. I couldn't believe you were working in a greasy spoon," she prodded, her gaze searching his. "Lennox Wilde, from the Wilde family clan. I didn't know nothin' about that until Jalil told me."

Jalil was a bus boy who'd put two and two together, much to Lennox's disappointment.

"We can't help the family we're born into."

Her gaze turned inquisitive. "You told me not all money is good money, but at the time that didn't make sense to me." She started fidgeting with one of her long pink nails. "Now it does."

"It sunk in, huh?"

"Yeah... so now that we're grown 'nd sexy, I want to ask why you got a minimum wage job when your parents had all that money? You wouldn't answer me directly back then, but I want an answer *now*."

He mulled on that for a second, then went with, "I want you."

"Yeah, you said that, Len, but that doesn't answer my question."

"Just listen. It's part of the reason why I'm going to answer you. You've always been the deep end of the pool to me. I want to damn near drown. I want the heat, the intensity, the heart and soul you possess. My wanting a chance with you is what will make me talk about this."

"So you don't talk about your family?"

"Sometimes, but not like this. I don't talk about my family's business."

"Respect." She nodded and reached for her drink.

"I don't discuss it with my friends, and not much with women I've been with in the past, either."

"Are you afraid of gold diggers?"

"Nope. If a woman is mine, she won't have to worry about being provided for. We'll work together to reach our goals, but she'll never struggle or have to be the main breadwinner. I'm not broke, and I'm working my way to owning that fitness center, but I do expect some things in return. Loyalty, love, affection, devotion. Anyway, to answer your question—long story short," he ran his hand along his leg, trying to find the right words, "My grandfather runs a large enterprise, a family business. Us Wildes are everywhere in Texas. Houston is still the main hub, if you will. Some are seen, some are not. People know us though, especially in this day and age."

"Yeah, I found that out after the fact. What type of

business does your grandfather run?"

"It's a, shall I say, arduous industry. Most people know that it's not exactly G-rated, so to speak. Some of it is legal, some not so much, and I'm not admitting to anything that the police and Feds don't already know. It is what it is."

"He makes pornos or something?" Lennox burst out laughing and shook his head. She looked so serious. "What?" She laughed lightly. "I do OnlyFans. I keep it on the low from people I know though. Shiiiiit, there' a lot worse things in this world."

"Nah, he doesn't make pornos. He deals with loans, you could say. Rentals…" He winked at her. Her lips curled in a smile.

"Okay. So big poppa is a land shark."

"That and many other things…" *Bookie shit, arms sales, extortion, online gambling enterprises, strong arming, middleman for feuding companies that owe money… the shit Grandpa is involved in and running would make your head spin. Satan in the flesh.*

"You didn't flinch when I mentioned OnlyFans."

"Why should I?"

"You pulled a stunt tonight and not only watched me dance, but tossed money at me. So you're okay with all of this, huh?"

"Sex sells. You're a beautiful woman. You use your feminine wiles to stack a bank roll. This isn't anything new." He shrugged, not certain what she was getting at.

Her brow rose in suspicion. "Why would someone like *you* be interested in a woman who does that?" Her voice was velvet, though bordered with sharpened blades. Through darkened eyes, she peered at him. Waiting.

"That doesn't have shit to do with me. And what is all this about, a man like me? I'm not better than you, and you're not better than me."

"I know you're not better than me. That's not what I'm saying. Women are superior to men, actually, but that's another topic for another day." They both laughed at that. "You seem more traditional is what I'm getting at."

"You think I'm a square?"

"No, not at all. But you always came across as having a certain, I don't know, expectation of the roles women and men play in relationships."

"Hmmm." He thought about that for a few seconds. "Yeah, but that doesn't mean it turned me off or swayed me in any way. I mean, I haven't deviated from when I told you that you're mine, even with what I know now regarding how you make your cash."

"You think if I give you a chance, you can change me, don't you?" She smirked.

He shrugged. "I don't give a shit about tryna change you, Nadia. You'd change for yourself."

"Oh, so you're just hopin' and wishin', huh? A change is going to come, like the gospel song says, right? Born by a river... praying to God, and wishing on stars. Thinking you can influence me in some way, maybe like a YouTuber lyin' about how good some product is that don't nobody else give a fuck about until they say it's incredible, and then they go cash a check off of folks' gullibility. Be slick with it, why don't you?" She sucked her teeth.

"You sound bitter and defensive."

"I am, Lennox. But I also can see a plot a mile away. My

mother raised hell and bail, but she ain't raise no dummy."

"Good, because I don't want a dummy. Stupid people are time consuming and energy draining. Raise? I don't raise women or try to. Women aren't children and I don't treat them as such. I'm the top dog, but I never try to boss my woman around."

"Nobody has ever been able to boss me around since I was a child, and you of all people should know that. That's the least of my concerns." She reached for another tissue. Perhaps she had allergies. Allergic to her own bullshit.

"Like I said, Nadia, you'd want to change your occupation on your own because this isn't what you really want. I don't have to do *shit* for you to come to that conclusion. But in the interim, it's your life, and I'm not really concerned about that. I've read a lot in the last few years about women. Relationships. Love. I had a lot to learn. I was wrong about a lot of things. You ever heard of Dr. Saint Aknaten?"

"Ache-gnat-tan who?!"

"No," he laughed. "Dr. Saint Aknaten. He's a sex therapist out of New York. I had an online consultation with him sometime back. I was goin' through something. Anyway, he wrote all of these books about how women think, how men should treat women and stuff like that. A friend of mine told me about him. He's brilliant. Some have said he's psychic, but in the interviews I've seen of him on YouTube, he dances around that question or acts like that's silly."

"Do you think it's silly?"

"What? That people say he's psychic?"

"Yeah."

"I would not have until it happened to me. I don't believe in psychics, well, I didn't. I'd still never go to someone claiming to be one but this guy, this man was different, Nadia. He is so in tune with people that it's scary."

"What happened?" Her eyes widened and she leaned forward, soaking in every word.

"He uh, he said some things he couldn't possibly have known about me. They were *very* specific. Like, you'd have to be a fly on the wall to know this shit. Super precise. The entire consultation was hair-raising. Not only is this man extremely intelligent and down-to-Earth, Nadia, the guy lives what he talks about. He walks the walk. I have some of his books if you wanna see them."

"Is he a cult leader or something? This some emotional pyramid scheme?" She smirked.

"No, of course not. I learned a lot from him. About the world. About women. About me. I'll just leave it at that." He shrugged. "I don't really wanna get too heavy into that right now, but just remind me about the books if you're interested." She nodded in agreement. "Back to the topic. My point is, in regard to you thinking I want to change you, like I said, I won't have to. There's a season for everything."

"I see you're still a deep thinker. I think people were always surprised about that... findin' out you're not just some meathead. You like to learn. To read. To discover. All of that aside, Mr. Universe, you don't actually know me anymore, not enough to be able to tell me what I want. No offense, and as far as—"

"None taken."

"And as far as you not being concerned about any of this, well, I find that hard to believe."

"Why?"

"I remember you being a little jealous and possessive when a guy would hit on a woman you were with, or—"

"You just said that I don't know you anymore. Alluding to the fact that too much time has passed, and you're all grown up. Well, that can go both ways. In some ways, like a leopard, a man or woman never changes their spots. Who we are at our true core rarely changes, but we can evolve. We can improve."

"We can devolve, too."

"That goes without saying. What's understood doesn't need to be explained, but I can control myself better now. You're not the only one who is older. Time snatches everyone at the same seconds, minutes, and hours of the day. We are all revolving around the sun. The same calendar rules every living thing. No one is left out. There are no Benjamin Buttons, either. Life is not happening in reverse. In honesty though, 'cause no other motherfucker knows me better than my own self, I'm still a little possessive, yet not jealous. Don't confuse the two."

They went quiet for a spell.

"I sell my body, but I'm not a prostitute. And I like how I look naked. I like it when people wanna fuck me, but can't."

Now she had to know she was poking at the bear. Saying things to try and gauge his reaction. She was almost getting off on the idea of tormenting him this way. Testing the waters. Not that she wasn't being one hundred percent honest, of that he was sure. She licked her lower lip as if trying to gather a drop of sweet nectar before it dried up. Her gaze narrowed on him as she did so, then she leaned forward ever so slightly, allowing her Asian style silk robe to fall open, exposing part of her breast.

"Are you trying to convince me, or you?" She didn't respond to his question. Instead, she grabbed her glass and took a sip of her drink. "Makes me no difference. Like I said, I don't have anything to worry about. One day, you'll stop, and not because I asked you to. Not because you're ashamed. Not because your mother didn't raise no dummy and I'm not the boss of you. Not because you were bullied into it, either. But because you'll remember that your body is worth more than any price you could charge to see or touch it."

"It's just skin. Who I am on the inside is never for sale."

"If it's just skin, then you wouldn't care if someone tattooed the word 'SHITHEAD' across your titties. If it's just skin, you wouldn't care about how moisturized and firm it was for your shows, and what clothing you put on it to make yourself look even more beautiful. The expensive perfumes… You wouldn't be concerned about piercings, covering scars with makeup and the like. You glow. You take damn good care of yourself. If something is worthless, you wouldn't put so much effort into it."

"I didn't say I didn't want my outer appearance to look good, or that physically I'm worthless. I'm saying that it's not as important as my mind," she pointed to her temple, "and who I am on the inside."

"You're right, but you're still contradicting yourself."

"How so?"

"If it's not important, give it away for free then. If who you are internally is the real pot of gold, treat that as such, and not the other way around."

She nodded with a taut jerk of her head, then ran her fingers through her mane.

"Let me explain something to you, Nadia. Everything we do in life, if it's not our ultimate goal, is just a stepping stone. You're an amazing dancer, that's trill, I can't deny that, but it's not the end game. No judgment." He raised both hands as if in surrender. "I'm not perfect. I've done my dirt. We live and learn. I decided I wanted to clean up my act and do better, though. No more chasing skirts, as my grandfather would say. Being a dog was in my nature. I was never shitty to you because I felt something different for you, and you weren't one of my conquests."

"I'm the one that got away, then. A challenge. Time has passed, and—"

"I don't care how much time has passed. You are the same, where it counts, Nadia. Look, you or I can read a book from thirty years ago, and though some of the jargon and music mentioned may have changed, the premise is still the same, and relatable. You are the same. In here." He pointed to his chest. "I could see it in your eyes right away. That little broken girl is still inside of you, Humpty Dumpty as you said, but you've been taking care of her the best way you know how. You took a detour. You're still traveling though, and that's all that matters."

"Oh, so you're Dr. Phil, Dr. Seuss, Mother Goose, and

a travel agent now, too? As I said, you don't know the real me. I wish you did, Lennox, but you don't. Do you want something to eat?" She glanced down at her watch. "You might be sitting here starving. I should've asked earlier, but I—"

"No, I'm not hungry. At least, not for food. Anything I don't know about you, I can learn. I have no problem being a student, especially when it comes to a woman I want."

Her lips pursed as she crossed her arms. "Why are you single?"

"Is this an interview for the position of your man? Why are you asking me that?"

"You're not supposed to answer a question with another question," she simpered. "Look how attractive you are."

"Okay. You got a mirror around here so I can?"

She snickered. "Silly. You know why I said that. You appear to be a good catch. You're employed. Two jobs. The gym and the club. You have some money saved up, I imagine. Your own place. Nice truck. You told me you don't have any kids, so that makes you a unicorn. If you're anything like you used to be, a nice guy, too."

"Wrong. I *chose* who to be nice to. That's a small number. Nice guys finish last. Anyway, it's simple, really. I'm single because I want to be. Then I saw you, and I no longer want to be so..." She swallowed. He watched her throat tighten, and delighted in her embarrassment and flushed complexion. "Name somethin' you think I don't know about you."

"I'm not that sweet girl just out here tryna make it anymore. I may look the same, but I'm different. And I'm okay with that." Her fingers twitched as if she were holding an invisible cigarette between them.

"Nadia, I didn't love you back then because you were sweet. I loved you because you were hurt, yet still motivated to move around that discomfort and elevate yourself. You're a survivor. You'd cry to me, but then do things to help yourself. I've never seen you as helpless or a victim. The hand you were dealt was unfair—still, you never believed you deserved that pain. I recognized that pain. I wasn't there for you just to be a shoulder to cry on. Rather, I could identify with it."

"What you know about that type of pain, rich boy?" she taunted, smiling big and wide—pretty, but there was a sinister quality behind it. "They say money changes people and is the root of all evil. I'm not so sure about that. Maybe if my mother had more cash and a happily ever after, she wouldn't have taken her frustrations out on me, and maybe if my father had had some cash, he wouldn't have treated me how he did, acted in such an ugly way. Dead men can't make no money, but he signed his own death certificate." She snorted.

Her choppy, cruel laughter sounded like an echo from an empty tomb.

"Money doesn't change anyone, Nadia. It just shows who a person *really* is. You wear dark humor like a suit of armor." Her smile slowly faded. Then he continued, "What do I know about that type of pain?" He gently grabbed his right earlobe and cured an itch. The hot swell of emotions made him sweat. "You didn't know much about me. Just what I wanted you to see. Like I said, I was nice to you, but

I'm not nice, by blood. It was a calculated choice. To love and protect you. That's all I cared about back then, and that's all I care about now. Always remember that…"

CHAPTER SIX

Founding Fathers

THE TIME WAS 4:12 AM. Lennox tossed his keys onto his hallway table. The echo of the metal hitting the wood reverberated in his home. On the outside, the one-story brick house was rather modest, with adequate landscaping, an American flag, and nice curb appeal, but on the inside he'd turned it into a modern spot, with state-of-the-art appliances and brushed metals and wood. He kept his place clean, airy, minimalistic, yet presentable.

The faint smell of coffee from the day before lingered in the air. He caught his reflection in a nearby wood-framed mirror hanging in the adjacent waiting area of his dwelling, and slowed as he removed his leather jacket. His eyes were slightly bloodshot, but full of hope. It had been a long night of hashing it out with Nadia, but that was much needed. In many ways, she was the same ol' Nadia, but in others she'd changed.

More mature, for one. She was upfront with her feel-

ings, not having to be coaxed to express her disappoint-
ments, mistakes and needs. She did not belabor any of the
details, and didn't share too much. She seemed more open.
Approachable. However, she was also an enigma. That
turned him on even more. The woman she'd once been and
the woman she'd become had merged into a beautiful
puzzle he was desperate to solve. The prospect that their
hours spent catching up were only the tip of the iceberg
was, for him, icing on the cake. She was intriguing. She
excited him. She was hardworking and a blend of old-
fashioned and contemporary.

If it were somehow possible, she was even more beautiful now than before. She'd filled out a bit, she glowed.
They'd gone back and forth for several hours, filling in the
holes of worn memories and dusting off the broken pieces
of glass from their pasts, trying to fix something that was
intended to be mutilated and damaged until they left this
thing called life. And yet, as a duo, they were patching it
back together, one jagged edge at a time.

He stood there in front of that mirror, replaying their
conversation in his mind. Remembering how, after her
second glass of Vodka and cranberry juice, her tongue had
loosened and the confessions poured out a little easier.

Like how she'd been jealous of him and an ex-girlfriend,
Vicki. He'd had no clue about her feelings. Nadia shared
that Vicki had threatened her, way back then—told her to
back off. Seemingly, it involved the woman's intuition that
Nadia had the hots for her man and their 'innocent' work
powwows hadn't been so innocent after all.

Nadia also admitted that she would check up on him

every now and again, too—such as asking people how he was, and trying to find any trace of him on social media to spy on him from afar. She had frustrations at his lack of a cyberspace footprint. Indeed, he kept his private life pretty much offline, so she'd been left with more questions than answers.

He hung his jacket up and made his way to his kitchen. He had to be at work in a few hours, but wasn't in the mood for sleep. His mind was running a mile per minute and showed no signs of slowing down. After washing his hands, he opened the refrigerator and poured himself a glass of filtered water. All he could hear was his own breathing and loud swallowing as he stood in the dimly lit room. When he was finished, he smelled a bit of her perfume on him, from when he'd hugged her goodbye. He pulled at his shirt, pinched the fabric between his thumb and forefinger, and brought the material to his nose. Closing his eyes, he inhaled all that was her, falling into a beautiful trance.

He ultimately released the cloth, and got back to his agenda. Placing the empty glass in the sink, he headed up the hallway to his bedroom, where he stripped down to his black boxer briefs and slipped under the thick comforter, cellphone in hand.

As soon as he opened the device to view workout equipment and routines, perhaps listen to a bit of music, he noticed a missed text message sent a couple of hours earlier, around the time he silenced his notifications while with Nadia. Rubbing his eyes, he brought the phone closer to his face, squinting to make out the words through tired eyes. It was his father.

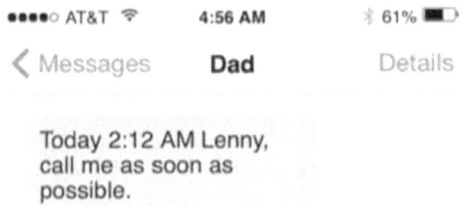

Raking his hair back, he loudly exhaled. He called his father's number, cleared his throat and waited.

"Good, you're awake," the man answered on the third ring. "How are you doing?" Dad's voice slurred as if he'd been drinking. His tone moved in sluggish waves.

"How am I doing? Dad, do you know what time it is? I'm in bed."

"Okay, I'll just make this quick."

"Please!" A strange emotion came over him, much like a sense of loss.

"Your grandfather is waiting for you to let—"

"Grandpa's terroristic attacks on this family? *This* is

what couldn't wait? This is why you texted me two hours ago?"

"I've waited long enough. I need to know what you plan to do. I figured you'd be home and besides, you're a night owl."

"The only calls or texts I want at two in the mornin' are for money or sex, and since you're my father and have been told by your own father that I can't have another dime, I can rest assured you ain't callin' for either one of those damn options."

"You were at his house, even though he's all but disowned you. I know things are going to get worse if you drag this out. The family is talking about it."

"I don't give a crap what the family is talking about! The family collectively kisses Grandpa's ass, like he's the second coming of Jesus!"

"I'm trying to talk to you."

"Well, now you've talked to me. Is there anything else? I have to go."

"Yes, there's somethin' else, boy! You've not answered him. This is serious! I love you and don't want to see you hurt, Lenny. What you don't understand is that this is for your own good. You work long hours and get peanuts. If you at least take him up on this, you'd be able to negotiate your schedule and make more money than you've ever dreamed of. All of the stuff you wanna do, the cars you wish for, the gym you want to own, the homes you want... it would be at your fingertips. You'd be set."

"Like I told an old friend tonight, and now I'm tellin' you, money isn't everything. My life isn't easy, but Grandpa is not the type of person I'm willing to sell my soul for."

Dad was quiet for a bit. All he could hear was the man blowing out smoke from his cigarette. Then, the sounds of him gulping down something strong and wet. "Lennox, I understand, okay?" His voice was clearer now as he tried to control himself, no doubt, and avoid saying anything to tip over the apple cart. "Yes, my father is a difficult person at times, but he loves this family, Lenny. You can't deny that. He's leaving behind a legacy. That's why he's bein' so stern. You're letting your stubbornness control your rationality."

"The only control I see right about now is how your corrupt father is trying to control me like he controls *you*. Nah, I'm good." His phone flashed with a text message from Nadia right at that moment: *I hope you made it home safely*. He was never really safe, but he appreciated her checking on him all the same.

"Lenny, you and I don't want it to be like this. But it is. A part of me would love for you to be able to just do whatever you want, throw caution to the wind, but that's not how life works. You've been hand-selected, chosen to help run an entire department of your grandfather's empire. The zoo."

"He wants me and several of my cousins to run it to-gether. None of us are interested."

"I'm not interested in a lotta shit I have to do, Lenny. That doesn't mean it doesn't need to get done. Money aside, do you know what all of this really means?"

"It means that your fear of him outweighed your love for me, and my mother."

Silence.

"...That's not fair, Lennox. I love ya... both of ya. What happened—that's not my fault." His voice cracked.

That's why Dad drank late at night now. He'd get shit-faced at least a few times a week in the comfort of his big ass, empty house. Running from memories. Running from guilt. He drowned in the recollections by sinking into a pint of something. A cold can. A tepid wine glass. He drifted to the bottom of his aquatic memories, lying low with the broken bones of dreams long gone. Only, he never fully died from drowning. He'd just lose his breath as his ocean of a father's wrath swallowed him, the dark world closing in around him. Squeezing him to death.

"Lenny, you don't know all the details. You didn't get to see all the times I stood up to him but lived to pay the price!" A knot formed in his stomach. "I tried to keep you away from this when you and Silva were children, but when my father sets his eyes on someone and wants them, he does everything he can to get them."

"I'm not some object on a shelf. I'm your son! Some-body from my generation had to finally tell him no. I and a few more of my cousins are the only ones who've said enough is enough."

"And now you're payin' for it. We *both* will be paying for it if you don't take him up on his offer."

"I want you to stop calling me Lenny, Dad. You only do it now when you're drunk. It's no longer a term of endear-ment. I associate it with your discomfort and anxiety. They both stink. As far as his offer and how I'm gonna move forward, I'm still sortin' this out. Some are even waitin' it out. That's not my plan, but I don't blame them."

"That's a dead man's game. He doesn't get better with age, Lenny. He's gotten worse with his demands. He is leaving a legacy behind," the man stressed again. *Fuck his legacy*. "He wants to make sure he hands over the reins to the *right* people. Out of all of our family, he chose you, me, and some others to help him achieve this. So we'd have somethin' to pass down to our own children and grandchildren. You know how big our clan is. You know some of your kin is resentful that your grandfather didn't want them on his team! They'd jump at the opportunity you have before you, Lenny... sorry, Lennox... but he wants who he wants. Just like you've always been a person who went after what you wanted. You have to respect that. You haven't responded to your grandfather's proposal. That's the only reason I contacted you so late at night. You need to, and you need to do it right away."

"It wasn't a proposal. It was blackmail, promises that I don't care to entertain, and his typical threats."

"Lennox! For fuck's sake! You know he's prepared to do exactly what he said he'd do! Did you hear me? This isn't the time to—"

"Don't tell me what to do. This isn't your decision. It's mine."

"But it affects *all* of us, damn it!"

"You never had the guts to stick up for Mom and yourself, then she died and it was too late. Now you want me to fall behind you, to get the same treatment. I know full well what he said he'd do, and my time is *not* up. You had to get wasted to even have this conversation with me because you know he is dead wrong. His own grandson tried to kill him! That should tell you something."

"Your cousin Kage is a damn lunatic. Certifiable! That sister of mine birthed a mental basket case. He's been nuttier than squirrel shit from day one. You can't really use him as an example." He snorted.

"Look, stay in your lane, Dad, and let me figure this out."

"There's nothing to figure out! My father is no damn bluffer. If he says he's gonna do something, he's going to do it. Good, bad, or indifferent. You think I'm some pushover when it comes to him, but I did what I did to protect my wife and children! That's strength! You're here, alive, because of *me*! I stood up to him when he said things about your mother, but because you didn't witness it, you think it never happened. And I'd do it again. I loved that woman! Damn you! You have no idea what she and I went through and the stressors we endured on behalf of you and Silva. How dare you, Lenny... how dare you..." Dad's voice trailed, growing weaker with each word spoken. "You're just like her though.

"Rebelling just to stick it to someone is foolish! You gotta have a plan. Now you listen to me, and you listen good! You tell your grandfather that you accept his offer, and you do it ASAP so we can move forward. If you give a damn about your mother, like you say you do, then you'll put all that past shit behind you, and do the right thing. Your grandfather knows your weakness... and he is using it. Don't lose everything, and all for nothing."

With that, the man abruptly ended their connection. Lennox stared at the screen, which now noted the time and how long the call lasted before it faded to black...

CHAPTER SEVEN

Mother Nature

"**M**AMA, I'M IN the parking lot. See you in a little bit." Nadia ended the call after leaving the voice message. She sat in her car for a bit, listening to 'Good Good,' by Usher, Summer Walker and 21 Savage. She grabbed her vape, but decided to put it down and just simmer in the moment. She whispered the lyrics to the song while snapping her finger to the slow, easy beat. After the tune ended, she grabbed her black and white snakeskin purse from the passenger seat, removed her key ring with the pink rabbit foot, got out of her car, locked it with her fob, and hightailed it towards her mother's townhome.

Once she reached the door, she slid her copy of her mother's house key into the lock and entered the dwelling. Inside, the cool air gave her chill bumps, and the alarm was going off. *Mama always keeps it cold as a polar bear's tits up in here...* She locked the front door and went to the kitchen, her silver and white Skechers sneakers squeaking on the floor as she headed to the control panel to turn off the security system.

Laying her purse onto the kitchen table, she stood there for a minute and took a few deep breaths. It had been several weeks since she'd been by, and the last visit she'd made was short and sweet as possible. She looked about to see if anything had changed since her last time here. Maybe a new end table, or vase?

Nope. Mama's home was the same. Mostly all white furniture and wall colors. Looked like a blank canvas. Few signs of life. Cold like the air conditioning that blew through. The place had all updated stainless-steel appliances, and little in the lines of décor. To the average eye, it was a lovely place, but it didn't breathe. It didn't move. It had no vibe. No flavor. No soul.

One cat palm plant lovingly named Lady, due to a ladybug that had been on it when it was purchased, had been growing in a corner for three years now, where a window blew abundant sunny kisses. At the deep kitchen basin, she pumped some soap on her hands and rinsed them off with hot water, then dried them on a paper towel. She tossed the thing in the trash and opened the refrigerator door, finding a bottle of water, and sat on a white bar stool at the kitchen counter.

Instead of messing around on her phone while she waited for her mother to arrive, she reached for one of the magazines on the counter. Nadia looked at the half-torn label on the front of the periodical that displayed her mother's name and address, then glossed over the shiny cover in colors of amber and orange. *Mama's subscription to*

002 Houston.

She flipped through the pages, her mouth instantly watering at the sight of the fancy food from various local restaurants, plated in ornamental ways. Moments later, she heard her mother's key in the door. She turned around in the chair to face her. Waiting. Mama walked right past the kitchen as if she hadn't noticed her there, but she knew she had. Nothing got past that woman. With a loud sigh and heavy thud, Mama's toolbox and bag hit the coffee table, as it always did for years. That toolbox, big, red and heavy, was Mama's pride and joy. She'd been an electrician for over thirty years.

"Mama," Nadia called out with a smile. "Have a good day at work?"

"This dumb man blew a fuse by fuckin' around with too many things plugged into an outlet in his first-floor bathroom. He didn't notice 'til this mornin' that his refrigerator was out. Groceries spoiled. He checked the fuse box but didn't see nothin' wrong, so he figured it was electrical. Turned around and called us and booked an appointment. Now, a normal person would say, 'Well hell, I ain't have no problems until my wife plugged in her hairdryer. Didn't put two and two together." She shrugged, then slipped out of her jacket. "So I go to the fuse box, flip his switch, then five minutes later hand him a bill. I was nice, ain't make fun or give him a hard time and even knocked a bit off 'cause of the coupon we had."

"Don't tell me, he got mad that he had to pay anything at all?"

"Baby girl, you already know. I ain't the help!" Mama

stormed across the room and turned down the air. "Little stocky pig-nosed White dude, about yea high." She put her hand out, indicating his diminutive stature. "This mothafucka, Nadia, had an attitude soon as I cast a shadow on his front do'e. Seing a woman and immediately thought whatever... I've seen that look ten thousand times. He was all up on me the whole time. Watchin'."

"Probably thought you were going to steal something." Nadia snorted, turning back to the magazine.

"Of course he did. Once he saw I wasn't no con artist, he eased up a bit, but then when I told him what the problem was, he laughed it off and just thought I was gon' leave. Like that was the end of the story. I set him straight. Ol' boy wanted to get in my face because I still charged for drivin' over there, problem solving, and my time. I work for a company just like most people, and they want their due. He felt like it should've been free. Shiiiid. Took ere'thang in me not to cuss his ass out." Mama snatched the remote control off the coffee table and turned on the television.

"Ain't nothing in this life free, 'cept death and aggravation."

Mama's whole face spread into a smile. "That's right, baby. I taught you well."

The tall, brown-skinned woman with straight, shoulder-length salt and pepper hair pulled back into a ponytail, stomped into the kitchen, and turned the water on to wash her dirty hands. After they were good and wet, she pumped three dollops of sudsy soap into her palms, vigorously rubbed them together, then rinsed.

"You talk to your grandmama? She asked 'bout you the

other day."

"I haven't talked to Nana in a couple of weeks. I knew she was recovering from her surgery, so I didn't want to get on her nerves too much. She was tryna sleep the last two times I called."

Nadia was close to her maternal grandmother. They had a lot of great conversations and good times, but Nana had been having problems with her arthritis and headaches. Mama reached into the refrigerator and pulled out a bottle of beer. Moments later, the top was off, and she guzzled half of it down in a matter of seconds.

"You hungry?" Mama asked after belching.

"No. I ate a couple of hours ago." Mama nodded in understanding then sat across from her. Her dingy blue jumpsuit with the company name, 'Ace Electric Heating and Air' and her first name, JoAnn, sewn on it was something that Nadia had seen for years. Mama mainly worked for several properties around town who hired her to do the electrical repairs in their rentals, but every now and again, the company would send her out to emergency calls such as this. It was always something, but the money was consistent, so the woman seldom complained.

"You gotta work tonight?" Mama questioned after a brief silence.

"Storm comin' in, so I decided to call off. I'm not pressed for the money or anything. I can skip a day or two."

"You called off?" Mama's voice rose as if surprised.

"You know I don't like getting caught in no storm." She turned another page of the magazine. Brazilian food.

"Hmph," Mama huffed, then mumbled something she didn't catch. Her eyes narrowed as she ran her hand up and down the beer bottle, caressing it like a lover. "What? You scared of a lil' rain for? Just drive slowly, and don't be switching lanes all crazy, treating it like some twerking contest."

"I just don't like it is all." She shrugged. She hated lying to Mama, but also disliked talking about things that hurt her as that conversation normally didn't go anywhere but downhill fast. All Mama would do was tell her to tighten up. Straighten up. Woman up. Fear wasn't in the woman's vocabulary. Fear was a four lettered 'F' word. Literally. When Nadia was a little girl, if she cried after falling and busting her knee, or got upset about a lost toy, Mama would raise hell. Mama despised tears. She made iron look like melted butter, and mountains look like pebbles tossed about in sand.

"You are still afraid because of that car accident you had in the rain in Atlanta, ain't you?"

The room suddenly felt colder than ever. Nadia kept her gaze on the open magazine, focusing on the image of an elegant couple sitting at a table covered in white linen, smiling at one another while holding the stems of fancy champagne flutes.

"It was impactful." She kept her eyes on that smiling couple. The two paid actors or models who pretended to be in love, and out on the town.

"Impactful?" Mama sucked her teeth, reached into the breast pocket of her uniform, and took out her cigarettes. "What the hell is that supposed to mean? A meteor hitting the Earth is impactful. That was four years ago. You had some cuts and bruises. You lived." She leaned back, looking somewhat disgusted. "So you just gonna let some rain talk you outta some money?"

Here we go. "You don't even like me dancing, so what does it matter?"

"I *don't* like you doin' that shit. Ain't nothin' changed." Mama lit her cigarette then took a drag and blew smoke out the corner of her mouth. "You out here busting it wide open for a bunch of mothafuckas who ain't about shit. Got wives that they lied to and told they had to work late, or they're standing behind some pulpit preachin' the word, talking about how bad lust is, but just the night before they were sitting in some cheap plastic chair that's probably got dried jerk sauce on it, and I don't mean from no Jerk Chicken appetizer, either." She rolled her eyes. "…Sittin' there all hard and sweaty, smellin' like piss, getting turned on by women like my daughter—who wouldn't fuck them in their *real* life, if yo' life depended on it. Throwin' money away at some fantasy! You're just a wet dream." Mama sucked her teeth.

"Movies are a fantasy, even the realistic ones. TVs shows, sitcoms, soap operas, game shows even, are all fantasies. It's not real. It's scripted. Rehearsed. Amusement parks are fantasies, and people pay for that too, Mama. There is no Mickey Mouse in real life, and there are no princesses living in tall pink castles, either. But it's okay to dream. Even if it's wet…" Mama grunted and tapped her cigarette. Ashes fell into the ashtray that sat between them. "You love going to the movies. Unless it's a biography, and even that has some creative license, none of that shit on that screen is real, Mama. Fantasies… sometimes that's all we have." Nadia shrugged. "I'm not knockin' nobody's coping mechanisms just to get through life. We all need to escape every now and again."

"Lookin' at naked asses bouncing to music ain't no copin' mechanism, and it ain't no fantasy. It's exploitation. It helps no-good mothafuckas cheat. Puts ideals in their head. If it was just dancin' and you were fully clothed, that would be one thing. But you strip down. They see *every-thing*… from your roota to your toota."

"Some men just enjoy being in the company of beautiful women, Mama. My body is only being looked at, not given away or even sold. I'm not a prostitute and besides, not everyone's story is the same."

"It's all about lust, like I said, so the story *is* the same. Don't matter that the book cover is different—the chapters all read identical, the pictures are carbon copies, and the ending is never a surprise. Music. Drinks. Drugs. Ass. Tits. Pussy. That's it, that's all." She tapped her cigarette into the ashtray again. "Most of those bastards got ass at home. Why they need to see yours? Why don't they shove some of that money into their own girlfriends' or wives' G-strings? I'm certain they'd appreciate it."

"That's where the fantasy comes in. Sometimes their wives don't look at them the way I do. We don't know them, so we can play up to how they *wish* to be perceived. Their wives and girlfriends don't dance for them and make them feel like they're the center of their worlds. Because they don't want to, or they can't."

"…And they shouldn't want to. I raised you, Nadia, to never love a man more than he loves you, and never love nobody more than you love yourself. It's not selfish, it's survival. It's best not to love they asses at all, 'cause men don't know how to love. They can't even spell love." Nadia closed the magazine and reached for another. "Their whole existence revolves around what a bitch can do for them. What she can cook for them. Clean up for them. Suck off for them. Indentured servitude. Slavery still exists. It's the woman. *We're* the slaves. First to a White slave master, then to our men. Take, take, take. Seldom give, except for plenty of grief. All these guys care about is money a woman brings to the table, and what orders she can obey.

"Shit, we built the damn table and set it, too! Our religion has been used against us. Your father became a preacher on account of him realizing he could manipulate people by saying it's the word of God. The purposeful misinterpretations of the Bible is the worst thing to ever happen to humankind." *That pizza looks good.* She flipped a page. "It's been used to teach us to tear each other apart, to always go wit' the man's side against other women, and to fight each other for some dusty ol' dick. We call our daughters fast, and blame them when grown ass men flirt with 'em, or worse. How we even know God a man, huh? Callin' Him Father. If He created us, then he's a woman. That's what makes sense."

"Why do you think that?" Nadia removed a glass lid from a matching candy bowl and popped a mint into her mouth, sucking loudly.

"Women give birth, not men! That's why. How we

gonna be somebody's children, but never came from a womb? That's patriarchy. A bunch of bull!"

"God isn't human."

"Right, so why should it be a He?! To control us. We don't assign a gender at all, and if we just must, why not call God, Mama?! Mama brings life into this world. We're the incubator. No seed can do anything without first being put into the soil, and given sunlight and rain. Semen has no life without us, and yet women create every time we open our damn eyes, and even in our sleep!" Mama's words shook that entire room.

The woman was crazy. She was opinionated and harsh, at times downright rude, but one thing was certain: she was also smart and a thinker, whether Nadia disagreed with her or not. The way she put ideas together was thought provoking to say the least. That couldn't be taken away.

"Nadia." She crushed her cigarette in the ashtray and shook her head. "They been lyin' to us since that ugly story of Adam and Eve. For all we know, Adam ate that damn apple, if there even was one, and we've been bamboozled."

Nadia was used to her mother going off like this. Since she was a little girl, Mama had made it perfectly clear that she was at war with God. Religion. Bible folks. The woman had been raised in the church, and had been a devoted Christian up until she gave birth to her second child, Nelson. She loved God, and claimed to still love God, but now, she had questions. Some of Mama's points, wild or not, couldn't be easily rejected. They had merit, and deserved exploration. Nadia dismissed most of them, but held onto a few. Occasionally, Mama would say something that would make her pause. Give her food for thought. She also knew that this was how her mother dealt with her animosity towards men, or mankind in general.

Mama didn't hate men—that would mean she still cared about them, or desired them on some level. But she would simply look past them in a crowd, as if they were a tree standing in her way, or just the invisible air itself. She merely saw no use for them.

Men are only needed to make babies... she'd say, adding that the world is already overpopulated, anyway. *Men are stronger and can build things.* Mama said women can build too, and, in fact, build better. The machines can do the heavy lifting. She'd taught Nadia how to change tires, put oil in cars, bake a fantastic cake, plunge a toilet, fix a leaking sink, change a fuse, sew on a button, kill a bug or set it free, and drive a stick like a pro. Yet, despite all of this, the woman didn't look how people imagined she would. She had a real pretty face, and rough hands, still gorgeous in middle age, with deep dimples, a pretty smile, and clear skin with a radiant, rich hue.

She'd caught plenty of men's eyes in her youth, and her attractive looks kept them coming. Her eyes were big and round, dark brown with naturally long lashes, and her lips were full, pouty, and a shade of plum, mostly from smoking so much. Oddly though, it only looked like dark lipstick on her. The perfect dark wine stain. She was tall and slightly muscular about the arms, and when she spoke, even when she was talking about something funny or lighthearted, her tone always had bite. Mama was habitually angry, but showed flashes of mercy to the ones she loved. Just enough to not appear cold-hearted to her core. She was intimidating. Gifted. Brash. Determined.

Everything she set her mind to do, she did it, and usually well. There were chunks of Mama's past missing though. Pieces she didn't share. Gaps in time. After Nadia's little brother, Nelson, left for the military, she'd rarely seen her mother entertain anyone from the male gender. Nadia rarely knew of any men Mama dated after her divorce from her father, but she must've because she'd gotten pregnant and given birth to her brother three years after she'd been born. Nelson came into the world, but Mama never talked about his father. In fact, she didn't even know her brother's dad's name. Mama refused to speak on it.

"Mama, you said women backstab other women for a man. How do you think that plays out? Give me an example." She looked up from the magazine. Their eyes met.

Mama gave her a brutal and unfriendly stare, but she knew it wasn't designed for her.

"Women put men before themselves, thinking they're more important than us just 'cause of what is between their legs. We hurt one another because we've been brainwashed. Throw our own worth away and lift them up high. We call men kings that haven't run nothin' but their mouths. It could be small shit, like giving them the big piece of chicken while the kids get crumbs. What matters is how he treats his family, and what he does to provide. Then and only then should his ass be getting a big piece of anything. Bein' born wit' balls don't make you no leader. Don't make you no better." Mama's tone lowered and she calmed, but her eyes darkened.

"Sometimes, Mama, I think love is overrated." A soft cloud of sadness hovered over her head.

"It is. Most men are liabilities because all that testosterone done made them feel like they gotta rule over women to get acknowledged, feel powerful, and like somebody. What women are calling narcissistic is what most men are, period. We just found a fancy psychological name for it. Out of every ten men, only one of them is half-way normal, and that's not saying much."

"Mama, you know you made that statistic up." Nadia chuckled, grabbing her bottle of water. "Narcissism is real. My ex is one. I know another man that's not, though. At least he wasn't a long time ago." The image of Lennox filled her mind. "Your theory might hold water, though." She shrugged.

Most men ain't shit. I don't want to add to Mama's indignation though.

"Listen to me. Even men know they're useless, Nadia. That's why they lie to us, play on our nurturing instincts, so they can use us for our natural resources. Our wombs. Our intelligence. Our ability to take care of everyone and everything. They're abusive overgrown children! Believing the lies they've told us has been our downfall, and we gonna keep fallin' for it. We keep tripping over each other as we plummet to Hell. You think I'm evil and bitter, don't you?" She offered a watered-down smile.

"You're not evil, but you *are* bitter, even though not everything you said today was wrong. I don't know why you're bitter. I mean, I know what my father did, but besides him, I have no context. No clue. You don't talk to me. Not about stuff like that."

"…Ain't no reason to burden you with my private affairs." Her jaw tightened.

"Mama, your private affairs are no burden. When I was a child and would ask you things about yourself, you'd tell me to stay in a child's place. I'm grown now. I'd love to know more about what makes you *you*."

Mama's world was framed in dark shades of blue, with no light at the end of the tunnel. The woman saw no gray areas. Just a sea of darkness. She spent most of her time working, being in school to learn how to make more money, or dedicating herself to her chosen occupation. She was one of the hardest and most self-disciplined women she knew.

When Nadia and Nelson were little, Mama often disappeared into her bedroom with her music turned up high. That was her alone time. Her dating life, so to speak. Mama didn't keep no man. There was no guy sitting at their table or on their couch when they'd get in from school. It was clear that this was by choice. But Mama did keep a daily schedule and followed it, made sure they did too, and she kept a clean house, while taking care of her children. She'd been authoritarian, hard to get close to, but at times funny. Lunches were packed. Clothes were ironed. Hair was combed. She showed love through action, seldom saying the words.

"What do you want to know?"

Nadia was surprised by this invitation. She closed the magazine and set it aside, this time not reaching for another.

"Why did you hate it when me or Nelson would cry in front of you? Kids cry."

It was like Mama couldn't understand sadness. Couldn't stand to even hear someone crying, or falling to pieces. Or maybe she understood it *too* well, but refused to discuss it. She might have thought that even uttering the truth of any pain she endured would somehow give it power over her life, once again.

"I *know* kids cry. I didn't hate when you'd weep." Mama looked downright confused by such an accusation. Maybe she had no idea that she'd behaved that way for all of those years? Was she that lacking in self-awareness?

"It sure felt like it. Mama, you used to always say, *'Don't let nobody turn you into a victim twice.'*"

"Yeah, I remember that. The first time someone hurts you, well, they did what they did. It happened. It cut you deep. The second time someone hurts you, you were already warned. You ain't no pig, so stop rollin' in slop. Learn your lesson before you have to get down in that mud and drown."

"Did another man, besides my daddy, get you down in the mud and make you drown?"

Mama got up from her seat, grabbed another beer, and sat down with it.

"Nadia, why do you think the women your customers are in relationships with ignore them, and they come to your place of business instead? Besides you stating earlier that they know the real them, and it's a fantasy and all."

Nadia ran her hand along the side of her neck and massaged a kink.

"Because women nowadays have too much to do and no time to cater to a man's ego and pride. She's raising children, helping to take care of grandchildren in some cases, working in and outside of the home. She got a full plate, and playing make-believe to a husband isn't on the agenda. The last thing she wants to do is look at the man standin' at the end of the bed butt naked, pot belly sticking out, talkin' about, 'Gimme some.'"

Mama glared at her, then they both burst out laughing. She watched as the woman who brought her into the world gulped the rest of the beer, then tossed it into the nearby recycle bin.

"Nadia, everybody has a storm they're tryna avoid. I've got mine. You've got yours. You shouldn't let some shit you survived already turn you into a victim again. Storm… hard rain. It comes. It eventually will stop. But you still replayin' all that in your mind. It's controlling you. You got a lot of me in you, whether you want to admit it or not. You can blame me for a lot of things. Some of 'em are my fault. Many aren't. You can blame your father, too. But there's no one left to blame now for any failures in your life, at your big age, but *you*."

"I never said I blamed you for anything."

"You ain't have to… you just sometimes enjoyed it when I was down in the mud…" Her face flushed. "We all get pushed down in the mud, baby, at least a time or two, 'cause we didn't heed the warning from God the first time. It wasn't just one man that tried to kill my soul—it was many. It's their nature. Startin' with the way my daddy treated my mama, all the way 'til I dealt with Nelson's father. You tell me I don't talk to you, but the way I see it, the details ain't necessary, and they're mine to hold."

"But Mama I need you to tell me why you—"

"I told you once, and I'll tell you again. I don't hate men, and I don't expect you to, either. I just don't love or like them much. And that's what they can't tolerate. The idea of having no control over me. To that, I tell all those penis carriers to suck my left ovary, and if they can't stand me, well then take a load off and sit the fuck down then…"

CHAPTER EIGHT

Music and Petals

Absolute power corrupts absolutely.

L ENNOX TRI-FOLDED AND tucked his grandfather's letter away in the top drawer of his bedroom bureau. Dressed only in the dark gray jogging pants he'd worn for work at the gym, he pulled back the curtains from his window and opened the blinds to take a look outside.

He stared at his front lawn, then the houses across the street as his thoughts gathered. Then he noticed his American flag flapping aggressively in the wind. The sky was ashen and ominous. The clouds spawned and spoke in broken English, breaking apart then clustering tight as lightning lit up the sky, followed by loud booms. The soft fabric from the black drapes slipped against his fingertips as he released it, and went to sit on the edge of his bed under the dim lighting.

The sounds of JamWayne's, 'No Problems,' played as he closed his eyes and held his forehead. The skin that tightened beneath his touch as each tendril of disgust, each strain of stress emerged. Grandpa had reached out. He'd called and left a voicemail. It was straight and to the point:

"I plan to kill some time."

He listened, then deleted it. This was a stark reminder that time was not on his side, and his peace was on the chopping block. After some time, he got up, stretched, and walked into his small work-out cave. It was an inviting space, after the remodel he'd put it through. He'd torn down the wood-panel partitions to replace them with ivory walls on which hung framed motivational posters, and on one side he'd filled a bookcase with health books.

He got ready to put on one of his favorite country or rock 'n roll music playlists, but then spotted the old CD that Nadia had handed to him when he was visiting her apartment after dropping in at her job. He'd joked how he hadn't seen a CD in a long ass time, but she had an old school affinity for them, due to her mother always playing them, especially on weekends, when she was growing up. Now she uses them to create custom mixtapes to practice some of her dance moves for work. Slow jams, rap and hip hop, a little jazz and whatnot.

He picked up the CD, noting the scratches on both sides. Curious to see what was on it, he found an old CD player that had belonged to his mother and plugged it in, hoping it would play without a hitch. He waited with anticipation, then heard a slight skipping and crackling noise, reminiscent of a record player.

'Make Love 2 Me,' by Lorenzo, started to play.

"Oh my God." He chuckled. "I haven't heard this song

in forever." He only knew about it from some of the parties he'd attended back in the day. Wasn't his typical kind of music, but some things had a way of sticking with you.

He hopped on the treadmill, his mind relaxing as stonewashed recollections of Nadia playing timeworn 1990s R&B came back to him. She'd had a portable CD player and headphones that she'd bring to work, and would sing as she cleaned and sometimes helped open the Red Rooster restaurant with him. *Damn, I forgot all about that. She didn't have a bad singing voice, either...*

'Come Inside,' by Intro was the next song. He went to his bench press, lay down, and began to lift weights, his breathing in time with the loud music. Heavy rain pounded against his windows. 'Moments in Love,' by Art of Noise shook his memory box within his brain once again. Out poured something haunting and beautiful. His muscles burned and strained as he concentrated on each rep.

The good pain radiated through his body as he pushed himself to and beyond the limit, while melting into the melody that put him right back in The Red Rooster—under the flickering lights, just him and Nadia in the stock room at four in the morning. Arms wrapped tightly around one another. The moisture from her tears soaked into his shirt as he cradled her braided head in the cusp of his calloused palm. Some days she smelled like Jennifer Lopez Glow Eau de Toilette and baby powder. She felt like a soft dream on a hard night. But we all have to wake up...

He finished his reps, drenched in sweat, and sat there, allowing the extended version of the song to play on, vibrating his speakers with the rhythm of years gone past.

When it was over, he turned the music up, loud as it would go as 'Fly Girl,' by the Boogie Boys, began to play. Then, he headed to his en suite bathroom. Turning on the shower, he made sure it was ice cold and on full blast before he got under the bursting stream.

The music was practically vibrating his entire house as he reached for the soap and started bathing. When he was finished shampooing his hair and rinsing off, he snatched a fluffy white towel from the rack and dried off. He used his mouthwash, brushed his teeth, and made his way into the bedroom. He turned on the nightstand lamp and put on a pair of black pajama pants.

He went to his kitchen and grabbed an apple from a bowl on the counter, on the way to his home office. The room was sparsely decorated—an old black metal desk, antique lamp, a few pieces of baseball and football memorabilia, stamps and envelopes for sending mail, and a box of pens and pencils.

'I'm Ready,' by Kano, now burst from Nadia's CD. Sitting at his desk, he took a deep breath, then pulled out a slightly crushed shoebox out of one of the desk drawers. Inside was a layer of dark purple velvet material which protected the items inside. Cherished old photos, a half-empty bottle of perfume in a satchel, and miscellaneous items he'd kept forever. He pulled a handful of the photographs out, reverently holding the corners of yellowed pictures, tracing them as he sorted through the pile, one by one. Pausing, he gripped one in particular a little tighter, and put down the others. He smiled.

It was his mother giving him a big kiss on the cheek. He

looked to be about twelve in the photo. He had shoulder length dark hair, sun-kissed skin, and innocence still in his bright gray eyes. He brought the picture closer, and his vision blurred as moisture filled his eyes. *I miss you, Mom.* With a trembling hand, he transported the photo to his mouth, kissed his mother's image, then set it back inside of the box. He turned down the music and picked up his phone.

"Thank you for calling Poppy Florist Shop. This is Selma, how can I help you?"

"Yeah, hey, Selma. I've never ordered from you guys, but I did a quick search on my phone and saw that you are still open tonight. I know this stuff is usually done online, and I know it's raining hard tonight, but uh, I wanted to speak to a live person because timing is important right now."

"Okay, sir, well, what can I help you with?"

"I want to know if there's any way humanly possible you can deliver some flowers to a special lady in the next hour or two? I want it done ASAP. I'll pay double…"

NADIA HATED STORMS. She didn't mind so much if she were indoors, or simply caught in the rain while walking, protected under the safety of an umbrella, but driving in one, especially in heavy traffic at high speeds, made her muscles tense and filled her with fear. One of the few things in the world she avoided. She was glad to be safely home tonight.

In that moment, she relived the experience of her car swerving, then fishtailing until she was spun around and flipping three times—the roof on the ground, and blood trickling down her face. That had been a long time ago, but it wasn't the only bad thing that had happened during a bad downpour.

She'd had another situation transpire, one that her mother, grandmother, and absolutely nobody knew anything about, and there was no point in discussing it because it wouldn't change a damn thing. Shoving the memory out of her mind, she put the rest of her fresh fruit and vegetables away. She hadn't been home long from the grocery store, and was completely exhausted for some reason. Funny how when she'd take an occasional vacation day from work, she felt more sluggish than ever. Earlier in the day, she'd gone through her storage locker where she kept some of her furniture, to try and find a few things she needed for her apartment—to no avail.

Mountains of boxes were crammed in the space, some of them she'd left unlabeled to her regret, in her haste to get the hell out of Atlanta. Now, sorting through the mess seemed overwhelming. Her move from Georgia back to Texas had proved more than she'd bargained for, but all in all, it felt good to be back home. The only problem with being here though was that nightmares had a way of chasing you wherever you went, regardless of whether you were fast asleep or wide awake. She looked outside her living room window and shook her head.

It had been raining practically nonstop for two days straight. At almost seven in the evening, it looked as if it were midnight. She turned on the television and sat back, a smile forming on her face. Not because of the cheesy Tubi movie on the screen but because of... *Lennox.* He popped into her mind often, more than she'd ever be willing to admit to him.

She'd been evading his most recent calls, but then longed for him to contact her again. When too much time passed, she began to worry, and then would respond via text—just timely enough to let him know she was still there, but not so fast as to stroke his ego. Make him think he'd won anything. *Childish?* Maybe. She wanted to be chased. Pursued. This time, she didn't want him to give up on her so easily. He needed to prove to her that he was for real, especially since she was now considering breaking her rule to stay single for a long while.

After he saw her dancing at the club, she felt a sense of vulnerability she'd hadn't experienced since she was in her early twenties. It wasn't shame. Not sadness, either. It was like a dark veil being lifted ever so slowly to expose the past, and let the light in from the present and future. He'd messaged her earlier in the day to see how she was doing. It was a nice gesture, especially since he'd been busy at work. She texted him back that she was doing fine. His response was short and sweet: *That's good to hear.*

The pursuit she desired? It was working. He was breaking her down. Whittling her to nothing but stardust. He'd said he was going to get her after all and now, she believed him. Every damn syllable he'd uttered. He was making it so hard for her to get him out of her system because he was consistent, still an excellent listener, and not too pushy. It was almost like he'd studied her and found out her weaknesses. She didn't want to be in a relationship, and she damn sure didn't want to be in love, but there was no way she could be with a man like Lennox and not fall head over heels. He was kryptonite even for the strongest of Super Women.

So once that door was opened, it was never getting closed. He was so ingrained within her, a part of her fabric of life, there was no way she could completely rid herself of him, even if she tried. *I'm so confused... Lennox, you were so easy to talk to back then. You were my friend. Didn't judge me. Just listened.*

She looked down at her phone and pulled up a picture she'd taken of the two of them while he was at her apartment. He was standing right behind her, his wide, hard chest pressed into her back and his chin resting on the top of her head as he held her around the waist. He was smiling into the camera, and she was smiling at the both of them. She looked... happy.

Damn, he is still fine. He looks even better. All muscular, tan, and sexy as hell. Look at his eyes... those lips. Shit. His smile used to always kill me. He smelled so good, too...

Her pussy tightened like a fist, then tickled with a trickle of sweet lust-fueled moisture.

KNOCK! KNOCK!

Her heart raced as the abrupt knock broke into the quiet of her daydreams, followed quickly by the doorbell ringing.

"Poppy Florist! Delivery!" a man yelled out.

She grabbed the television remote control and put it on mute. Standing up from her couch, she made her way over to the door and looked out the peephole. There, on the other side, was an older man sporting a gray hat with stitchwork of flowers, and 'Poppy Florist' written beneath it. He was holding a large bouquet of pink and red roses, a thick pink sash wrapped around it, and a small matching pink bag.

"I didn't order any flowers," she barked from behind her locked door.

The man chuckled and shook his head. "Ma'am, they're for you. From a... hold on..." The guy struggled to hold the flowers and bag steady as he pulled a crumpled piece of paper from his pocket. "...From a Lennox Wilde."

Her heart hammering within her, she undid all three locks from the door and opened it. The man handed her the flowers, then a piece of paper to sign. Off he went while she stood there holding the huge bouquet and little boutique-style bag.

She closed the door, set everything down on the hallway table, then locked the door again. Collecting the items in her hand, she grinned until her face hurt. In the kitchen, she placed the flowers in a large vase, then opened the card that was standing on the front of the bag.

Baby girl, you've been avoiding me a little, and that's okay. What's meant to be will be. You're mine, like I told you. As soon as we saw each other again, sparks flew. I'm not a patient man, but I've waited for you for over ten years. A few more weeks won't matter. I know you're scared, but you don't have to be. I'm not the storm you fear, but I promise, I will still get you wet...

CHAPTER NINE

The Perfect Storm

LENNOX WAS IN a deep, dark sleep when he realized that the music he was hearing wasn't a part of some dream. It was his default ringtone. The one that everyone over the age of thirty with an iPhone seemed to choose as their default tune, including himself. Opening one eye, he stretched across his king-sized bed, half-naked beneath thin sheets. He clumsily lunged for his cellphone, knocking over something in the darkness.

Whatever it was hit the floor hard, then rolled away. He brought the phone to his eyes as the side of his face pushed hard into the pillow, struggling to make out the words on the darkened screen. It was no use. He sat up and rubbed his eyes. Yawned. Increased the brightness. Now, he could see. Two missed calls from Nadia. A voicemail, too. He listened to it as he slipped his arm behind his head and leaned against the headboard.

"Len, you're somethin' else. Wow... It's late, I know.

Um, just uh, just wanted to tell you that the flowers are beautiful. Gettin' flowers at night is different. I didn't expect that. Hell, getting flowers period is out of the norm nowadays. I didn't think men sent flowers anymore." She chuckled. "But yeah, Thank you… thank you so much. I want to talk to you about something you had written on the card." She took a deep breath. "I don't know what your schedule is like this week, but if I can meet you tomorrow sometime, would that work? Let me know either way. If not, we can plan somethin' for another day this week. I know with your two jobs 'nd all, and my crazy schedule, it might be hard sometimes to link up without more advance notice… Well… goodnight."

And that was that.

He sat there for a little while, gripping the phone. Then, he set it down. Taking a deep breath, he leaned over and grabbed his bottle of water to drink. He chugged it, crushed the empty plastic bottle, and tossed it into the trashcan. Back under the covers, he allowed flashes of Nadia dancing on stage to enter his mind.

Spinning red lights had glazed her limbs in hues of magenta, burgundy and crimson. A seductive glance from over her glittery bare shoulder and a shake of her ample ass sent his dick into beast mode. He ran his fingers along her bare, slick flesh as she gyrated against him. The scent of sweat blended with her intoxicating perfume, filling his nostrils as he gripped her from behind. There were so many men in that gentlemen's club, but for a split second, it felt like it had been only the pair of them. Cigar smoke eddied past him as he squeezed her and gave her flesh a tender slap, a firm pinch, before paying her what she was owed. He knew he was falling for her fast and hard when he stood amongst other ravenous wolves and felt not a shred of jealousy.

In his mind, he was the leader of the pack. It was obvious: They couldn't compete where they couldn't compare... She was his and his alone—and anything she did, spoke of, or contemplated before they reunited didn't matter. It was vapor. Gone with the wind. As he pondered their time together at her place of business, an unexpected pang of guilt seized him out of nowhere. *I've been plotting against her.*

Everything he did in the last few weeks was calculated. A slow dance to a fast takedown. A beautiful manipulation. A spirited chase with a deep, dark, nasty mean streak. He was hunting. Afterall, that's what men did, right? *We pursue.* He was hiding in the shadows, then pounced at just the right time.

I mean, shit. I guess I felt a little guilty because she's happy about the gesture, but I know she understands what this is about. Men are made to provide, dominate, and conquer. Most women seem to crave that and resent it at the same time. But this was nature. Yet, he could not fight his instincts when it came to Nadia, but he could control how he went about it. This was no ordinary conquest. He could feel it in the depths of his soul.

Yeah, she was right. She *was* the one that had gotten away. But it was more than that. Deeper than that. He was now at a crossroads. In deep shit. His life had gotten terribly complicated, and in some way, she was the only thing that felt right at that moment. With all of her hurdles, Nadia was the easiest person to understand in his life.

My own father wants me to abandon my values. The ones he and my mother instilled in me and my sister, not tellin' me that when it came to old man Wilde, all that shit went out the window. One set of rules for the world. One set of rules for Grandpa. I was expected to do what was predictable in this family: fall in line. I prefer to stand in my own circle. The other option is to live my life the way I see fit, regardless of the consequences.

Dad had fallen in line, and was miserable. He was wealthy, could buy practically anything he wished, but his life wasn't his own. He'd never remarried after mom died, but he had a slew of women he fucked just to get his basic sexual needs met. Mama was gone, and all Lennox had was his sister, Silva, who now barely spoke to him. He had his clients at the gym, but they didn't know the real him, and neither did his friends. He kept everyone at arm's length.

I'm all alone in this… No, I have my cousins, too. We need to come together. We're all in the same boat.

He wasn't as close to the majority of his cousins as he'd have liked to be, but he believed that had been planned to some degree. Now that he was mature, he could change that. Grandpa was getting older and more desperate, too— just like Dad had said. He didn't care about Lennox's dreams and goals. No doubt his grandfather only viewed him as a commodity. A tool to be used and if need be, abused. Someone he could mold into his own twisted and contorted image, and train up to orchestrate destruction amongst the masses. Grandpa knew he could do it because he'd done it before… He had blood on his hands that would never wash off.

He wasn't happy about those prior "engagements", but

they were part of his growth as a man. He'd had so much rage in him back then, it seemed the only way was to get it all out. Now, his past had caught up with him. Lennox replayed the words written on the letter from his grandfather in his mind. The promises. The threats. The blackmail. And the most important part: what would happen if he didn't conform. He sat up once again and reached for his phone. He sent a text message:

Nadia, you're right. We do need to talk.
I can make time for you tomorrow. Let me know your
schedule. Sweet dreams.

He placed his phone back down on the nightstand, closed his eyes, and pushed all the bad shit swaying through his mind aside. A smile crept across his face as he fell into a dream. This time, there were no other eyes on Nadia in the club except his own. It was just them—all alone. Soft music playing, in a private room for two...

SHE'D ASKED HIM not to, but he insisted. Nadia checked the time on her phone, then returned her attention to the storage unit. She'd planned to ask him the pressing question that was on her mind, but that all got derailed when she mentioned that she needed some things from her storage unit but was having a hard time getting stuff situated. Lennox was putting box after box onto the bed of his truck, tackling them with the greatest of ease as Dusty Leigh and Bubba Sparxxx belted out, 'OAB,' from the radio in his ride.

"That should do it!" He shut the back of the truck, dusted his hands off, then gripped the bottom of his shirt and maneuvered it across his face, removing a veil of sweat. In the process, he exposed some of the tightest abs she'd ever seen. She scanned his body and heated up from head to toe with scorching hot approval. "I'll follow you back to your place."

She nodded, thanked him, and got into her car.

As she drove away, she looked at him a couple of times through the rear-view mirror. He donned a Houston Astros baseball cap on his head, now completely shirtless, a chain dangling from around his neck. He bounced a bit when he went over a speedbump. In that moment, she could have sworn that his pecs jumped. When he realized she was looking at him, he tossed her a seductive wink and cheeky smile. She reached for her phone.

"Hey, Danielle. I need a favor."

"What's up, girl?" Danielle was an associate of hers at the Sweet Soiree Gentleman's Club. Another dancer. She was one of the few women she confided in from time to time, and was just an overall chill person.

"Hey! I know I've been off the last couple of days, but I might be late tonight. Can you cover for me in case I am?"

"…Late? Yo' ass ain't comin'. You either have a drug problem all of a sudden, Nadia, or you got you a brand-new fuckbuddy 'cause you don't miss no money fuh shit!" All Nadia could do was laugh. "Yo' stage name might be Velvet, but it should be Velveeta 'cause you about gettin' that cheddar, baby. Ms. Cheese! You rarely miss a day!"

Biting her lip, she looked away from the mirror and placed her eyes squarely on the road ahead. "You're right, but this couldn't wait. I was just getting some stuff out of storage and things are taking longer than expected."

"Mmm hmmm," Danielle said in disbelief, followed by a husky laugh. "Okay, girl. I got you."

"Thanks, baby! See you later."

"Bet. You owe me a drink, heffa." The call ended.

Nadia turned up her radio which was playing a local commercial about a gas station's fountain drinks. Some two for one special.

About twenty minutes passed and she pulled into her parking lot, with Lennox right behind her. She parked and he drove past, looking for a visitor space. Once she was at her door with her key, he was walking towards her, a few boxes in his arms, his steps easy and slow. She opened the door and stood there until he caught up. Moments later, they were both inside, and she turned on the lights in her living room and hallway area. She stood by as he brought all the boxes in, setting them exactly where she wanted.

"Thanks so much for all of your help. You're a lifesaver. Are you thirsty?" she asked as she made her way into the kitchen, flipped the light, then washed her hands.

"I could use somethin'. What do you have?"

"Everything," her nerves tensed when she noticed him toying with his necklace, the pendant a dark, shiny tooth. He was rubbing the chain between his thumb and forefinger, and biting his lower lip. *Damn.* "Um, I've got iced tea, water, beer, some Pinot Noir, uh… water, of course. Apple juice, too."

"I'll have some iced tea. I drank a little too much the other day, so I am laying off until the weekend." She nodded in understanding, grabbed a can of Lipton Brisk iced tea, and cracked it open. As she opened a cupboard to pour the beverage in a glass, she heard him approach and the faucet turn on. She removed the cup, closed the cabinet and stood there as he washed his hands.

"I need to ask you something, Len."

"Yeah? What is it." He pumped soap into his palms.

"How'd you know I don't like storms? You said it on the card with the flowers."

"Because some records are public."

She swallowed, walked around him, and reached for the bottle of wine.

"So, you checked up on me?" She grabbed a wine glass from a cabinet.

"The same way you'd checked up on me. Looking on social media websites. Askin' some of our mutual associates about me. Yeah. I saw the public record." He dried his hands, took the glass from the counter she'd poured him, and sat down at the small kitchenette table.

"The details aren't public."

"The initial charge *was*. I paid for them to be public. To me." He said those words without flinching. Without a care in the world.

"When?"

"Recently."

"Why?"

"Because I needed to know why you disappeared from me, Nadia, all of those years ago, and I knew what you were tellin' me was only half the story when I was over here the first time. I know when you're telling the truth and when you're lying. I always have."

"How?"

"Because you rarely lie to me. It's not in your nature to make up shit, or omit important parts. Therefore, you usually resort to just tellin' half the truth when you have something to hide. That way, you aren't directly lying, but definitely skipping key details. The times you have lied to me, it was when somethin' was too unbearable to share. You'd eventually come clean, but it would take you a while. We were friends. Close friends. Good friends. Regardless of you havin' a crush on me, which apparently I was too stupid at the time to notice, I know you would have stayed in touch. Nope. It had to have been something else. You pulled away, and it always bothered me, but like I told you, I don't chase women who don't want to be bothered."

"I wasn't lying though when I told you I was afraid it would ruin our friendship, and you'd be a distraction."

"I know. Your answer about being distracted and all of that I don't think was a lie, but it wasn't the *full* story. Your book is missing important chapters, Nadia, and I want to read the ones you snatched out."

They sat there, across from one another, drinking. She blinked tears away.

"I've had bad luck with relationships, Len."

"I understand."

"I don't think you do. You couldn't because you're not a woman. You're a White man in a White man's world. You have a courtside advantage. The world sees you as the most powerful, while women like me are seen as low on the totem pole."

"I'm not rich. My family is. I'm going through shit that doesn't fit what you think of me."

"It doesn't matter. When people look at you, they see power. Privilege. People that look like you make the rules. People like me have to abide by them. Take it or leave it. I'm Black. I come from humble beginnings. My parents eventually split apart. So, I ended up being raised by a single mother. I grew up in a bad neighborhood. I suffered … you knew about that because I told you way back when. Not once though did I feel sorry for myself, and I still don't, so don't get it twisted, this is far from a pity party but unfortunately, things didn't improve for long."

"You escaped the life you were dealt. You went to college. That says somethin' about your toughness and perseverance."

"Yeah, I went off to college, then started law school, but dropped out." She tossed up her hands. "I'm a stripper and do live videos for money. I am fine with that. But I'm not stupid. I know how judgmental people can be. On paper, I am the classic stereotype of a loose Black girl. The only thing missing is a bunch of kids from a bunch of different baby daddies." She shrugged. "I know how this looks… I know how people perceive me. People don't understand me, but there is a rhyme behind the reason."

"Perception and reality are rarely completely in sync."

"On this, we agree." She took a taste of her wine. "I'm going to tell you what happened. The parts you couldn't have seen from that report." She stroked her glass with her fingertips. Looking down into the wine, she studied her reflection in it.

"Okay. Fill me in." He leaned back in his seat and crossed his arms. Waiting.

"I was a junior in college. Things were going okay. I met this other student and went on just a couple of dates with this guy..." She closed her eyes briefly, then continued. "When we first met, I saw him as attractive. Seemed smart. He started flirting with me, and everything was normal. We kept talkin' and getting to know one another, and I realized we weren't that compatible, so I told him I just wanted to be friends." She reached for her glass and took another sip. "That didn't go over too well. He started yellin', accusing me of being a tease, shit like that. I thought he was crazy, and moved on. Thankfully, he wasn't in any of my classes for the next semester.

"So, weeks pass, I barely see him, I am thinking everything is fine. One day, I am goin' back to my little studio apartment, and this guy is standing by the door. It's raining so I'm in a hurry to get inside. I go up to him and ask him what in the world is he doing, and he proceeds to tell me that he wants another chance and that I was too hasty. I tell him I appreciate that, but I'm not interested. He says okay, that I couldn't blame him for trying, and he wishes me well and walks away. Then I tell him bye, open my door, and he bum-rushes me. I remember... I remember how hard it started to rain. It was like... a dream. A bad one. He tried to drag me inside my apartment, but I fought. I kicked! I screamed! No one came to help me. Suddenly, I felt intense pain at the back of my head. I started blackin' out, but saw him looking down at me. Drenched. Holdin' what looked like a small bat. I don't... I don't even know where it came from. I blacked out completely.

"When I came to, I was in the hospital. He'd beaten me so badly that the doctor said it was a miracle I was still alive. Two broken ribs. Brain swelled up. Bruises from my forehead down to my ankles. Deep cuts. Chipped tooth. Inflamed. Battered. Bloodied. Everything hurts. Rape kit showed nothin', so I guess I should've been grateful he didn't do that to me, too. Would've been easy while I was unconscious. So eventually, the police came to the hospital. I said who did it." She looked down into her glass of wine. "Told them that the guy's name was Corey Elroy. They said they'd follow up. Long story short, I was nobody. There were no witnesses. His word against mine. He claimed to be studyin' and in his dorm room all night. His roommate vouched for him. He got away with telling a big ass lie."

She sighed and shook her head.

"Did the police actually interrogate the roommate, or just ask once?"

"I have no idea, but I doubt it would've mattered. Nobody believed me, Len, and the police treated me like I was crazy. They even asked me many times if I was on any kind of drugs. Like I beat my own damn self up!" She sucked her teeth and rolled her eyes. "He was popular. His parents were loved in the community. I was this girl that nobody knew. A stranger. He was used to getting what he wanted. Nobody told him *no*. He was royalty. Some high yellow golden-boy with good hair who was gonna be goin' to medical school, and he came from a great family. Here I was, this skinny, brown-skinned, knock-kneed child with unruly coils and big lips. I had a thick Texan dialect at this prestigious college, sounded even more country than the Georgia peaches. It was assumed I got in due to affirmative action or some quota, versus the fact that I was just smart as hell, and my high school test scores proved it and I remained on the Dean's list until the day I graduated. Even after this incident. I tried, Len. I tried...

"I stayed with it, you know, the whole college thing, until the end of my senior year, but my grades were droppin' fast. I went on to law school, had gotten accepted into Georgia State University College of Law. I tried to keep up with my studies, but I couldn't sleep. Had nightmares of him attacking me. It started slow, but I think the stress from school, my grandmother getting sick, my father gettin' sick too, with all of our unresolved issues, it started to stack up. The pressure mounting. Started remembering bits and pieces of the assault. Stuff I had forgotten or blocked out. Him tryna pull my pants down. I bit him... I didn't even know that at the time. Couldn't tell my mama, so it was all bottled up inside. I was a wreck. I needed to talk to her."

"Why couldn't you tell her what happened? Before you left for college, you told me you were working on your relationship with your mother."

"I was... but it takes two to make a relationship improve. My mother was still closed off. She is who she is, Lennox. Anyway, I didn't think she'd understand and hell," She shrugged. "Even if she did, there was nothing she could do about it anyway. No one could erase what happened to me. I was never the same after that. I was paranoid. Felt like folks was staring at me. Talkin' shit about me. A man tried to kill me, Lennox. In the rain. But somehow, *I* became the villain. I was lyin', right? Just tryna take a good man, down! Oh, and here's the cherry on top. This mothafucka had a girlfriend the entire time. So a new rumor spread that I was trying to break them up. I didn't even know about her ass! People were playin' on my phone. Threatening me. Calling me names. I had only gone out with this damn demon twice. Like I told you. Our personalities were far too different, but even more importantly, something about him didn't seem right. I paid the price for listening to my intuition. Some people can't take rejection. Telling them 'No,' sends them into overdrive." She gazed once more into her glass.

"Don't I know it. Always trust your gut. Believe it or not, the consequences could have been worse if you hadn't."

"What did that report say to let you know there was a storm that night he attacked me?" She slowly looked up. Met eyes. He was looking at her as if she were the sun chasing all the clouds away. With that one look, she felt warm all over. Cherished. Believed.

"Someone had the wherewithal to write it down. It said that you just kept screaming in the hospital, according to the staff and nurses, saying *'I hate the rain!'* They said you were having some sort of breakdown. Had to give you medicine to calm you down at one point."

They both drew quiet. Only the knock of the water pipes broke the silence for a long while.

"I was on academic probation in law school. I went from a 3.9 GPA down to a 2.1. It plummeted like a rock in an ocean." She gulped the last drop of wine. "I used to love rainy days, but after that car accident, and then this? Naw…" She blinked back tears. "…I can't stand the rain. Sho' don't want no storms."

"What if I told you that rain is just the tears of a clown, and you ain't got nothin' to be afraid of?"

"Unless you can prove that to me, I won't buy it." She said with a chuckle.

"The proof is in the pudding. You know why?"

"Why?"

"Because a blade of grass ain't afraid of another blade of grass, and lightning ain't afraid of other bolts of lightning, Nadia. You are one of the strongest people I know. Few are more resilient than you. Don't allow something you loved now to be hated because of a person who has already stolen your time and peace of mind. Every time you avoid the rain, you let him rob you."

"What does that have to do with grass not being afraid of grass, and lightening 'nd such?"

You can't be afraid of no storm, baby, because you *are* the storm. You blew back into my world just in time…"

CHAPTER TEN

On Talking Terms

AN HOUR PASSED, and Nadia went from fighting back tears to holding her belly as laughter seized her body, shook her hard, and wouldn't let go.

"Len, stop!" She dabbed at her eyes with her knuckle, ridding herself of the waterworks of mirth. "Joseph wasn't like that."

"The hell he wasn't. He was a player. I'm not hatin' on him because in a way, back then, so was I. I wasn't a big cheater, ya know, but I moved on fast. Real fast. I felt like spice was the variety of life." Joseph was another guy they'd worked with back in the day at The Red Rooster.

"Someone said he has like four ex-wives." She snickered as she reached for her glass of wine from the coffee table.

"Five ex-wives. He's currently remarried again, last I heard, but that was a year ago. He was completely anti-marriage, but did it over and over. Said he wasn't going for it again, but of course, that obviously was a lie. He also said that his last ex-wife gave him the only food that reduces sex drive."

"And what food was that?"

"Wedding cake."

She tossed a couch pillow at him. It bounced off the side of his head and they both erupted in laughter. He snatched the pillow from the floor, tucked it under his arm and stared at her. Across from him, she sat with her leg tucked beneath her and her second glass of wine half gone. Every time his gaze met hers, her heart flipped in reaction.

"My aunt used to say, 'I spent a lotta time child proofin' my house, but y'all bastards keep managing to get back in.'"

He burst out laughing. "That was a pretty random thing to say." He slipped his arm behind his head and leaned back against the couch, a lazy sexiness in his gaze.

"It was I guess... Oh, I know what made me think of my Aunt Dee Dee!" She snapped her fingers. "The bit about the weddin' cake. She made weddin' cakes for folks. She was good at it, too. They were so pretty. Just like her." Images of her Aunt Dee Dee entered her mind. Oh, how she missed her. And her delicious cakes, too. "She was my mama's sister. The youngest." They drew quiet.

"Nadia." He leaned forward and clasped his hands. She noted his set face and fixed eyes. "I want to tell you that, uh, I've been through some things, too. It ain't been just you."

"Of course you have. You're human. I never thought that you hadn't." She debated on calling off work for the whole night as she got more and more comfortable sitting there with this beautiful man in her living room.

"You don't know the real deal, though. I kept it from you. Didn't want to talk about it back then. I want to talk to you about it now though, 'cause I need you to understand that one day, you're going to my life partner. My wife. Because of that, I need to come clean. Be an open book. That's not in my nature, but I'm steppin' out on faith that what I'm feeling and thinking is right." He spoke without a hint of immodesty. It sounded as if he were merely stating a fact, in the humblest way possible. His gaze swept over her.

"Your wife? Lennox, stop it. I see that whole wedding cake thing and talking about Jacob had messed with your mind. We haven't even—"

"You're scared."

"No, I'm not."

"You are. You're scared of commitment, not because you don't want to be tied down, but because being tied down leads to vulnerability, and people get hurt when they're close and exclusive." He spoke like some therapist, and she was on his couch. He cocked his head to the side, then linked his fingers together. "That's why dancing is so easy for you."

"Dancing is easy for me because I'm good at it, and I get paid well for it."

"That's just what you tell yourself. You get to have the attention you want from men, with no strings attached. They can't kiss you, hug you, or fuck you. When they see a woman like you, most men want to do all three. You're beautiful, and out of many men's leagues based on looks alone. Out of most men's leagues if you include how damn smart you are. Naw, the average Joe can't have you... They just have to sit there and watch. Horny. Dicks hard. Pockets empty. You win. You're in control. Just how you like it."

"You think you know everything. You don't." She covered the words with a big smile, perhaps wanting to soften the blow. She was met with an even bigger smile as he looked straight through her.

"Let me tell you something about me, then I'll get back to the topic. You see these hands?" He held up his fingers, then made double fists. "My hands are deadly, baby. I can knock a motherfucker out cold with just one hit. I caught a case. My father and grandfather managed to get it buried. Money talks. I was young back then. My father got involved. My grandfather knew some people. Pulled some strings. I should've been doin' a bid."

"You beat someone up. So what?" She took another sip of her wine.

"...I killed a motherfucker."

She crossed her legs and set her glass down, then crossed her arms, too. The room turned suddenly colder. "Why'd you do that?"

"Because I was paid to do it. It was a job. I had been approached and asked to do it, and I, at the time, was angry enough to accept the challenge. I had been itchin' to hurt someone anyway, Nadia, so it was the right place and time. I had no self-control back then. I did some other shit, too... but that's the incident that landed me in big trouble."

"Was this durin' the time I knew you? Like, before or after?"

"Right before. That's one of the reasons I was workin' there. To get out of the spotlight. Start over. I was an angry young man, Nadia. Mad at the world. I was mad that my mother was gone. Mad at God. I was mad at my father for other shit that would take too long to explain right now. I just wanted to fight the whole world."

"Who asked you to do this?"

"Some rich kid needed help. He paid me a lot, and I did it. I only got caught because his dumb ass was bragging about it later. He got confronted by the police all that time later after I did the kill-for-hire job, and sang like a bird. Threw me all the way under the damn bus. At least that's what the police told my father."

"Damn… like, how did you feel about doing something like that?"

"I didn't feel anything at all. As sick as it sounds, it was like a relief. I wanted to murder something. Make somethin' bleed. The guy I killed I found out wasn't a good person no way, but that still didn't make it right for me to do it. The relief was short-lived, too. I needed some healing, and that wasn't the way to go about it. It took me years to get right in my head, and in my heart. Normal therapy didn't work, so, I started reading. I started workin' on myself. I found a couple of people that could help me. That could relate. Someone to talk to, that had walked in my shoes. God gave me these hands, Nadia. I'm strong, but the Devil made me use 'em. That made me weak. I can use them to hurt people real fuckin' bad, or I can use them to help. Like bodybuilding, and building things. Or giving a hug, maybe helping someone up when they fall. Or maybe, offer some healin' by touchin' a woman in just the right way."

She looked at his big hands… his nails were cut evenly,

his knuckles large, and the tops of his hands were covered with veins and old scars.

"These hands had the honor of touching one of the most precious jewels I've ever seen. You." Her cheeks warmed. "I wasn't even supposed to touch you that night while you danced on that stage, but you let me. I saw how you quickly waved the security guard away when he tried to approach as I put my hands around you while you were performing. You gave up control and handed it over to me… because you *want* to trust me. With all that I am, even confessing to you the terrible thing I did, you *still* trust me, 'cause after all these years, you know my heart."

She hung her head. "I *am* scared. A lot has happened. I don't trust men, and I barely trust myself when it comes to y'all." It was hard to let the words come out. To let him hear them with all the disappointment and pain bubbling forth within her. She turned away from his scrutiny, feeling judged and loved all at once.

"It's okay to admit that you're scared, Nadia. Shit, I didn't put much thought into settling down, either, until I decided to grow the hell up. What solidified it though was when I saw you again. I told you I literally asked God for help, then saw you less than twenty-four hours later. I don't look a gift woman in the mouth… Ain't nothin' else I can do with you 'cept make you mine. The writing is on the wall, and the signs all point straight to heaven. Ain't your middle name Heaven?" She nodded, surprised he remembered that. "Well then, ain't nowhere else to go but up."

"Lennox, you've made your intentions clear. I think it's also clear that I'm interested now. I'm entertaining you after all, but I have some questions for you."

"Ask me anything you want."

"…This open book of yours. What's in chapter one?" She hugged herself a bit tighter.

"Chapter one would be my parents. They're the genesis. My father's side of the family was considered basically White trash back in the 1940s. That all changed once my grandfather was about twenty-three years old, and got some land. He was smart, self-educated. A business tycoon. He worked under some important people. Learned a thing or two, and applied it to building his own company. That company grew into other ones. Those were legit businesses, until they weren't anymore." His eyes darkened and narrowed. "Grandpa Wilde built an empire and married beautiful women to hang on his arm like trophies. Had a bunch of children with most of them.

"My father is the product of one of those marriages, and he's wealthy because of him. My father was selected to help run the business because he has a head for numbers, and knows how to keep his mouth shut. He's loyal to a fault."

"You've never been asked to join the business?"

A strange look came over the man's face, followed by a twisted smirk and a dark chuckle.

"Oh, he's asked, baby. He's demanded, too. In fact, Old man Wilde, good ol' Grandpa, has put me between a rock and a hard place. If he can't have me, nobody can."

"What? Is he threatening you? Your own grandfather?"

"Oh, yes, but that's a long story. I promise to get into that later. For now, let's stick to Chapter one." She nodded in understanding. "Onto my mother. The woman who brought me into this world… Aaliyah Abdallah."

"Hold on, that name sounds Muslim."

"Yeah. My mother was Lebanese. She is Sunni."

"Really? I never knew that." She looked at him curiously now.

"I know. Most people didn't know."

"Now that I look at you, yeah, I can see that. Your skin is tan all year long." He laughed at that, but she was serious. "You look like you could have some Indian or Middle Eastern in you. Yeah, I can definitely see that. I never thought much of it when we were younger. Just thought you were fine as hell. Why did you never tell me that your mother was Muslim? My uncle is, too."

"It wasn't somethin' I was tryna hide—it just wasn't relevant. Not only that, but I also kept details about my mother away from most people, friend or not. She was a very private person, and raised me and my sister to not discuss anything about her with outsiders, unless it was completely necessary."

"Was she paranoid or just secretive?"

"Neither. She was trying to protect herself and her children. She'd been disowned by her family after she married my father, and she didn't want any information about herself getting back to them if it was in a negative light. Honor and reputation were very important to her family, and even though she was the type of person to think for herself and do her own thing, she still wanted the approval of her family. She wanted them to be proud of her. She always wanted to prove them wrong about their reservations regarding her choices and actions, so she guarded information carefully. Her marrying my father really pissed them off, but she was determined to prove that her marriage was good."

"Oh, wow. So was she disowned because your father is White? Wait, is Lebanese White, too? Excuse my ignorance, baby, I just—"

"No, it's fine. It depends on who you ask, but America, to my mother, is one of the few countries that is hung up on complexions and race. My mother explained that it was never really talked about like that in Lebanon. For all intents and purposes, my mother's ethnicity is Middle Eastern. Her race, by most people, would be considered White, but when asked, she always said Arab or Mediterranean. She never, ever considered herself White, and to my recollection, never claimed to be."

"What did she look like, if you don't mind me asking?"

"Her skin was olive. She had jet black hair and was mistaken usually for bein' Italian, sometimes Latina. Her eyes were a grayish green color. A little darker than mine. She didn't look White, in my opinion, but because she was Muslim, and there's a lotta anti-Muslim feelings 'round here, some folks don't see her as American, either, even though she got her citizenship long before she got married to my father." Nadia nodded in understanding. "Anyway, nah. My mother's family didn't get mad because my father was White. It was because he was Christian. They wanted her to marry a well-educated, financially secure Muslim man. Funny thing though, Nadia… She kept a lot from them when she moved from Lebanon to America on her own. Like the fact that she worked as an escort before I was born. I told you about that. "Yeah, and I know what you're thinking."

"What am I thinking?"

"How did I find out if my mother was so private?" *He was right. She was thinking just that.* "Well, let's just say a family member made sure that I knew, and it wasn't out of the kindness of his heart."

"Do you know why she did it? Or was no reason given?"

"She was havin' money problems, and her family didn't want her to move here in the first place, so she couldn't ask them for help. She was about to be evicted from her apartment. Her family was very traditional, and to them, she should have kept her ass in Lebanon, marry a Muslim Lebanese man by the time she was eighteen or nineteen, and have a bunch of children. Instead, she wanted to study abroad and go to college. Be a doctor, like one of her brothers. A friend of hers told her she could make money by escorting so she could pay for school. She was desperate so she did it, and because of her beauty and exotic looks, the clients came fast. Pun intended." He smiled sadly.

"That's the same thing I did...I was trying to re-enroll in law school after I dropped out due to my bad grades and emotional issues, and I needed money to get back in. It just never worked out that way. Is that why you weren't as judgmental as I thought you'd be when I told you that I danced and do OnlyFans?"

"Maybe." He shrugged. "I don't think I would have reacted any different, either way. As far as my mother is concerned, unlike you, she was ashamed about her past. It's not something she wanted discussed. She'd done it for a short time, less than a year, but it still happened. If that kind of information got to the wrong people, and to her family, her life would have been in danger. She'd literally be killed."

"Killed? But why?"

He sighed and closed his eyes for a brief moment. "You don't understand it because these are very different cultural customs, Nadia. This ain't Texas. Like I said, she came from a strict, traditional family, and she was always looked at as a trouble maker because she insisted on doing her own thing, but up until that point, nothing she did was worthy of her being burned at the stake. Escorting though?" He sucked his teeth. "That's a guaranteed scarlet letter. A woman's virtue is everything to my Lebanese side of the family. Virginity. Purity until marriage, and definitely not sleeping with rich men for money and gifts, no matter the reason. Her family would be judged and there'd also be consequences, like them being shunned in their community."

"But death?! I mean, yes, I've heard of this sort of thing, I'm not stupid, but it seems so extreme. I bet the same rules aren't applied for men that sleep around."

"I don't know, you're probably right, but what I do know is that if this information got out, it would cause such high humiliation, the family would be snubbed and possibly no longer allowed to even worship with their friends and neighbors. Because of that shame, what could have taken place was a mercy killing because of an Islamic belief called

Zina."

"What's that about? Zina?"

"There are four categories, but they all have to do with lust, or physical intimacy—extramarital affairs, fornication, homosexuality, and another talks about premarital sex. It differentiates all of them. Lust is considered the catalyst for Zina, and unfortunately, the women carry the burden. Even if a woman is raped, in some of the old republics, she is blamed for it. Like, questions come up asking what she was doing out that time of night, or what was she wearing to entice the man, things like that. Men are believed to be unable to control themselves, so women are urged to take precautions to not tempt them to lust."

Nadia shook her head in disgust.

"I hate that your mother went through that. I hate that all women shoulder that burden because quite honestly, this ain't just some Lebanese thing. They do that same shit here in the USA! Supposed to be Christians, though." She rolled her eyes. "As soon as someone comes out on the news claimin' to be raped, women and men wanna ask, 'Well, why she wait so long?' or, 'Look what she had on, she fast.'"

She was sure he could sense how personal this was to her—a story that didn't bear repeating in her personal experience.

"You're right. All of that is true, Nadia." He ran his hand over his face and exhaled loudly. "If my mother's family found out about her being an escort, according to how my mother explained it, they'd feel compelled to get rid of her. We're talking complete termination of life. Like that would somehow right the wrong. So because of all of this, Nadia, we all made sure to never discuss it."

"Okay, I get it now. Enough of that. I'll get mad all over again. Tell me more about your parents."

"After my parents got together, and my mother got married against their wishes to my father, they stopped talking to her because he was Christian, like I explained. But then they came around towards the end of her life."

"What caused the switch?"

"Well, she had me and my sister. We were gettin' older and they never met us. She was living nicely. Big, beautiful home. My mother always said she wanted for nothing. My mother apparently would send them pictures. Much to their pleasure, she was still Sunni. Still practicing her Muslim religion. She was a good mother, too… A damn good mother. A loving, beautiful person…" He hung his head, clasped his hands and swallowed.

"How'd she pass away?" He ran slightly trembling fingers over his gorgeous crown of dark hair. "Hold on, baby. Here I come." She got up from the couch, crossed the room, and sat next to him. Placing her hand in his, she intertwined their fingers. His shoulders slumped as he cried softly. "Take your time."

"Aneurysm. It was sudden. No one knew she had it. She didn't suffer with high blood pressure that we were aware of." He shrugged, blinked his tears away, then ran his thumb along her palm, deep in thought for a few moments. "To this day, we're not a hundred percent sure of how this happened, but it did, and at the end of the day, that's all that matters."

"Can I see a picture of her? You got it on you?"

He nodded, grabbed his cellphone, and scrolled through his camera roll. She saw flashes of pictures of cars, exercise equipment, some screenshots of what appeared to be typical X-rated materials such as a close-up of some titties, and some silly memes.

After a minute or two, he handed her his phone. "Here's a few of her. You can look through them."

She gently took the phone from his grasp, then began sliding her finger along the screen. One after the other, she saw many pictures of a gorgeous woman with long dark hair, bright greenish gray eyes that she obviously passed down to her son, and a lovely smile. In some of the photos she was in what appeared to be their home garden—gloves on her hands and a sunhat. In other photos, she may have been on vacation. Airports. Monuments, shrines, and statues. In another photo, she was in her doctor attire, seemingly at work. One picture made her pause. Lennox's mother was with who she presumed was his father, who was tall, thin, and handsome, smiling proudly as he stood beside her. There were also two children: Lennox at perhaps age eleven or twelve, and a little girl with big light brown eyes and thick dark hair, who she surmised was his little sister.

"Y'all look happy."

"We were." He reached over and abruptly took the phone from her. That was the end of an era.

They sat in silence, looking at the same stain on her rug. She regretted not turning on any music. All she could hear was his breathing, and her heartbeat that throbbed in her ears. Perhaps he could hear her heartbeat, too.

"I understand now," she finally said, running her palm along her upper thigh. "You lost your best friend."

He nodded, another sullen smile across his beautiful face. "She liked you."

She turned to him curiously. "She liked me? I never met your mother."

"I had a dream. This is going to sound ridiculous. Strange. Nevermind. I don't want to scare you or freak you out."

"No, go ahead. I'm listening."

"In the dream, my mother was still alive when you and I were workin' together. It was so realistic. Anyway, one day, my car was actin' up, so she came up to the restaurant to drive me home. That happened in real life a few times, you know, my car acting up, so it made sense in the dream, too. Well, in the dream, you were still inside The Red Rooster. She sat there in the parking lot and watched us interacting as I clocked out apparently. That was kind of, what's the word?"

"Symbolic?"

"Yeah, that's it. Symbolic, because it's like a mom looking over her kid. Anyway, I got in the car, and she said, *'You like that Black girl.'* Then, she'd start driving. That's exactly somethin' my mother would say. So, in the dream, I remember I said yeah, you were my friend. She said, 'No, you like her *more* than just a friend.'" I didn't deny it in the dream, and if she were to stand in front of me at that time, I would not have denied it to her, either. She told me you seemed like a real nice young lady, and she felt like we'd be good together. She said, as she was driving, that she'd heard us talking on the phone when I was home sometimes, too."

"That's symbolic, too. Like she can hear you without seeing you."

"...Yeah. You're right. Is this bothering you? Making you uncomfortable? I'll stop talking about it if it is. I know some people don't believe in stuff like this, and that's fine." His watery, sad, beautiful eyes captured her soul as he looked deeply at her.

"Nope. Not even a little bit. I like hearing it."

"Okay...Like I said, it was just so damn realistic. My mom and I would talk like that when she was still alive. I could tell her anything. It was like... like she was sending me a message in that dream. This dream was old though, not recent. I had it before you even moved back into town, but I never forgot it."

The shock of this discovery hit her full force. Her spirit fluttered and heated within her core at his words. Lennox was many things, but a liar wasn't one of them...

"It's like she was tellin' me you were the one." He sniffed, dabbed at his eyes. "I forgot about the dream until recently. My mother didn't like most of my ex-girlfriends, but I think even in heaven, she knew I loved you before I even did." He pursed his lips, as if quelling emotion. "I miss my mama." Another tear fell from his eye as his voice cracked. "She was too good for this world. God took her away. Think about her every day...Mothers know our hearts, Nadia. They *always* know."

"They always know," she repeated, squeezing his hand. His jaw tightened as he slowly turned towards her.

They drifted closer and closer to one another until their mouths met. His supple lips made her melt. Her pulse skittered as the soft wetness of his tongue joined hers. An enchanting shudder of want and need ran through her. His kiss was so slow... so warm... so sultry and sexy... She savored his flavor: traces of mint and sweet tea.

His skin smelled like 'Fucking Fabulous,' by Tom Ford, and a dash of vanilla. Her back slightly arched as he ran his big hands along it, up to her shoulders. He pulled her closer. Thick fingers parted her hair, gently massaged her scalp as he deepened their kiss. He was devastatingly erotic, dripping with swag. His kiss was insistent, yet somehow patient.

Filled with a flood of desire, she broke their kiss, then reached for the hem of her t-shirt. Pulling it over her head, she exposed her sheer red bra. Lust in his eyes, he traced her face with a tender hand. His fingers drifted to her breasts to circle her nipple and make it harden to his touch. She briefly closed her eyes and waited in anticipation. She shuddered when he leaned in and sucked her breast over the fabric, his oral embrace soon becoming hard and fast. She placed her hand along his groin, her curiosity tearing her apart. She started at his balls and worked her way up. *Shit, yes... he's got a big one...Damn. It's huge.* His dick was hard as a rock. Long and thick.

The sounds of his working tongue along her nipple reminded her of a rabid animal. The heat and wetness of his mouth made her pussy pulse, and she hoped and prayed he'd remove her bra soon, and suck her breasts with no barriers between them. But then, as quickly as he began working her into a frenzy, he stopped cold.

"What's wrong?"

He slowly lifted his head from her breasts and caressed her neck with a gentle hand, concern in his eyes as if he'd seen something in her that she'd been trying to hide, or keep at bay. She felt suddenly sick inside. Unwanted. Shunned. His eyes glowed with some energy she couldn't understand, decipher, or read. It chilled her. Unnerved her to the bone.

"What'd I do wrong? You don't want to have sex with me?"

He kissed her cheek, then ran his thumb slowly along her lower lip.

"You did absolutely nothin' wrong. I *definitely* wanna have sex with you, baby. There's nothin' more that I'd rather do right now other than pick you up, throw your ass on your bed, and fuck your womb clear out the fucking frame."

"But?"

"But you're used to men not caring about your needs, and thinkin' only about their own. You're used to men not havin' any self-control when it comes to you, so much so that they attack you in the rain, and cause you to have mental storms. PTSD. You're used to being used for your body, and nobody givin' a fuck about what's in here." He pointed to her head, then to her heart. "Well, I'm not like everybody else, Nadia, and I'm not what you're used to."

"But I—"

"I want you bad, Nadia. My body is on fire for you. I have had my share of wet dreams about you. My heart and my mind wants you, too. It took all of me to stop just now. But no matter how much I want to know what you taste like, and be buried deep inside of you, right here, right now, all night long, I know damn well that the timing isn't right. When we make love, baby girl, it's going to be something like you've never experienced. You're not ready for this dick."

"Boy, please!"

"I'm not playing, Nadia." He gripped her chin, made her face him head on. "I'm serious. I'm not the type of man a woman just wants to fuck once, and leave alone. Because of our chemistry, our pasts, our friendship, and everything we have with one another, we're going to be addicted to each other once we start a sexual relationship. We won't be able to stop. Our connection is so strong, and that's the last component to bring this all together. We can't rush it. I need to know in my heart that the timing is right. Not for my protection, but for yours. I refuse to lose you, all because I couldn't control myself. When we *do* get together, the universe is going to explode."

She rolled her eyes, "But I *am* ready."

"You're close, but not quite there yet. This is a spiritual connection. You and I are serious – I know myself so well now because I've done the work to get to this point. It took a long time, but I got there. I know who I am as a man. I know what I stand for. I know what I'm going to put up with, and what the hell I'm not going to put up with. I love you! I loved you from the moment you cried on my shoulder by a big ass bag of flour in a little diner that most people barely knew the name of. And here's the thing: I'm going to be the next man, and the last man to *ever* be inside those sugar walls. So I'm not worried, and you shouldn't be, either. I'm not going anywhere unless you want me to. That's a promise." He caressed her chin, nothing but love in his eyes. "I've got over a decade of love and lust built up inside of me over you. This has to be handled carefully. I'll know when you're ready, honey, and when you are, when that day comes, you best believe I won't hesitate. But today isn't that day."

He got up, slipped his phone in his pocket, and made his way to her door. She watched him, burning with anger and budding love. But she was rendered speechless. She wanted to curse him out, but she couldn't. Wouldn't. He opened the front door and helped himself out, then closed it behind him, without a goodbye. She got up and watched him from her window. He walked towards his truck then disappeared out of sight.

How could she describe what she was feeling right then? Her emotions flipped and changed from one second to the next. She went back to the couch, still smelling him in the air, and smiled. A tear streaked her cheek, and then another. He had the self-control of a priest, and the sex drive of a beast. She'd been in the company of an alpha. Supreme big dick energy. She'd kissed a top dog. No ifs, ands, or buts about it. His bark was as big as his bite.

Lennox was the definition of a *REAL* man...

CHAPTER ELEVEN

The "Kaged" Saint

A few days later

KAGE'S LIPS CRIMPED beneath a curtain of salt and pepper hair. His unruly mustache and mountain man beard made him appear older than his years, yet gave him an uncanny sophistication. A thick layer of long blond hair streaked with premature silver covered one of his mischievous light blue eyes as a curl of thick cigar smoke escaped his crooked mouth. He tapped the ashes into a dark brown ashtray, then fidgeted around in his worn chair, half the stuffing coming out of the cushion. Stretching a long leg forward, he slumped down a little and half of his body was gobbled up by the shadows.

"You can stop lookin' at yer phone, Lennox. Ain't no good signal out here in my neck of the woods, lest I turn it on."

"I can't believe you live like this. It's like a time machine..." Lennox looked around his cousin's two-room, hand-built, off-the-grid abode. "A dirty, small, strange time machine."

"And I can't believe you ain't on steroids, with your big, beefy, bison Burger King lookin' ass! Ya look like a white-skinned gorilla. More importantly, where I live should be the least of your fuckin' worries, brawny boy. Take a piss test for me. What's your blood type? Vanilla protein shake?" Chuckling, Kage grabbed a small plastic trashcan and spit into it.

Lennox took a deep breath and slipped his phone in his pocket, staring at his cousin.

"We gotta do something about Grandpa."

Steely eyes met his. The mood turned suddenly cold and somber.

"I tried. More than once. He's got too much protection around him, and he's attempted to kill me at least twice. What was his ultimatum to ya?"

Lennox paced the small house, darkness beginning to consume him, too. He moved closer to a small window that allowed a few meager streams of light into the dwelling. Outside, past the bright red curtain, he could see the forest. It was beautiful. Peaceful. Like something that would be on a postcard with a picture of Bambi frolicking in the woods with butterflies. On one wall of the room, about eight guns hung on a log wall, near them a big box which he presumed was filled with ammunition. A small electric refrigerator buzzed, but knowing Kage, it was probably only full of beer and wilted produce.

"He's threatened to tell my mother's family some things about her... some things that will get her buried body dug up from the family cemetery and sent to a place they reserve for evil people. That's a big deal where she's from." Kage brought his cigar to his mouth, and rested it along his lips. "He's also threatened to get me tossed into prison for that murder way back when. The same strings he said he pulled to ensure I had no record and didn't serve a day in jail, after my dad begged for his help on my behalf without my knowledge, he said he'll tie those same strings in a knot that'll never unravel, and never be turned loose." He dropped his gaze and fiddled with his cuticles for a moment or two.

"Well, he might be able to swing it if you don't do something." Kage exhaled a dense cloud of smoke that sailed past his blue peepers real slow, like lazy storm clouds. "Lennox, your problem is, you're now the good guy. You got this thing about not wanting to go back from where ya came. New age therapy. Spiritual journey shit. The mother-fucker that was out here bustin' heads open with baseball bats and cussin' everyone out is now some yoga master with a gun." Kage smiled big and wide as if he much preferred that version of him.

"Something had to change. I was a danger to myself more than anyone else." Lennox crossed his arms and sighed. "He's hellbent on destroying my mother, too. Even beyond the grave. Really, he doesn't give a damn about her, but she's just collateral damage. He knows my mother is my weakness, so," he shrugged, "he's using it."

"Does this have something to do with why Grandpa is always callin' your mother a whore?"

Lennox cracked his knuckles, then rolled his shoulders.

"Yeah." They were quiet for a spell. "The place my mother is buried in was important to her, Kage."

"Why? She's dead. Just like my ol' man. What does it matter now?"

"It's a cultural thing. She talked about it a lot. How she wanted her family's forgiveness." Lennox began to pace back and forth. "She finally got it, and I believe in spite of what happened, she died peacefully because she knew my father would honor her wishes and have her sent back to Lebanon to be buried, as she and her parents requested. She got to lie next to her grandmother and grandfather. Considered an honor. It's a sacred cemetery for good souls and all of her family is there. She got a beautiful ceremony and the whole nine. My father, sister and I are accepted as family now, too."

"Silva and you talk to your Lebanese side? I never knew that. I thought y'all were still estranged."

"Not anymore. Not since I was like ten years old. They acknowledge us often, and my grandparents, uncles and aunts even call a few times a year to check on everyone. My father has forged a solid relationship with his father-in-law that exists outside of my mother. Something to stick to. They actually seem to like one another, oddly enough. Family was so important to my mother, Kage. This was all despite her choices to find out what life was about on her own. She wasn't one to take orders from other people, even those she cared for, but she never lost the love she had for family, her religion, and the traditions she held dear. Mama was a little complicated, but at the same time, I understand her. Completely." *Dad was right. I'm just like her.*

"Grandpa won't let me close enough to him without ten guys in the room with guns." Kage chuckled proudly. "I hate him with every fiber of my being. I'm no longer his golden boy, and haven't been since I tried to off him. But you? He still trusts you. You may be the one to end this nightmare for all of us. Take him out."

"But I don't want to take him out. I just wish he'd disappear and leave me the hell alone. I don't necessarily want him to die, just... go away. If I kill him, it'll cause too many problems in the family. It'll be taken out on Silva and Dad, too. Not only that, but I'd also probably have to go into hiding. He could ruin everything, Kage. Everything." He threw up his hands.

"Well, all of that is hypothetical, but what he'll do to you sure ain't. Ask yourself what's most important to you, man? Him still breathin', or your mother's wishes and her family name? He must have somethin' pretty bad on her. Don't let him dangle that over your head. Either tell him you don't give a fuck, or do something about it. You can't cut off a snake's tail, cousin. Ya gotta cut off its head. There's no half steppin' with Grandpa. You either have to make things so hard for him that he backs off willingly, or make your choice to hurt him so easy that he fears messin' with you. I chose the latter."

"...And we all see where that got you."

Kage laughed, a deep, raspy, rumbling laugh, then violently smashed his cigar in the ashtray. "Lennox, you say you came here to look me in the eye. You say you wanted to talk to me directly, pick my brain, cousin to cousin, man to man, because you know that I was close to Grandpa many full moons ago. You know I understand things about that man that some of y'all don't. Six of my cousins, including you, are being blackmailed and threatened. He's not fuckin' around." Kage's eyes narrowed. "Every time I turn around now, I get strange, creepy phone calls, dead animals at my doorstep, or direct threats from the chief himself. He won't kill me just yet though because he wants me. He had no doubt when he set my other home on fire that I would survive and rebuild. It was a challenge, a punishment and a test. He is aware I'm not stupid, and that I know how to survive."

"So do I, but I have to be strategic about this! I also have to trust my heart."

"And what's your heart saying?"

"To trust the Lord. Always stay packin'. And by any means necessary."

"Sounds like your heart is smarter than I thought." Kage leaned forward and glared at him. "I'm tellin' you that you can't go halfway with him, Lennox. If ya swing on him, you better knock his fucking block off. If you miss, you're dead. He told you straight out, in that letter, what he was gonna do. Now, I don't know exactly what your letter said, the small details and all because I didn't read it, just like you haven't read mine, but you're telling me the gist of it now, and I understand he's got you over a barrel. Sounds like he knew what buttons to push. Do you wanna tell me what was on those buttons, or keep pussy footin'?"

"If my grandparents find out that my mother had sold her body for money soon after she moved here, it would be a disaster. This all happened before she became a wife.

Mother. A doctor."

"Well holy shit. She went to medical school?"

"Yeah. She was a family medicine physician. She decided to stay home and raise a family, so she left the clinic she was at and started a private practice, halftime. She became the doctor that she wanted to be. Her plan was to return to work fulltime after my sister and I were both out of high school. But, she died. If it gets out what she did, Kage, her life as an escort, that will cause enough chaos to remove her from the mausoleum. It would bring such shame to that side of the family that they may even be run out of town. I know it sounds like something from the 1800s, but this is just how it is. I can't let him do that to them. I can't let him ruin my mother's name. Me going to prison pales in comparison to that. I can do time. I don't want my mother to do time like that, from the grave, too."

"So Aaliyah was a prostitute?" Kage smirked and shook his head. "I wonder how Grandpa got a hold of that tidbit?"

"I have no idea, but you know he can find out just about anything he wants."

"Yup. He's a resourceful son of a bitch. I remember he hated Aunt Aaliyah somethin' fierce, too."

"He hated my mother because she was strong-willed and told him to fuck off. She didn't like his ways, or his politics. She disagreed with my father working for him, too. She saw that Grandpa was taking interest in me, and she made sure my visits were supervised from that point on. You know how grandpa is. He doesn't like strong women. He doesn't like independent women. He doesn't like anything or anyone that stands up to him. She walked into a hornet's nest when she met and fell in love with my father."

"Speakin' of dear ol' dad, what does my weaselly Uncle Scott have to say about all of this?"

"He wants me to sing like a fucking bird. He is terrified of me going to prison, his only son, and he doesn't want his wife's name dragged through the mud. He called me and begged me to just do what Grandpa says so we can move past this. But I can't, Kage." His tongue was heavy with burden and grief. "I just can't."

"And you shouldn't. All I can tell ya, because each of our situations is a little different, is that you have to play the hand the way he doled out the cards. The key to winning this game with Grandpa is to get a running head start on your next move. One thing I know about him is this: He hates defiance, but he respects a calculated maneuver. So much so that if you figure out how to get him off your back, he'll let you go, top dog. He lets us know that in his own way, too. Double check the paperwork."

"That means I need to figure out his weaknesses, just like he figured out mine. I know his ego is inflated. That's a weakness. He's narcissistic. That's a weakness, too."

"Yeah, but those aren't the type of weaknesses that can be exploited and dismantled quickly though. You have to find something personal to you *and* him, Lennox. Look at the shit you two have in common, versus how you differ. Think outside the box. Your situation, in my opinion, is less complicated than mine, because there's far less bad blood."

"That might be true but I'm not backing down, and he hates that."

"Wouldn't matter anyway. Backing down from him doesn't work." Kage stood up slowly. The man was tall and lean, with a muscular build. He was so sinewy that when he stood in that semi-dark room with only a few lanterns and candles lit, and the setting sun's rays filtering through the window, he looked like an eerie tree. His eyes were electric with hatred, and his smile infused with evil joy.

"How would you know? I can't 'magine you backin' down from nothing. Not even from a mudslide sure to suffocate you with a cold, clammy hand."

Kane ran his tongue along his upper teeth as if trying to fish out a piece of gristle. "It's elementary, little cousin. We know he don't respect no fuckin' body who follows his commands. He didn't like your mother, my Aunt Aaliyah. But he damn sure respected her backbone. Few 'round here have one." He slipped a knife out of his jeans pocket and began flipping and flicking it around like some toy.

"He don't respect her or he wouldn't be pullin' the stunt he is now."

"You said it yourself. This ain't about her. It's just a way to get to *you*."

"I read that love kills hate. That's gotta be the bullet in my gun, Kage. Every cell in his body is filled with aversion. I don't love him, I can't love a demon, but I know how to love, and he doesn't. No matter my past... all the men I've injured and killed. The ones he knows about, and the few he may not, I'm still filled with love." He placed his hand over his chest and bowed his head as if in prayer. "And no matter my mama's past, she's worthy of being buried in a beautiful place. She's a wife and a mother. A sister and a friend. She's a queen. I have always loved my mama. Grandpa can never take that away from me, Kage. If I work for him, I'll go back to my old ways. I'll lose my soul."

"And that's what he wants. He's like a vampire. Suckin' the life out of everyone who foolishly crosses his path. He's just about destroyed my life." He cast his eyes downward. "He can sniff out softness, Lennox. Soft men make him sick. Me too, matter of fact. My mama is soft. Your daddy is soft. Pliable. Able to be manipulated like putty."

"Every now and again, he calls me dog, or top dog, Kage. He's called me that since I was kid. Dogs are loyal. They do what they're told. He's made it clear how he sees me, and since I didn't follow the command, he wants to break me. Like some stray puppy."

"Top dogs are leaders, man. You're looking at this all wrong. He tells on himself every now and again because what he calls us gives us clues as to how we can survive his fucked-up games. You being able to love and being loyal as hell doesn't make you soft, cousin. It makes you strong!" Kage beat his chest with a fist, forcing his thick beard to shake as he moved. "He can smell strength, too. He could sniff you out as soon as you were born. He's a user, so he saw your potential immediately. That mother of yours was the key. She gave birth to a bad son of a gun." Lennox couldn't help but smile. "The seven of us smell damn good to him. Like tender meat on the grill. By us cousins standin' up to him the way we've done, all it did was make him want us more."

"We're marked for life."

"Ya damn straight, but each of us has to do our part, or

he'll never turn us loose. We can't break. We can't fall down and not get back up. You were the first one he called to the carpet. He's hoping that if he can break you, the rest of us will fall in line. Out of all of us, he believes you have the most sense. The one we'll imitate. There's always a reason to this bastard's madness." Lennox leaned against the log walls, next to the guns. His guts churned with hot anger. It felt like there was a tangled ball of bloody tendons and he had to unravel it. Figure this all out.

"Kage, let me tell you something. No matter how high this mountain is, I've got a ladder. Somethin' told me to not work my normal shift one night at the club, and take someone else's. I did, and ran into a woman I hadn't seen in over a decade, but have loved just as long. I got up this morning, full of rage, and somethin' told me to be still. To calm down. Something said, 'Talk to your cousin Kage.' Something said, 'That old man wants to keep you two apart.' I listened to that voice and picked up the phone. Without hesitation, you told me to come to you. It took me over two hours to get out here, but if it took two hundred hours, I still would've made the journey." Kage nodded, his eyes sharp on him. "You and I have more in common than I realized."

"All seven of us have things in common. That's why he chose us, even though we didn't choose him. He called you Top Dog, and me a Lone Wolf... I'm your ancestor, and you're the newer generation. Dogs come from wolves... you and I are related in his eyes, and I ain't talking about just blood. We've got that leadership shit that he wants. We can sniff out an opportunity. We aren't swayed by money, pussy, and power. We're motivated by lovin' someone that is now gone. We dig in the dirt for bones. The dead. For you, it was your mama, and now, this woman that you feel something deep for. We love out loud. We defend it in public. We hurt over it in private. That's our weakness.

"When we think ain't nobody looking, we're howlin' at the moon. You gotta make some noise, but this time, not behind closed doors. You need a jury of your peers. That'll be us, your cousins. And you'll need someone to vouch for you. Bear witness. Maybe this lady is your witness, little cousin. Maybe she gotta be sworn in, so she can defend what she knows to be right, just, and true."

A chill ran down Lennox's spine. Though it was a simple metaphor, the fact that Nadia wanted to be a lawyer and had been going to college for that before she began dancing gave Kage's words an uncanny quality.

"Our blood makes him believe we are bound to him, Kage. I'm bound to no man. My loyalty does have limits. He knows that he's the reason for the season. The brainchild behind the mayhem and money. He likes the chase. Just like the dog and the wolf."

"He sees a bit of himself in all seven of us. You're nothin' but a pretty, shiny thing to him."

"I know that."

"Then if you know that, use it to catch him in his own snare. What you've told me makes it clear in my mind." Kage pointed to the side of his head, his brows rutted as if slightly annoyed. "I know what you need to do, you just gotta figure out how. That is what I don't have the answer to."

"Survivin' Grandpa Wilde. Coming to Netflix."

They both had a mirthless chuckle at that.

"Look, Lennox, you've been out of drama and bullshit for a while now. It makes you a bit out of practice for these things, but you better get your head back in the game, and you better get it in there fast. Keep focused, and hold on to this frame of thought. Make it so that when Grandpa grabs you, like the pretty shiny thing you are to him, he'll find out you ain't no golden toy buried in the soil after all. You're a gotdamn grenade."

"Use what he thinks you are to turn it back on him. Like I said, I don't have that advantage. He knows I'm a fuckin' bomb. You, on the other hand, look more promising in his eyes, and agreeable. That also makes this all the eviler. He called you a dog? Yeah... He's making you hunt for your own death. So, turn it around on him and serve him justice on a platter. Make it the worst thing he's ever consumed in his entire life." Kage placed his hand on Lennox's shoulder. "Make your flavor bitter, your texture dry, and for God's sake, you better be more poisonous than a witch's kiss because the mission ain't to make him sick, little cousin. It's to make him regret the day he ever tried to dig up the top dog's mama's buried bones..."

NADIA STOOD IN the book store, lost and confused while 'L.I.E.' by N'Dambi played. It had been a long time since she'd purchased a book anywhere other than online, but when her grandmother had stated she wanted a new cookbook for her birthday, it seemed like a great idea. Besides, she did miss the scent of books, new and old, and her Kindle simply couldn't compare to that nostalgia. She made her way to the cooking section and found plenty of recipe books Grandma might enjoy. She got several of them to cover all bases. Grandma loved trying new recipes. It was the cutest thing. Now that she had what she needed, she still found herself practically rooted in place.

The mission wasn't over. Over the past couple of days, she'd become obsessed with the whole question of, *'What if?'* Had she buried her dreams in the ground and covered them up with fake peace of mind? Perhaps her last encounter with Lennox had sparked this feeling. The way he left her heated like an oven on a thousand degrees and didn't bother to turn her off when the humiliation was cooked to a nice golden brown was downright diabolic. Sure, he'd called the next day like shit didn't happen, but something *had* happened. Something major. He'd turned her down, but for all the right reasons. There was something else at play, too. She began to resent some aspects of her business. Her loyal OnlyFans client, Pedro, who'd she'd entertained for over four months, told her after he climaxed from her teasing gyrations that afternoon that she was *the oldest broad he'd ever paid for a nut.*

The sleepy-eyed son of a bitch had meant it as a compliment, stating she looked good for her age, but instead of taking it as nice words from a wealthy Hispanic man who just didn't know any better, one who had a belly button fetish and money to burn, it fed into her concerns that the expiration date on this filming for funds ride was soon approaching. *I can't be doing this forever. I don't WANT to be doing this forever… I can't believe this, but I miss law school, too. I want to look into going back, and getting my degree.*

She realized after that encounter with her client, tense conversations with her mother as of late, and a man who she was torn up about who had the audacity to walk away from her good, wet pussy, carting a full-fledged hard on to boot, that her feelings for Lennox were clouding things, too. She now didn't have a strong desire to be naked in front of strange men. She had no feelings about it all, in fact. It didn't feel bad, or good—just something she did, going through the motions.

Feeding their kinks, getting paid well for their weaknesses, and taking control of their libidos didn't give her the zing she typically enjoyed. She'd mulled this last night as she stripped down to her bare flesh on that stage—a thought she'd never entertained before when her clothing hit the floor and her legs fell open into splits. It was as if Lennox was wielding some sort of spell over her now, and she'd never even fucked him. Frustration crawled up her neck like an insect, biting hard—an annoying tingling sensation that was now tapping on her shoulder and whispering bullshit in her ear. Reminding her that her journey wasn't over. It had just begun.

Maybe that's what they call a conscience? No longer fighting it, she made her way down the legal books aisle and studied the offerings. Some paperbacks offered textbook legal advice, others were self-help in nature, and a few were geared towards those going professionally into law. Students interested in a particular field. She picked up a book and read the title: *The Tools of Argument: How the Best Lawyers Think, Argue, and Win* by Joel P. Trachtman. Flipping through it, she discovered a few passages that caught her interest, then closed the book and placed it in her basket to purchase along with the cookbooks. Minutes later, she found herself in the romance book aisle.

Her body warmed as she checked out some of the steamy covers. She considered her reaction to be amusing, yet refreshing. It took a lot to get her turned on nowadays, but something about the glossy covers of smooching paramours in lust-fueled embraces gave her all the feels. Corny, cute, or sexy as hell, they called to her, bringing forth memories of her early teenage years where she and her girlfriends huddled together at the local Walgreens after school, giggling while reading sleazy words printed on off-white pages in romance novels, and flipping through cheap magazines that published poorly edited erotica aimed to titillate and arouse such as Bronze Thrills, and similar periodicals.

She stood there for a moment, eyes closed, traveling Memory Lane as the smell of hot coffee wafted around her. *The magazines always smelled like wet newspapers, and the pages were thin. That drugstore smelled like perfumes, bubble gum, and cherry candies. That old Chinese pharmacist, whose head was shaped like a misshapen egg, would glare at us from over his glasses.*

On the covers of the magazines she and her friends found so amusing were people that never matched the descriptions in the stories printed inside the pages. Like older guys with greasy Jheri curls being passed off as the sexy lead role, while in the actual story, the guy was only twenty-two, built nicely, and had a fade. Pointing out the stark differences, they'd laugh hard, then point to the dirty passages and crack up all over again:

Jerome laid Delilah down on the small, rickety, iron bed in his prison cell, and said, "I'm gonna bust your tight little cherry tonight, girl. You about to take all dis dick, bitch. All ten inches. And you gonna like it."

The probation officer was a virgin, but madly in love with the dangerous playa. Jerome was the sexiest and most ruthless man in the prison, and he stuck up for her when no one else cared. She owed him so much. She wanted Jerome to be her first, and now was the time to give herself to him before it was too late. He took her handcuffs from her belt and tied her wrists to the iron bars of his cage, then made her lick on her baton.

"That's right. Suck it. Practice makes perfect."

He tore off his prison shirt and her pussy got even wetter at the sight of his hard, chiseled hairy chest. All that chocolate was for her and her alone. At least for one night. He grinned down at her, exposing his gold tooth with the bright diamond in it.

Jerome was a big-time neighborhood drug dealer, and all the women around town had been talking about how good he was in bed. The one detail that stuck out the most though was when they were bragging about his big, long, juicy black dick... Jerome said his dick was always hungry, and that it had a mind of its own. Some of the girls had admitted how that big, swinging snake of his had sent several women to the hospital. She didn't mind being taken away in a gurney and admitted into ICU if it meant she could finally be with the bad boy of Baton Rouge...

She opened her eyes and burst out laughing, then caught herself. *I can't believe I still remember that! Word for word!* She'd stolen the magazine from the store, jamming it into the inside of her jacket. *Me, Kim, Jeisha and Angie must've read that thing a million times, passing it between us! We were far too young to have such things. I masturbated to it a thousand times!* She moved slowly down the lane, grabbing various books from the shelves based on cover alone. *Oh, this looks good.* She'd scan a few, put them back, but every now and again a blurb or two would have her intrigued enough to place it in her cart. 'Chosen,' by Darie McCoy, 'Blind Spot,' by Olivia Gaines from her Technicians series, and Bound Through Time: Past (A Viking Brothers Novel Book 1) by Twyla Turner, to name a few. She'd perused practically the entire store, enjoying herself, falling in love with the rare treat of pleasure reading, when she stumbled across the psychology and sex education books section.

Normally, she'd have kept it moving, but the name of one of the books as she passed by caught her attention: *'Sweet Black Pussy'* by Dr. Saint Aknaten.

That has to be in the wrong section! Shouldn't that be in the erotica area with the romance books? She snatched it off the shelf and read the cover again. It was a smooth, matte hardback cover, black with an embossed black rose on it, with a red stem and leaves. The title font was also raised, printed in red and gold. *Gorgeous cover.*

She flipped it open and began reading, not stopping until she realized her damn foot had fallen asleep. Tingly and all. She gasped when she looked at her watch. *Oh my God.* She'd been standing there, practically in a trance for over an hour, devouring the book. What had felt like ten minutes was in fact much longer. She'd drifted into another world.

A sex therapist, psychologist, and advocate for Black women by the name of Dr. Saint Aknaten had written this gem. When she turned to the back of the book, she saw his picture and hummed. *Well, surprise, surprise. This motherfucker is fine as hell. Damn. A real zaddy. Where have I heard this dude's name before?* It was killing her, trying to remember. She placed the book in her basket, not caring about the price, and made her way to the register. As she was standing in line, she got a text message from Lennox.

I want to take you out for dinner and a movie soon, baby. Let me know your schedule.

She quickly texted him back: *We can go out this Friday or Sunday. I'm going to pay you back though, and walk away just like you did me. LOL.*

As she was pulling out her wallet to pay, he wrote back: *Not so fast. When I'm done with you, you may not be able to walk anywhere. LOL. Jokes aside, we'll see how the date goes. I still have to make sure that you're mentally ready, and emotionally capable to handle all that I have to offer. I'm playing for keeps.*

Her lips curled in a smile, and her stomach erupted in butterflies...

CHAPTER TWELVE

A dog-eat-dog world

G RANDPA WAS DRESSED in a ghost-white suit and a healthy dose of vintage swag. His white tie hung from his neck, the silver flecks in the design glowing in the currents of sunlight. A white cowboy hat donned his head, large oval-shaped diamonds wrapped around the white silk band. He gripped his white marble cane with a beringed hand as he made his way to the fitness center front door. A slight look of strain and angst shone in his eyes. One white and gray snakeskin cowboy boot stepped leisurely in front of the other as he made his steadfast approach. Jasper, one of the two men that accompanied him, dressed in black and dark gray camouflage, opened the door for the old bastard, both sporting guns on their hips.

Uncle Danny was the second flunky. Enslaved blood. Lennox snatched his large jug of water from a nearby counter, tipped it to his lips, and took a big gulp as he leaned against the white wall, waiting for the circus act to begin. Thankfully, his ten o'clock client had just left—a lady he personally trained every Tuesday and Thursday. Minutes prior, he'd seen Grandpa lurking in a dark blue Lexus with tinted windows, parked right outside his place of business. Yes, he knew it was him without seeing him. Grandpa had many cars that his sons and grandsons would drive him to places in. This was one of his favorites.

He sensed the old bastard approaching before he even saw him. Lennox figured it was a gift and a curse. This feeling he would get deep inside of him that burst free, ringing the alarms whenever something nasty was slithering his way.

"Grandson," Grandpa said proudly, raising both arms as if about to initiate an embrace. "So good to see you!" Lennox took another gulp of his water. "I'd like to speak to you privately, if you don't mind."

Lennox kept drinking, then belched. "…I mind."

"Well, isn't that a shame? Don't tell me I've come all this way for nothin'?"

Lennox could feel the eyes turning his way as people began to eavesdrop and look on. An older man was standing there, fit as a fiddle, donning expensive, flashy clothes covered in jewels and gold. Grandpa Wilde plucked his hat from his head with a slightly shaky hand, and held it modestly against his stomach. Thick, long waves of silver hair with snow-white highlights fell across the man's face, partially concealing one of his snake-like blue eyes. His silky white beard appeared more lustrous than usual as the bright gym lights hit it. What a conniving and contradicting sight to behold.

"I 'spose, since you've left me no choice, I'd hate to have to talk to you out here then, in front of all of these good folks about such a sensitive matter." The old man dramatically sighed as he slowly moved his arm about the room, waving the marble cane with the gold tip about like some magician wand. *He don't even need that fucking cane. Just has it for show.* A darkness flashed across his face as his faux frown stiffened while pretending to be wrought with sadness by being turned down.

"If you hate the idea of it so much, leave."

"You know I can't do that, Lennox. They'll be an audience I guess for us to discuss private affairs. Like how your whore of a mama's lovely, long Lebanese legs were spread wide fuckin' open, exposing that black, hairy bush you came out of, but then it was for every Tom, *definitely* Dick, and Harry to slide into and—"

"Shut up." Lennox barked, slamming his bottle down on a nearby counter. "In the back."

Grandpa and the two-armed men followed him into a small storage area filled with yoga mats and dumbbells. Lennox closed the door behind them, then faced them, arms crossed. He and Grandpa stared each other down, eye to eye. He imagined they looked like two rival fighters right before the big brawl. In fact, they were.

Grandpa's lips pursed, and his salt and pepper thick brows bunched as his icy stare intensified. His lips suddenly bowed in a warm smile, as if he were some robot and someone had flipped a switch. He then slapped Lennox's shoulder hard.

"Look at you..." He scanned him from his face down

to his feet. "You've grown up to be incredible. Strong. A fortress. I couldn't take my eyes off you when you came to visit the other day."

"You call that me comin' to visit? You kidnapped me, and the rest of my cousins that you've labeled AWOL, at gunpoint."

Grandpa ignored him and went on with his spiel. "You've grown into a strapping young man. You've got a ruggedness about you. You're so damn robust." Grandpa's eyes narrowed as he looked him up and down. "...You don't have any children, though. And you're unmarried. Maybe you still like to play the field?" He could tell Grandpa was fishing, trying to elicit a response. He remained quiet. "You've endured. Lost your mama... got caught up in some legal tangles. Had no money. Cut off from the family. My grandbaby wants nothin' to do with her big brother. Y'all used to be close. Silva... she's doing just fine though. Grandpa's precious baby girl."

"What is this? A phony psychic reading? And Silva isn't a baby anymore. She's a grown woman, and you turned her against me."

"I did no such thing. She just lost respect for you is all. That's none of my business." The old man rocked back on his heels. Smug as ever.

"You can ruin my relationship with my sister, cause all of the mayhem you want, but you can't boss me around and run my life. I'm my *own* man."

"See? That fight in you, that strength, both physical, emotional and mental, is what I love about you, Lennox. The problem is you need to understand that family, your blood," Grandpa softly poked him in the chest, "are the only ones you can truly trust. That's why I have only a handful of staff that I share no bloodline with. It ain't worth the hassle, and it damn sure ain't worth the risk."

"But if someone doesn't wanna work for you, you should respect that. Love is an action word. You don't force folks to do stuff they don't wanna do if you love 'em. That's not love. That's selfishness. Control."

"Well," Grandpa shrugged nonchalantly, "I strongly disagree. Parents have to tell children to do things they don't wanna do all the time, boy."

"I'm not a child."

"You aren't… but you're mine. *My* grandchild. You belong to me." His voice hardened. "The elders always know what's best. Why do you think things always go to shit when the younger folk are runnin' things? If you look at ancient times, it was the elders, the grandparents and great-grandparents, who made all major decisions for the clan. Wisdom only comes with experience. Experience only comes with time. Time only comes with age. People say all the time how blood will treat you worse than a stranger, and that may be true in some cases, but that blood is like a code. It stands for somethin', Lennox, and it can't be broken. Code of honor and respect. The blood of Christ… Flesh of my flesh, blood of my blood." He placed his hand across his heart. "Family is the answer."

"You're the answer? Then I'll never have a question. In fact, I have nothin' to say to you. Consider me mute." He leaned forward and lowered his voice, while the subdued sounds of 'Love Me JeJe,' by Tems played in the background.

"Lennox, you can pretend to be deaf, mute and blind, but the Lord will open your eyes and force you to see. This is my last appeal to you."

"Grandpa, the Lord will force us to do nothing. I have free will, as do you. You've been exercising your free will," He placed his hand on his hip and leaned slightly forward. "And I'm just doin' the same. There's something called Jahannam, and according to my mama, it's a bad place for evildoers in the afterlife. Islam's definition of hell. I'm not Muslim, but I respected my mother's beliefs. You wanted to talk to me about my mama's legs bein' open when you first got in here making a ruckus. Well, guess what? The doors of Jahannam will be wide open for *you*. I'm sure most men would prefer the legs... My whore of a mother, as you like to call her, will be looking down on you from Heaven, and when she does, I 'magine you'll beg her to spit on you to help put out the fire. But instead, she'll grab some gasoline, pour it all over your writhing body, and laugh as you burn." Lennox cackled.

"Watch it now." Grandpa's chest rose and fell faster, and his complexion deepened. "You watch your tongue, boy... I see you've been takin' lessons from crazy Kage! Yeah... I know you two been slippin' and slidin' 'round one another like blobs of snot. Family are also the only ones who can get close enough to hurt you, Lennox, but the blood saves. It heals. You better hope and pray I choose the latter."

"If you respected family so much, Grandpa, you wouldn't have treated my mother the way you had. She was married to your son. That made her your daughter, too. She was married to the son that did just about everything you asked, and you couldn't even let him have *that* in peace. You were jealous that he didn't love you as much as he loved her, and angry that she didn't care about you or your twisted opinions about her. You want to be worshiped. Your ass kissed. I ain't gonna do it. You can come up here with the army brigade, National Guard, and Scooby Doo and Shaggy, and it won't change a damn thing. My mama was the same way, and you couldn't stand that she wasn't afraid of you. Now, if you don't mind, I need to—"

"Boy, I've heard about enough of your lip." Grandpa jetted his finger in his face. "I want to make somethin' quite perfectly mother-fuckin' clear to you. I don't know what mountain you think you're standing on, but this ain't the hill you want to die on. And let me clear that shit you said about your mama up. I *never* had any ill will towards your mother. Did I like that Aaliyah was one of dem Muslims? Abso-lute-ly fucking not. Did I think she was good enough for the likes of my son? Hell no. I also didn't give a shit about her bein' no doctor and havin' all that education. But you're right. Your father loved her, so I didn't touch one hair on her head. I have two simple rules. First rule: Any of my children or grandchildren can love whoever they want to love as long as that person doesn't interfere with me and my business.

"Second rule, I won't cause any intervention with anybody y'all are married to, as long as they don't cause significant, intentional harm to me, or any of my family members, especially those that are involved in the family business. Let's be fair because your mother broke both of those rules. She knew what was expected, and she decided to do the exact opposite. Multiple times. I gave her ample opportunity to shut the fuck up. Sometimes that woman put silly ideas in your father's head. He'd get ballsy, and then he'd have to be set straight." Grandpa placed his hand back on his shoulder. This time, with a bit more pressure.

"Set straight? Like some doll that fell on its side. Toys. Little GI Joe men. That's all we are to you. Green army soldiers made of cheap plastic. A bunch of damn toys!"

"Nonsense. Nothin' I do is for play—"

"You want to *use* family, and not regular ol' people because family is a commodity to you. You want blood because we're easier to control, manipulate and extort. You accuse me of standin' on some mountain, but you can't even stand on an anthill on your own. This mountain of mine? This thing called life? At least I climbed it by myself! You're a tyrant and a coward! You couldn't do a fraction of what I've succeeded at, and the best achievements in life have little to do with money, Grandpa. Greedy men like you sit back and count your cash while sitting in the middle of your bedroom, alone, not noticing the stench of burnin' flesh. You never realize a flame is spreading until it's too late, because you're so engrossed in your greed and power trips. You totally miss the fact that your ass is on fire!"

"Get it all out, boy!" Grandpa cackled. "All of this make-believe stuff you've concocted in your head! No, I want family because family are the best men for the job!"

"Bullshit. It's gives you an advantage that can't be compared. You know our full history, from five generations back, maybe even more. You know what we've achieved, and where we've failed. You know many of our secrets, the things we've done. Like you knowin' about me driving out to Kage's house. Case in point, I am sure you know now that I found the little tracker you had one of your fuckheads put on my truck. It's been removed. Proof that you are watchin' us every chance you get. In some cases, you were even at the hospital while we were bein' born. You know our ticks, pet peeves, temptations, advantages, gifts, and limitations.

"With a new person you meet, or some stranger that you get to know, you still would have missed a lot of that important information. Only could take their word for some things, because not every detail about a person can be charted or verified unless you were right there, when it happened. With your children, grandchildren, brothers, and cousins, you were there, in some capacity, every step of the way. Getting the play by play. Watchin' them like some Boogeyman. The more you know about someone, the more power and leverage you have over them. You want to be king of the mountain. That's why you're pissed that I'm tryna climb it. This just in! Breaking news... Guess what, old man? I don't have to climb the mountain, or be king of the mountain. I *am* the mountain..."

Grandpa's hand slipped from his shoulder, and he gripped the top of his cane with both palms. Picking it up a wee bit from the ground, he slammed the tip with might down onto the concrete floor.

"Lennox, your fucking mama is dead. You probably blame me for that, even though it was her own health that took her out of here. Your father is not to your liking. You probably blame me for that, too. Nothin' I can do about that. Perception is a skewed lens. You blame me for you and your sister's falling out. Ain't my fault that I spoil her. Take care of her. She's a good lady, and deserves my love. Now, I told you very clearly what the situation is, as well as the consequences. This was a courtesy visit. The last opportunity you have to do the right thing." He pointed his finger in Lennox's face. "I will tell your mother's entire family about her whore ways.

"I'll tell them about what a foul-mouthed tramp she was, and about the disrespect she showed me as the patriarch of this family. I will then let a few important folks know that you ain't kill just *one* man, you killed several, and I have the proof. You're a fucking killing machine. And you liked it!" He sneered. "Your father *begged* me, cryin' his eyes out for them to not take his boy away. You'd gotten yourself in some shit you couldn't get out of. The boy wasn't no kin to you, and that's why he told on you faster than a Cheetah on roller skates. I agreed to help my grandson out of a jam, even though you and I were on the outs.

"You yelled at me for your mother's American memorial service, here in Texas, that the family had after her body was shipped to Lebanon so that her friends in the states could say goodbye. I was her father-in-law, for God's sake, regardless of how she and I didn't see eye-to-eye. You made a big ass scene. Told me to get out. Four of my men had to drag you away."

"Four of your men?" He scoffed. "They were my

gotdamn younger cousins! More blood on your payroll!"

"Doesn't matter. You proved how ungrateful you were, boy. After all I have done for you over the years."

"I didn't ask you to do a damn thing for me. My father did, and he did so behind my back. You did it not to help me, but so I'd owe you one day. You must think I'm a fucking idiot. I'm not rollin' over for anyone, especially not a psychopath who sends men out to murder families on Thanksgiving, then pretends to be Santa on Christmas."

"Don't you stand there and act all high and mighty! You could've turned down my help, but you didn't. You're no better than what you're trying to pretend you're not. A cold-blooded killer. You were a gun for hire. You were willin' to work for those yuppies, but not for your own grandfather doing pretty much the same damn thing! I would have paid ten times more, and there'd be no trace! You did that to spite me!" Grandpa tossed his cane on the floor with a big crash and jeered.

"…And you did it so sadistically, too. Rubbed it in my face. Lennox, in spite of all of that, I know you're one of the pure ones. Deep down. You have such a beautiful soul." *Pretty little things…* "You want to do the right thing. You want to be loyal." *Like a good little dog…* "So, you think long and hard about what's on the line."

"If I come from your bloodline, how pure, righteous and loyal could I *truly* be?"

Grandpa sneered as he got in his face. "I will take your dead mama down, and you right along with her. I will have you spend the rest of your days practically under the prison, and then drag your mama's tattered, tramp skeleton out of that lopsided grave in that piece of shit country of her's, set it out under the blazing sun, and let the crows fuck her pelvic bone until it turns to dust! Her final act of servitude as a lady of the night.

Don't.

Fuck.

With.

Me!

Now, you fetch, and roll over and play dead. Only messin' around with me, you won't be playing for long, boy. It'll be for real. For eternity. It's a dog-eat-dog world, Lennox, but you just remember this: Every dog has its day..."

CHAPTER THIRTEEN

A Rose Garden and a Sprinkler

N ADIA REACHED FOR the tissue on her nightstand, brought it to her nose and dabbed at the trickles of snot forming in her nostrils. She could feel the dry sting of her eyes, certain they were red without seeing her reflection. Taking a deep breath, she flipped to another page of the book…

...And this is why a woman, who created the entire world, sees herself as a mere speck of nothingness. A woman has forgotten her place in the universe. She's been programmed to do so. She has allowed herself to be used without reciprocity. She's allowed her ideas and inventions to be stolen, without apologies, compensation, and reparations. She's allowed herself to be reduced to dust, told she is here to only serve, when she is the main addition and supreme. She's allowed herself to be taught incorrect information, incorrect morals, incorrect standards, all so that it may please the one that is incorrect in his mindset. She has been taught to worship the one that is physically stronger than her, but emotionally weaker. The womb is the center of life. Not the seed. We are mere sprinkler systems to their garden. And deep down, we know this.

Men, we have fooled ourselves into believing our own lies. If you lie often enough, you begin to believe it yourself. So somehow, along the way, we, the sprinkler, convinced womb-man that WE are the garden. We did that.

We did that through our laws of the land. We did that through warping the true intent and word of God. We did that through calculated lies, manipulation, and brute force. Women form soul attachments to men, and men to women, but women bond harder. It's because they are nurturers, but it also puts them at a disadvantage, making them easy targets. So then we essentially tell an ocean that she is nothing more than a muddy puddle.

I hate to tell you fellas, but we are not the creator. We are merely *a part of* creation, and yet, we have placed our feet on the womb-man's neck. We come from her. Not the other way around. The sperm does not have the same mission, abilities, and duties as the egg. The egg existed first. It is inside our mothers, grandmothers, daughters, aunts and female cousins when they are created in their mother's womb.

Therefore, if you think about it, we all are older than our birth years because we should start counting our existence from when the egg was formed inside our mothers. A part of us was already in existence. We were not yet human, but the blueprint was drafted. Being fertilized and being whole are two different things. We know this, though. Somewhere deep inside of ourselves, we've always known it, and that is in fact why we collectively treat our women the way we do.

We are jealous of the woman's biological power, and instead of uplifting and protecting her, we have convinced her – due to her desire and hardwiring to cultivate and satisfy – that it is WE who are in charge. Our prayers call the Creator Father, and yet, we understand that in all major religious texts, God has no biological sex, nor a gender. So, which is it? And if it is true that there is no gender or biological sex when it comes to God, why is Father the chosen appellative? Who decided this? We did. And why did we decide this? Because if one is falling to their knees and worshiping male energy, a male image and male personification, it is that much easier to control and manipulate women into falling in line and following our demands. All it took was a few confused women who were leaders to help spread this lie until it became an accepted truth because trust me, gentlemen, nothing we accomplish can take place without some sort of co-signing and approval of a conquered woman with some power and influence amongst her sisters.

There will always be those out there that cannot be saved, but when they are in power, they are dangerous. I am talking to my fellow men – trying to break down to you how this happened, and discuss the karmic repercussions and spiritual debts that we now owe. This is why we're seeing a rise in women becoming angrier, more disengaged, and more combative to the point that many are vowing to wash their hands of us, period. And what is our reaction? More manipulation, gaslighting and control. We make more and more rules to tighten the reins. What is the woman's reaction? More disengagement. What is our response to that? Abuse. Violence. We are losing control, and instead of coming to the table to talk and work these things out, understanding that men and women benefit each other in a fair system and playing field, which currently does not exist, we will become more and more violent.

When we as men lose dominion over the women, we become increasingly mentally unstable. She is the one thing we always had, always relied on, and when she packs her bags and leaves, and takes our children with her ... we see it as our investment, our property walking out of the door instead of our soulmate departing due to a broken heart.

We can't even understand the basic psychology of a woman because we refuse to shut the fuck up and listen. Women tell you that they are leaving long before it is said out of their mouths. We don't observe. We don't care until it is too late. Now, I don't like to get too heavy into religion, and I'm not going to do it now, but it is impossible to discuss the breakup of the human family, and the destruction of our marriages and romantic relationships, without at least touching on it because it is one of the tools used to direct us into what we should and should not be doing with our mate. I've said for years, I don't dislike religion. Just because I do not prescribe to religion, it does not mean that I don't believe in God, because I firmly do. I know firsthand, without a shadow of a doubt, that God exists. That is the main reason why I was able to wake up from my own fog and cease my destructive behavior towards myself, my best friend who I've known since childhood, and the women I sexually and romantically engaged with.

We are all entitled to worship as we wish. Spiritual beliefs are not the problem. They become the problem when we utilize them to govern others who do not benefit from said philosophies. My point in bringing this up is to give an illustration as to the brainwashing, warping and conditioning we use to keep our women in check. It used to serve us well, but now, the women are waking up. They realized that they are not being served in return. We complained about having to provide. We complained about having to protect. We complained about having to help one another, and respect our partner. Now, we're standing around dazed and confused as to why bags are being packed, and we're coming home to empty houses.

My wife is at home. I'm not having these motherfucking problems with her because I am doing what the fuck I promised her I would, when we exchanged vows. So when men complain to me and tell me I am just pandering, or trying to get women on my side, that's bullshit. My life speaks for itself. My wife, Xenia, is in the public eye. She is very outspoken, and has been open about various aspects of our marriage. I drive her crazy, but she loves me. She respects me as a man, her husband, and the father of her children. She trusts me. It took work to get where we are in our marriage.

We have two completely different backgrounds, but also some commonalities. I grew up on the East Coast, she grew up on the West coast. Two completely different vibes. If you know, you know. She was affiliated with gang activity, I was affiliated with gang activity. Meaning neither of us were gang members, but we hung with gang members. I had a troubled childhood, she had a period where her childhood was troubled. I had problems with my father, her father was non-existent for most of her childhood, and that caused her a great deal of distress and trauma. I had trauma due to butting heads and not getting along with my father for the majority of my life. At the time of our initial meeting, Xenia was against interracial dating and marriage.

She is a Black woman, devoted deeply to her African American culture. I obviously am not a Black man. My father is Egyptian, and has no genetic African ancestry, and my mother was North Korean. Xenia was used to being able to use her amazing control of language to express herself to her prior relationships. She wasn't used to men who are able to articulate what they want. She wasn't used to men who didn't play mind games and were decisive. I told her soon after I met her that I was going to marry her, and she didn't believe me. Here we are, all of these years later. Married. Happy. Healthy. I did the work. If you don't do the internal work, you will fail.

Men are failing. We pushed them too far. We've done too much damage. We're completely out of control. You can be a true alpha male without dominating your soulmate. In fact, true alphas, gentlemen, do not dominate their Queens in the first place. That goes against code. That's out of pocket. That's desperation. By the time you pound your fists upside your Queen's head, screaming and cursing at her, you've already lost. There's no coming back from that. Even if she forgives you, you've already proven you can't be trusted. That you're a loose cannon. You've shown her that you are weak. Abuse is not strength. It's a frailty. A deficit. You've proven that you're extremely toxic and too emotionally unhinged. You've proven that you can't handle the truth. You can't face that you lost because you gained her by lying about your true intentions. You were conniving.

All lies are eventually revealed. We may be dead for decades before the truth comes out, but like a hard dick in some wet, snug pussy, it's cumming whether we like it or not. We've tried every trick in the book, except offering the gotdamn truth. That's because we want to keep

them in bondage. And the truth sets people free...

Nadia placed the book down, leaned back and closed her eyes. Her mind reeled and her body warmed from burgeoning, confusing emotions. After a few minutes, she reached for her phone and made a call. Lennox answered on the second ring. She heard rock 'n' roll music playing in the background, people talking, and what sounded like weights and machines moving.

"Hey, baby. I'm workin' right now. Can I—"

"I know honey, sorry about that. I'm not gonna hold you, Lennox. This'll be super quick."

"Okay. Hey, Rick, hold on a sec, please... thanks... Okay, I'm here. You alright? What is it?"

"Yeah, I'm fine. Just have a question. Didn't you tell me you had read some books, or talked to some therapist and author named Saint Aknaten?"

"Yeah."

"How'd you find out about him?"

"Uh... it was an accident, actually. I was online and some of his videos popped up. Like some conferences he'd spoken at."

"How was that an accident?"

"I had misspelled a word in the search field. Whatever I typed caused him to pop up instead. I got curious, so I watched a video, and then before I knew it, I was spendin' whole days watching him and listening to interviews and stuff. That made me go on and buy some of his books. I could relate to what he was saying. I read like three of his books, and then I found out he had like a program, a system for healin' trauma that affects our relationships with women. He was talkin' about all trauma affects our relationships, and I hadn't ever really thought about that.

"How I avoided settling down. I didn't want to be committed, but I told myself I did. I had been in denial. I was a mess. I would abandon perfectly normal relationships with no warning. It was crazy. I decided to have an online appointment with him. It was kinda expensive, and there was a long waitin' list… but, uh, he squeezed me in, and it changed my life. He's the real deal."

"Hmmm, what did y'all talk about if you don't mind me asking?"

"Hold on… let me get out of earshot… Okay, I'm back. I mean, we talked about a lot. My session was about two hours long, and he called me a few months later to check on me. He has a very aggressive style of therapy, Nadia. He will curse you the fuck out, and then love on you, but that shit works. He doesn't mess around, and he knows what the hell he is talking about. He's brutally honest, will point out every fucked-up part about you, but that man has a heart of gold. Anyway, he explained to me that I avoided deep connections because of losing my mother—and a part of me feels like no woman can ever compare to her. Funny. You're like my mother…"

"Yeah… that's crazy. I can see the parallels. We were both in school and… well, anyway, what else did y'all talk about?"

"He, uh, let me think for a second… I'm trying to sum up a very intense and long therapy session on hydraulics basically. Okay. He also said that for some reason I blame my father for her death even though he didn't have anything to do with it. I knew that logically, ya know, but on a subconscious level, I blamed him anyway. I never even thought about that, Nadia but damn if he wasn't right. Once he explained what I was doing and why, it all made sense. It was an eureka moment."

"So, what happened after the therapy session? Did he just say, 'Good luck!' and hang up?"

Lennox chuckled. "Nah, it didn't work like that. That was just the beginning. He gave me some work to do, some exercises and assignments, and it made a huge difference. I had to do these daily questionnaires. I had to pray and meditate, and keep reading. It helped me a lot. I became true to myself." He laughed nervously. "What's this all about, girl? Why are you askin' all of this anyway?"

"…I was just curious."

"I don't have time for this, Nadia."

"Alright! Alright! Remember when I told you I was going to the bookstore to get my grandmother a cookbook? You won't believe this, but I was in another aisle, and his book stuck out like a sore thumb. I picked it up and started reading it, and before I knew it, a whole damn hour had passed. I was sold. I couldn't remember where I had heard his name mentioned before, but then I remembered what you had said. That's why I called you. To double check if I was right."

"Oh, okay. Yeah … cool. What book did you see?"

" 'Sweet Black Pussy.' The latest edition. I bought it, too. Been reading it."

"That's a good one. One of his best, actually. He has a new edition, huh? I might snag that from you. Anyway, I gotta get back to work, baby."

"Yeah, yeah, of course. Sorry. I look forward to seeing you for our date soon."

"No problem. Ditto. Can't wait to see you." And then the call ended.

She sat there still with so many questions. What drew Lennox to this man? What made him realize he needed help in the first place, and when was he no longer afraid to get the assistance he needed? On top of all that, she had no idea that Lennox was even into interracial dating, let alone open to speaking to a guru about it. Most of the girlfriends she'd seen of his when they were younger had been White. It was burning her up all of a sudden to not have more clarity on the matter. Unable to shake it, she shot him a quick text message:

> You don't have to answer right away, and I never thought to ask before now because I guess it just didn't matter. Why would you take courses from a man with expertise on interracial dating? I mean I know he speaks about relationships and marriage in general, but I never saw you with any Black women. Am I your first? You can be honest. I won't be angry either way. I just want to know.

She poured herself a cup of hot tea, then returned back to reading...

> **...There was a time when some so-called scholars tried to imply that the woman's brain was less intelligent because on average, it is a little smaller than her male counterparts. Well, of course it's smaller on average, dumb asses! Women typically have a smaller bone structure than men, so naturally, her organs, protected by the**

bones and muscle, would be smaller than ours, too.

There was another theory that women are slaves to their emotions. Some are, some aren't – just like some men are, and others aren't. Yet, men are far more likely to be a loose cannon, and that is because of our hormones. We are literally manufactured to pop off when we feel it is necessary, so how can we claim that women hold the heavyweight title on this?

All of this confusion is designed to once again keep women in check. Trying to use so-called medical evidence that is skewed and proven unfounded to drive a weak point home. Trying to use divine intervention and religion. Trying to use guilt trips. All of these are tools of the game. The tactics are endless. Pimping at its finest. We say: *How dare you question me, woman! Your brain is smaller than mine. You're mentally slower than me. You're too damn emotional. You're a nincompoop, and thank God that I am here to guide you, or there is no telling where you'd be!* Uh, happy. That's where they'd probably be.

Nadia burst out laughing.

We tell women: *You are too weak to build and create. You need me to tell you what to do and how to do it because you have no direction and are easily confused.* And you know what? All around the world we say this shit, and we get away with it. This all started because of our own insecurity, but now we've placed the disease of insecurity onto the backs of our lovers, forcing them to carry the weight.

The Black woman is the first portal of life on the planet Earth. We've convinced her that she's less rational than us. We've convinced her that she needs us to direct her every step of the way. We even have her going to church mostly by herself, so more of the same scare tactics can be driven into her head. We trained her well, like a dog. All we ended up doing in the long run is teaching her how to walk right the fuck out of our lives. We've become the bitch to our own egos. Stop reacting. Don't yell. Don't cry. Don't martyrize. Don't hit. Don't threaten. MOTHERFUCKER, JUST DO BETTER!

Nadia paused and shook her head, fighting tears of elation. Some things that her mother said, Saint was saying too, only in a different way, with a better explanation. *Mama may not be wrong about everything after all.*

Most of the time when a heterosexual woman is insecure, it is tied into the approval, validation, or endorsement of the male gender. She feels she isn't pretty enough. Her hair isn't nice enough. She's too fat. Too skinny. Too short. Too tall. Her ass is too little. Her breasts too small or too big. It's always something. She compares herself to other women and will fight another woman for an unworthy man who is playing both of them. She's trying to meet unrealistic expectations, imposed by someone who doesn't even know where the hell her clitoris is.

Nadia burst out laughing again, from the gut.

The majority of the Black woman's trauma, in America in particular, comes from two roots: Racism and Men. Black women traded in one slave master for another. Can you guess who that is? '*Well, that's not fair, Dr. Aknaten!*' I hear that shit all the time from men. I don't give a shit about something not being fair if it is accurate. The truth is not fair, men. It is not unfair, either. It simply IS.

So many men have approached me, upset when I make that statement about women's suffering. This is a biological male problem, regardless of race, ethnicity, or creed. I am talking about *all* of us. All men feed into the dysfunctional system of controlling our women. We first have to understand what we are doing, then the second step is to understand WHY we are doing it.

Another reason, besides insecurity, is because we're threatened if they don't help us. If they don't give us what we want, when we want it. We are intimidated if they start to collectively think for themselves. Some of the men at my seminars and conferences say, *but Dr. Saint Aknaten, how can you say all of this when there are horrible women out here, too? There are mothers having children that we didn't want, and raising them wrong. Teaching them how to take advantage of men, and not taking care of their responsibilities. How can you say that, Dr. Aknaten, when there are women lying, scheming, keeping our children away from us, and playing us, too? It's not just us.*

They scream this from the rooftops. They call me a panderer, and a simp. Never to my face, but online all day and night, because they are cowards and don't have the fucking balls to look me in my eye and say this silly simple Simon shit. I'm not above beating a mothafucka's ass, but I digress. All jokes aside, I really don't care about name-calling from boys masquerading as men. You're a damn child. You're nowhere near my level if you have this sort of remedial reasoning. And I don't care about your fucking feelings, either. Fuck a feeling. Feelings don't change shit. They improve nothing. They are completely unreliable. I care about logic, facts with substantiated data, and reality when it comes to decision making and accountability. I care about making improvements, rather than pointing fingers at the wrong shit just so we don't have to do the work of self-improvement. We are not victims. We are perpetrators.

The reality is that 90% of shitty women became that way due to having derelict, absentee, or destructive fathers, as well as mothers who put destructive men above themselves and their children. IN 90% OF THE CASES, A MAN STANDS BEHIND THE FUCKED-UP BEHAVIOR OF A FUCKED-UP WOMAN. WE ARE ALWAYS SOMEWHERE IN THE FUCKED-UP MIX, AREN'T WE?

Most women in prison right now are there due to some dealings with a man. She was either a drug mule for a man, or she was on drugs because of trauma from either a romantic partner or male family member... which led to a life of self-abuse and crime. She was introduced to drugs by a man, or killed him in a crime of passion, after perhaps finding him in bed with another woman.

Perhaps she took the fall for a guy and didn't actually commit the crime herself, or she participated in a crime orchestrated by a man in her life, or she had to off him because he was doing insane or violent things to her or her children. When women steal, kill, hurt for a thrill, I can promise you that in most cases, a man is involved. That's just how the ball bounces. 90% of these scheming, lying, manipulative, dirty, horrible women are created from a botched core memory – bad or absentee fathers is a common one. It's more often than not traced back to the childhood in the majority of these cases, and then fed from other incidents throughout our adolescence and adulthood ... but the thing that got the ball rolling was dear ol' dad.

The sprinkler system, remember? That's us. The sprinkler system that wants to be adored and worshiped and treated like the garden sometimes stops working and watering the flowers and plants, then gets angry when those flowers and plants grow up crooked, dry, and damaged! We blame them for being fucked up! We judge and sneer in disgust.

DADDIES! DON'T CALL YOUR DAUGHTER AN IDIOT. A WHORE. A CUM DUMPSTER. DON'T ACT LIKE YOU DON'T KNOW HOW SHE GOT THE WAY SHE DID. DON'T SAY THAT HER MOTHER TURNED HER AGAINST YOU, OR TAUGHT HER WRONG. YOU SHARE THE BLAME IF THAT IS TRUE! IF YOU TRULY WERE CONCERNED AND BELIEVED THIS, YOU WOULD HAVE DONE ALL YOU COULD TO BE IN THAT LIT-TLE FLOWER'S LIFE! YOU WOULD HAVE FOUGHT AS HARD TO BE WITH HER AS YOU DO FOR YOUR VICES: WEED, BEER, LIQUOR AND WINE, ATTENTION, FOOD, WOMEN OR JUST SOME RANDOM PUSSY THAT YOU RAW-DOGGED.

YOU WOULD HAVE WOKEN UP IN THE MORNING, BRIGHT AND EARLY, AND TOOK YOUR ASS TO COURT INSTEAD OF SLEEPING IN! YOU WOULD HAVE BEEN FIGHTING TO SEE YOUR BABY INSTEAD OF COMPLAINING, STARTING BOOTLEG, DUSTY ASS, IGNORANT PODCASTS SCREAMING FOR HOURS ABOUT HOW, *'THESE BITCHES AIN'T LOYAL.'* ! YOU WOULD HAVE BEEN FIGHTING TO GET AT LEAST JOINT CUSTODY! FIGHTING FOR THAT BABY THAT DESERVES BETTER IF YOU THINK HER MOTHER IS SUCH GARBAGE! INSTEAD, YOU LEFT HER THERE. YOU ABANDONED HER. YOU PLAYED THE VICTIM. YOU GOT MAD THAT YOU HAD TO PAY $100 A MONTH IN CHILD SUPPORT. YOU WERE ANGRY THAT SHE KEPT THE BABY AFTER SHE TOLD YOU THAT SHE WAS PREGNANT – AND HAD THE GALL TO BE SURPRISED WHEN YOU KNOCKED HER UP, AFTER RAW-DOGGING HER FOR MONTHS.

IF YOU TRULY CARED, YOU WOULD HAVE WORKED TWO OR THREE JOBS TO SAVE UP MONEY TO HIRE A

GOOD LAWYER, FIND A BETTER PLACE TO LIVE, GET A RELIABLE CAR SO YOU COULD HELP RAISE YOUR CHILD! AIN'T NO WAY I WOULD LET MY WIFE RAISE MY CHILDREN WITHOUT ME IN THE PICTURE TO HELP. IT'S NOT THAT SHE'S NOT A GREAT MOTHER, SHE IS, BUT EVEN THE BEST OF MOTHERS STRUGGLE IF THEY HAVE TO DO IT ALONE! MY CHILDREN NEED ME! THEY NEED US 24/7! THEY'RE NOT JUST THE RESULT OF BUSTING A NUT! IT'S A JOB BEING A FATHER, AND AN HONOR!

THESE ARE SOULS THAT YOU HELPED USHER INTO THE FUCKING WORLD! THEY TOOK A CHANCE ON YOU. THEY BELIEVE IN YOU. THEY THINK YOU ARE THE CLOSEST THING TO GOD! THIS IS SERIOUS! DON'T SAY DEROGATORY SHIT ABOUT THAT YOUNG LADY YOU HELPED CREATE. YOU FORFEITED YOUR RIGHT TO TALK SHIT ABOUT THAT BABY GIRL WHEN YOU DID NOT WATER HER! WOMEN CAN'T WATER! **WE** ARE THE FUCKING SEED AND WATERING HOSE! SEMEN IS MORE THAN FLUID! IT'S THE FIRST WATERING. IT TELLS THE EGG THAT WE ARE THE FATHERS, AND WE'RE READY TO GET TO WORK! THE EGG SAYS, 'BET. I GOT IT FROM HERE. MEET ME AGAIN IN NINE MONTHS!' WE POUR INTO THAT VESSEL, AND THAT WOMAN, AS ALWAYS, MAKES SOMETHING BETTER! WHEN THAT BABY IS BORN, YOU CAN START WATERING HER OR HIM AGAIN. GIVING KNOWLEDGE. LOVE. UNDERSTANDING.

BUT YOU DIDN'T! YOU LIED! THEN YOU GET MAD WHEN THAT MOTHER HAS TO BE TWO PEOPLE INSTEAD OF ONE, AND YOU SAY SHE IS EMASCULATING YOU! SHE'S ACTING LIKE A MAN! WELL, OF COURSE SHE IS BECAUSE SHE HAD NO CHOICE! YOU WEREN'T THERE! YOU CREATED A DROUGHT! FATHERS, IF YOU HAND ME AN EXCUSE, I WILL HAND YOU A MAP AND ASK YOU ONE QUESTION, MR.

WERE YOU?!

Oh my God! I have never heard anyone speak like this about my life! He is talking about ME! Tears kept forming and her mind spun, her heart bursting with emotion. Taking a deep breath, she continued.

I am coming down hard on us men because we made a promise, with our bodies and our souls, and we're not honoring the contract. In the case of male children, the results are just as bad when we are not around, or emotionally shut off. In fact, with boys, all we do is create more versions of ourselves – our unhealed selves, and the fucked-up cycle continues. A father can be in the house, but not really present. That is exactly what happened to me. I was an exception, though, because I didn't blame my mother for the things my father did. Many times however, that isn't the case. That young man grows up and blames the garden, not understanding that if the sprinkler had stayed and did the work needed, there would not be so many fucked up, damaged, trauma-bonded, mentally deranged, neglectful, manipulative people on this planet.

The mother can't move! She is the garden – rooted. She has no choice but to stay there with the children while the sprinkler gushes and goes rogue. The hose starts spritzing and waters someone else's lawn, with no remorse. Garden after garden after garden have been given seeds, with no water. Lawn after lawn.

That's the legacy we're leaving behind as men. We make families we don't want. Enter marriages with

**women we don't love. And we're never satisfied, con-
stantly moving the goal post. We don't want
relationships. We want robots with pretty faces, maids,
live-in chefs, wet pussies, and mouths that only open if
they're kissing our asses or sucking our dicks. We have
done a terrible thing, and the punishment will be harsh.
In this lifetime, or in death. Payment will be rendered.
God will question us, and we will be forced to answer.**

Nadia placed the book down once again and blew her
nose. Reaching for the bottle of water she had on her
nightstand, she took a big, long gulp. Her face was so wet
with tears, she simply gave up wiping it. She'd hated her
own father for so long that when he died, they were still at
odds. She had regrets. Guilt. And yet, the anger remained,
so fresh. It ruled her. She hadn't even bothered going to his
funeral. The anger for men began with him. Of that, now
she was certain. She didn't feel loved by him, only dismissed or judged... *I WASN'T WATERED!*

The anger continued and grew when she was beaten by
a fellow college student and fought to stay alive. She wanted
the tables to turn. *What goes around comes back around though. I
wanted my power back.*

She tried to take control and make men beg for her.
They now had to pay her to even *see* her. Even in her
romantic relationships, she realized she always wanted to be
in control. It was hard to give fully of herself. She wanted
to twist and turn them, and it worked for a long while. She
became Velvet, and revenge fit like a glove. But then she
realized the pain was still there, right under the surface.

Deep down, she really just wanted to love and be loved.

She wanted to heal, but didn't know how. She no longer aspired to remain chained to her own trauma and pain. She wanted something to change, but she didn't always feel motivated. At least not until she ran into a man from her memories. He re-entered her life and offered her a beautiful future. A man who gave her his heart freely, and not once asked her for anything in return…

…Women who have active fathers. Good fathers. Caring fathers. Fathers who spend time with them and teach them about men, about making their own money so that if their relationship falls apart, they can survive, be self-sufficient. A man to teach them about loving themselves and keeping their standards high, about what it means to be a good wife to a deserving man, about how to spot a man who isn't about shit, are far less likely to succumb to corruption, ruthlessness and all the things men don't like about certain women.

You sons of bitches can't talk to me about the fucked up things women have done to you – because I've had some fucked up things done to me by women, too. You're not the only one to go through some shit! Some shit happened to me, at the hands of a woman, that you wouldn't even believe! In fact, one diabolical incident was so traumatic for me, it almost destroyed my marriage. I almost lost my woman over something I hadn't even initiated or agreed to. It was so serious, that my wife had moved out for a time being. I was at my fucking lowest. I had lost so much. She took my babies with her. I was crushed, so you motherfuckers sitting around being keyboard gangsters, writing me shit about how I don't know what's going on in this world regarding how the women are acting, can go eat a dick.

Don't come to me harping about the evils of women and how they're Satan's spawn, when I know even regardless of the incident that happened in my own life, which was criminal, iniquitous, humiliating, and disturbing for myself and my wife, it pales in comparison to what we as a gender have done to our female counterparts. Most of us men are the ones doing the most heinous, diabolic shit out in this world. Most of us who have no issues getting women, can count only a few incidents, or less, of a woman doing us wrong. But the times we've done women wrong are probably in the hundreds!

And worst of all, we are doing it because we can! If the woman says no, we can physically make her. We weren't created stronger than them so that we could assault them! We were made stronger so we can protect them! Shame on you. We set this bullshit in motion! And even in my own personal situation, the one I've been discussing in a roundabout way, a terrible thing happened to me because of shit I had done to HER. I wasn't innocent. I had fucked her over, a woman that loved me while we were together, and instead of appreciating that, I mentally abused her, and she never forgot it.

She lost her mind and vowed to get revenge on me, and boy, did she ever. No, I didn't deserve what happened to me in the least, and I did receive justice, but I understand cause and effect. We as men will dog women out a thousand times. The one time a woman wrongs us, we forget about our own pasts, and focus on the one time we were done greasy. Then every woman after her has to pay for our broken heart. That's bullshit. Shift how you treat people, and people will treat you better. You'll attract better vibes and energy. Now, let's continue...

The statistics prove what I am saying to you is true. I

don't have to make up any of this. The facts are already proven, and I have my sources at the end of this book, should you be inclined to do the research yourself so you can reach your own conclusions as I did.

Nadia quickly flipped to the back of the book and began skimming the eight pages of sources listed. *Wow.* She then landed on his photo again and smiled. *I know his wife has fun with him. Whew! It should be a crime to be this fine.*

...Whether something is fact or just my opinion, I will state that. Women who come from caring homes with two loving parents where both are devoted, and the father is active in his children's lives, are far less likely to be volatile as adults. Period. Don't argue with *me*. Argue with your daddy. Some of you motherfuckers are quick to say, 'Single mothers are the worst.' Or, 'I bet she came from a single parent home. That's why she's screwed up!' If she did, and we believe your theory, then wouldn't that make the father partially responsible due to his absence?

I don't want to hear about all of these unfounded historical theories about the man being kept out of the

home due to governmental interference, either. Those are half-truths that were used to emotionally manipulate people. The full story, with sources, as to what happened are cited in the back of this book, but to play Devil's advocate, let's pretend that these tall tales were true – I still say unto you: Where there is a will, there is a way. We as men manage to do so many things, and if there is something not getting done, then that means we don't want to put in the effort to get it done! Period.

If it takes two people to create a baby, then why in the king kong fuck are you just blaming the women? I can tell you why: because you want to be a victim. You want to wear the skirt. You want to be coddled. You want it both ways. You want to go 50/50, but be treated like you brought 100. You want to be treated like an alpha and a baby at the same damn time, when really you're an incel with a God complex because your own father wasn't shit, either. I swear some of y'all are out of your fucking minds, and you're too dumb to know it. I said it. Don't like it? Close the book. I don't give a fuck.

I can't even see you right now. I'm probably watching movies in my man-cave as you read this, on vacation enjoying myself under the warm sun while drinking Pina Coladas on a beach, in my office helping someone who actually gives a damn about improving their life, on a golf course or basketball court showing off my athletic moves, or better yet, fucking the shit out of my beautiful queen on our brand-new silk sheets. I ate this discussion and left no crumbs, and the only thing left up in the air is my woman's legs. You think I care about you getting mad because I told you that YOU are the fucking problem, and that you're an idiot? I see you're still reading. Maybe you're not so dumb after all.

She cackled at that.

This is simple. Unless someone is a raging sociopath with a neurological disorder, it is extremely rare for a biological woman to sit up here in this big, wide world and destroy it. She cannot willingly destroy that from which she is! The bitch (female dog, literally) does not chew off its own tail and then wonders where it is. The lioness does not eat her own heart and wonders why she is dying! A mountain does not crash on itself and then ask why it crumbled! Self-preservation is key with all womb carriers, regardless of whether they are fertile or not, because they are programmed to create, not destroy! We cannot destroy that from which we are!

Men can do that because we are not the main creators, contrary to what we at times believe, and we are programmed by nature to conquer and destroy. This is because that's how we had to protect our families, especially in ancient times, since we are naturally more physical and violent. There's nothing wrong with that if it is utilized in the correct way. It has to be controlled, though. These hormones, called androgen, include testosterone. They are what make us men. They can cause us to be extremely destructive if not kept in check. That is one of the many reasons we need women! They have the power to stop us from annihilating ourselves! They are our balance, and we are supposed to be theirs. But instead, we decided to try and take over for the '99 and 2000s! We are angry. We are horny. We are physically strong. That's a bad combination if we're unhinged. We are unable to be multi-taskers efficiently for long periods of time.

Again, research it. There are always exceptions to the rules, outliers, but I am focusing on the large majority.

Not the small percentages that are contrary to the rule. As men, we need purpose. We are the ones who need direction.

We need someone who knows how to soothe us and calm us down. Feminine energy is required to do that. We need someone to place our seed inside of, too – whether that is reproductive-wise, or simply our ideas. Someone to bounce concepts off of, world building, goals, plans. A partner in crime. In other words, men need vessels to pour into. That's a woman. We pour into her and then, she takes it and makes something better. On the other side of that coin, women need to be able to nurture, grow, and make things. It doesn't have to be a man or a child, but they need something to create and take care of. In other words, someone needs to guard the gate while they grow their garden.

Someone must build the gate that keeps the garden safe and stand before it to protect it. We as men need something that is beautiful, that we can come home to. It doesn't have to be beautiful to everyone else, but it must be beautiful to *us*. I don't just mean physically; I am talking about a woman's essence. Something that is nothing like us. Something that balances us out. If this system is disturbed, this divinely created arrangement that was formed since human creation, it breeds confusion. It breeds contempt and violence. It breeds cultish mentalities. The blind will lead the blind, thus bringing out the worst in people, especially the need to control and manipulate. To bully. This state of affairs enables trauma bonding, feeding the people that get their rocks off behind creating, instilling, and encouraging *more* trauma.

Women and men are not the same. We are equal, but not the same. I don't give a monkey's chaffed ass about being politically correct. Facts and truth do not care about politics. Politics are a game. They are lies to control the masses. I've never tried to win a popularity contest. We are biologically different, and there is nothing wrong with that. It's beautiful. It should be celebrated instead of denied or shunned. I'm not apologizing for it, either.

Men, we have to be better sprinklers. Women are the fruit of the earth. They are the product of a perfect ecosystem. When you yield a bad crop, it is because of WHAT IS BEING PUT IN IT, WHAT YOU NEGLECTED TO DO, OR WHAT YOU DID NOT CONTROL THAT ENDED UP DESTROYING IT. An apple does not become foul on its own. Something happened. No apple chooses to rot. A flower does not choose to wilt and die! Who was manning the gate?! Who allowed an infestation to ruin the crops?! Who turned off the water?! Come on, men! Think! We created this bullshit, so it is up to us to turn it around. We are in big trouble, and we know it. Women are choosing to be alone in the woods with a damn bear, versus with us. This is all in direct response to the rising violence against women, and men not allowing them autonomy.

We are afraid right now. Men find themselves in desperate times. I know all about it, because I'm getting massive amounts of calls and emails. MAYDAY. Our gardens have entered a premature winter, or maybe this is long overdue. Regardless, the garden is figuring out ways to get watered without us. Everything in nature finds a way around a problem if it directly impacts their existence and ability to survive. It's called evolution.

Where is the fucking water? Women are no longer asking us that because they know the answer. Men have drank it, and most of what's left, we've contaminated with manipulation and lies. Where is the gotdamn sun?

We have destroyed it with verbal abuse, known as gasses and pollution. Where is the soil? We've dug it all up, slung it at each other in dick slinging contests, and poisoned the rest with pesticides and pettiness. Then we have the audacity to be upset about the jacked-up produce and foliage of the garden.

No, sir. You don't get to throw stones and hide your hand. Fruits are a direct reflection of their environment and care. Rather than look in the mirror, we deflect. We make up irrational reasoning. We blame our mothers, and their mothers, too. Meanwhile, fathers get off scot-free, only to go on and make the exact same mistakes they did last decade, and the decade before that. When you don't reprimand wrongdoing, the wrongdoer believes they are right. Men say they are doers, even though they – WE – do every fucking thing except take accountability.

The worst thing the women of Earth ever did was hand us the keys to drive. Since then, we chose to drive them over the cliff. Look at the world. Murders all over the damn place. Sex exploitation and sex trafficking. Robberies, senseless attacks, theft, elder abuse, and sexual assaults. Men hitting women in the face with closed fists when they turn them down for a date. We have run our countries, our continents, our world and our women into the ground. Look at all these wars and all this poverty across the globe. We did that. Nothing has been solved. The same wars have continued for what seems like a lifetime. All for the three Ps. Pussy. Power. Pennies. Our families are destroyed. We run the world, and the world is now running away from us.

We can't blame women for that, too, though we try to. The Earth is a hellhole because of US. Because of you. Because of me. This is the aftermath of trauma. When you try to dominate that which you were never supposed to have dominion over in the first place, eventually, the oppressed will rise up. They will find a way to either hide from you or defeat you. At the end of the day, it comes down to this: They don't want you. Not because of how you look, but because of how you behave. That's why I am here, gentlemen, after all of these years of protecting the Black Queen, encouraging men to pursue women the right way. And I am still learning. I too fall short at times.

Protecting and loving hard on your woman is a sign of potency, not limitation. The fact that we believe this is a flaw in this day and age shows just how messed up we are. Who told us this? Who taught us that showing emotions in a healthy way, openly expressing love and desire for a woman rather than anger, is a pathetic thing? We're so afraid of other men thinking that we're weak, we've allowed fragile men to define what is power.

Who told us that we no longer have to earn a woman's trust and body? You have so-called relationship experts who have not stepped one foot in a class about human psychology or relationships, telling people with a straight face that all women need to be putting out. That they've hit the wall. Every straight man isn't promised pussy! That's some incel shit because let me tell you right here, right now: No true alpha male has ever had to force himself on a woman, or demand pussy. The panties drop when we walk up in the motherfucking room! Half of you motherfuckers shouldn't even be fucking in the first place, and quite frankly, half of you in that same percentage shouldn't have even been born if the correct rules were actually in place and being adhered to. You're a liability! An embarrassment! A walking disaster! You can't cut it, and you blame women instead of yourself. All you're doing is wasting that woman's time, and standing in a real alpha's way.

Who told us that women have to submit to us, just because we have a dick? That's not how this works. I am a scholar. I am a learner. I am a teacher. I am a sprinkler, trying to be a farmer. A garden provides beauty, health, and nourishment. But you have to water it. If you take care of her, she will grow.

Gentlemen, it's time to water the garden within you, that hurt little boy. You are ill. Do you want to get well? It's possible. You can't help but be sick because we are all born into toxicity. The world is ailing, so we have no choice but to enter it in a state of trauma from day one. Dysfunctional lovers trapped in toxic relationships happen long before the two people meet. They start in our childhood. We dream of the past, but the nightmare we keep creating for ourselves must end today, or there will be no future...

She closed the book and looked off into the distance. She wanted to read the next chapter, but a mental and emotional break was warranted. Rather than taking a shower or napping, though, she found herself up on her feet, staring at a picture of her father that she had saved on her phone. He was handsome. He was laughing in the photo, a twinkle in his eye. She could see a bit of herself in him. Actually, a lot of herself.

Daddy, I'm trying to forgive you. I just wish I knew where to start. I'm sorry that I was such a disappointment to you. I hated you for what you did to me and Mama, and for the fact you were a terrible father all of my life. Then, after you got out of prison, you created a new family as though I didn't even exist. You became religious, found God, and I wanted to punish you for abandoning me.

When you did come around, it was only to judge me. When I called to tell you that I had been assaulted, you answered the phone, told me you were busy and would call me right back before I even got a single sentence out. But you never did call back... I lay in the hospital bed, in terrible pain, and cried myself to sleep. I didn't try to tell you what happened after that. That night, I needed my daddy! But you weren't around. You didn't water me. You didn't even bother to spit in my direction...

CHAPTER FOURTEEN

The Wisdom of an Older Woman

"I 'VE GOT A date tomorrow," Nadia blurted as her grandmother returned from the house, the screen door slamming behind her. She leaned back on the white veranda swing with the chipped paint, happy as she could be on Nana's porch.

"Thank you." Nana handed her a big glass of iced tea. Two thick wedges of lemon floated at the top, and the fresh lemon juice made it a bit cloudy. She took a sip and hummed, just like she used to as a little girl. "This is soooo good! You make the best sweet tea in all of Houston." She kicked up her feet and swayed back and forth real slow, the swing squeaking and squawking from years of use, rust, wear and tear as she basked in the warm sun rays. There was a nice breeze, too.

"I didn't catch that, baby. What you say 'fore the 'thank you' and 'best sweet tea?' I was comin' out the door and feelin' a little sidetracked." Nana sat close to her on an old green folding chair with a plump floral cushion. The deck furniture had a retro bloomy design, but was fairly new. All of the furniture on the porch was in muted tones of orange, lemon and lime with bits of white throughout.

Nadia took another sip of her sweet beverage—this taste was even better than the first. The balance of lemon, ice, sugar and tea was just right. She gleamed up at the clear blue sky.

"I said I've got a date tomorrow."

Nana's narrow mahogany lips curved in a smile. Knobby, rich brown hands circled her slender knees draped beneath a black and white striped dress that was two sizes too big. *She's lost a lot of weight since she got sick.*

"Isn't that somethin'? I thought you was turnin' into ya mama for a minute there," Nana hooted, slapping her thigh. "Swearin' off menfolk. The way you went on about that ex-boyfriend of yours made me think that was it for you." The beautiful old woman with plaited salt and pepper sighed, set her glass down on the small table beside her, then shook her head.

"He somehow got me to change my mind. I think he has superpowers, Nana, because I meant what I said about being done with men. After LeRon, I didn't want to be bothered. At least not for a long, long while."

"Mmmm hmmm. I understand. I told you that man was trouble. The way he was all up under you. Wouldn't let you outta his sight. Some men will make you wanna get on yo' knees and pray God to snuff 'em out in their sleep." She cackled, though a part of her believed Nana wasn't kidding. "You ain't mentioned no man in a long time. Say he got superpowers. That's cute." Nana took a slow sip of her tea. "Found someone you like, huh? That's nice. What's his name, and where'd you two meet?"

"Well, I've known him a while, many years really, but we ran into each other again a couple of months ago. His name is Lennox." Nana nodded in understanding. "And yes... I *really* like this one. A lot, actually. We were kinda young when we first met, so it's probably best things panned out just as they did. I think I told you about him a long time ago. It's nice to get butterflies over a man again."

"It shole is, ain't it? I tell you, no other man made me feel that way but Samuel." Samuel had been Nana's third and final husband. He'd passed away a couple of years prior. She'd been first married at age sixteen, then again at twenty-two. The first husband, who she only called devil, used to beat her and was double her age. The second one, Princeton, was a cheater and would be gone for weeks at a time, with all the money gone right along with him. "I love to see you smilin'. I hope you have a fun time. Make sure you tell me all about it."

"I'm sure I will, and you know I will." Nadia took another sip of her drink. "Nana?"

"Mmmm hmm?" The old woman clasped her hands and yawned.

"Mama was willing to talk to me a little more the other day. Told me I could ask her a question. You know, about the stuff I used to complain about to you. How she wouldn't open up and speak to me. You've always told me that it wasn't your place to fill in the gaps. That she should tell me in her own time. Nana, that time has come and gone. I could tell she was trying though, and I appreciate that for what it's worth."

She leaned forward, set her drink down and clasped her hands, her gaze piercing. The sun hit the reflection in her dark-rimmed glasses, almost blocking out her inky, slanted eyes completely.

"You say you appreciate it, but it wasn't enough. Yes, I said for years I wanted you to give her time. I suppose you feel time is running out. I've spoken to my child about this. She don't wanna hear nothin' I got to say about it, though. We ain't promised tomorrow." Nana's complexion deepened, and she looked away.

There was a stillness between them. The wind even seemed to slow down, giving room and space.

"There wasn't enough time in a day, a week or a year to make this make sense, Nana. I need something bad, but I'm not sure what it is." She shrugged. "I used to feel selfish. I had most of what I wanted growin' up. Naw, we weren't rich or anything like that, but I didn't struggle like some folks did. I felt bad for complaining. Mama used to tell me to stop all that fussin' and cryin'. I'd ask her for things, but I didn't *want* anything. I wanted *her*." A deep pain buried inside of her was unleashed. "I am searching for a lot of things, Nana, but I think I'm partially blind. Maybe even if I saw what I was searching for, I wouldn't recognize it."

"You would recognize it. Don't doubt yourself."

"Well, let me rephrase it. It's like a treasure hunt, you know? But like I said, I don't know what I'm lookin' for. Maybe I will when I see it, just like you said. I don't like this."

"Like what? Feeling helpless?"

They smiled at one another. Smiles of pain. Smiles of recognition. Twin grins beaming bright.

"Nana, you my soulmate, you know that?" Nadia giggled.

"…And you're my favorite granddaughter from your mama. Keep that to yourself though." The old woman brought her finger to her mouth in a shushing motion. "Wouldn't want none of my other grandbabies gettin' jealous."

"I'm your *only* granddaughter from my mama! Nana, you so silly! Goodness, I love you!"

They had a good laugh at that, while a bird chirped in a nearby tree. *She must have her babies in there.*

"I'm figuring some stuff out, Nana. I feel like I'm learnin' about myself at a rapid rate. I still don't know what to do with the information, but I'm learnin' it anyhow."

"Well, what clues do you have? Maybe I can help you out." Nana winked at her.

Nadia felt warm within, as if she were being hugged from the inside out.

"Work. I like the money. I've saved up a lot. Financial insecurity scares me, and I never want to have to depend on anyone else to make it." *I learned that from my mama. Not everything with her was bad.* "I don't like work as much all of a sudden, though."

Nana shook her head. "Naw. It ain't all of a sudden. I don't believe that."

"You don't believe me? I'm not lying though."

"I know you aren't lyin'. That's not it. It may *feel* like you just woke up and felt this way, but it ain't. It's been building. I know, because I know *you*." Nana pointed a finger at her. "You been chewin' on this meat for a minute now. I am curious though what got the ball rolling."

"You might be right, but I don't remember the starting line. I imagine it was a bunch of things that led me here. I feel some type of way. Because of that, I've started being unreliable. Fickle with it. That's not even in my nature. I stand by my word, and an appointment is my word. I've canceled a few of my appointments recently, and I am not looking forward to them as much anymore."

"Appointments?"

With her fingertips, she chased a rush of prickly heat that crawled up the back of her neck. "You know, the online stuff I told you that I do."

"Showin' ya milk and cookies?" They looked at one another and burst out laughing. Just then, 'Pride,' by Kendrick Lamar, played from someone's parked car a few houses down. For a split second, she recalled hearing that same song while feeling lonely in a crowd of people.

"Yeah… that. Chocolate milk and chocolate chip cookies. No nuts." She smirked.

"You feel guilty?"

"No, not really." She reached down and ran her hand over the top of her white sneaker. A pair of Pumas with gold trim. "I never felt ashamed about it, and still don't. It's art. A performance. So, it's not guilt. I just… I just don't want to do it right now." She offered a weak smile. "Thank you for never judging me about it, Nana. When mama ran and told you about it a long time ago, hollering and carrying on after I was honest and told her where I worked, I just knew you were going to hit the roof, too."

"Baby, I ain't got room to judge nobody!" Nana snatched off her glasses, grimacing. "You dance for menfolk. Show skin."

"Some women come, too."

Nana shrugged. "I don't know much about all of that, but I do know that men look at pretty women all day and night, and most of the women being ogled are none the wiser, and aren't even getting paid for it. A man screwin' you with his eyes alone... Lust." Grandma gritted her teeth. "It ain't what I want for you 'cause I know God want better for you." She threw up her hands. "...But I ain't God. I ain't surprised you've made a killin' at it, though." Nana's lips curled like handlebars. "You're a beautiful girl, and you're my grandbaby, but there are worse things in this world."

"According to Mama, me being an axe murderer is the only thing that would be worse," she teased.

"Oh, that's hogwash. There's plenty worse. Like making the whole world pay for something one person did. That's the *wrong* way to make a livin'. Can't no debt that big be repaid no how. In the end, it just leaves everyone broke." Nana reached for her own drink once more and slurped it loudly. Nadia waited while the old woman got her fill, and simmered in the words Nana was cooking. The stove was hot like white fire.

"I like that. Good food for thought. I'm changing. Change is good, I hope," she scoffed.

"Nadia, we all change over time. Well, we should."

Nana rolled her eyes as if thinking of someone specific that had arrested development. "Some folks act like five-year-olds all their lives. Ain't nothing anyone can do about it. My point is, we're supposed to grow as people. As for me? Now, I could make a lotta excuses for myself." She pointed at her chest.

"Excuses for what?"

"For some of the ways my life turned out. Like, for instance, I could talk about how my mama didn't protect us from our daddy. On and on I could go about all the things she didn't do. Or how our daddy worked so hard that he resented us being extra mouths to feed. He hit us, just like he hit my mama. He died in a nursin' home with nobody caring about him because of all the wrong he'd done. I could use that as a reason for some of the mess-ups in my own life. Yo' mama could make excuses, too.

"Blame it on her daddy's bad blood that runs through her veins, the devil that he was, and me bein' overprotective of her as she grew up—never letting her breathe, as she used to say. Said I suffocated her, and was so religious that I didn't use common sense." She shrugged. "Your mama been fightin' with God since she was a lil' bitty thing. Her 'nd God was on good terms for a long while until your Daddy come along. Everybody's mama, Nadia, got a reason as to why they're like they are, but the bottom line is this: nobody is perfect. One day, if you're ever a mother, you'll understand me firsthand."

"…I know. I never expected faultlessness though. I just wanted her to be truthful with me about her feelings. About how she felt 'bout life. About my father. About everything.

She only wanted to talk about right here, right now, and when the day was done, she was done talking about that, too."

"I know you didn't expect perfection, baby, but a tiny part of us *always* wants our mothers to live up to the fantasy we have of them in our minds. That's what you had. A fantasy. We all fall short, honey… we fall short, and then the pedestal crumbles." Nana sighed, then continued. "I do know that my daughter loves you and Nelson something strong. She sacrificed a lot for you two."

"I know, Nana. I've thanked her for that many times. We were never homeless or starving."

"I didn't always agree wit' how JoAnn went about things, but she was trying her best. I also know that she's a hard nut to crack." Nana coughed, snatched a balled-up tissue from her dress pocket, and blew into it. "Yo' mama was the first. JoAnn is my oldest child, and her soul is old, too. People used to call 'er the teacher." She smiled sadly.

"Yeah, I remember you telling me that. 'Cause she was real brainy, and a little bossy, too. The bossy part is definitely still there." Nana burst out laughing.

"Yes… She taught me some stuff, too. She's the one child that taught me just how awful I was… and in her own way, she never lets me forget it." Nana's forehead crimped.

"What do you mean by that? I never knew that mama resented you. I know that she didn't like going to church every Sunday, and some little stuff here and there, but not her being angry at you. She never said anything like that to me personally."

"Of course she didn't." Nana crossed her ankles. "That

would then be her admitting, in her own way, that she was hurt by something that I had done to her *personally*. And you know JoAnn can't dare do that." Nana sucked her teeth. "She never told me directly that she despises me, can't stand me, nothin' like that. It's the way she looks at me… takes forever to call me back… I can see it. I can feel it. She don't want me to have no power over her, so she won't say nothin.' Confessions to JoAnn is weakness. Silence is power."

That's why the caged bird sings…

"Point taken."

"When she was a child, well, that was a different story. Your mother always had a mouth on her, Nadia. Back then, when she was a kid, I didn't take no sass, but it wasn't because I thought it was disrespectful of children to talk like that to grown folk. If we're being honest, baby, it's because I know that is what us adults used to say to our children so we didn't have to answer for our own short-comings. We ain't wanna be questioned by something we made. Something that came from us, but smaller than us. We wanna rule over that, control it 'cause everything else in the world feels bigger than us."

Nana dropping gems today!

"We didn't want to tell the truth, either. Pride and ego. Kids can be blunt. They'll speak they mind. Ask why ya Aunt Toya always asking to borrow money when she got a job, or why Uncle Demarcus ain't got no teeth, or why yo' cousin Nita always yellin' at her babies when they ain't done nothin'."

"That's the truth right there. Who wants to explain that

Aunt Toya is bad with money and spends it all up at the club and on weed, then expects the family to bail her out? Uncle Denny ain't got no teeth because he drinks wine all day, and the sugar ate his grill up. Nita always yellin' at her kids because she's afraid they'll end up like their father if she don't get their butts in check right now. Nobody in their right mind wants to get gritty like that with little kids. It'll break them into the realities of life. The real world. We wanna keep them in a protective bubble for as long as possible. At least that's how I feel about my little cousins. Keep them away from heartbreak."

"Yes we do want to keep them in a bubble, and that's what I did with JoAnn." Nana's lips crimped in exasperation. "Despite your mother being so resilient, smart as a whip and independent as she was, she was a delicate child… felt things deeply. JoAnn was a sensitive soul. Right to her core." This news hit Nadia by a big, whopping surprise. Mama didn't come across as ever possessing a sensitive bone in her body. "But then, something in her changed, honey. The lights inside got dim. JoAnn got a hold of the family curse it seems. I wanted her to break it with you. But now, you're upset and lost, too."

"What family curse?"

"The one you tryna get up and around from, apparently. Got you thinking about life and your decisions. I pray every day, baby. Sometimes God answers. Actually, God answers *all* the time—it's just sometimes the answer is no, and I don't like that. I've learned that I gotta accept the no's though. They're there for our own protection. Struggle sometimes is a part of life."

"Misery ain't though, Nana, and we should never get used to it. Too many of us Black people have accepted misery as part of our lifestyles. Like, it's part of a normal day for us. Despair is a death sentence."

"You're right, baby, and that's why I don't want you to end up like... never mind." Nana began to fiddle with a loose thread on the side of her dress. This was the most she'd spoken of her mother, and Nadia was so grateful for it, but it was evident she still wouldn't come clean. She was holding back.

I need all of it. I need to know more about my mother. It's been part of the reason why she and I butt heads. Why do I feel like I can't talk to her, or go to her when things get tough. I don't know who she is deep down. When I get too close, she barricades herself, tells me to stop it, or goes silent. Nana knows the real JoAnn. I want to know the real JoAnn, too...

LENNON MOVED SLOWLY through the aisle. He paused, slipping a shirt over his arm as he continued to shop in the upscale store. 'Back On 74' by Jungle played through the speakers. He glanced down at his watch, went to the cash register, and paid for the nice sage green Polo shirt, as well as a bottle of his favorite cologne. As soon as he walked out the front doors, an attractive older Black woman, shaped like an old-fashioned Coca-Cola bottle was coming into the store. Being the perfect gentleman, he held the door open for her, allowing her to enter.

She thanked him, her long platinum blond hair swinging

with each step on silver stilettos. Dark smooth skin wrapped around a physique that was straight out of a dream, defying her age. As he turned to release the door, he felt a gentle tug on his arm. He paused and looked into her eyes.

"Boy, you smell *good!* What is that?"

"Thank you, I just bought some more, actually." He waved the bag about. "It's Tom Ford's, 'Fucking Fabulous.'"

"You're damn right it is." They both laughed. "I've smelled that on other men and it always smells good, but something about the way it blends with *your* chemistry just takes me there. You're easy on the eye, too. Tall, dark tan, and handsome."

"It's what I always wear. Thanks for the compliments."

"You're welcome. You like older women, baby? A little flavor, too? The Blacker the berry, the sweeter the juice." She placed her hand on her hip and leaned back, sizing him up as if he were some new outfit she was debating on purchasing and taking home.

"I'm flattered, but uh, I'm kinda seein' someone right now."

"Well, now you can't blame a cougar for trying. Yum, yum, yum. Wit' yo' sexy self. You take care now." She made a sort of growling sound as she looked him up and down once more, winked, then headed inside the store. A Chanel bag rocked back and forth over her arm as her ass bounced from side to side in a form-fitting cream dress.

He chuckled and made his way to his truck. He could appreciate another woman's beauty, but something about the interaction made him even more excited for his upcoming date with Nadia. Once he was seated in his truck, he turned on some music: 'Frogs,' by Lucy Chris. Taking out his cellphone, he proceeded to get directions to another store he'd heard just opened. They specialized in baseball caps. Before that though, he re-read the strange text message Nadia had sent earlier in the day. The interaction with the lady at the store solidified that he needed to go on and respond instead of ignoring what he considered a silly question.

This is pointless… I'll answer though. Obviously she feels it's important.

He began to type:

No, you're not the only Black woman I've dated, Nadia. Just because you never saw me with one didn't mean it wasn't happening. A lot happened before and after you were in my life. Rest assured, I've flirted with Black women, dated Black women all of my adult life, had sex with Black women frequently, as well as a few relationships, too. I have dated many races of women. I love ALL women. I wouldn't say I've dated more White or Mexican girls than Black girls. It's probably been about even. I have a type – but skin color has nothing to do with it. See you tomorrow xoxo

He lit up when KARRAHBOOO', 'Running Late' came on. Placing his dark sunglasses over his eyes, he turned up the music and rolled out.

CHAPTER FIFTEEN

Don't Go Chasing Waterfalls

THE RATTLE FROM the gold chain attached to the side of Lennox's jeans made a song with the wind each time he took a step forward, his long legs possessing natural born swag. Nadia gripped onto the edge of the big steel door of his beautiful truck as he boosted her inside. One big, strong arm snatched her from behind, holding her close around the waist, and the other rested on her thigh as he guided her onto her seat.

After making sure she was comfortable and secure, he closed her door and claimed the driver's seat, his window cracked, and the tune of, 'Million Dollar Baby,' by Tommy Richman blasting through a set of powerful speakers that vibrated with each pulse of the base.

Before he pulled away from her apartment building, he turned towards her with his sexy, hooded gray eyes, licked his lips, then leaned closer to her.

"I've got excellent taste." He smiled wide, showing his

bright teeth. "You look good."

"Thank you. So do you. I like that dark blue jacket. It's well made. I had—"

Soft lips pressed firmly against hers, cutting off her words and thoughts with the pressure of passion. Then, he leaned back in his seat and drove towards the main road. His sexy cologne wafted in the air, leaving her breathless.

"Uh, I was going to say…" She smacked her lips a couple of times, smiling from ear to ear. "I wanted to thank you for responding to my question about your dating past with Black women. I know it may have seemed strange to you for me to ask, but—"

"You didn't want to feel like a guinea pig, right?" He swiped his hand along his short black beard and scratched a spot near his jawline.

"I mean, no, I guess not, but because I have already known you for a long time, if I was the first," she pointed to herself, "it didn't mean I was going to throw in the towel. I'd be lying though if I didn't admit that I'm more comfortable not being the first one."

"I got it. Understood." He grabbed a pack of gum and shoved a piece in his mouth. "You want one?"

"No, I'm good. Wait. Are you trying to say my breath stinks?"

He burst out laughing.

"No! I would just be honest and tell you straight out. I love to kiss, so if that was somethin' I noticed I would have addressed it right then." *He's probably right about that. He never really had much of a filter.* "It just would've been rude to not offer you a piece since I took one out for myself."

"Okay. Just makin' sure." She giggled. "Well, don't you wonder if you're the only White—well, White *looking* I should say now that I know that your mother was Lebanese—man that I've ever dated?"

"Nope."

She burst out laughing at how quickly he answered, then shrugged.

"Well, I guess that settles that. So, where are we going? When I tried to get it out of you last night, you attempted to act all secretive about it." A part of her loved every moment of the mystery. She couldn't recall the last time she'd been on a real date.

"I've got this all planned out. I want you to just go with the flow, though," he stated casually as he approached a red light. "Here." He handed her a chilled bottle of water. She side-eyed him, then took the bottle and broke the seal. As she gulped down the water, he merged onto Interstate-610. Marcellus The Singer and Cecily Wilborn's, 'You Baby,' began to play.

"Oh, this is my song! I nevah liked country music that much 'til Marcellus got on the scene. Whew! You like this too, huh?" She smiled excitedly as she put her bottle in the cup holder, then figured out where the volume control was on the LED lit control center flatscreen panel.

"Yeah! You're late, Nadia. I love country music. Country rap. Country blues. All of it. He's one of my favorites. Saw him in concert last year."

"I bet he puts on a hell of a performance. I'd love to see him in concert one day."

"That can be arranged." His eyes on the road, he took

her hand and squeezed it. She felt all warm and buttery inside.

She sat back enjoying the pretty atmosphere. The sun was shining bright, and the sky was streaked with shades of deep blue and pastel pink, reminding of her cotton candy. She swallowed, recalling the taste of that sweetness. *Haven't had any in years.*

As he drove past other cars and trees turned into blurs, she began to daydream. *The sugary scent of a summer day… Back then, the air was infused with the smell of grilled burgers, hotdogs, and sauteed onions. I remember eating my aunt's homemade strawberry pound cake. Ohhhh, it was sooo good! The smell of kiddie sweat was all over my body, and my friends', too. We smelled like earthy soil and peanut butter, and chlorine from Nana's above-ground pool that she used to have in her backyard… Our hair had been dyed colors from the chemicals—dusty redheads and rust colored curls with dark mahogany tans by the time the summer came to an end.*

A part of her longed to be a child again, running through sprinklers with her little brother and cousins. Getting her hair braided, adorned with tiny colorful plastic beads while sucking on an orange frozen popsicle. Mama would let loose and drink cheap wine and hula-hoop with them. Her heart flipped. She glanced over at Lennox who seemed oblivious that she was dancing down memory lane. With him present, all of those reminiscences rushed back to her. Innocence. Sweetness. Heartbreak. Pure, golden joy.

It wasn't long before they pulled up at a restaurant. Her face split into a smile, and as soon as they were parked, the smell of a damn good time filled the air around her. He'd driven them to a well-known BBQ dive that many of the locals and out-of-towners loved: Truth BBQ. And best believe it—it was the motherfuckin' truth. She surveyed the area. Barely any parking and as usual, and there were plenty of people milling about waiting to be seated.

"I haven't been here in years!" She reached for the door to jump out, but he told her to stay put. Moments later, he was at her passenger's door, helping her out of his ride, then walking with her up to the establishment. He put his name on the waiting list. They waited for a little while, enjoying small talk and plenty of flirting.

"Sorry for the wait, baby. They don't accept reservations, so…" He shrugged.

"Oh, naw, that's okay. I figured they didn't. I know they have some of the best BBQ in the city so I'll do my time and wait." He pulled her close, arm around her waist, then kissed the top of her head, placing an invisible gold crown upon her tresses which she'd parted down the middle and flat ironed, allowing it to flow like a dark brown poncho. Every time he touched her, she felt like the most precious jewel in Houston. Like glitter that never lost its sparkle. Like the next best thing since bright sunshine and sexy full moons.

"I love barbecue."

"I remember."

"I like that. You make me feel good. I really love it when we get together. I touch myself, I mean, I'm touched by the little things, too." Her cheeks felt flushed. *Did I just accidentally admit that I've been taking myself on clit trips and to Pound-town on account of him?! My vibrator has been getting a workout lately, that's no lie, but that is my personal business!* He threw her a mischievous, sneaky look. She playfully punched his shoulder. "You know what I meant!"

He laughed lightly, kissed her cheek, then reached for her hand. It was the sexiest, sweetest, and yet most innocent gesture.

"Len, do you remember when we slow danced in the pantry of The Red Rooster that one time?" He looked down at her as if he wasn't certain. "Remember? I was in there crying. As usual." She rolled her eyes. *I was such a crybaby... going through bad times...* "You rarely asked me what was going on after realizing I wouldn't tell you what was wrong the majority of the times you'd catch me in there. This one particular time, you turned on the radio and we started slow dancin'."

"I remember." His deep voice rumbled close to her ear, making her insides purr.

"You were so much taller than me, but I managed to relax my head on your chest. I remember how warm you were... how you smelled like Cool Water and flour." His lips curled at that.

"I was in charge of making the biscuits back then."

"Yeah...You didn't try to grope me or nothing like that. We just danced real slow. I kept crying for a while and then, I stopped. I felt alright. A sense of peace came over me. I remember the song that was playin', too. It was—"

"Sam Smith's, 'Stay With Me.'" Raw love glittered in those gray eyes of his.

She brimmed with the tips of sunbeams, radiating joy from within, and the kiss of honey-flavored raindrops soaked into her soul, seasoning her with love.

"...Yeah. You *really* did like me more than a friend." She whispered the words, the middle breaking like a twig beneath the weight of a deer hiding from prey.

"Of course I did. I knew you were goin' through stuff though with your mom, and your father's situation wasn't any better. You were having problems. You trusted me after a while. Confided in me. I wasn't going to mess that up by putting the moves on you."

He wrapped his arms around her and buried his head against her cheek, swaying with her as he hummed that old Sam Smith song in her ear. By the time he was finished, her body ached for a more intimate touch.

"Wilde! Party of two!" the hostess announced.

She was still riding on cloud 9 when they were alerted that a table had opened up. In fact, the declaration sounded like a train trying to screech to a halt, snatching her out of the soft edges of the sound of his voice and embrace. She blinked a few times and approached the hostess right alongside him while 'Rude,' by MAGIC!, started to play. Once inside, their selections of meats were cut right in front of them and served on lunchroom style trays. They ordered their sides and beverages, but it was a hard decision. There were so many delicious items to choose from. It wasn't long before she felt the bubbles of her fizzy drink tickling her nose as she snorted from laughter, both of their faces hot and red from the hilarity of their silly dinnertime discussion.

"You're lying!" She cackled, then jammed her fork into a slice of tender brisket.

"No, I'm for real. This really happened. My whole family was there, and the turkey was only chasing my cousin.

Roman couldn't have been no more than fourteen. For some reason, it had its anger directed at him exclusively. They went around and around some trees until finally, it caught up with him. He tripped, and that was the end. It was attackin' him. All you saw were feathers."

"Your grandfather had turkeys as pets, or was he raising them for food?"

"Not either of those. See, it was a wild turkey. It just popped up outta nowhere, but my grandfather lives around a bunch of woods so there's all sorts of wildlife back there. Deer. Coyotes. Bobcats."

"What were y'all doing while this turkey was being a menace to society?"

"We were laughing and not much help at all." She snorted and shook her head. "Our parents were inside the house, not payin' much attention 'cause it was just us kids outside playin'. Somebody called for Grandpa eventually. I don't remember who. He came tearing outta the house with his shotgun to settle this once and for all, but then my sister started cryin' and begged him not to shoot it. He gave in to her little girl tears," he chuckled, "and decided to try and shoo the bird away by throwing stuff instead. Some of the rocks and what not hit Roman in the process, and that made us laugh even more. He was screamin', 'Ahhh! Ahhh!'" His laughter floated from his throat as his complexion deepened. Nadia could barely speak for a bad case of the giggles seized her stomach and squeezed. "The turkey finally turned him loose and ran off. Roman got to his feet, a few scratches here and there, and said, 'It's okay. We'll see your ass come November on the damn table.

Right next to the taters.'"

She burst out laughing again, almost to the point of choking. When they quieted, they settled down and enjoyed their food.

"Mmm, this meat is thick and juicy… so good. Suckin' it right off the bone." After she uttered the words, she realized her mistake. She'd done it again. Their eyes locked, and they both started laughing again. "Lennox, your mind *stays* in the gutter. Mine is only in the gutter for work—I don't mean that shit, but yours is authentic and true!"

"Hey, you were laughin', too!" That vein of his popped out in the middle of his forehead as he chuckled all the harder. She sat there watching him lick his fingers, wishing he was licking on her, too. She loved that he didn't weave anything about her personal profession into a tawdry play on words, seedy jokes, and sexual innuendos. He acted as if it was never even on the radar. She was just a regular person, sitting across from him, enjoying a meal. She loved that. She loved that a lot.

They finished their feast and she dismissed herself to go to the ladies' room. As she walked, she noticed some of the older songs that were playing in the restaurant were ones that had been popular around the same time they'd met and were working together. It was rather uncanny, a coincidence perhaps, but of course, maybe Truth BBQ always played tunes like that? She used the restroom, washed her hands and dried them, then returned to the dining area.

"I went to the bathroom while you were gone, then paid the bill and got us some refills to go." He pointed to her cup filled with Sprite.

"Thank you, partner." Wrapping her hand around the Styrofoam cup, she slurped some from the straw and walked out. He helped her back into the truck and when he got inside himself, he removed his jacket and tossed it in the back. He was wearing a nice short sleeved Polo shirt, the buttons open and a gold chain tucked beneath it. She glugged noisily on her drink. When she went to put it down, she noticed the water bottle she'd been drinking from earlier in their date was in the way.

"Where can I put this, Len?" He glanced in her direction as he expertly pulled out of the tight parking spot. Taking it from her hand, he set it in the cubby area of his door.

"Can I listen to something?" She pointed to the radio.

"You don't have to ask."

She leaned in and began to switch to various radio stations, finally landing on 'Bad Habit,' by Steve Lacy.

"What movie are we going to go see tonight?"

"No movie tonight."

"Oh, well… okay. I had a great time." She shrugged. "Thanks for dinner. What are your plans later? Work?"

He shot her a glance, his brow raised as if in bewilderment.

"Huh? I said no movie… the date isn't over. We've just gotten started. Nah, I took off from the club tonight. I plan to entertain you all night long. If you can hang, that is. We'll see." A sexy smirk spread across his face as he made a fast left turn.

She leaned back in her seat, crossed her legs, and squelched her smile by sucking on the straw of her beverage cup. Then, she began to shimmy her hips as Kendrick Lamar's 'Humble' came on the air. He snuck glances from the corner of his eye when she rocked her hips to the beat of the music.

"I see you lookin'," she said in her most seductive voice.

"I see you teasin'."

"If you look, then I charge a fee. I don't dance for free."

"I'm not your little 'only fan'. I'm tryna be your man. If you charge me, then you won't get the D." She burst out laughing.

"What are we, Dr. Suess? Both of us are silly!" Moments later, he pulled into an area she didn't recall ever visiting before. He turned the car off. "What is this place?"

"It's called Smither Park. It's a really cool spot. They've got all kinds of local artwork and fun stuff." Before she could respond, he was out of the truck and slamming his door shut. Seconds later, he was once again helping her out of the big vehicle.

"Oh my goodness, look at all of these! Mosaics, right?" She pointed to shiny tiles all over various stone statues and the like. Some of the mosaic creations were adorned with shiny shells, coins, broken pottery, cloth, and what appeared to be costume jewelry. She raced around, touching and studying so many colorful pieces of art. "Even the sidewalk is covered. This is so pretty... Are those bottles? Oh my goodness, they are." *How'd he know I'd like something like this?* "I knew nothing about this place, Lennox. Has it always been here?" she called out to him, having run at least thirty feet by now in the opposite direction, her eyes feasting on the funky and cool artistic renderings.

Lennox observed her from afar, a smile on his face and his hands shoved into his jeans pockets. It was as if he was getting pleasure just from watching her enjoy herself.

"I don't know the exact time this place opened, but it's been here a while. If I were to guess, maybe 2014. Somewhere around then."

"How'd you find out about it?" He caught up to her and they stood in front of one another, a large mural close beside them. "My sister. She's into things like this. I came with her a couple of times a long time ago. Silva told me about this park when we were still on speakin' terms." His eyes looked a little bit less bright when the hurtful words rolled off his tongue.

She was getting ready to ask why they don't communicate anymore, but instead, she placed her hand along his chest and looked up into his sad eyes. She recalled him talking about his little sister often when they worked together. He'd absolutely adored her, and had seemed to be the protective big brother that many girls dream of.

"Do you want to talk about it?"

He looked down at her for a good while, silent, then placed a perfect, soft peck on her lips. When he lifted his head, he was smiling faintly—so unsure and a tad hopeless. But his eyes now seemed full of courage and desire. He shook his head and made his way slowly around her, arms crossed and looking about as if he'd lost something.

Side by side, they viewed the artwork and sculptures together, their steps in unison. To her right, she spotted an arched area, set up like a theater.

"They have plays and things like that in there," he offered. "I've never been to any, but I know that they have them."

They walked inside and she was impressed by the art that covered every inch of the place, from floor to ceiling. After getting their fill, they left from the theater area and came upon some wide swings. Lennox walked away from her, wrapped his hands around each chain, and called to her.

"Come here."

She happily jogged over to him, then plopped down into the swing. Her tight jeans crept up her legs ever so slightly, and a nice breeze caught inside of her baggy white shirt. He began to push the swing, higher and higher until she was giggling and screaming bloody murder at the same time. The sun was going down, and now the sky went from blue and pink to orange and muted red. As she pumped her legs, she could see above the world. She'd go up and kiss heaven… fall back and sense the butterfly wings fluttering in her gut, like the kind one experienced on roller coasters.

She slowed down until she was finally level with the ground again, the ride coming to an end. Then, he joined her on that wide bench swing with enough room for two. They pumped their legs in harmony, each one holding on to their side of the swing cable. Her hair blew around wildly in the wind, but she could still see through the whipping tresses. He was looking right at her, gray eyes beneath thick black brows, paired with a suggestive bright smile.

At last, they both stopped pumping their legs, and the swing slowed until it was barely moving. The wind kept sweeping through their hair, and soft kisses were bestowed on them from the setting sun.

Their free hands intertwined, and as if on cue, they leaned close and pressed their lips together, tasting each other in an oral embrace. The kiss was searing, passionate, hungry. Romantic. Lust-fueled. Obsessive. Emotional. She could barely catch her breath because it got more demanding with each second. They sat there, feet dragging against the ground, lips locked until they slowly pulled away from one another at the same time... but their hands remained linked.

"We've been away from each other, but some small part of us never separated," she said softly, moisture forming in her eyes.

He kissed her nose, then stood and helped her off the swing. Hand in hand, they walked back to his truck. Once she was situated inside, the sun had vanished and the sky looked down on them in shades of dark blue. He was soon steering the vehicle again to the sounds of Khamari's, 'These Four Walls.' He reached for her hand, kissed it, then intertwined their fingers. Her insides turned to jelly. She felt like a girl falling for her first love. Like a child with her first crush. Like old friends coming together and exploding like a supernova in attraction and lust. In love.

"...One more stop." His deep voice broke through her thoughts.

She nodded, but kept quiet. Her emotions wrapped around her mind and heart like a weighted blanket. He pulled up to the Gerald D Hines waterpark. It was dark out, but there was still a fairly good amount of people milling about. He kissed her again, tasting like her best dream with a side of comfort and epicurean ice cream for dessert.

The sound of the rushing water from the man-made waterfall was loud, yet it still didn't drown out her pulsing heartbeat. He broke their kiss gently, then turned her to face the waterfall. Lennox stood behind her, his arms wrapped protectively around her body, and rested his face against the top of her head.

"What do you see?" he shouted over the rush of water.

"A horse-shoe-shaped waterfall. People like to come here 'cause it's pretty. At night, the lights are on. Never been here after sunset."

"Yeah? Well, that's just the thing, Nadia. You've been here at night, just in a different type of way. You don't like storms." Her muscles clenched as she stared straight ahead while he spoke close to her ear. "All this water pouring down is pretty. Some find it relaxing. Since it's not fallin' on you and it's contained, you feel safe. But when you're pushed under, it triggers you. Your storms in life came before the first drop of rain ever hit you. They started with your mother and father, and continued with you bein' attacked by someone who had no idea that he was a mouse tryna take down a lion." She smiled sadly at his words. "Storms in our lives aren't meant to beat us down, baby. They're meant to make us stronger, so when the next one comes, we're better prepared.

"Storms are teachers. Trainers. Enforcers." She nodded in agreement, and wrapped her hand around his forearm, squeezing. "I want you to know though, there ain't a storm comin' your way that you have to face alone ever again. "I'll be your umbrella. Your shelter. The roof over your head and heart. You've got *me* now."

She quickly spun around and looked him in the eye.

"…And you have me." She placed her hand against his cheek, looking deeply into his eyes.

"Nadia, I'm attracted to daring women. Strong women, beautiful on the inside and outside. I'm attracted to you because you are all of those things and more. I was your friend before I was anything else." He took her hands into his, folding them between his palms as though holding them in prayer. "I'm always gonna be your friend, for as long as you do me right."

"I plan to do you, all right."

They both burst out laughing. He deposited a gentle kiss on her lips.

"Let's get outta here."

Hand in hand, they walked towards the lot where the truck was parked. Soon, they were cruising, the lights of Houston all aglow.

"I hate that the night is going to end." She yawned. "I had a great time."

"Me too," he said, his eyes keenly on the road.

"What are you about to do?"

"Well, I don't have to work security at the club tonight, so I will probably go home and play a little Xbox or PlayStation, depending on my mood."

"Oh, really? You got that Assassin's Creed Valhalla?"

The man literally gasped, and he snuck a shocked glance her way. She laughed.

"What in the hell did you just say? What do you know about Assassin's Creed?!"

"I know I'll beat yo' ass in about any game you might have. I don't care if it's Resident Evil, Diablo IV, Assassin's Creed, or Call of Duty. I will wipe the floor with you."

"Oh, really?! Let's see you put your money where your mouth is! How about a healthy wager?"

"No problem, Top Dog. How 'bout fifty bucks to the winner and whatever drink of our choice? I've got expensive tastes, so be ready to go broke fuckin' around with *me*."

"Oh, I ain't never scared, baby. It's on. Strap up. I'm takin' you to the crib. You'll walk in but leave limpin'."

"Well, take me home then, big boy! All that big talk. Bark and no bite. Be prepared to be embarrassed. Humiliated. I specialize in breakin' big mothafuckas like you."

"Let's see about that…" Lennox chuckled, then turned on some different music: 'Like That' by Metro Boomin, Future, Kendrick Lamar, DaBaby, Ye…

CHAPTER SIXTEEN

Head Games

MEGAN THEE STALLION'S, 'BOA,' blasted through his living room speakers while Lennox beat Nadia's ass like a drum in a game of Resident Evil. He was able to set it to multiplayer, and though she was getting slaughtered, she was still holding her own.

"Turn that shit up!" she barked, dark rage in her eyes as her bruised ego swelled and angst grew.

"Hey, don't catch an attitude. You did this to yourself." He tossed up his hands, stifling a laugh. "You wanted to play against me, instead of us working together to kill these motherfuckers. Teamwork makes the dream work."

"I work alone." She cackled. "Seriously though, I'm just not familiar with this version is all."

"Another one is coming out soon."

"I'll play that one, too. See, you have an unfair advantage 'cause you play this a lot and I'm rusty. This is Resident Evil 4, right?"

"Nah, baby. This is Resident Evil 6. I've got Resident Evil 7, too. Biohazard. That one is totally virtual reality though, and freaky as hell. I also have Resident Evil Village/Shadow of Rose. That one is pretty good, too. R.E. 7 though I'd have to say is one of my favorites. It takes place in an old house where an experiment went wrong."

"That actually sounds fun. I may want to look at that later on."

"I have 4 though, if you want to play that instead."

"No, this is fine. I didn't like the one set in Africa."

"Yeah, a lot of people feel that way, but it helped the storyline move forward. I'm more of a Call of Duty man, but this is cool, too."

"I guess. Anyway, I'm *still* a better player than you. Just watch!" she snapped, her eyes glued to the large screen as she barely avoided yet another run-in with a dangerous beast.

"Pshhh! I got way more kills than you, girl. Doesn't matter how quick or pretty you move. A dead man is a dead man. You suck. Just admit it. Don't get mad, get even." He poked the bear, loving taunting her. She shot him a crossed look. He winked at her, she rolled her eyes, licked her nail, then presented her erect middle finger with the same hand. *Sexy, mean ass…*

Laughing, he grabbed his stereo remote and turned the volume up so loud that he could barely hear her cursing him out now. She began swaying to the music while she played the game—laser-focused as she aimed at several aggressive zombies that were gunning for her.

He noticed his favorite baseball bat rolling from beneath the couch, pushed it aside, then sat back down next to her. Here they were. Two thirty-something-year-olds playing video games... No judgment. No shaming. It was so natural. As natural as day and night. She said she wasn't a gamer per se, and he didn't coin himself as one either, but he enjoyed it. It was something to do. Something to concentrate on. Something to drown out his troubles in.

"When d'you first start gettin' into this?"

"Resident Evil?"

"Well, no. Video games in general."

"Oh." He yawned and leaned back. "There's no story, really. I just... wait." A memory resurfaced, one he hadn't mulled before. "You know what? I take that back. I actually started playin' them a lot more after my mother passed away. Silva and I were showered wit' a bunch of gifts from our father when Mama died. I guess he thought that would ease the pain. A bunch of materialistic shit. Got pain? Throw money at it." He made a gesture as if he were making a free throw in basketball and shook his head.

"Money don't do shit but train us to not feel anything, but that's short-lived. Sounds like your father was trying to help, but didn't really know how." He nodded in agreement. "My mama didn't have money to throw at me and my brother when upsetting things happened to us, but she'd turn on the TV and allow us to watch somethin' we wanted to see, or cook a bunch of food. A damn hot dog and a Tyler Perry movie ain't gonna make me any less sad that my daddy was with a whole 'nother family... and he accepted his new wife talkin' to me any ol' kind of way, which made my mama all crazy." She sucked her teeth.

"Anyway, this isn't about me. I hear you. I hear you loud and clear. Thing is, you don't have to be sad by yourself no more. I'm here… We can be sad together. We can talk like we used to, only now we're better able to get through it. Oh, shit!!! He's on my ass!" She kept playing, her eyes on the prize. And yet, he felt heard. He felt under-stood.

…Thumbs smashing the controllers… Shit talking… Wine glasses empty, then PAUSE. Refilled. More wine. More shit talking. Smoke floating in the air from a blown out white candle and incense burning… Laughter.

"Shit! He almost got me! Len, how the hell do I get out of this area? I'm runnin' outta ammo! Damn it!" She was practically beating the controller to death, her face twisted in concentration so deep, it rivaled the lower bowels of the pits of hell.

"You are being too aggressive with my shit, Nadia." He was torn between wanting to laugh and tell her to calm down and cool it.

BAM! BAM!

"A! You're about to break my shit and still get killed anyway! Slow the hell down. Relax."

"Would you *please* be quiet?! You ain't even answering my question, or helping. You're just messin' up my concen-tration with all that background noise coming out of your mouth! Rah rah rah rah… Sounds like the Charlie Brown teacher." And then she burst out laughing when she looked back and caught him staring daggers at her.

He laughed lazily, biting his lip and shaking his head. He remembered way back when the two of them had funny little spats like this... She was always competitive, but mostly with herself. Maybe her internal storms were the scariest of all? They outrivaled zombies, killing machine robots, rabid monster werewolves, and any dystopian apocalypse on the silver screen, or between written pages. So much so, nothing scared her. Except perhaps not being heard, and not being believed... Therefore, she made certain that she was at least *seen*.

The reality of that being a true possibility hit him like a ton of bricks.

Nadia focused back on the game. She bit into her lower lip so hard, it looked as if it would bleed. The woman's hands were moving fast and she was completely zoned in. *Beautiful, nasty devil. Competitive little demon.* And he loved it. She was actually quite good at the game. He simply was better, and wanted to make sure she knew it since she'd sold all of those wolf tickets. Besides, they both were competitive as hell. It was one of the things that drew them to one another, and all in good fun.

"Damn it! That's it. They got me. You got lucky because I'm out of practice, Lennox." She tossed the controller down onto the couch, pointed her finger in his direction, then stormed off towards the kitchen as if she lived there. Instead of taking his turn, he put the game on pause and followed her in. She opened cabinet after cabinet, looking mad as hell as she closed them with vitriol, but not quite a slam.

"Hi, my name is Lennox Wilde. I don't believe we've met. I live here. Can I help you find something?" he joked as she fluttered from cabinet to cabinet.

Her chest was heaving when she slowly turned in his direction. A smirk creased her face, and then she burst out laughing.

"I figured I wasn't a guest." She shrugged. "We've known each other too long for that, and you know all about me. I thought I was just your girl, one that you can also kick it with."

"My girl, huh?" He crossed his arms. "I like the sound of that."

Her complexion deepened, and she turned to look inside of an open top cabinet filled with nothing but old plates he'd purchased from Target years ago but never used, and a vast collection of shot glasses. "You think it's strange that a woman likes video games like that, don't you? The violent ones?" She opened another cabinet before he could respond. "I want some Cheetos or Doritos. Got any?"

"No, I rarely eat that shit. Full of sodium and bad ingredients, but I know that you're not in the mood for a nutritional lecture." He walked behind her and opened up his small pantry door. "And no, I don't think it's strange that you play violent video games, and are good at them. We're in a new day and age. Plenty of women enjoy playing boxing games, battle competitions, undead, military or whatever video games with plenty of guns, guts, and glory, and are amazin' players. I was just joking with you out in the living room. I think you play well, actually. How'd you get that good at it?"

"I used to play it with my brother, and then I got my own system. It relaxes me."

"Relaxes you? I can't tell. If that's relaxation you

showed me out in the living room, then I'd hate to see what you being worked up is like."

She sucked her teeth and rolled her eyes.

"I'm just warmin' up. I'll get you next time, but tonight, I will throw in the towel," she stated breathlessly, as if she'd just run a marathon. "I lost the bet, so I'll Cash App you the fifty dollars."

"I'm good. Take it as me lettin' you off with a warning. A warning for talkin' shit." He winked at her.

"Naw, fair is fair. I'll send you the money. But uh, yeah… I haven't played in like seven or eight months though." She kept wanting to drive home how rusty she was… Now as she said it behind hooded eyes, he wondered if it had a double meaning? He looked over his shoulder at her as she shrugged, then leaned against his kitchen counter, ankles and arms crossed.

He turned back around and scanned each shelf. He had boxes of granola, keto-friendly cereal, and protein bars. Nothing he was certain that she wanted. Then he spotted some chicken crackers. Grabbing the half-empty box that he often used when he fixed his delicious chili on cheat days, one of the few things he cooked to perfection, he turned around and handed them to her.

"Are these okay?"

"Mmm hmm." She set the box on the counter and tore into them, not making much eye contact "Thank you." She began shoveling them into her mouth, her glossy stiletto-shaped nails dragging along her lower lip. "When I play video games, my appetite soars," she explained. "I'm a naturally hyper person, but competition? That makes it worse. Somethin' about the adrenaline rush, I guess." She stood there digging into that box, stuffing the crackers into her mouth, one after the other.

A bit of crumb gathered around the right side of her lips, and she licked it away with the tip of her slick pink tongue like a lizard going after a fly. Her bare feet moved about nervously against his floor with each fast and furious chew. The toe nails were cut short and perfect, a glossy light pink color coating each nail, sparkling and gleaming. The top of her right foot had an Ankh on it. The left, an Egyptian beetle and hieroglyphics. Everything about her dripped with beauty, enigmatic energy, and femininity. She kept bouncing about, as if she had ants in her pants. And yet, she remained sexy in the midst of it all. Munchies aside, something about her was different tonight. In a good way. He could feel it. See it. Hear it.

"You didn't have to take off work tonight," she stated as she finally began to slow down and chomp softer. "I would've understood." She swallowed the last bit of food in her mouth. Apparently she'd overheard him on the phone when his boss called soon after they arrived at his house, asking him to work that evening.

"Nah." He waved her off. "They called me into the club last minute and I just let 'em know that I already had plans. I was already scheduled off. I wouldn't have missed this for nothing." She looked like a cute little mouse standing there, blushing, turning colors like a prism, holding a half-bitten cracker up to her juicy lips. Looking up at him with big, dark, doe eyes. Eyes so pretty, he wished he could strip down and swim in them. Eyes he believed in his heart were now ready to see more... A *lot* more.

Her vibe is right tonight. She's been thinking. She's been reading. Studying. She's opened up more to me about a lot, too. She accepted what I told her about my past, and still wants me. I know about her past decisions, too, and never wavered in my desire for her. At one point in time, we were practically best friends. This woman has always had my heart.

The other day she even told me she wants to go back to law school. They weren't empty words—she was online looking and began making calls and sending emails. That was always her dream, and I want her to have it—but never feel as if I'm pushing her into doing anything. Into being anything she doesn't want to be. I want the soul of the person I met ten years ago. It's still there, just wiser now. I want the fucking best for this woman, even if that isn't me, but I know damn well that it is. Yeah, it's time. She's ready...

He leaned forward and caressed her chin, then her cheek.

"Nadia, you're so damn real, you know that? And so beautiful. I just love everything about you, girl."

Their eyes hooked, but then she abruptly turned her back to him, barreling towards his refrigerator. She slipped a bottle of Gatorade out, broke the seal, and stood there, now facing him again. Staring him down. Gulping. He watched her throat move. Constricting. Her cheeks compressed as she guzzled the clear liquid. Holding the bottle around the thick center like a dick. She swayed ever so slightly... pirouetting slowly. Barely moving. She had complete, measured control of her body. It was a thing to see, a sight to behold. An unhurried, enchanting dance. She moved like a liquid whisper. Her eyes were full of black smoke and choked him in hot, seductive flames. Her body, her mind and her electric vibe put him in mind of a seductress, a seasoned snake charmer, and he was definitely rising to the occasion.

"You paused the game," she stated. A loud crinkling sound rent the air as she crushed the plastic bottle with one hand, then threw it in the recycle bin without looking. Score.

"Yeah. And?"

She closed the gap between them and flattened her breasts into his chest. Looking up at him, she appeared so fragile, yet so strong. *Her vulnerability is showing. On purpose. Emotional panties down around her ankles. She's open. Wide open.* The soft warmth from her body sent his into a heatwave.

"Why did you stop the game?"

"That's a silly question, Nadia. Because you came into my kitchen and we were still playin'. Or so I thought. You came in here."

"Ain't no such thing as a silly question." She smiled, her voice soft, sexy, and a bit raspy. "I came. I saw. I want to make you cum, too. Fuck that game." She bared her teeth and made as if she were going to chomp the tip of his nose. "I want to play with *you* now instead." She took a small step back and smiled, ogling his groin. His dick was semi-hard, and he felt it twitch as her eyes rested there. He ran his hand slowly over it, breaking her scrutiny. Her eyes gradually drifted back up to his. "Am I allowed now?" Her lips curled upward, but her tone seemed tinged with a touch of resentment. "You said I wasn't ready for you. You had turned me down. Do I finally qualify?"

"That question goes both ways…"

Wrapping one arm around his neck, she pulled him in for a kiss. He bent down to pluck his flower, and their lips pressed against one another as their breathing became mutually louder and choppy. She groaned as he backed her up against the wall, slamming her in place.

"I'll take that as a 'yes'…"

NADIA WALKED INTO Lennox's dark bedroom and leaned against the wall. It was modest. Extremely clean. A little chilly, too. *It smells like starch, a little bleach and fresh laundry in here.* He smacked the wall and a dull orange light bathed the room. In a matter of moments, he turned on two blue lava lamps, then lit a stick of incense and several candles he'd taken from a small cupboard in his dining room. Arlo Parks', 'Caroline' played from large pulsing speakers hanging from two corners of his bedroom.

He looked at her a couple of times, but didn't say anything. She walked to a large window to the left. Tipping the curtains open, she looked out, loving the view. The highway appeared small in the far distance, a cocaine line of light blue and red dust, but the speeding cars lit the sky as 'Take You There,' by Pete Rock began to play. She swayed to the easy, lax rap beat.

In the reflection of the window, she looked up and saw a tall, muscular figure coming up behind her. She slowly turned in his direction and took him all in. He was naked from head to toe. Only his necklace and gleaming watch remained.

Thank God for a man...

He stood so close to her, she had no choice but to etch this magnificence from the one above that stood before her. He reached for her and took her hands into his, eerily quiet, but his eyes were nothing but gray smolder and lust. Her heart beat a bit faster as she studied him, wishing she could read his mind. Sex had been nothing more than a game, a means to an end in the most recent years of her life, but with Lennox, no... This was different. This was real. He leaned ever so closer to her, to the point that she could hear his slow, rhythmic breathing over the melody playing. Jet black facial hair, naturally tanned flesh, freckles on his broad, muscular chest, incredible pecs, an eight pack that was so hard it rivaled concrete, tapered waist, an Adonis belt that made her salivate, thick, but well-trimmed black pubic hair that haloed a generous, long, veiny, gorgeous dick, muscular thighs, long legs with unbelievable calves, big, well taken care of feet. The man was not eye candy. He was an entire buffet...

Her voice disappeared as he grabbed the back of her hair, tilted his head, and placed a hot kiss on her lips. She shivered when his tongue plunged deep inside her mouth. She forgot she was still dressed until she felt his hands roaming her body. Not once did he speak since he'd brought her inside of his bedroom. His hands, the music, the vibe and his mouth said it all. The old school song, 'Mind Blowin'' by Smooth, now serenaded them. She smiled at that. *He knows me so well.* She used to dance to that song as an introduction when she'd come out on the stage.

But then, her smile slipped. How'd he know?

She shoved the thought out of her mind, her body on fire for him as he ravished her. He kept kissing her as he glided her belt from the loops and forced her pants down to her ankles. She rocked into him as the touch of his big knuckle dragging along her stomach awakened every cell in her body. She felt so small next to him, and yet so safe and protected. A cool nip of air slipped between her legs as he freed her of her underwear. The searing kiss came to an end then and he stepped back, dragging the fabric down her thighs to meet her pants.

She stepped out of them, and he cast them aside. Then, she brought her shirt over her head and let it drop to the floor. A hot, wet heat circled her breasts. She gasped as the coolness of the window hit her when he gently guided her to it, then pressed her against it with need. He licked and sucked her breasts over her bra, and her eyes fluttered as she fell under his spell. She looked down at him devouring her twin peaks. Teasing her. The room glowed in cerulean shadows and lights from the lava lamps, making his skin appear blue. And hers, too. They blended together like two oceans, their edges watery and cool.

She trailed her lips against his shoulder, then placed a kiss on his flesh. His large hands began to roughly drag against her skin, massage the globes of flesh, and squeeze her breasts. He pushed one out of the confines of her brassiere, then sucked it slow and hard until her nipple was erect with his ministrations inside of his wet mouth.

"Mmmm, shit," she moaned as she rested once again against the window. "You do that so good, baby…" G-

Unit's, 'Wanna Get To Know You' drifted from the speakers. Once she felt him lifting her off the floor, she quickly wrapped her arms around his neckline, clasped her legs around his midriff, and went along for the ride. He walked her to his bed and tossed her down onto her back. She bounced a couple of times, and playfully looked up at him as he stood there, stroking his big dick.

Damn.

It was impossibly harder, making her mouth water just at the sight of it. Snoop Dog's, 'Let's Get Blown' serenaded them. Waves of incense smoke shifted past their bodies like low flying clouds and lovestruck ghosts. His eyes glistened. She imagined him being some vampire on the prowl as he placed one knee on the bed. She smirked, then crawled until she was sitting in the middle of the bed.

"What you about to do to me, boy?"

His chin tilted upwards and one of the evilest, yet most beautiful smiles creased his face. He slipped his tongue real slow out of his mouth. The damn thing was so long, it went past his fucking chin. It was like he was rolling out the red carpet… He waved it real fast, creased it, made it roll like a fruit rollup, much to her amusement and delight. 'Motivation,' by Kelly Rowland, practically broke the speakers as the smooth bass dropped on them. She went to lean back further, but he caught her beforehand, circled his arm around her ass, and ushered her to stay in place.

Lying on his stomach, and she sitting with her legs spread open in the middle of the bed, he settled between her legs. Running a rough, possessive touch along her legs, he pushed her a bit further back onto her hands, which were extended at her sides, her palms pushing into the sheets. This forced her pelvis to tip forward. Now wrapping his arm even tighter around her waist, he slipped his tongue out of his mouth and swayed it back and forth all along the crease of her pussy lips. He took his sweet time and then, he nudged her further open with a wave of his tongue, skating it against her clit, then dragging it against the entrance to her honey walls.

"You taste so fucking good, baby, but I always figured you had some mouthwatering pussy between these gorgeous, long legs of yours..." The cavernous rumble of his deep voice and the slow rise of heat from his warm breath massaged her pussy folds. Her eyes rolled from the sensation, and then he was right back to work. She'd lost track of time, but realized according to the puddle of her own making forming beneath her that he'd been lavishing her with oral affection tirelessly. Her orgasm built slowly and she came quietly, but then another one followed as he sped up and used his fingers to rub her in all the right places.

"Ohhh, that feels good, baby. Yeah... that's how I like it." The fast, wet slips and slides of his tongue had pressure, not too hard and not too soft. She ran her fingers through his dark, silky strands of hair, pushing him further into her pussy. "Mmmm! Yes... eat my pussy, baby..." She could feel the warmth and perspiration from his scalp as she dragged her nails through his shiny tresses.

She gyrated her hips from left to right ever so slowly, swinging them like a pendulum. Lennox V'ed her garden open with two fingers from his right hand, his eyes completely closed as he devoured her, one fast and furious nastily delicious slurp at a time. Her pussy filled with nectar as he made her hot all over, his working lips and tongue sending her to a place where only orgasms dwelled, and women yelled. He seemed to know exactly what to do and when to fucking do it. He'd go from long, slow, oral strokes up and down her clit, as if sauntering down a country road, to fast tongue fucking like city slicker talking the talk. She squealed when he brought two fingers to his mouth, sucked them to get them wet, then shoved them inside of her. Thrusting deeply.

"Fuckin' beautiful as ever... you're kinda tight, baby. I need to open you up. Make sure you can handle this dick. I don't fuck fair."

"Uhhhh!" Gripping the sheets with one hand, she held onto his crown with the other, squeezing him to her with a determined clasp. He held onto her all the tighter as his tongue danced against her clit. Her libations poured, dripping from her open foundation as he tasted her over and over. He groaned then swallowed. When he rose from her, he slipped his finger down his chin, collected her juices, tasted them, then smiled. His body was covered in a thin sheen of sweat, and his chest rose and fell slowly.

Her insides rattled with exhilaration as he reached for her, snatching her off the bed and bringing her into his unrestrained embrace. She shivered as another soft orgasm radiated from her love and spun around in her body like a tornado when he wrapped his strong arms around her and squeezed. She buried her face against his throat as he stroked her shoulders with a gentle hand.

After a few seconds, she broke the silence. "…Shoulda asked this earlier, I hate to break up this, uh, situation… but when was the last time you got tested? I get tested every couple of months. I can show you. I'm on the pill, too."

He slowly pulled away, slid out of the bed, and grabbed his phone. She laid on her side as she watched him playing around on it. Marcellus TheSinger, 'Until We Meet,' began to play. Less than a minute later, he handed her his phone. She read his most recent test results. A little less than six weeks ago, tested negative for everything. She handed the man his phone back, got out of the bed, retrieved her phone from the pockets of her pants, and found the latest email from her doctor, too. She handed it to him, and he read her information. He placed their phones side by side on the nightstand, then opened the top drawer. She slipped under the covers as he brandished three Magnum XL condoms. When he faced her again, his erection was full blown, curving slightly to the right. Her pussy clenched at the sight of it, and her mouth watered. He joined her back on the bed.

His breath fanned her face as he kneeled on the bed before her, stroking his dick. She ran her fingers over the pronounced veins across his chest. She sighed as he cupped her head, and kissed and sucked her neck while still stroking himself. It turned her on so much… the way his big hand barely wrapped around his nature, and the slow and long caresses of his hand along the shaft.

He pressed his mouth to hers, leaving the velvet warmth of the perfect kiss. When he released himself, she stared into his eyes and touched his dick with a delicate hand.

They focused on one another as she stroked it the same way he had, wanting to please him. Make him feel good. Her body shrank as she lowered herself until at last, the rounded smoothness of the large head of his cock slipped between her lips. He looked down at her as she licked him like an ice cream cone… the same intensity dancing in his eyes, making her heart skip a beat. Her pussy dripping, she finally saw his eyes clench closed, and a choppy groan escaped his mouth.

"You like how I suck this long, fat, juicy dick of yours, baby?"

"Mmmm hmmm, baby… keep goin'…"

She went down farther. Deeper. Faster. Gagging herself as saliva dripped from the sides of her mouth. He gripped a chunk of hair as she slurped and sucked him, bucking his hips and ruthlessly fucked her mouth. His balls pressed into her chin as she went so deep, she almost choked. She loved how he sounded… deep, masculine growls… how he smelled… musky and clean… how he tasted… salty precum and smooth skin…

"Ahhhh… shit, baby…" he roared.

Eyes still closed, that vein in the center of his head popped—such passion and control on his face as he neared climax. Love surged in her and from her like hot honey. Her mouth burned from the monster pummeling within it. She didn't care. Her need for him and her love of pleasing him spurred her on. She wanted to taste his story, feel his warm cum fill her mouth, and swallow his worries, but he grabbed her dreams and tossed them aside. She shrieked after he abruptly slipped out of her mouth. In a flash, he'd torn the condom open with his teeth and sheathed himself.

He tossed her on her back in the middle of the bed and forced her legs wide open. Her inner thighs burned as he placed her spread-eagled and pressed his heavy weight into her body, delivering urgent kisses along the way.

"Fuck me. FUCK ME, GOOD, LENNOX!"

He wrapped his hand around her throat as if she told him she needed that, wanted to feel him take control, and then...

"AHHHHH!"

He mercilessly breached her, the lunge sharp, hard and deep. She clawed at him, her voice caught in her throat as she glared at the ceiling. She held onto his slick, wet body, drowning in the lovely scent of his cologne and his sweat. Her body jostled and slid roughly towards the headboard as every inch of his delectable, hard-hitting dick pumped so angrily, yet beautifully, inside of her, bottoming her out. This was how she wanted to receive him. Strong. Hard. Deep. She'd been so wet that he slipped right in, but once he was inside, he touched parts of her that she'd forgotten even existed.

"...Len! SHIT!"

"You told me to fuck you good, and that's what I'm doing. I'm gonna fuck you so good, baby, you won't remember any other motherfucker except for me. Mmmm!" He pushed harder, then slowed, gyrating his hips to the rhythm of the music—BadGir's, 'Steppin' Out,' featuring King George.

"Mmmm! Ohhh, baby! Oh, shit!" She orgasmed, and he cradled her like an infant, slowing his plunges and jabs to a gentle rocking. She blinked as her body shook like a leaf. A tender sweet kiss against her lips.

He buried his face against her cheek, and that sexy ass voice rattled against her eardrum. "Baby girl, I've loved you since our days in that pantry at The Red Rooster. I've loved you since you soaked my shirt with your tears… I've loved you since you gave me my first rap mixtape and taught me how to do your favorite dance. I've loved you since you broke my heart when you closed me out of your world… I know why now. But all you need to know is *this*: I *never* stopped lovin' you. You'd best believe me."

"I believe you. For the first time in my life, a man lay on top of me and told me somethin' beautiful 'bout myself, and it wasn't a lie." Her voice shook and her eyes watered, betraying how she fell apart on the inside, but tried to hide it with a smile. He was not a human ATM for her to use and abuse. She was no pump and dump machine. This was a waterfall. A storm. This was the reign of the rain.

"Ain't nothing to lie about. You've been mine since God created the earth, girl. Names written in the stars. Lennox and Nadia forever. I found you and this time, I'm not letting go."

She laughed through the tears. A sweet release of healing mercies. They wrapped their bodies around one another as he began to move faster, increasing his speed once again. The man's stamina and self-control were mind boggling. He drifted to her breasts and sucked lightly on her nipples as he crashed into her, over and over again.

"My dick looks so good goin' in and out of your pretty pussy, baby. I love how you take it… You feel so damn good."

He'd slow his thrusts, move in circles, take his dick out and stroke her clit with the tip, then shove it back in, fast and hard. She orgasmed so many times, she'd lost count. Her pussy clenched and squeezed his wide shaft as he fucked her so fast and deep now, she knew she was going to pay the price in the morning.

"Mmmm! I'm 'bout to cum, baby!" He roared as a rush of warmth filled her, cocooned in the condom. He pumped inside of her in jerky plunges until he was emptied. Throbbing inside of her, he lay there on top of her, panting. Seconds later, they were holding one another tight and kissing. Talking. Laughing. But it didn't last long...

He snatched the condom off, tossed it in the small trashcan near the bed, and slipped another one.

"Stand up, then bend over the bed."

She did as he asked, and purred when he stood behind her and fucked her doggy-style to the sounds of, 'Lay Low Play Slow,' by Young Guy, tearing her pussy out the frame.

"You beatin' my shit up, boy..."

"Your pussy is too wet and perfect for me to *not* to beat the walls down. Feels good to you, baby?"

"Feels so fucking good! Got a big dick and know how to use it!"

"Mmmm... this pussy of yours was made specifically for my mouth, hands and dick, baby girl. Now that I know what you taste and feel like," she looked over her shoulder as he spoke. He rested his hand against her lower back, dipped low, and drove inside of her real slow... "I'm guarding this stuff with an AK-47. BOOM!" His hips shot forward like a piston as he rammed hard inside of her with purpose and direction. He held onto her shoulder, forcing her into his harsh lunges.

She screamed and hollered, clenching the sheets with teeth and hands. He lifted one of her legs high in the air, pivoting inside of her at an angle, hitting her spot as his balls slapped hard against her swollen pussy lips.

She fell apart, a full body orgasm making her feel as if she were dying and being reborn all within a matter of seconds. *I've never come this hard in my life!* The man knew how to fuck. He knew how to touch her. He knew how to love her...Lennox followed close behind her. A low growl escaped his mouth as he ignited his manly release.

They must've fallen asleep because before she knew it, she was lying on his chest, and he was snoring lightly. She stifled a laugh. It sounded a bit like a broken flute. One of his long, heavy legs was wrapped around her own, and his arms cradled her against him as if she were precious cargo. She knew it before then, but this made it all crystal clear. She was in love with him. Things would have to change. He deserved that much, and more. Worries clouded her thoughts like billows. She disappeared under the sheets...

"Uhhhh..." He groaned hoarsely, coming out of a sound sleep.

She wrapped both hands around his rotund dick and sucked slowly, needing him. She flung the sheets to the side, wanting him to watch her at work, and paused for a brief spell to look at him. His eyes were half open, and he flashed a crooked smile as he looked down at her. His dick went from soft and flaccid to stiff and massive in no time.

In his groggy state, he soon drained into her mouth. A warm, velvety expulsion of cream. She gobbled his appreciation and swallowed as he jerked inside of her mouth and held the back of her head to his groin while voiding the last drops into her mouth.

The sun had come up, and they didn't discuss plans or parting ways. Instead, he laid her on her side, stroked himself into a new erection, and entered her, their foreheads pressed together. Breathing harsh and loud. They held each other as he pivoted inside of her until they climaxed simultaneously. They were quiet, yet speaking to one another, in some strange way. Reaching over her naked body, he covered her with the sheets and grabbed his phone to make a call.

"...Heeeey, Ashley. I have a lot going on today... No, everything is fine, just need to alter my schedule. I have an eight o'clock appointment with Bernard Benton today. Can you offer him a reschedule today, for... uh, one PM? ... Yeah ... Benton. Also, I was supposed to cover John's spin class today at ten. Please call David and I'm sure he'll do it since he wants to teach that class anyway... right ... I won't be in until one... I need a half day to take care of something... Okay, thanks."

He disconnected the call and lay down next to her, wrapping his arms firmly around her, then kissed her forehead. His stomach grumbled loudly. They both laughed at that.

"So I take it, you want me to cook breakfast?" she teased. "Tryna domesticate me, huh?"

"Nah, not at all. I'll order some Uber Eats for us, and

get some coffee, too. I just, uh, want to talk to you some more. Spend more time with you before you rush off." He kissed her shoulder. She nodded in understanding. She didn't want to get up anyway. To leave the warmth of that bed, or his side. He took her hand and squeezed it. Then he rolled on top of her, pinning her down as he grabbed his dick and aimed it at her pussy. She immediately opened her legs wider for him… as well as her heart…

CHAPTER SEVENTEEN

Hit Me With Your Best Shot

H E LEANED AGAINST the living room wall, studying
Nadia, who sat Indian style on his couch, wearing one
of his Houston Cougars jerseys over lace panties. She
puffed on an e-cigarette, holding it loosely with a limp wrist
draped in gold chain bracelets, while her gaze focused on
the matter at hand. He crossed his ankles, taking sips of his
coffee to wash down the lingering taste of pancakes, then
placed the cup on the end table. She flipped the paper to
the opposite side, continuing to read the creased letter
covered in old food smudges and oily disdain that had
collected since the moment it was thrust upon him.

With a slow, long exhale, Nadia placed the letter down
by her side, picked up his stereo system's remote control,
turned up the music, then went right back to reading the
document. Anycia's, 'Back Outside,' featuring Latto, drifted
from his speakers.

Minutes grew long in the tooth, and then, it was over.

Unsure of her stance on the contents of the letter, he didn't dare blink. She cleared her throat and delicately folded the paper back the way it was with her pretty little fingers. Shiny, long nails dragged along the folded edge and for a brief moment, a flash of irritation crashed her expression, then faded into a dark smile. Leaning forward, she placed the letter onto the coffee table, sighed loudly, shook her head, and leaned back, arm extended along the length of the couch. A clear look of disgust on her face.

"…And I thought *my* father was a motherfucker. The devil sho' is busy, ain't he? Your grandfather makes my daddy look like Ghandi. Tha fuck?" She chuckled, though it was obvious she was not amused.

Lennox sucked his teeth, laughing mirthlessly while he nodded in agreement. The devil was definitely busy, and the devil was Grandpa. Always on the clock. He sat down beside her, and they remained quiet. He liked these moments with her. They spoke to one another without a need for extra filler. No desire to fill in gaps. Instead, their minds took in the crumpled information and tried to make something smooth of it.

He glanced her way as she looked down at the floor. Sunlight filtered in through the living room curtains, giving her a pinkish halo. Her flawless brown skin with undertones of amber and yellow glowed like a lantern. Soft fine hairs framed her hairline, flowing into a mass of dark brown wavy tresses that were now gathered in a sloppy ponytail after an evening and morning of beautiful, lust-fueled debauchery. She looked simply gorgeous. She stopped his heart just from a mere glance. Her natural state, devoid of the fluttery lashes and dark red lipstick was just as lovely, if not more so.

"…And you have six other cousins going through the same thing as you right now?"

He nodded. Taking another sip of his coffee, he set it back down. "He wants all of us."

"Why y'all?"

"Because we're the best, and we told him no. He hand selected each and every one of us from the moment we were born. He watched us closely, making a decision as we grew into teenagers, and then into men."

"He only chooses the boys?"

"Mmm hmm."

"So chivalry is not dead after all," she teased. "He's got the nerve to be sexist in his evil ways, but in this case, the womenfolk should be happy."

"He sees it like a war… Women shouldn't be on the frontlines. He keeps women around in the business for different purposes, but they're never front and center."

"So, what usually happens when he decides one of his chi'dren or grandsons is a good fit for whatever position he wants y'all to fill in his company?"

"Most people choose to comply." He shrugged. "We're the seven that didn't."

"Bad men seem to always want what they can't have, Len."

"Yeah… and I wanted you at one time, but knew I couldn't have you. I agree with what you said. I'm not who I was back then, but he doesn't seem to believe that."

"Why do you think you were a bad man, versus confused and hurtin'?" She cocked her head to the side.

"...Because I did bad things. I knew they were bad, and I didn't care."

"But you care now, right?"

"I do about most of the things I did. Some of them I *still* don't care about."

"They say, once a gangsta, always a gangsta, Len." She crossed her arms and glared at him, as if trying to gauge his reaction.

"I don't deny my bloodline and what that means. I'm just saying that I acknowledge that some of the shit I did back in the day was evil, but in some ways, it was necessary. I just shouldn't have been the one doin' it, is all. The difference now is, I've made a choice to be better."

"Maybe being better is being truthful about who you are, too."

Their eyes locked. His body warmed and his muscles tensed.

"I know who I am."

"You do, your self-awareness is admirable, but you don't look deeper into the darker pieces of you, Len. You are so busy tryna run from your past, you ain't slowed down enough to really see it for what it was."

"What I did back then, Nadia, was out of character. Up until that point, I had been a good kid."

"I know that you chalk it up as you mournin' your mama and actin' out. That might be true, but everything we do is *in* character, Len, or we wouldn't have done it in the first fucking place." She took his hands in hers and rubbed them, the most peaceful smile on her face, and yet he was filled with so much unease.

"Regardless, none of those things I did will happen again, Nadia. I've come too far and I have too much to lose."

"Fair enough... So, what are you going to do about this little grandpa problem of yours?" She released him and leaned back against the couch.

"I have a plan, just need to get the details down pat. Can't go in half-cocked."

"Tell me what your plan is, 'cause maybe I can help you."

"The less you know, the better. I don't want you embroiled in this bullshit."

"I can handle myself just fine. I've entertained big time drug dealers and gang bangers... been in a room full of hate-filled horny men with guns, when fights have broken out. Bullets flyin'. Ain't met a mothafucka that can spook me yet."

He leaned forward and caressed the side of her face with a gentle hand. She had the heart of a lion, the beauty of a butterfly, and the compassion of a lamb. She was his sword, his sunshine, and his rock.

He glanced at his watch, then cleared his throat. Time to address another situation that couldn't wait a second longer.

"Not to get off topic, but uh, is there anything you wanna tell me, Nadia?"

She looked at him curiously. "About this letter?" She pointed to the coffee table.

"No, about your life. About anything you got goin' on right now."

"Huh?" she shrugged, then took a draw from e-Cig before turning it off. "I've been an open book."

He grimaced and crossed his arms.

"Let me move back before lightning strikes."

"Okay, not right away," she chuckled, "but *lately* I have. I don't know what you're getting at. Just spit it out."

He pointed to the table. "I showed you that letter so you'd understand that I've got a serious situation I'm dealin' with right now. It was only fair. I can't be in a relationship with you without you knowin' that my grandfather is this kind of person. He's a dangerous man, one of the most known and feared in Houston. He's got half the damn police paid off to stay outta his business, and he's never hesitated on blowin' someone's brains out if he felt threatened. For most of my life, I have dealt with this stigma. This black cloud.

"That is why I didn't talk to people at work, and still don't, about my family, especially *him*. I've been workin' a long time because I had to make my own money since I kept refusing to join him in his nefarious and often illegal activities. I can't hitch myself to him. He'll then own me. My father is one of his many lapdogs. It's pathetic." His throat burned as his pancakes repeated in his system. "I don't ever wanna end up like my old man. So, with all of that, I had to tell you about this. Because I love you, and I'm serious about us being together. He doesn't have a history of messin' with folks' girlfriends and wives, but it still wouldn't be fair to keep that from you."

She nodded in agreement.

"He doesn't have a history for it unless they're dead."

She pointed to the letter. "Threatening to tell your deceased mama's family about her little stint in sexual services and ruining her family's reputation and lives in the process is nasty work."

"Yeah." He sighed. "True, but you know what I mean."

"Yeah, I know what you mean, baby. Look. Thank you for tellin' me, but it doesn't change anything about me. You. Us. You've made your decision to stay the hell away from this family business, and I stand beside you every step of the way. I support your decision. Instead of being retired and quieting down, your grandfather seems to be just getting started. Old and evil is a hell of a combination. He don't know how to love, but he sho' know how to hate. He does it well. Angels need to be cultivated. Demons never need even one day of trainin'. Funny how bad shit comes to folks so naturally, but being good 'nd righteous we got to work at. Anyway, It's a lot on yo' mind right now, and a lot on your table, even without the stress of this mess."

"Yeah, it is, but I'm okay. I choose to be okay. I have no choice, because I'm laser focused on what I want. Breakin' down and falling apart won't fix this shit. Me being smart about my next move will. I gotta plan all of this, all while he's makin' my life a living hell. I'm trying to save up the money to open my own gym and get approved for a low interest loan, as I already discussed with you. I just finished two certifications for personal training and I have a business degree that I haven't used but need to put to work. This is my vision, Nadia, and he's trying to ruin it, so I can make *his* dreams come true. He doesn't care that his dreams are my nightmare.

"I've worked my ass off since I was sixteen years old, and I haven't had handouts from my well-off grandfather. I haven't always had the support system that I need, either. I've got a broken relationship with my father that is goin' downhill fast, and the truth is it's because I don't respect him."

"Why? Because he works for his father?"

"Because I find him cowardly and embarassin', and he knows it. Because he is trying to get me to go along with this, knowing it's not what I want, and it's not what my mother wanted, either. Dad knows if she was still here she'd kill him before she let this go on. He's gutless. But he's still my dad…" He took a deep breath then continued. "Everything family wise is fucked. My sister still refuses to return my calls. Another result of my grandfather's brainwashing. He's a wrecking ball."

"Why is she upset with you?"

"Silva thinks I'm making trouble for no reason. She thinks I should be honored that I was chosen by Grandpa Santa Claus to be in his little Christmas club. Only he isn't Santa, despite the white beard, and the only thing in that sack over his shoulder are bullets and obituaries. She thinks our grandfather is like Mr. Rogers," he scoffed. "He never let her see the *real* him, and she never believed what I'd tell her. Even my father kept her from the truth of his own dealings, and that's because Grandpa told him to keep the girls out of occupational details. He has enough legit business ventures to lean on and claim that they are his keys to the ponderosa, but it's all a farce."

"What does she say when you try to talk frankly with

her about y'all's grandfather?"

"Every time I tried to explain to her that the man is a maniac, she either accused me of flat out lying, getting fake information to try and use to defame him, or insisting that whatever I presented to her wasn't as bad as I made it seem. Hell, even to this day, she has no idea that the fucker is a career criminal, let alone serial killer as far as I am concerned." He tossed up his hands. "He's good at playing different roles for different people, Nadia."

"Chameleons are smart... They know who to show their true colors, too."

"Definitely. He's good at protecting his fake image, too. Silva and I have a lot to catch up on, and I could use her support right now, but she's dancin' with the enemy and can't see the forest for the trees. He will stop at nothing to get his way, unless I come up with somethin' that's better, or somethin' so terrible that he decides to leave me the hell alone. I don't want any more blood on my hands." *But he may not leave me any choice.* "Now, back to you... do you have any loose strings, Nadia? Put it all on the table."

"No." She shrugged. "Like what? What are you accusin' me of?" He could tell she wasn't lying. She genuinely didn't seem to know what the hell he was talking about. "I'm not hiding anything."

"Oh, really? That's not true according to this." He slipped her phone out of his pocket and handed it to her. "Looks like you've got an ex-boyfriend who can't take no for an answer." Immediately, the vibe changed. Her shoulders slumped and her complexion deepened. "And before you accuse me of anything, no, I wasn't goin' through your shit. When you were in the shower, your phone kept going off. I saw some of his messages flash on the screen—well, part of them—and I got the gist of it. Now, do I need to handle somethin'?"

"…I thought you said all of that violent shit was behind you. In the past."

"I've evolved. That doesn't mean that I'm a fuckin' doormat or pussy. I protect what's mine."

She pursed her lips while reading a few of the messages the fucker from her past had bombarded her phone with before putting it down abruptly on the table—next to the letter from Satan.

"Let me put it like this. I have a lot of upset boyfriends, Lennox. I tend to rub men the wrong way when I'm not dancing for them, or doing some performance to cater to their fragile egos. The 'real me'," she gestured with air quotes with her fingers, "gets under a lot of men's skin. Some say I'm too loud. Too opinionated. Too independent. Too unemotional, I guess. None of that is true except the opinionated and independent part.

"What is true is that I have a short fuse for bullshit, and I call out all red flags as soon as I see them. I was a people-pleaser as a child. Life taught me to cut that shit out quick. When I end these relationships, if you want to even call them that, usually I just get a 'Fuck you, bitch,' and they go on their merry way. Sometimes I get drunk butt-dials or whatever." She rolled her eyes. "But it eventually stops sooner than later, and then it's over. This one isn't working out that way. This one just happens to be crazy and a little unpredictable."

She picked up the remote and turned the music back down.

"Why is he threatening to hurt you if you don't give him some money?"

"Because LeRon thinks I owe it to him, but we already went to court and the judge ruled in my favor."

"Then he's using it as an excuse to still be in contact with you?"

"Yeah, but he really does want the money. I think he wants to see if I'll break. If I told him right now I wanted him back, I believe he'd drop this."

"So he wants you more than he wants the money?"

"No. He doesn't give a shit about me. It's what I represent. What I can do. Some guys get off by dating strippers. It's a kink for them. Especially one like me that had to be booked in advance, made a lotta money, and was a crowd favorite. Dancing is highly competitive in Atlanta. I got a lot of top billing for shows. My name was well-known in these stripper streets. He enjoyed that. He doesn't want me, though, Lennox... not really. He wants the lifestyle."

"He wants to ride your coattails? This is ridiculous."

"It is, but it's true. The riches. The glamour. Atlanta strip clubs hit different. It's a part of the culture. A way of life. I had a nice apartment. A real nice one. A penthouse, actually, and I had just about all the things that money could buy. I have a nice savings, and he wants a slice. Says he deserves it. Says he helped promote me, get me bookings. He ain't do shit that I was already doing by myself before I even met him, and I was doin' it well. I didn't benefit from being with him. He benefited from being with *me*. He got to go with me on trips and rent expensive cars to floss in. He's a schemer and a user. Now he's callin' me every week from blocked numbers threatening me."

"Just tell me his full name. I promise I won't do anything."

They both burst out laughing.

"Boy, stop. Lennox, I *know* you. I ain't tellin' you that boy's name 'cause you'll end up on the news. You've got enough problems as is. Anyway, like I said, he's not even here, so chill. He's in Atlanta. I ain't worried about him." She scoffed. "And besides, if he is dumb enough to bring his silly ass over this way, I got Dolly and Parton waitin' for him, and trust 'nd believe, they work 24/7, not just 9 to 5."

"Who's Dolly and Parton?"

She smiled at his question as if she'd been waiting to be asked.

"My Glock 43X and Springfield hellcat. They can sing their asses off, too. Got a mouth full of pretty, shiny bullets, and both of 'em can foxtrot through any dancefloor. I hold one in my left hand, and the otha in my right. I say… 'Jolene, please don't make me put a hole in dis here man…'"

"Cheers to that." They tapped their glasses and cups together. "Do you shoot well?"

"Does a bee like honey?"

"Who taught you how to shoot or did you just learn on your own?"

"Didn't learn on my own. Got it from my mama."

"Of course." He laughed.

"…You already know." Her face flushed deeper and her

high cheekbones rounded when she smiled. "She taught me and my brother how to use a gun. I was fifteen. Mama said, *'Listen you two. Y'all gonna learn how to fight, and how to shoot a person dead, today.'* My brother piped up and said, *'But we can just call the police like Nana says.'* Mama laughed and put her hand on her hip. *"Boy, the world don't give a fat fried fuck a duck on a truck for good luck 'bout no black folks getting justice in this world. So, we have to make our own justice 'cause it's JUST US. Now pay attention or you'll wish you did.'* Mama grabbed some bottles, pop cans, and some of my old dolls, took us out in the mornin' to a field, and we stayed there for hours until we could shoot those dolls square in the middle of their glassy eyes. There was a lot of tears and yellin', swearin' and not caring, but we did it. She made sure of it."

"Being able to defend yourself is important. I'm glad she taught you two early."

"Mmm hmmm… I can fight, but fighting sometimes ain't enough. Too bad I ain't have that heat on me when I was in college. Woulda made a world of difference. The storm would've never came." Hatred blazed in her dark eyes. "Now, you'd be hard pressed to run into me without a piece on me. You ain't got to teach me that I can't have my guard down but one time." She raised her finger. "Lesson learned."

"You ever have to use Dolly and Parton? Or have to shoot anyone, period?"

She was quiet for a long time, then reached for her juice and took a few gulps.

"This woman broke in my house one time… said I was messin' with her husband. I ain't even know who her damn husband was. At first I found it kinda funny, but I was mad too, 'cause she was in my house. My sanctuary. To this day I don't know how she got in my apartment, she ain't never say when I asked her, but I got a hold of one of my guns and gave 'er a warning shot. She got up outta there real fast. Thought I was gonna stand there and wrestle with her weird ass. I saw the car she drove off in, filed a police report, and they saw on somebody's store camera who she was not that long afterwards. She got arrested at her job. Bitch was a whole ass teacher. Throwin' her good career away over some bullshit.

"Come to find out, her husband was some fella that used to come to the strip club all the time and had gotten a little obsessed with me. He was a chiropractor. Plain lookin' and too handsy. That's all I remembered 'bout him. He was lying to himself, and to her, and believed me and him was in a relationship I guess." She shrugged.

"What happened to the husband after you figured out he was the one that caused this mess in the first place?"

"This fool had the nerve to show back up to the club and try to pretend he didn't know what the problem was. Had his ol' lady going crazy over a lie and some movie he had playing in his head. She was in jail, lost 'er job, and he was back at the spot like not a damn thang had changed. I made sure the bouncers had the 411 as soon as I spotted him. They took him out back and beat him down to the mothafuckin' ground. He ain't come 'round there no more after *that*." She chuckled. "Had to let these mothafuckas know, Len, don't let the pretty smile fool you." Her grin faded into the darkest alley and the deepest valley. "I'm 'bout that life.

"My father was a killa 'foe he got saved and said he was called to preach the word. My mother ain't no angel, either. She on that eye for an eye type shit. I made it clear to that lunatic that next time I wuddn't giving just no warning shot to his ol' lady. I felt a lil' sorry for her, so I let her live, but there would be no second chances. On soul. Next time, I'll be shootin' to kill, and he wouldn't be walkin' away from that club if I saw him again, neither. I told him straight up that he'd be leaving in a body bag, and I *might* toss a few dollars on it."

She polished off her juice and got to her feet.

"Anyway, baby, I gotta run some errands and what not before work tonight. I know you have to get ready to leave soon, too." He got up and walked back with her to the bedroom so she could put on her pants she wore the night before, and her shoes. As she collected her belongings, he glanced at his watch one last time. He slipped out of his jogging pants and whistled to her. She turned around, her sock in her hand, and her eyes widened at the sight of him stroking his dick.

"'Jolene' ain't the only Dolly Parton song that needs to be discussed today."

"Oh, really? I never took you for a Dolly Parton fan. What's another one we need to talk about?" She put her hand flirtatiously on her hip, tilting her head back as she belted a laugh.

"'Here You Cum Again,'… because you're definitely about to be cummin'." She spun around and burst out laughing. "Take that shit off. All of it. Right now. You're gonna give me some more pussy before you leave up out of here."

"You ain't the boss of me." She smirked. Taking a few wobbly steps back.

"Ain't tryna be the boss, just tryna get ya ass ate and ya salad tossed."

"You a fool!" she hooted, letting that sock slip from her hand back onto the floor.

"Dolly got it wrong."

"Oh, did she now?"

"Mmm hmm. Tennessee ain't the only places with mountains. Why don't you come on over here and ride this Houston peak? I got somethin' you need to climb up on, and slide down, all right."

"Lennox! What's gotten into you?" soft laugh lines creased around her eyes, and her lips curved in amusement.

"Don't worry about what's gotten into me, I'm tryna get into *you*. You got me all worked up, hot and bothered with all that gun and gangster talk. Dolly and Parton ain't the only ones that like to shoot their load. I'm ready for target practice RIGHT NOW, and trust me, I never miss."

"So you want a chance to hit the doll between the eyes, too, huh? You wanna play paintball, and tint my face white, don't you, boy?" She teased, reaching for her panties, and slowly sliding them down her thighs.

"Not your *entire* face. I would *love* for you to see me cummin'."

"Oh, honey, I *insist* on keepin' at least one eye open. Just make sure your one-eye soldier shoots me right. I'm picky and hard to please."

"I'm hard, too, and I'm reportin' for duty. Trust and believe, I aim and fire to please."

With that, he slammed and locked the bedroom door behind him...

CHAPTER EIGHTEEN

Roll of the Dice

IT HAD BEEN a long but fairly uneventful night. The buzzing of the music at work kept spiraling in Nadia's head while she fought a mild headache. Perhaps it was the cigarette and cigar smoke, too? She hadn't consumed any wine or liquor so her mind was clear, yet she felt a wave of dread, as though some trouble was afoot.

She pushed it aside and reached for her water as she made a left turn at the light, taking a couple deep gulps of the refreshing, cool beverage. The street lights beaming onto the quiet street gave her a sense of peace. It was a little after two in the morning, and most people were tucked in their beds.

Looking in the rearview mirror, she noticed the car. Again.

She'd noticed it a few minutes prior, too. A vehicle was sticking behind her, making the same turns as she had, going in the same direction. She decided to make another left at the next light, which caused her to double back where she'd already driven. A perfect block. She casually looked at the rearview mirror for a third time, and watched a man's profile behind tinted glass make the same exact turn. *So this is what we're doin' tonight, huh?* Polishing off the water, she tossed the empty canteen onto the passenger's seat.

Nadia maintained the same speed limit, driving an even thirty-five miles per hour. She then calmly reached into the center console of her car and pulled out Dolly. She placed the cool metal of Dolly's sleek steel body against her hip. Nadia had two decisions to make. Take the chance on driving to the police station to lose the person pursuing her, or send them a clear message so they'd never bother her again. Deciding to give peace a chance, she headed in the direction of the police station, and made a hands-free call.

"See? This is why I need to move to Kingwood," she mumbled under her breath as the phone rang. On the third chime, a woman answered.

"Houston Southeast Police Department, how may I direct your call?"

"Hi, I just need to speak to someone in general. This isn't a 911 situation." She glanced quickly in the mirror at the car behind her. "Yet. I just need a police officer to meet me outside your station."

"Why's that, ma'am?"

"I have someone followin' me on the road. I made several turns and they made the same ones, and ain't hardly nobody out here but me and him."

"Okay, what's your name, honey, and what is the color

and make of your car?"

"My name is Nadia and I drive a black Ford Fusion. I just got off work."

"Do you happen to know who is following you, or is it a stranger?"

"I've had this happen before, it kinda comes with the job, but this time I am ninety-nine percent sure it's a customer of mine."

"A customer?"

"I'm a dancer at a gentlemen's club, ma'am. Sweet Soiree."

"Okay, I understand. Do you know his name by chance?"

"Only his nickname. Dice. Tall guy with a beer gut, and a mouth full of gold teeth."

"Can you tell the make and model of his car? The color, too?"

"It's a white Mitsubishi Eclipse with some white dice hangin' from the mirror."

Suddenly, Dice got right on her bumper, riding it hard. The headlights blinded her. She winced, and quickly flipped her rearview mirror in his direction to reflect some of the light back at him. He stayed close. She swallowed and looked ahead, gripping the steering wheel a bit tighter.

"Can you see his front license plate number, Nadia?"

"He's too close right now for me to see it, but when he was farther away, I did see a lil' bit of it. The first four numbers, I believe, were 4722. He's got—"

"Okay, how far away are you from our station?"

"'Bout eight minutes, according to my navigation

screen. Now he's doing some strange stop and start motions, like he's drunk. He's stoppin', then runnin' up fast on me, tryna scare me."

"Okay. Try to keep calm, and I'll stay on the phone with you."

"Alright. I'm calm, though, just giving you the play by play." She approached another light on a desolate tree-lined street and suddenly felt her car jolt forward. The maniac bumped her vehicle with a light tap. "Damn it! Ma'am, he just hit my car." Now, she was no longer calm...

She slowed down.

"Don't get out of the car, Nadia. It may be a trap. Make sure your doors are locked, too."

"Doors are locked. I'm well aware that this is a set-up, but now he's gettin' out his car. The door is opening. Probably about to lie about accidentally hittin' me."

"Is your car too damaged to drive away?"

"No."

"Drive forward. Act like nothing happened."

"Okay." Nadia knocked her gear out of park, and kept driving as before. The man quickly jumped back into his car. She sped up, and so did he, then she approached another light, her heart knocking against her chest.

The light turned red. She had to stop.

Suddenly, the bastard put his car in reverse. For a split second, she was hopeful he would abort mission and leave, but then she saw him barreling towards her at an ungodly high speed, and he rammed into her a second time. This time, much harder.

"Nadia, what was that noise?" the woman questioned.

"This mothafucka hit my car again!"

"Nadia, I am dispatching an officer to meet you. Keep driving towards us. Stay on the line."

"At this point, my life is in danger, and I won't make it there in time. Nor will the police officer you sent to intervene."

"Nadia, he's almost there. If you can drive your car, do so now."

"I don't have time for none of that because this son of a bitch is backing up again!"

BOOM! The man hit her car a third time. The jolt forced her forward, almost knocking her out of her seat into the windshield. Her head became dizzy and her seatbelt dug into her skin, burning her flesh, but keeping her secure and in place. She quickly gathered her bearings and then saw his driver's side door slowly opening.

"Ma'am, he's comin' again! He's approaching me. The light has went a full cycle and is red again, and he's about to be red, too. YOU GOT THE RIGHT ONE TONIGHT, BABY!"

"Nadia... Nadia!" the woman screamed. "Don't get out of the car!"

"Oh, sweetheart, that won't be necessary. I can do this all from the comfort of my seat."

Nadia sucked her teeth, rolled her window down, gripped Dolly like the bitch owed her money, and stretched her arm out the window, directly at the figure emerging from the lights and shadows.

She aimed it at his head. He was nothing but a menacing outline due to the bright headlights of his car, a shadow full of darkness, but light illuminated all around him like a chalk outline. Perhaps foretelling of things to come?

"Dice mothafuckin' Incel the Third!" He stopped in his tracks as he seemed to suddenly realize she was holding a metal friend. "I ain't wanna do a VIP with' yo crazy ass tonight, turned you down, and THIS is what you do?! Bet! I got somethin' for that ass!" In a flash, he turned around and ran. She shot in the air as he jumped back into his vehicle. "NAW! WHERE YOU GOIN'?! You don't want a lap dance no more, boy?! Dance to these bullets, bitch!" She enjoyed watching him panic, his shadow bopping around in the car like a nervous wreck. "I WILL BLOW YO' DUSTY EGGLANT-HEADED ASS RIGHT BACK INTO THE SNATCH THAT BIRTHED YOU, MOTHAFUCKA!"

She got out of the vehicle and fired at his car, shattering his back window as he hauled ass past her in a blaze of smoke from his squealing tires. Heart pumping, chest rising and falling like an accordion, she slipped back into her seat and closed her eyes, her throat sore from screaming, and her chest radiating dull pain from the adrenaline rush.

"Nadia, are you okay?" the woman on the phone asked.

"Yes ma'am... he's gone now." She took a deep breath. "He was gettin' out of his car after he tore my back end up. I shot at him. My gun is licensed and registered, and I know how to use it."

"Officer Duncan is one minute away. Do you believe you injured him, ma'am?"

"No, I purposefully did not 'cause I don't want no media attention and no court case. Just did enough to make him go away." She put her car in drive to see if she could finish her route, shave off a few seconds. She could, but she heard a lot of reverberating, knocking, and dragging from her ride. "He damaged my car real bad, but I can still drive it I think."

"No, stay right there. Officer Duncan will meet you, assess the situation and damage, and go from there." Nadia could hear the sirens now. "Another officer has already been sent to find the person in question. It's okay, darlin'. Everything is fine. Help is on the way."

"Help was already here." She glanced at her gun now lying on her lap, and smiled sadly. "But I appreciate you all the same…"

Shaking her head in disbelief, she wiped a tear from her cheek. A tear born of pure rage and misery.

…A short time later

IT WAS A little after three in the morning and Nadia found herself on Nana's porch. Nana was a notorious night owl. Tonight, she was happier than ever about that. She needed the woman's warm arms around her. She needed an angel on earth.

Nana didn't ask any questions when that doorbell rang. She looked out the peephole, opened the door, and welcomed her grandchild inside. Now they were once again sitting on the porch while rap music played from next door. They enjoyed the blanket of blackness and stars, the insects singing a tune, and the balmy night air, with a nice breeze passing through every so often.

"Well, you filed the police report so it'll be only a matter of time fo'e they get him."

She sensed a trace of irascibility in her tone.

"I'm done, Nana." Nadia took a sip from the glass of freshly squeezed orange juice her grandmother had given her.

"Done with what, baby?"

"Done with it all." Nadia waved her hand, her jaw tightening in disgust. "I asked for a sign, a *true* sign to be finished with this career, and this was it. I have been followed home many times over the course of my dancin' career. It's not that within itself—it's the energy it attracts to me. Dancing can be beautiful but what it attracts ain't so pretty all the time." Nana nodded in understanding. "I have had bodyguards from the club I worked at in Atlanta escort me so I'd make it home safe.

"I've had men somehow get my number and harass me. I've had one guy try to rob me while I was still at work. He saw me comin' out of the restroom and tried to hem me up against the wall. I kneed him in the nuts and got away. I've had to help other dancers not get their asses beat by crazy boyfriends or some pimp that had gotten his hooks into them." She placed her juice glass down and shook her head.

"You were a friend."

"Well, that's another dark side to this. Nana, I ain't got many friends." She lifted her hands in the air, then let them fall against her thighs. "I know plenty of folks. Got a whole lotta associates. But friends? Naw. Some women are intimidated by me because of what I do. I do it well. I ain't the prettiest, but I'm one of the best. I'm a foodie, but I work hard on my body, and I practice what I'm doing. I keep my mind sharp. I do what needs to be done. I don't have a drug or drinkin' problem like some of them do, and this isn't me thinkin' I'm better than nobody, 'cause I'm not. I'm just sayin' that I'm not as broken as some folks, and it makes things easier for me. Women can be funny acting sometimes."

"Well, when you live in a world that tells girls they ain't worth nothin' if they not married and got babies, that's bound to happen. We see ourselves through the eyes of men, baby. Read a magazine, and the cover say, 'How to drive yo' man crazy in bed!'" Nana chuckled. "Or, what do men like?' And then it gives a long list of the perfumes they like on us, the makeup, the hairstyles."

"It's called male centered."

"Huh? Male centered?"

"Yeah. What you described, Nana, is what my mama found out is called 'male centered,' and she told me about it. It's when we hurt ourselves, our best interests or other women, just to get or keep the attention of men. Some folks in the black community call 'em mammies, or Pick-Me. Another variation of that term, is a Pick-Me-Esha."

"Hmph!" Nana shook her head and crossed her ankles. "I ain't know they had a name for it."

"Yes, they sure do, and it keeps us women apart from one another. Makes us compete with one another, for scraps. Like gangs over streets that we don't even own. I think I have a friend, one minute, you know? And then she starts acting strange. Think I'm going to take her man, so then all of a sudden, they don't want to hang with me no more." A flush of heat consumed her. The thought of that reality made her madder than what had happened that evening—the whole stalking and police situation.

"My only friends, Nana, are other strippers, and some of them ain't really friends either because they might have jealous or hateful hearts after somebody done them wrong in the past, too. 'Fraid me or someone else is going to get all the money. Some of these dancers are worse than everyone else, as far as friendships are concerned. If you're pretty, they hate you. If you can dance yo' ass off, they hate you. If you are a crowd favorite, they hate you. If your body is nice, they hate you. I can dance, and I'm a crowd favorite. I also keep to myself. So now I get called stuck up. Don't get me wrong. There's a few ladies at the club that I get along with just fine, like even, but that's not the norm. One young lady I actually mentor. Her name is Lydia, and she's a doll baby. Her mama died when she was young, and she ain't have nobody, but she's more like a niece than anything else.

"Sometimes you'll meet a sweet one though, and I know a few right now that I have drinks with every now and again, but I end up pullin' these types of girls aside, just like Lydia, and tellin' them to get their money and leave fast. Take that money and go to nursin' school, or shoot for the stars and become a doctor. Invest in a business. Buy some property and rent it out. Go get your real estate license, or move somewhere nice. Don't stay in this shit like I did."

The two women were quiet for a while.

"Why do you think you stayed with it so long, Nadia? I thought you was happy? You never told me all of this. You never told me you hated it."

"I don't hate dancing, Nana, but I don't love it any-more, either. The plan was to stack my money so I could finish school and live well. Then, after I dropped out, it was to start over. I wanted to travel the world, too. I wanted to eventually finish school, but first, I had all of these plans to see places. I *did* travel a little…but it would have been better with friends. Real friends. Like I said, I can't keep many friends, Nana—not while doing this sort of work—so girls' trips were sometimes out of the question.

"Relationships have always been strange for me, too. Once a man knows you strip, he thinks he can buy anything from you, including your soul. I never date anyone from the club. That's a rule of mine. When I meet a man outside of the club, I'm honest about my profession. If the guy knows you are a stripper and says he's cool with it, he won't be for long."

"I imagine they get jealous."

"Soon as he starts fallin' in love with you, he starts act-ing possessive and crazy. I'm not putting up with that. I'm not about to sit around and baby somebody, or spend my life tryna convince them that I'm loyal. You either believe I am, or you don't. I don't move like that. I'm too old for this. My fuse is short now, and like tonight reminded me, if I don't pull away from this, someone is gonna end up dead, but it won't be me. I got the sign I prayed for, so that's that."

Nana's lips thinned, and she swiped at her eye before offering a stiff yawn.

"I want you to do whatever makes you happy, Nadia.

You tol' me the otha day that you wanted to go back to school. Seems to me all the signs are there for you to let this thang go, and do just that. You're still young. You got time to start ova."

Nana offered an exaggerated wink, making her feel better.

"I see your mama all in you right now, girl... I mean that in a good way." Nana's lips curled in an approving smile. "You've got a different path than hers, but y'all are similar in so many ways. Beautiful like your mama, too."

"Thank you, Nana. I need to know *how* and *why* you see my mama in me. You told me about some family curse the other day, but I want to stop this thing. I feel the need to connect with something. It's a spiritual thing." Nana nodded in understanding. "I need a lifeline. Can someone *please* give me a map?"

"We all go a different route, Nadia. My map don't look like yours, and yours don't look like the baby that you may one day carry."

They glared at one another.

"Our maps are different, Nana, but we're all tryna get to the same place. As a teenager, I didn't listen to you or Mama. Now, I'm listening. I promise I am." She swiped a tear away.

"You don't need any guidance, sweetie. You've fallen but always got up."

"I get up, yeah, but each time I fall, I am a little less steady on my feet, and have more bruises. Some injuries can be avoided with education. I don't need you to be my crutch. I don't need you to be my ride to the destination. I need you to just point the way. Who *is* JoAnn?"

"You're askin' me to betray my daughter, baby."

"Nana." Nadia closed her eyes and fought tears of anger. Grief. Sadness. Her body shook like a bone rattling song. "I don't know nothin' about no family curse, sounds like an excuse, but at this point, anything is possible. What I *do* know is that I'm full of piss and vinegar, as you like to say. I'm on the verge of ending up like my mother, in the bad ways, too, but I don't want to!" She blotted away more budding tears. "Is that what JoAnn would want? Is that what *you* want? I got a change comin' outta me.

"I'm sittin' on yo' porch at this crazy time of day—it's still dark out, and yet we're up drinking orange juice as a bird sleeps with her babies up in that tree. My car was messed up and got towed to an auto shop due to some asshole who couldn't take rejection, and because of that, I had to Uber over here. My boyfriend is none the wiser and may hit the roof when I tell him what happened to me tonight, 'cause when I tell him, it's going to take me, the National Guard, and five professional wrestlers to keep him off of Dice. Something has turned a light on inside of me, and it is tryna make me see! I'm hurting! I'm proud of my progress, but I gotta keep moving. I'm ready! My pain ain't just from Mama. My daddy broke my heart, Nana, and now he's dead. I've got a lot going on inside! My car and filling out a police report are the least of my concerns right now!"

"Nadia, as far as your father, he can't do nothin' now because—"

"That man had a whole 'nother family and left me in the dust. He was my first example of how a man should behave. I have had countless chaotic relationships. I've been raped before. It happened when I was sixteen. Maybe if he was around, it wouldn't have happened." She saw a little life and light leave Nana's eyes. "Same age you got married the first time. You know about the assault in college now, Nana. It was a medical miracle that I had even survived that attack. You and I have had the same crap happen to us, Nana. It ain't right. Different journey. Same map! Closed mouths do more than not get fed. They keep horrible secrets. Closed mouths keep the hurt alive!"

She quickly wiped another tear away, holding her head high. Her voice quaked as everything crashed down at her feet. Nana also seemed on the verge of breaking down.

"I've got LeRon harassing me still, too..."

"LeRon?! But I thought that court case was closed?"

"It is. He don't want to accept the verdict, and he can't accept that I don't want him no more and moved away. Mind you, this is the same negro who cheated on me, gaslit me to smithereens, and all sorts of devious mess. He's a narcissist, and I didn't even know what a narcissist was until after I got rid of him. I'm saying all of this to say, Nana, that my life has been a big ass dumpster fire from the time I was born, up until now. I'm not feelin' sorry for myself. Please don't think that." She put out her hand as if to say 'stop.' "I'm just venting. Expressing myself. The hurt. This is part of my healing. Finally telling the truth about it, and facing it. Taking it for what it is."

"I know that, uh, your daddy hurt you, baby." Nana leaned forward and tapped her knee. That light, warm touch was a soothing balm.

"It wasn't just that he hurt me, Nana. He hurt my mother, too. I know that my father asked my mother to abort me. He told me." Nana's complexion lost color. "Yup. I've known for years. Even pitched a fit when she refused. I asked my mother about it. She admitted it—said he was cryin' and droppin' to his knees, talking about he don't want no babies. He hated me before I was even born." Nadia dabbed at her eyes.

Her grandmother hung her head again, shaking it. "What else did JoAnn tell you?" She then sat a bit straighter.

"I know that he was married to someone else when he got with my mother, too. I know that mama was not aware until his divorce was final, but by then she was already pregnant with me, and forgave him. She was in love. He was in lust. She lived to regret it."

"She shole did." Nana huffed and flopped back in her seat. "He tricked us all though, Nadia. I thought he was a good man way back then, too. I was dumb." She chuckled mirthlessly. "We didn't have no online searches, Facebook, and Instafame and stuff like y'all got now to check people out. See if their story is right."

Instafame? She means Instagram. Nadia kept her laughter to herself. *Same but different, really.*

"I get it, baby. Nadia, yo daddy was a man of many faces. He only showed us two of 'em. The liar, and the conman."

"When he found religion, he doubled down on that,

306

selling snake oil. Some things I've been through I definitely brought on myself. Other stuff?" She vehemently shook her head. "I ain't deserve it, Nana. I ain't deserve none of it!" Another tear fell, and Nana got up, dug in her pocket, and handed her a scrunched-up tissue. Nadia took it and patted at her eyes and nose. The tissue smelled like cinnamon and Cherry blossom perfume. Nana sat back down, quiet, her gaze set on her.

"I'm sorry about all of your pain, Nadia. If I could take it away, I would!" Now her voice trembled, too.

"You can't take it away, but you can help soothe it. If high blood pressure and certain mental illnesses can be hereditary, Nana, then so can other things. Like this thing we don't have a name for, but some call it a generational curse."

"I don't know what the hell is going on in this family," Nana shook her head. "Why we end up choosing the wrong men, have men turn crazy over us, and having regrets about life in general."

"Me, you, Mama, my aunts, my female cousins, just about all of us have never had a successful relationship or marriage, except for you with Samuel. Maybe we're not the problem, and maybe this isn't so unusual after all." Nadia shrugged. "Maybe most families are like ours. But just because something is common, or happens all day and every day doesn't mean it's okay. Don't make it right. People jump off bridges and plummet to their deaths all over the world. That doesn't mean we too should jump. Especially when someone cares enough to talk us off the edge. That talk, no matter how painful, should always be the truth. The truth is the map. The truth is what sets us free."

CHAPTER NINETEEN

Old and New Curses

G RANDPA WILDE SAT in his opulent office, the scent of his cigar blending with the odor of fresh paint. The corridor was being repainted, and the knocks and bangs of minor repairs made his brain throb. 'Nights in White Satin,' by the Moody Blues, serenaded him. He leaned forward, his cigar in hand, and grinned at the photos sprawled all over his desk as Beverly kneeled before him, resting on her knees, her tight, wet perfect mouth wrapped snugly around his throbbing, thick shaft. He flipped to another photo on his desk, his eyes drinking in all that was before him. A beautiful heat flushed his body, each muscle burning with anticipation.

"Take all of that cock, honey. Down your throat it goes… You know how I like it… Mmmm… that's it…" he grunted as he neared climax. Slipping a beringed hand beneath the desk, he grabbed a clump of hair from the back and wound it tightly around his fist, ushering the red-headed siren down his shaft as she held the base with both hands. Her ruby red nails dragged slowly along his pubic hair. Echoing sounds of her feverish sucking and slurping filled the room as he rocked his hips slow and easy, delivering more of himself into her mouth. His hips bucked faster, and he groaned as he gripped the edge of the desk and ejaculated inside of her mouth.

"Uhhh! Uhhh...." He breathed hard and heavy as she swallowed his cream, then released him and got onto her feet. Snatching a tissue from the box on his desk, she dabbed the sides of her mouth, quietly got dressed, then re-buttoned his shirt for him. "Thank you, darlin'." He popped her on the ass, and her lips curled in a pretty smile.

"Anything else you need, baby?" she asked as she leaned over the desk and looked him in the eye.

"Nope. Nothin' except for you to get the fuck out of my office." He chuckled and ran his fingers tenderly along her chin, but he meant every word he said.

"Okay." She shrugged, looking a bit disappointed. "I guess I'll see ya when I see ya, Mr. Wilde." She stood straight, blew him a kiss, tossed her hair to one shoulder, then exited his office, closing the door behind herself. Fact of the matter was, there were too many women biting at the chance to be his next wife. He was never getting married again—he'd sworn to that after the explosion of his last marriage. Now he had beautiful women who would practically beg for him to fuck them—all to get a piece of that Wilde money, and a taste of the good life. No one had made him turn his head more than once in a long, long while. Besides, gorgeous women were a dime a dozen.

He was in great shape for his age. He played golf twice a week, swam, ran, and lifted weights. He didn't need any of those fucking blue pills, either. He ate right most of the time, and as long as he was able, he was going to continue fucking, but with no strings attached. It made things far too messy. Why should he buy the cow when he could get the milk for free? Grabbing a tissue from his desk, he dabbed at his now limp dick, tossed the wad in a gold trashcan, tucked himself back in and zipped up his pants. The sounds of 'Morning Has Broken,' by Cat Stevens, appeased him.

As he adjusted his clothing, he came to a decision. After reviewing the information from the private investigator for a second time, he was ready to make his move. He reached for his phone and dialed.

"Boss," came a gruff, yet youthful voice on the other end. "How can I help you today?"

"I've got some news." Grandpa grinned as he stroked his beard, then brought the cigar to his mouth. "Looks like Lenny boy is just like my son. Chip off the ol' lusty block. They like, shall I say, exotic fruit. Darker berries." He chuckled.

"Dark berries? What do you mean, boss?"

"He's got himself a fucking woman..." He was met with silence.

"Uh, really? Lennox? Are you sure?"

"As certain as an ant's attendance at a picnic."

"Not to question you or anything, but Lennox is *always* around women." Sam chuckled. "I mean, it's part of his job. How can you be sure that this is a serious thing and not some fling? In fact, he had a threesome about a year or two ago and—"

"Oh no, Sam. This is different. Much different. Lennox was definitely a bit of a playboy some years back. Besides, it's in his blood. Can't fault him for that—being all beefy, good lookin' and all—but this little chocolate chip spent the night." He burst out laughing and slammed his fist against his desk, giddy as can be. "Bitches never spend the night over Lenny's house, Sam. He gets them the hell out right after he fucks 'em. When he's serious about a lady, he keeps her… lets her stay. I've watched him over the years. I know his patterns when it comes to these things. He even ordered her breakfast… He's been taking her places, too. They look like salt and pepper love birds."

He gripped one photo of Lennox standing at his front door, looking all lovesick as the beauty to his beast left his home. "He's in deep. Got it bad for her." *Got himself some good, juicy, black pussy, I see…* He sneered as he examined Nadia's face. *It can be addictive, Lenny. Best be careful.*

"Well, isn't that interesting. You called her a chocolate chip and mentioned somethin' 'bout salt and pepper. Is she Black?" Sam laughed.

"Can't get nothin' past you, can I? You genius, you." He rolled his eyes. "Yeah, Sam. She's Black. Pretty little thing, too… Nice ass. Nice tits. Gorgeous legs…" He flipped to other zoomed-in photos of her. "Ya see, that's Lennox's weakness, besides his mama. He has a soft spot for women, but especially women that come from the wrong side of the tracks. Just like his daddy. Lennox is captivated by beautiful things, Sam… Just like me. He loves him a pretty filly to have on his arm. He's not quick to fall in love, but when he does, he's done for. He falls hard. He likes 'em rough around the edges, too… and nasty." His tongue jetted out as he squelched the urge to laugh. "This lady seems to be just his type."

"Nasty? What makes her nasty?"

"She's a fucking whore!" he yelled. "A gotdamn stripper and sex worker on that site… what tha fuck is it called? Only Friends?"

"OnlyFans!"

"Whatever! She shakes her ass at some big time Gentleman's Club where the ballers have to pay top dollar to even get in the door. Supposed to be the best of the best. I don't go to strip clubs myself. Haven't been to one in probably over a decade." He cleared his throat and sat taller. "If I'm gonna pay all that damn money, then *somebody* is going to suck and fuck me before I walk outta those doors."

"Hell, yeah!" Sam burst in laughter. "Just a bunch of teasin'."

"She's been a stripper for a while, too. A veteran. Even teaches pole dancin' classes, it appears. She's went national." He laughed. "Can you believe they have awards for this shit? Regardless of her entrepreneurial spirit and good looks, she's a fucking slut. Just like my grandson's mama." A wave of anger rolled against his throat. "I finally found the wild card. Lennox is playing hardball." He tossed down the stack of photos and swayed back and forth in his chair. "From my understanding, he's spoken to an attorney, too. Still tryna verify that."

"Really? I would've thought he'd avoid that sort of

thing, to try 'nd not get his father wrapped up in this."

"You'd think, but obviously he's up to something. See, Sam, that's the thing about your cousin, Lennox." He drummed his fingers against the desk. "People think he's just some gym rat, when in actuality he's exceptionally clever. The boy's looks can be deceiving. He's awfully wily and duplicitous. He's also made appointments with some law folks. I'm not certain who they are, but I don't like what I've been seeing. Now, this could all be for the gym he's tryna open for all I know, but I doubt it. He's making moves. I gotta give it to him." He shook his head and smiled dismally. "I didn't think he'd go that route. I figured he'd try and strongarm me, since he can't buy his way out. He's broke."

"I thought he was middle-class?"

Wilde rolled his eyes. "That's broke to *me*, Sam!"

"…Oh."

"Now I've got some leverage. I've got the girl's name and address, but don't know a lot about her yet. We need to get to diggin' on her, find out her story."

"Okay, got it."

"I want you to go to the club she works at, Sam, and also check out her OnlyFans page. I'll fill you in on the rest of my strategy in a little bit, but first confirm her work schedule."

"Okay, yeah, just send me her info and I'll get right on it."

"If I can't make him move to my side of the field by shaming his mother and her family with the truth, or exposing his crimes from the past, then I'll make him move because of his dick and bleedin' Liberal heart. I may still do all of that, but this thing right here? *This* he'll definitely care about."

"Boss, I have a question."

"Yeah, Sam…"

"I thought, uh, I thought you said you didn't care who any of us dated and married?"

"I don't."

"Well, uh, why is this—"

"Because it's the only way to get what I need! I will fucking destroy him and this woman if Lennox doesn't do what I tell him. Either way, he is gonna move, Sam, gotdamn it, and then, he is going to fall into a hole he can never climb out of! He's been evading me! He's become more emboldened, too! He's gotten influenced by Kage, of all people, and his own father can't get control of him! Lennox was my show pony. He's the calm, level-headed one, but now he's diggin' in his heels and doing strange shit behind the scenes that I can't just yet figure out. Lennox went as far to threaten to rat himself out, beat me to the punch, in order to remove any clout I had in regard to contacting the right folks about all of those murders for hire he has tucked under his belt. He looked me in my eyes and told me this, and I'm a lie detector, boy… He *meant* it.

"That tells you right there that he's committed to fuckin' with me every step of the way, and making this as hard as he can! Now, it's war. It's the principle! THAT MOTHERFUCKER WOULDN'T EVEN EXIST IF IT WEREN'T FOR MY NUTSACK! He's an ungrateful son of a bitch!" His entire face went red hot, and his body felt like an inferno. "Sam, let this be a lesson to you, too. As in the story of Adam of Eve, boy, you know a woman will always bring a man down." He panted, and then exhaled, calming himself. "If it wasn't for his mama, then it had to be a different bitch altogether, right? As the song goes, 'What you won't do, do for love' and Lenny, you've tried everything, but motherfucker, Grandpa Wilde won't give up…"

…Later the next day

NADIA HAD FALLEN asleep while talking to Grandma on the porch. She vaguely recalled the old woman helping her onto her feet and shepherding her inside. When she woke up, she was in the guest room, covered in thick pastel sheets with old fashioned flowers painted on them.

The stuffy room was full of doilies, lace, and fake flowers jammed into plastic vases. A big painting of a White Jesus hung on the wall, and beside that was the Lord's prayer with a torn Dollar General price tag still on the corner of the gold frame. She got up, ate some breakfast, then had some coffee with Nana. Nadia loved visiting her grandmother in the old house that smelled like coffee, fresh linen, spices, and lemon Lysol. Even though she was there under not the best of circumstances, it still felt right. Magical. She always recalled it smelling that way, and that gave her comfort. Made her feel all warm and gushy inside.

When she was there, she felt so safe and at ease. Like she could breathe. The only time she felt the same was when she was with Lennox.

"I'm proud of you." Nana leaned lightly into her, her face tipping towards hers as they sat across from one another on the porch, enjoying the early morning sunlight.

"Thank you, Nana. That means a lot to me. I'm proud of you, too."

"Proud of *me*? What for?" The woman beamed.

"Proud that God chose you to me my grandmama. I couldn't wish for a better one." Nana's complexion deepened. "Here I am sittin' on this porch the morning after bein' at the police station, then here for the rest of the night. What a difference a day makes. I can't do this anymore. This has to stop, Nana. I've had warning after warning, sign after sign. Today was my last day workin' at that club. *Any* club." She sighed. "I've overstayed my welcome."

"You can stay here long as you wish, baby."

"Nana, not here, I mean with my job." She grinned, then gave a light laugh.

"Oh, I see. I heard you on the phone with your new boyfriend this mornin'…" Nana's lips curled in a mischievous grin. "You ain't tell him 'bout last night."

"Not yet. He'll raise the roof." She bit into her lower lip, not looking forward to that conversation. "The past came back to haunt me. The past's name was Lennox." She smiled sadly. "That man knows the best and worst of me. Running into him drudged up a bunch of old memories."

"Good or bad?"

Nadia reached for her coffee. "Most of 'em good. Some of them, not so good." She brought the rim of the cup to her lips. Its heat made her upper lip feel prickly and moist. "He asked all the wrong questions for all the right reasons. He wants me, Nana… He wants me as a friend." Her stomach stirred and butterflies took flight. "He wants me as a lover. As an everything. Said he's gonna make me his wife." She took another taste, then set it down. "He's movin' too fast. At least that's what I tell myself, and yet, at the same time, the pace seems just right."

"I can't have nobody else hurtin' my grandbaby. You believe in your heart of hearts that he's sincere?"

"Yes, ma'am. He's sincere. I can feel it. We love each other." She smiled so hard, it hurt. "When we first started seeing each other, he turned down sex. With *me*. Can you believe that?" Nadia asked sarcastically as she pointed to herself, and they both burst out laughing.

"He must be a keeper then 'cause you know ain't no hot-blooded man gonna turn down no cookies from a pretty girl." Nana slapped her knee. " 'Specially a man that's been pining over you for years."

She loved that she could speak to her Nana about anything and everything. No subjects were off limits, except for JoAnn's Pandora's box.

"So, an old friend opened new doors. That's beautiful, baby. Walk through them then. See what's on the otha side."

"I will. I've got to."

Nana sighed. "So, you're makin' moves. What's the plan for the future, baby girl?"

"Well, I've been reading a lot lately, mostly self-help stuff, and thinking about my life in general. Health, career, everything. Thinkin' about getting a therapist, too. I know our family don't talk about that sort of thing."

"I don't know much 'bout that, baby. We was told to let God carry our burdens, but I 'spose God gives man gifts, too. We're supposed to help one another. Maybe it does some folks some good." Nana shrugged.

"Mama said a therapist don't do nothin' but make you feel worse than you already did fo'e you walked in their door, but then turn around and charge you for fallin' apart in front of them. Said she'd charge me half that price, give me a Coke, and throw in a free pretzel," she scoffed. "Anyway, I even looked at taking online law classes while I work. Now that I'm quitting, I can focus on it full time. I got enough money saved up to last me while I do this. Should be able to pay for it, too. Maybe that was God's plan all along, you know? For me to learn some things, go some places... then try again. I guess I'll find out soon enough."

Nana's eyes lit up like bright stars. "Oh, Nadia!" She brought her hands together and rocked back and forth. "My prayers have been answered. All I wanted you to do was try 'nd get back into your schooling, 'cause it was so important to you. You were doin' so well, too. I told you back then and I'm tellin' you now, you'd be a great lawyer." Nana's eyes narrowed as she drew serious. "You're so smart. Just like your mama."

"I miss school, Nana. I finally admitted it to myself. I love learning, and I would enjoy trying to get back into the swing of things."

"What type of law was you goin' into again, honey? I

can't remember."

"I was focused on family law. That's what I'm plannin' to return to. I know I learn fast… and… and I have a good memory. I test well. I always did well in school, actually, ever since I was a little kid." She ran her thumb along her palm, warming the flesh to an unnatural heat. "I just feel so old to be starting over." She hung her head, feeling some type of way. "But I'm also too young to stay put. I've been praying lately, too. Ain't prayed in a long while. I got my answer last night."

"You're doing some spiritual traveling, huh? Only you don't have as much baggage as ya Mama. Your load is easier to carry."

…And there it was. The first rock unturned. Nana reached for her coffee, the one with extra cream and too much sugar, gripping the black mug tight, and mustered a shaky gulp. She'd inadvertently shined a flashlight on the dark mystery of all that was Mama. Or maybe it wasn't inadvertent at all? Now, the theater curtains were opening.

They were quiet for a spell, letting the silence do the talking.

"…Did I ever tell you about the time I almost died?"

"No. I would've remembered a story like that." Nadia leaned back and got comfortable. She could see in Nana's eyes that she was going to gift her; with the truth.

"My first husband was the hot-tailed devil walkin'!" Nana's face balled up like a brown paper bag wrapped around a liter of whiskey. "He wanted to keep me pregnant, but I kept miscarrying. See, back then, big families were more common. Less birth control 'nd such. If I stayed pregnant, it would be harder for me to get away from him. He never said those words, but I understood the situation just the same." Nana's eyes glossed over with an emotion that Nadia couldn't read. "Besides, I wouldn't be able to afford to leave him, not with children up under me. By the time I was eighteen, I had three of 'em already. I love all of my children, but I wasn't ready to be no mother, Nadia. Back then, we'd dabble with different concoctions for this or that, including home remedies to get rid of a baby we didn't want to bring into this world." Nana fretted with that same thread that hung from her robe again, her gaze averted. The breeze picked up, blowing curly bits of her hair around that weren't bobby-pinned in place.

"It worked? The home remedies?"

"…Sometimes. Made you sick as a dog, but you had to catch the pregnancy early for it to have a chance. In the first three or four weeks was best. That wasn't always easy to do. After that, it was far more difficult. Risky. Well, one day, I came home after havin' one of the ladies that did such work take care of me, and—"

"How'd they do it? The women that would help with things like that?"

Nana's eyes hooded and her complexion drew ashen. "All sorts of ways women tried. Teas. Oils. Those were not always successful. I wanted a sure thing this particular time around. I went to Ms. Claudette who'd vacuum you out… the uterus." Nadia nodded in understanding, keeping a straight face, though her heart broke deep on the inside. "She was an old woman. In her nineties, I believe. She was from Sunnyside.

"She'd been a nurse. I'd had it done a couple times by her. It had worked. She wasn't free, though. I would have to steal the money usually. Couldn't wait too long by workin' an odd job and savin'. She charged twenty dollars. That was a lotta money back then. I'd take a lil' bit here and there outta your granddaddy's wallet, but not enough for him to notice. It still was never enough. I'd make up for the rest by stealin' tips off restaurant tables... things like that. On the third time I needed her, something didn't go right."

"What happened?"

"She did her usual thing, but afterwards, I was havin' troubles. I was bleedin' a lot. I went on home with some herb medicine, and pads she gave me. She tol' me it would be the last time 'cause my body couldn't take it no more. I went home and blacked out. Well, that man found me on the kitchen floor."

"Shit."

"Right! Took me to the doctor right away. Doctor say, 'She was pregnant and miscarried.' That devil got me home, put me in the bed, and gave me the medicine the doctor gave me to stop the bleeding. I could see in his eyes he *knew* what I'd done... He ain't say one word. He sat down 'side me for a long while, even held my hand. Then, soon as I second guessed myself and got ready to fall asleep, he stood tall like an oak tree. He looked down at me, balled his fist real tight... weak as I was. Hate brimmed in his eyes. I couldn't move. Scream. Say nothin'. He swung his arm back," Nana imitated the gesture she described, her eyes wide and dark, as if she were reliving the nightmare, "and he punched and slapped me so hard that I passed clean out.

When I came to, I realized he'd beat me up some more, and had his way with me."

Nadia's stomach dropped, and she felt her lunch repeating. The juice from breakfast. The coffee, too. The sunshine from that morning. The night stars from last night. The bird that had been chirping, before it was just a swallowed memory. Everything repeated and burned her throat, heart and soul. She pushed herself to the back of the swing and squeezed her eyes shut so hard, it hurt.

"Nana…" She finally built the nerve to speak.

"I know, baby. I know… But you need this. The truth. So, I'll tell you." Nana blinked back tears. "I looked at myself the next morning and saw he'd beaten me black and blue from the neck down to my thighs. I ain't recall none of it, 'cept for that first punch and slap. I told you a long time ago that I only married Lawrence to get out of my mama's house, away from her and my uncle. She ain't want me in there no way because her husband was making passes at me, and she blamed ME for it. 'Member? My daddy was dead soon after I was born. This was her *new* man. Frank."

"Yes… I remember." Nadia's soul was filling with rage.

"I had to get away from this man, baby, but I ain't have no money and nowhere to go. Not with all three of my babies. I didn't have Dee Dee and Percy 'til later when I married Princeton. Anyway, it was just me, JoAnn, Tina, and Larry Jr. After a few weeks, I went to my mama, asked her if I could stay wit' her. I told her what had happened. She said no, just like I figured she would." Nana crossed her arms and sucked her teeth. "Said that Frank don't want a bunch of kids in his house. That wuddn't none of Frank's house. He ain't lay one brick, or pay one mortgage statement. That was my daddy's house! His blood, sweat 'nd tears got that place. Not Frank.

"Anyway, I told her that if I ended up dead, it would be her fault. She pushed me out into the world, and the world swallowed me up. I told her she could write that in my obituary, too. I ain't say nothin' else, Nadia. I turned to walk away, leave from that house and never return, and she called out to me. She left outta that room and returned with a gun. She placed it in my hand. Squeezed my fingers around it. She ain't say nothing else, nor did I. We understood one another just fine.

"For the next two months, I managed to save up 'bout fifty dollars ironing people's clothes, scrubbing floors, making soap and sellin' it, doing hair, anything I could. I would give your demon of a grandfather half the money, and he thought that was all, but I kept the rest. He ain't never want me working, but he allowed this 'cause he could use it to go gamble or whatever it was he was doing after work that didn't involve a bottle. I packed up a few things, set 'em aside, and was planning to get me a one room place to rent. It was all I could afford. As long as it had a sink with running water, a hot plate, and some place clean for my babies and me to lay our head, it would be okay.

"I already had talked to the landlord and everything. I was allowed to stay there for six months until I could get on my feet, as long as I paid the rent on time and kept my children quiet."

"How were you able to pay the rent?"

"I made dresses and clothing for children outta scraps

of cloth." Nadia smiled at that. "I was good at it, too. And odd jobs. That way, most of the time I could stay wit' my babies. I always paid rent first and saved a dollar here and there so we could get an apartment later on. The landlord of the room for rent was an old Catholic man. I can still remember his voice and see his face." Nana smiled sadly. "Mr. Sullivan was a widower. He ain't even like Black folk according to the neighbors, and I heard him curse, spit and let that 'nigger' word slip out towards other folks quite often, but he had a soft spot for me for some reason. Even gave me free butter, cookies for the babies, and day-old loaves of bread on occasion, and he ain't ask for no cookies and milk in return, either.

"Just the rent paid on time, and peace and quiet is what he wanted. I imagine racism for him was a complicated idea. For some reason, he didn't see me as no nigger. I guess some racist White folks can do that inside their heads. Think, this Black gal right here a nigga, but that Black gal over there, ain't. Anyway, I got everything just so to move into this place, and your grandfather wasn't due home for a long while. I called a cab. Borrowed money from a neighbor for it. And me and the kids, with our bags, a little baby in tow, made our way out the do'e and to the car waiting for us. That devil pulled up to tha house, tires screechin'! I ain't tell nobody I was leaving him, so I don't know to this day how he found out.

"Anyway, he jumped in my face like a toad on a pogo stick, and swung his arm back again to slap me. Nadia, everything inside of me exploded. It was like an out of body experience. I pulled out that gun my mama gave me and pointed it at his face. Pushed it right into his big nose. I said, 'I'll shoot yo' ass dead as a doornail and send you to meet yo' maker, you nasty, greasy mothafucka!' And I meant that shit, too."

Nadia stifled a gasp and fought a bit of mirth, too. She seldom heard Nana curse, but it was evident as the old woman relayed the story, she was knee deep in a flashback. PTSD at its finest.

"I was ready to shoot that pistol, Nadia, and I wanted *any* excuse he gave me to do just *that*. If he'd even breathed wrong, his face was gonna be on the ground in a thousand bloody pieces. That monster stepped tha hell outta my way, I promise you that! He was cussin', tellin' me I was stupid, that I'd be begging him to take me back, and that I couldn't take care of no three kids by myself no how. On and on he went. I ignored him, got me and my babies in that cab, and I ain't look back. Next time I saw him was in court for the divorce. I tol' that judge, a big ol' White man, everything that yo' grandfather done to me. That big White man with big ol' jowls, and little thin bird lips, wearin' that black robe looked over at yo' grandfather and told him he deserved to die, but the law wouldn't let him do it. Granted me my divorce on the spot."

The coffee was gone. Her throat was dry, her mind whirling. Nadia got to her feet, grabbed both of their mugs, and entered the house. She refilled them with more fresh coffee and returned to her grandmother, only to find her looking towards the tree where the chirping bird had been earlier that morning. Last night, she didn't see the bird but knew it was there, sleeping in the nest in the darkness. The tree in the sun looked alive, fresh and vibrant. Last night, it was a big, tall thing in shades of black.

All birds have to eventually grow up, fly towards the sky, and find their own way, even if it's in the dark of night...

"Don't be so hard on my JoAnn," Nana mumbled, her eyes still on the sparrow that once was... "She come from a mean ol' father who hated her, too. He ain't want no girls. I gave him two of 'em." She chuckled. "I was young, didn't know what I was doing. I made mistakes," Nana said in a low voice, her eyes sheening over. "Your mother had a hard life. No support or relationship with her biological father. We barely saw him. That was for the best, but it still hurt her so. She wanted to make everyone happy, but couldn't. Now, here's something else. Don't you ever repeat this." Her eyes grew right serious.

"I won't, Nana, I promise."

"My baby never admitted it to me, but I think one of the delivery men touched 'er when she was 'bout eleven or twelve. I asked her over and over about it. She said no."

"What made you suspect it in the first place?"

"'Cause other girls in the building was getting hurt by him. She started acting different, out of the blue. That delivery man disappeared all of a sudden after word was getting around about him messin' with little girls. I remarried. My second husband wasn't too keen on JoAnn 'cause your mama spoke her mind, even as a child. She didn't like or dislike her stepdaddy, though. I think Princeton felt the same about her. They just tolerated one another. Eventually, she grew up, met your father and fell in love. Then she found out he already had an old lady." Nana shook her head.

"That about broke her in two because she was pregnant, and had no clue she'd been gallivanting with a married man." *I thought mama said she found out after they were divorced?* "Ya mama told me she felt stupid. She hated that more than anything in this world… feeling like someone had pulled the wool over her eyes. As you know, your father's first wife left him after she found out your mama was in a family way. *Mama definitely didn't tell the story that way when I was little…She must've been embarrassed for me to know the truth. Maybe she thought I was too young to understand?*

"Yeah, she never talks about it much."

"So, the two of them got married when that was all settled. He seemed right apologetic and convinced me and her that his marriage had been over a while back—it just wasn't official. Well, wasn't long after they exchanged vows that she found out he was cheating. That about sent her over the edge. After that, I saw her change yet again, Nadia. I asked her about her feelings, and she wouldn't talk." Nana sighed. "Your mama was never the same afterward. That was it. I never heard her speak of no man again. Obviously she'd entertained them a time or two 'cause your brother came on down the pike." They both laughed at that. "But I imagine that was a one-off situation."

"Nelson was an oops baby." Nadia smiled sadly. "At least that is what he calls himself. He acts fine about it, you know, and Nelson's life is good, but I think deep down it disturbs him that he doesn't know who his father is. Mama tried to fill in the gap. All she said was that his father went away and she couldn't find him. We both believed her. I imagine she'd let him if he wanted to be active in his life."

"Baby, I believe yo' mama, too. JoAnn is many things, but she never lied a lot. Everyone tells a tale now and again, but I can't say my child was big on makin' up stories. Nelson may have been an oops baby, but she loves him just the same." Nana blinked slowly and sipped her coffee, her gaze fixed on that tree.

So that's how JoAnn became JoAnn... She moved in silence. Her feelings stayed close to her heart, after it was broken. First, by a father who was using her existence to enslave a whole living soul: Nana. That's the curse. Souls trapped by pain. And rain.

That's the kiss of spiritual death. It's not the fists that land on your gut. The open hand that cracks you across the face. It's not the curse words, and damnations. It's not the emotional and psychological abuse within itself that tears you completely down. It's not the retraction of love. It's the fear of becoming a victim once again, of losing yourself. Fear of trusting someone who then turns around and stomps on your innocence. Perhaps it was a grinning delivery man who offered you a cherry lollipop in the hallway of your apartment building, then slipped his dirty, calloused hand up your skirt and made you promise not to tell? Maybe it was the father who never wrapped his arms around you, unless it was to subdue you for a spanking that was more for his own needs than yours?

The family curse is a venomous beverage. It's a jinx drink, a dark spell punch, a strong, bright red brew spiked from the juices of foul fruit and fermenting fear. Many are forced to drink it, and it burns on the way down. It's served like communion, with a death wish and a half-hearted prayer representing the body of Christ.

The curse falls upon those that are not watered in the garden, their dry roots twisting around them, strangling who they were truly meant to be, and who God intended them to become. The curse blocks blessings. The curse is knowing that you're in pain, but pretending you are not. The curse is pride and prejudice. The curse is staying in a bad situation because it's all you've known, or you're afraid to be alone, with your angels and your demons. The curse is saying yes, when the correct answer is no. The curse is getting in bed with old scars, picking at them to make them bleed all over you once again, and bathing in the blood of the past. Never allowing yourself to move on, grow, and heal for the future. The curse is covering emotional ache with acts of physical violence.

It's lashing out at an invisible demon that won't turn you loose. The curse is hiding behind toned, glitter-covered limbs and painted mouths under the electrifying glare of seductive, spinning lights, obscured behind a fortress of lust, so that the saving grace of love won't find you...

The curse is a liar and a thief, masquerading as a truth-teller and a giver to the world. The curse is created from our own unjustified hatred of ourselves and others who resemble our suffering and failures. The curse thrives on torment and anguish. The curse is not the blood that flows from between a woman's legs, but that which flows from that woman's heart. Because the heart is open and free, until the first trauma erupts. It's a venomous vine that pushes out of thick concrete and destroys all hope in its wake. It creates desperation and a skewed reality, and yet, it is protected by its victims at all costs, even while we watch it sink all of our hopes and dreams like quicksand…

The curse is a disease of the soul. Shame of it all, is that we don't even know that deep inside of us, we've always had the cure…

Perhaps the bird in the tree wouldn't mind your malodorous fungus, dented sides, and putrid, sweet flesh as you rot from the inside out, filling the air? Maybe she'd serve worms from your decaying soil to her babies after all, and then you dying within won't be in vain? Or maybe you'll sip orange juice at night with your Nana, or coffee in the morning time, and smile inside and out because you've looked the curse in the eye, refused to drink another drop of that fucking Kool-Aid it serves and finally stood up to it and said, "WE ARE DONE. NO MORE. I WON'T DRINK FROM YOU, EAT FROM YOU, TAKE FROM YOU, OR GIVE TO YOU. I AM TAKING MY LIFE BACK…YOU ARE DISMISSED!"

CHAPTER TWENTY

A Big Shot with a Smoking Gun

THE AIR CLUNG to the thick odor of gun smoke as Young Guy's, 'Take Heed' pumped through the speakers of Lennox's parked truck. He stood in an abandoned Tom Thumb grocery store parking lot at 10:07 P.M., in the zone. Loading his TISAS 1911 Night Stalker Double Stack 9mm SF, he emptied the clip, turning one of the target silhouettes he'd set up into shreds.

He slowed down as he heard a car approaching. The music from the vehicle blended with his 'Take Heed', creating a strange mixed melody with 'All There,' by Jezzy, featuring Bankroll Fresh. Taking his keys out of his pocket, he turned his truck off remotely. At about the same time, Jezzy's song cut off abruptly, too, ending the impromptu amalgamation of the two tunes.

Nadia's car door slammed then she marched towards him wearing heels that clicked against the cement, sounding much like heavy raindrops smacking the hard gray surface.

His gun boomed as he shot the target once again. Now the woman of his prayers stood beside him, though he didn't look directly at her. Out of the corner of his eye, he could see her jostle her hands into the pockets of a shimmery red Starter jacket.

"Two inches above the ear." He held up his gun, aimed, then fired, shooting directly in the area he'd declared. "So, let me get right into it, baby. I called you out here to have a discussion. We both have to be at work soon, and it won't take long. Just listen."

She cleared her throat, crossed her arms, and stared straight ahead at his target.

"I've killed many men." Sucking his teeth, he reached for the bandana in his jeans pocket and swiped it across his forehead to collect his sweat. "Most were for hire." He shoved the blue and white scarf back where it came from. "I told you about this, but I want to elaborate a little bit. For starters, I needed the money. The pay was good, but I was also angry. We had that in common." She nodded in agreement. "I felt like killin' somethin' would make me feel more alive. It didn't. I don't enjoy killing people. In fact, I hated it, though I do understand that sometimes certain ones have to be wiped from the face of the earth." He sighed. "I just always hope that I'm not ever put in a position again to be the one to have to do that. Play God, basically.

"Life and death coexist. They rely on one another. So, even though most of my activities, I'll say," he laughed dismally, "were for resources, there is an incident that doesn't match this. I killed one man for playin' in my face."

He shot at another target, this time landing the bullet right in the center of the chest. "My heart is not that of a killer, but when you come from my kind of family, and you live the life I've lived, it changes you. I've worked very hard to get away from that—to be a better person. I used to run from my past. Now, I accept it for what it is. Usually, I can resist any urge to take someone outta here that I believe is so evil, they need it. Some days though, it's a struggle."

All of us cousins have killed, actually, but that's a different story for a different day.

Nadia coughed into the palm of her hand, but kept her eye on the target as he held up his gun once again. "Chin." He shot and nailed the chin dead on. "Nadia, baby, listen. These are things I'm not proud of, and even though I've already discussed this with you, I wanted you to understand my mindset at the time, and why it happened in the first place."

"Can I say something?"

He brought his arm down, resting the gun at his side.

"Yeah. What is it?"

"You told me why it happened. Actually, you explained yourself very well when you first confessed your sins, so to speak, to me. I think maybe you don't trust my reaction… because I didn't run for the hills and tell someone. I didn't freak out. I know you've never admitted this to anyone before. Not to anyone you've dated anyway—but your secrets are safe with me."

She reached for him and gently rested her fingers along his wrist. "I've been 'round killas my whole life, Lennox. Thieves. Liars. Rapists. The way you see me responding to you is how I am. It's my authentic self. You have nothing to worry about. I am not gonna act differently and you explaining yourself for your past conduct is even more unnecessary. I already accept you for who you are, and know by nature that you're not a violent person. You have to be pushed to it."

"Baby, I don't think you understand what I'm saying. I get that, but I don't expect you to act any differently than you normally would around me. That's not what I'm thinking or saying. I don't expect you to spill your guts in return, if you don't want to, either, but I *do* expect honesty when I ask you a direct question, and you should expect the same from me. I don't play about my family, Nadia. My father is a fucking coward, but I love him." He bent down, reached for his water bottle, and took a big gulp. "My sister is a traitor, but I understand her situation, and I love her and would die for her if I have to. My cousins that are in the same boat as me, I'd take a bullet for each of 'em, too.

"With me it's about loyalty, but in the name of fairness and love. It's about justice and standing up for what's right. My cousins and I've been talkin'. Strategizing. Planning. I have a plan, and I'm going to talk to you about that tonight, too. In fact, it's already in the works. There are certain people my grandfather doesn't want any smoke from. He ain't scared of nobody, but he has too many enemies. He wouldn't expect me to tap into that, but this is exactly what I'm going to do because he doesn't play fair, so neither can I. There's too much at stake. My grandfather is about as evil a person as you can come across. The reason being is because he is charming.

"He can sell oil to a greaseball, and he can lie with a straight face. He's Satan's henchman. He's also fucking insane, brazen, and brilliant. One of the smartest men I know. Therefore, I know goin' in that whatever I do he's already considered it, but it's the *way* I do it that counts. We're playin' Chess, not Checkers. In order to fool the Devil and survive his games, you have to be taught by God. There has to be divine intervention. See, the Devil is a narcissist. Anyone he can habitually control is usually a narcissist, too. My grandfather is a supreme narcissist. The scary part is that unlike most narcs, he is keenly aware of it. That's a weakness, and it must be exploited if you want to outlast him in this mental endurance race."

"You seem to know him well. Like, deep inside of his mind."

"Well, it's not because anyone told me about this aspect of him, per se." He shrugged. "I've always had a kinda of sixth sense about people… like, not psychic or nothin' like that, but I can feel when people mean me no fuckin' good, or they've got a bad vibe. It's helped keep me alive. I can pick up on who is a snake. Who is a wolf. Who is a lamb. And who is a dog. That's funny, actually." He chuckled.

"What's funny?" The woman's eyes warmed as her lips bowed.

"I told you a while ago that my nickname from my grandfather is 'Top Dog.' He named all seven of us, the ones who went AWOL, after animals. He wants some of us to work in his faction of the company that he calls 'the Zoo'."

"The Zoo?"

"Yeah. It's where the baddest of the bad roam within his organization. Want someone killed? He goes to the zoo. Want someone shaken down or blackmailed? He goes to the zoo. Need to collect a debt with two hundred percent interest? He goes to the zoo. Need someone knocked off? He goes to the zoo. His security team. His muscle. The guys who do the dirty work and have no qualms about it."

"Ohhh, okay. I get it now."

"I will say this… My grandfather can read people very well, Nadia, even as children. It's a sick talent of his. I must've gotten it from him."

"Maybe you did because this Zoo group of his seems well planned and calculated. A little scary, too."

"Yup. He's already got a few of my uncles in it. A few cousins, too. Anyway, here's what's interesting about this. My grandfather, believe it or not, in his twisted mind, is actually quite religious."

"I believe it." She rolled her eyes. "The holy rollers are sometimes the main ones out here causin' havoc."

"Yeah, sometimes that's true. That's not a true Christian though. That's cosplay. Anyway, he, uh, he has inadvertently told us what he sees as our weaknesses and strengths through these nicknames." He raised his gun. "You pick the target."

" …In the dick."

He turned towards her and they locked eyes. He met her twisted smirk. Turning to his task, he shot the crotch of the target, then paused to reload—after which, he handed her his gun.

"Now, your turn. Left hand."

She held up the gun and aimed. The left hand of the target smoked after she'd blasted it away with one clean shot. She attempted to hand him the gun back, but he pushed it back towards her. Opening a bin, he pulled out another gun, a 12 gauge.

"Ever shot one of these?" he asked.

"Yup."

He handed it to her. "This'll be tricky, Nadia. You claimed to be able to shoot with both hands, right?"

"I can. So what?"

"That's not common. Most people have a dominant hand. Are you ambidextrous?"

"Not really, but I can shoot well with both hands for some reason. It came to me naturally."

"Interesting. Can you shoot with only one hand?"

"It depends on the gun."

"Let me see you do it."

"Fine."

"Okay, you've got two different guns there in your possession." He took a step back and wiggled his finger at her. "Different pros and cons to each. One is significantly longer than the other, making this even more difficult. What's your target?"

"You name it."

"Are you going to try 'nd shoot one after the other, or simultaneously?"

She stood there for a moment, mulling his question. "Considering the size difference, let me do one after the other."

"Let's time it. How many seconds do you need between

the switch?"

"Two seconds max."

"Only two? Oh, you wanna show off, I guess." He grinned. "Right upper thigh. Right temple. 3… 2…1. Go!"

She held both arms up in a bit of an awkward pose, but he was trusting the process. The seconds warred on like dripping paint. Slow and easy. Rhythmic heartbeats against a desolate night. The air rent with shots as she took fire, barely a moment between both shots.

"…Well, shit." He beamed in approval. "Got me a good ol' Annie Oakley. That's the right middle portion of the thigh versus the upper thigh, but it's definitely the right temple." He pointed at the target. "I imagine if both guns were similarly made, the thigh shot would have been more exact. Cleaner. You were rushing, but it's close enough. I love that for you."

She laughed lightly and handed him back both guns, one at a time.

He placed them down onto a blanket he had sprawled out, then faced her. They stood before one another, gun smoke swirling all around them. The air was thick with lust, resentment, admissions and smolder.

"Thank you for tellin' me about the guy following you home." He grabbed her around her waist and brought her flush against his erection. "I know that wasn't easy for you to do." She nodded. "…Because we have a history, and you know how I am… and you know he's thankful to be alive right now because I saw him, Nadia." He felt her tighten in his grip. "I paid him a little visit, and followed him. I wanted to shoot his brains out. In fact, I stood there with my gun in my holster. I took it out. Aimed at the back of his fuckin' head. But then, I turned around and let him be. It wasn't easy. It took all of me to turn around and go home. God's not through with me yet."

They stared one another down, both quiet for a while…

"You know I'm not new to this. I will set the world on fire just to keep you warm. You remember what happened."

She rested her face against his, and nodded.

Many years ago there was a man who walked into The Red Rooster in the wee hours of the morning. They weren't open yet, and wouldn't be for at least another two hours. Instead of turning the poor soul away, Lennox let him inside and went to the back to get some supplies. Nadia was nice and offered him some coffee on the house, to help him sober up. He was drunk out of his mind, yet lucid enough to have a fairly coherent conversation.

The man sat down on a stool at the breakfast bar. He began laughing loudly—he could hear him from the back. He could also hear Nadia pouring the coffee—the comforting sound of the brew being delivered to a clean mug for one's enjoyment and aid.

Then, he heard the sound of something crashing.

Lennox came out from the back with several cartons of eggs, and set them down. Coffee was everywhere. "This bitch don't know how to make coffee! The shit was too hot! It burnt my lip!" the man spat.

"Don't call the young lady out of her name, okay? I know you're drunk, but you know better. She was just tryna help. Coffee making isn't really her expertise."

"Not her expertise? She's the same color as it!" the guy guffawed. "Nigger black! I ain't even ask for no cream or nuttin'."

Lennox let the first insult go with a warning. The second one? There was no cautionary communication to be had…

The man ended up with half of his damn teeth knocked out of his mouth with one fist to the kisser, and soon became an unconscious, bloody mess as he pummeled him nearly to death. Nadia screamed for him to stop but Lennox kept bashing the fucker in front of her to the point that he was unrecognizable. Just a bloody heap of blood, tissue, flesh and broken bones. It was a vicious, nasty, fast, horrific assault, and Lennox enjoyed every second of it…

And then, without even asking, she helped him drag the bastard's body out the back of the restaurant, put him in the trunk of his car, and drive him deep into the woods. Nadia splashed water on the fucker to make him wake up from his dark slumber, more than likely to ensure he was still alive. They left him there with his wallet full, and his ego bruised and beaten, just like his face and body. Lennox drove them back to the restaurant just in time to clean up the mess, put on a fresh pot of coffee, and turn the sign on the door to 'Open'.

Another secret. Another bond. Another ugly moment in time: formed from terror, solved by love. They'd never spoken of it since it happened. It was a quiet understanding. An oath of silence. He was her friend, and he was in love with her… but, she didn't know it, and he refused to cross that line. Now, the line was so far crossed, they were running a marathon, side by side.

He gathered her in his arms. The fabric of her jacket rubbed against his palms as he pressed his lips to hers.

"My grandfather knows about you."

She pulled back, cocked her head to the side, and a darkness came over her eyes. "How?"

"I just know. There's been strange cars drivin' past my house... strange men poppin' up at the club. The gym. They're only there for a second—I make eye contact with 'em, and then they're gone. I'm sure they've seen us together."

"So... what are we going to do?"

"My grandfather has these rules, I guess you could say. He never breaks them. One of 'em is that he doesn't bother our wives or girlfriends unless they interfere with his business. He may threaten to, but he's never actually hurt anyone's wife to my knowledge. No physical violence against women. Take my mother, for instance. He never liked her, but he stayed out of her way until she told my father to stop workin' for him. So, one thing I know for certain is that he's not gonna try and get you killed or anything like that, but he may try to make your life miserable to the point that you won't want to be bothered with me anymore."

"That's crazy."

"Crazy and sly as a fox. Or, he may think he can dangle some cash in front of ya and you'll vanish." He shrugged. "It'll be a punishment to me, basically. A way to prove that he can take anything and anyone I love away from me, and he'll keep doing it if I don't fall in line. I want to tell you, right here, right now, that I love you enough to understand that you may walk away because of this."

"Lennox, no! I—"

"And that would be your right, okay? Nobody in their right fucking mind would want to be dealin' with something like this." His heart quickened as he looked into her beautiful, worried eyes. "You owe me nothin' but your love and honesty, Nadia. Your loyalty is to this relationship, not to you being in the crossfire no matter what. I would never jeopardize your safety, all because I want you so badly."

Her lips curled in a pretty, sassy way. "...And who the fuck said I was in my right mind?" He dropped his head and smiled at that. "You know a little toxicity turns me on. I'm unbalanced. Disturbed. Hurt. But healing." He slowly lifted his gaze to hers. Reached out and stroked her soft cheek. Her makeup was all done, and her hair hot-combed and sleek. "So, tonight is your last night dancin'?"

"Mmm hmm. Quit Only Fans last week. I was going to turn my stuff in, but I want to do this right. Have some integrity about the situation and give a proper sendoff. I want to say goodbye to a couple ladies who were good to me, give my favorite security guard, Shack, a hug, and give one last dance for a few good customers who come there just to see me, too." He nodded in understanding. "Lydia is there, too...you know, the girl I told you I was helping. I have to say farewell to her. Once that is all behind me, everything starts new. My first class is in two days." He loved the excitement in her eyes. How giddy she sounded. "And the student advisor said that most of my credits will still transfer over, so I'm not starting from scratch."

"I've told you a million times, and I'm gonna keep telling you. I'm so proud of you, baby."

"Yeah, it's going to be hard because I'm tryna do the

accelerated program, and I haven't been to school in so long, I'm rusty, and I—"

"You can do this. Stop thinking about how hard it's going to be. If anybody can handle this, it's you, Nadia." He pointed at her.

Her complexion deepened, and her eyes sheened over. "Thank you."

"What are you thankin' me for? I should be thanking you for giving me a chance and rollin' with the bullshit that I call my life. This shit isn't for the weak."

"No, no." She shook her head. "Thank you is definitely in order. Thank you, Lennox, for letting me cry on your shoulder about troubles with my mama, my daddy when he was alive, and just… my everything. Thank you for making me laugh back then, and now. Thank you for forgiving me when I moved away and didn't contact you anymore. Thank you for being my friend, *before* you were my lover."

He swallowed hard. His heart swelled deep inside.

"Thank you for always being there for me even when I wasn't there for myself," she continued, toying with her cuticles. "You'd show up when my heart didn't even make an appearance. Sometimes I probably didn't even indicate any gratitude because I was just expecting you to wipe my tears with no questions asked. I got spoiled by how well you treated me. That was selfish, but I still had the mind of a child back then. Pardon me for that. I," her voice cracked, "I *always* loved you, boy… I always thought you were what a man 'sposed to be.'"

"I know you loved me. Somewhere deep inside of me, I knew, and that's what kept me wanting to be there for you.

You taught me a lot of things. How to laugh at myself. Be more open-minded. You were more mature than you gave yourself credit for. Wise beyond your years. You were just a little lost and hurtin'. You taught me how to even want to love, even when that love isn't returned. You taught me how to look beyond my circumstances, and believe I could start my own life, with or without the support of others."

"Well, thank you for tellin' me that. Glad to hear I was of some assistance to you, too." She smiled sadly. "I had nobody in my life to show me how a man is supposed to treat a lady. But... I did have you. I had so many excuses and reasons why I didn't follow my heart with you, but sometimes, every blue moon or so, I used to wonder if would have followed my heart back then, could I have avoided that car accident, and then avoided that rain? I know the answer to that now. Rain waters us, don't it? It makes us stronger. We are gardens that need to be irrigated, and without the rain, we can't appreciate the sun.

"I know deep down I would have had to have gone through all of that misery to *truly* appreciate and understand you, Len. I wasn't ready back then, nor were you. You were still too broken, but you were trying to start over and mend. Now, just like you said, we *know* that we're broken, and that's the first step. Broken crayons can still color. You're much further along than me in your healing journey, but at this point we can pick up the damaged pieces together and help each other along the way."

She leaned in and kissed him. He fell deep into her oral embrace.

Once he'd gotten his fill, he broke her romantic spell

over him and stepped back to size her up. Then, without a warning, he grabbed her wrist and dragged her towards his truck. The woman screamed and twisted, unable to break free and demanding to know what he was doing. His hard dick practically broke through his jeans, standing at attention and chomping at the bit. He opened the passenger's side of his vehicle with the fob and forced her in the back. She screamed, laughed and yelled as he shoved her on her back and slammed the door behind them. Breathing hard and with dire need, he pressed himself onto her warm, soft body, trapping her in place, and claimed her mouth.

He sensed the thrill of her arousal as he pawed at her clothing with one hand, undoing buttons and zippers and snaps along the way. She writhed beneath him as he kneed her legs apart, resting comfortably between them. He tossed her bra and shirt aside, and the pants flew somewhere onto the front seat. When he'd stripped her down to her panties, his eyes pierced hers.

All he could hear was their breathing, and all he could feel was her heart racing beneath him. He delivered a tender kiss to sweet lips as he pushed her panties to the side. Undoing his pants, he dragged them down to right below his ass, freeing his hungry, thick, long beast. He grasped the base, and as she moaned and sighed, he dragged his dick up and down her pussy until he could feel the warm wetness he so craved.

The piercing pain of her long nails digging into his shoulders only encouraged him as he pushed deep inside of her, her wails and whimpers of pleasure echoing all around them. He pivoted in and out of her, drawing himself out in long strokes, and returning with power and need. He nestled his mouth against the crook of her neck, gyrating and rocking faster. Her cries of delight shattered him in the most beautiful ways. His whole being flooded with desire as he rode her both easy and hard, her face a canvas of ecstasy and delight as she moaned his name.

She dragged her hand along his arm, sending tingles up his spine. He rose ever so slightly, just enough to consume one of her taut, dark chocolate nipples. He moaned as he nursed from her, loving the feel of her soft, beautiful titties in his mouth. The warmth of her soft flesh all around him was intoxicating, and her even softer walls grasped his dick, squeezing and choking it as his thrusts increased and deepened. He ran an unsteady hand through her hair, brushing it back from her face, forcing her to look up at him as he made love to her.

"Look at me..."

She blinked hard, as if struggling to focus.

"I want you to stay in the moment. Don't float away from me." He gripped her chin hard, making her face him. "Memorize how I feel deep inside of your pussy, baby." Her pussy pulsed against him as he articulated the words. He slowed, bringing her leg up and resting her foot against his shoulder. He started up again, pivoting inside of her, watching his dick, slick with her juices, disappearing inside of her and then reappearing coated in her nectar. Slowly pulling out of her, he dipped low, slicking his tongue along her clit. She sighed and twitched as he ate her pussy for a short while before resurfacing and placing her warm thighs around his waist.

She shivered, the uncontrolled trembles of sensual awakening transcending... exploding into a full body orgasm as he held her tight. Her lips were agape and a faraway look shone in her dark eyes. He fell back on top of her, shoving himself in and out of her at a feverish speed. The truck rocked from side to side as he lost control—his need for her so strong, his heart felt as if it may burst. He could feel the heat of her body course down the full span of his. Their limbs were slick with sweat, mouths and chests dotted with saliva, his dick glazed with her pussy liquor and her pelvis and pubic hairs moist from his glistening drops of his precum. A wet orchestra of human delight and nasty nature.

Groaning and choppy moans crashed and overlapped as they ravished one another.

He ran his hand along her clitoris as he fucked her, the side of his thumb an instrument for pure satisfaction, building her up into a passionate frenzy. Fashioning his arm and hand around her head, he cradled her crown while plunging within her dripping wet, sweet, sugar walls. She cried out and clawed at his flesh as he fucked her so good, he could barely catch his breath. She wrapped her thighs around his waist, crisscrossing her legs and ankles against the small of his back.

"I want to feel your warm cum all up in my pussy, baby!"

"You feel so damn good, girl. You drive me crazy!" His body ached for hers, and he'd been thinking about fucking her all day. He grunted as he neared detonation, chasing a high that was right on the horizon. "I'm about to cum!

Ahhhh! Uhhh!"

Reaching beneath her, he squeezed her soft, ample ass with both hands, forcing her body into his wild lunges. His hips jerked and propelled back and forth like a pendulum as he released his torrent of pearls, delivering his copious seed deep inside of her.

She stroked the back of his head as he slowed, a strong desire to snooze beginning to take over. Fighting the urge to fall asleep, he rose from her beautiful body. He looked down at her, watching as a thin stream of his cum began to roll out of her hot chasm. Moments later, he had a few wet wipes in hand and was cleaning her up, then himself. He sat back, his chest rising and falling slowly as she put her clothes back on.

It wasn't long before he was helping her out of the truck while she attempted to fix her hair by looking at her reflection in his window, and running her fingers through her tresses.

"You want me to follow you home tonight after work? I know I'm supposed to stop by afterwards, but I can leave the club early and—"

"No. I've got this under control, baby. Dolly and—"

"Parton... yes, I know." He chuckled as he reached down and zipped up his pants. "I like a good music concert, too. I just didn't want Dolly or Parton to have to sing alone."

"Oh, don't you worry about that, baby. I can carry a tune, too. In fact, it can be a trio."

"As impressive as you are with some heat, it could never be a trio because you only have two hands."

"Oh, it's always a trio when I have my girls with me, honey. I can fight. I can bite. I'm handy with a knife and can turn almost anything around me into a weapon. That rain did more than just soak me the night I was attacked. It prepared me for the future. Hard knock life. *You* are part of my future, Len." She placed a sweet kiss against his lips, and he rocked her in his arms, squeezing her tight. "A *big* part of it. I'm not allowing a damn thing to come between us. Can't nothin' make me walk away from you unless you do me dirty."

"We've waited too long to be together, been through too much to get where we are, so that definitely won't be happening."

She nodded in agreement.

"If Grandpa Wilde wants to watch me from a distance, Lennox, then I plan to put on a show that he can see up close and personal. I'm the wrong one to sneak a peek at, because Nadia and Velvet ain't free. *All* mothafuckas, except my man, gotta pay. I take payment in cash, credit, or blood, and you best believe I'll be paid in full…"

CHAPTER TWENTY-ONE

The Final Dance of the Jezebel

...Later that evening

NADIA STOOD IN a black and silver see-through bra with red lace trim and matching G-string with diamonds around the waist. Thigh high black leather boots gripped her legs like a vise. She paced around her small dressing room that smelled of roses from over a dozen farewell bouquets as music thumped from the walls and vibrated her soul. 'Demons,' by Doja Cat. She sat down for a moment and reapplied her matte dark red lipstick. This moment in time was bittersweet. Like chocolate with a touch of lemon. It would be her last time on that stage...

She glanced in the direction of her closed dressing room door. The curtain drawn taut. Her name was written on the wall in bright pink nail polish, along with the names of a host of other girls that had come and gone before her. Twirling a strand of her cherry-scented hair, she fell softly into a daydream.

No more pounding, sexy music. No more dizzying flashing lights. No more gyrating for a crowd full of sexually crazed men who have money to spend and fantasies to unfold.

But it was time. Time to dig up the pain and heal. Time to bury the hatchet. Time to forgive Daddy and create her own sense of closure. Time to show Mama how to love and forgive her for not loving her in the way she and her brother needed. Time to absolve herself of her bad decisions. Time to get revenge when warranted, and have no regrets. Time to allow love into her life—and she did. Love's name was Lennox…

She went over the conversation she'd had with her man before coming into work and read the writing on the wall— only it wasn't written in lipstick or fingernail polish. It was written in the smolder of gun smoke. She was no fool.

Nadia reached for a glass of sparkling water with a wedge of lime floating atop it, and took a meager sip.

Mothafucka thinks he's slick. Lennox wanted to double check that I could defend myself and wasn't just talkin' shit. See it with his own eyes.

In fact, as soon as she drove into that parking lot, she knew the fuckery was about to commence, and that Lennox was burdened with a doozy. Once he told her the reality of the situation, she refused to admit to him that she was a little unsettled by the prospect of this powerful, ruthless White man who used guerilla and gangster type tactics to get his way, and stay in power. She tried with all of her might to exhibit a brave face, but she wrestled with the information. A knot formed in her gut.

If Lennox is the good guy, as violent and crazed as he could be, what would that make Grandpa Wilde? Life is lifing…

She shook the thoughts out of her head and came back into the moment when she heard a new song begin: 'Enough,' by Cardi B. She got to her feet, shook imaginary dust off her shoulders, and made her way out of her dressing room to get blinded by blue and purple spinning lights. To her left she saw someone practically hugging the wall. She turned and met eyes with 'Lady Lick', AKA, Lydia, one of the young women she'd taken under her wing. Lydia stood there in a bedazzled navy-blue leotard with the tits and crotch cut out, her long black curly hair clipped up in the back, and beads of perspiration and glitter covering her shoulders and breasts.

"Oh, Lydia." She took the woman into her arms once she caught her lower lip quivering and tears welling in her eyes. "Don't cry, girl." She smiled into her hair, stroking her. "Stop. You're gonna make me cry, too."

"I'mma miss you, Nadia."

"I'm going to miss you too, baby." She pulled away and looked into deep set, dark brown eyes.

"You've been so nice to me. You were the only one that talked to me when I first got here."

"I told you they did you like that because some of these hoes saw you as competition." She pointed in the direction of the stage. "Your face is gorgeous, your body is bangin', you can dance your ass off, you don't need no BBL, and you're smart, girl. Those things together make you a threat. You betta believe it."

Lydia had lost her mother at an early age, and had been raised by her grandmother in a house full of boys. As such, she'd experienced hardly any discipline and had to learn to fight. A budding flower in a garden of broken sprinklers. She ran the streets, looking for love in all the wrong places.

"Thank you for always keepin' it real with me, but being nice about it, too."

"Don't nobody lose no sleep over someone they can beat with their eyes closed. I can keep it all the way funky without bein' a bitch, if I choose to. At the end of the day, we all gotta answer for the shit that we do. I ain't your mama, but I know I was supposed to step in where she couldn't. God rest her soul. It's time for you to leave the nest. Now you take heed regarding what I told you a long time ago, okay?"

She placed her hand on the young lady's shoulder. Lydia nodded and wiped at her tear-streaked face.

"I will, Nadia."

"You go on and follow your dreams. You still want to be a medical esthetician, right?"

"Yes, I do."

"Then I better see you do it. I want to be right there when you graduate. This is a steppin' stone, Lydia. Never forever-land. There's nothing wrong with dancing, but for women like you and me, it's supposed to be temporary. Never make this place yo' home. Out there ain't good for you, 'cause it ain't real." She pointed towards the platform from behind the curtain. "Nothin' we do in this place changes the world on a big-scale basis, but this place changes *our* world forever. Keep the mission in mind. What is it? Say it back to me. E.L.B."

"To entertain, line our pockets, then bounce."

354

"You're damn right. You get yo' money up and put deposits down. Watch the weed and the alcohol, and never do any hard drugs. A little wine goes a long way, don't overdo it. I used to smoke cigarettes for a few years, then I started with the e-cigarettes, but now I do that, like, once every week or so. I'm not addicted, and that's important. Watch your vices. It'll do you in if you use it for a crutch. It'll make you too comfortable and allow you to run from your feelings, rather than face them."

"I gotta lotta bad feelings about stuff, but I'm getting better."

Nadia leaned forward and kissed her cheek. "Honey, bad feelings never go away. They just take naps, baby. Then they wake up refreshed and stronger than ever, ready to do us in when we least expect it. Best to deal with it instead of runnin' away. Hell, I don't have it all figured out, but I at least have a plan, and I'm trying. You don't have to be perfect. You just have to try to do a little bit better, day by day."

"You give the best advice." Lydia offered a sad smile. "You're my favorite therapist," she joked.

"I'm not a therapist, but I know a little something-something because I've lived it. Now, here's the last thing I'm going to say to you about this, girl. Give yourself a firm deadline on this here vocation. When that deadline comes up, you stick to it, no matter what, and don't you look back. When the milk is expired, don't keep chuggin'. You hear me, girl?"

"Yes ma'am!" The woman sniffed before thrusting herself back into her arms.

"Don't let me find out your ass is still here, Lydia, or any club for that matter, two years from now."

"I won't be here. I promise."

Nadia blinked back tears as she held her in her arms. "Now, you've got my number. Call me anytime." They embraced tightly, and she patted her crown as she rested her chin atop the young woman's head. She reluctantly broke free, and then faced the closed black velvet curtain. The odors of dense smoke and perfume surrounded her as her heart fluttered. She nodded to one of the bodyguards, letting him know she was ready.

Moments later, Megan Thee Stallion's, 'BOA' began to play. Nadia went to move, but was halted when a swarm of some of the other ladies wrapped their arms around her and hugged her.

The words, "...and now, comin' to the stage, for the final curtain call, is blaaaaaack and beautiful, Veeeeeelvet!' were yelled out from the DJ.

"BITCH, YO' TIME UP!" she yelled as she burst onto the stage, full of energy and charged with passion. She descended towards the middle of the stage, squatted down low, and rocked her hips from left to right as she mouthed the words to the melody. The tune blended into 'KEHLANI,' by Jordan Adetunji. She slowed down as she got to her feet and made her way to the shiny silver pole adorned with lights at the very top and bottom.

She jumped on the pole and twisted her body around it. Faster and faster she went until she was all the way at the top. The crowd of men broke out in whistles and applause as she worked her way back down like a snake, her tongue flicking in and out, and a look of dangerous seduction on her face. Once she hit the floor, she danced, bucked, spun, and gyrated with all of her might.

Her long clear nails wrapped around the pole as she spun around on it upside down, driving the crowd crazy. While she worked it, she removed her top and tossed it on the floor. Her full breasts sparkled from all the perfume oil and glitter she'd applied, bouncing with each maneuver. She made her way to the front of the stage, taking in the usual suspects who showered her with ten, twenty, fifty, and hundred dollar bills, sending her off in style.

As she moved her hips and bent down, she looked between her legs and noticed one man who seemed out of place. And then another, a few feet behind him. The two men didn't favor nor look familiar, but they had a similar vibe...

She replayed Lennox's words in her mind.

She kept dancing, her eye on the tall, thin White guy with a dark baseball cap. A dude who'd never been there. The other guy was wearing a button-down shirt and jeans—he also looked way out of place. He stood in the back looking about, as if he'd lost a friend in the crowd.

White guys were not the norm in this club, but they did show up from time to time. They were either older gentlemen—big ballers who had a penchant for Black, Asian, and Latina pussy, and often had a wife with these attributes back home. Or they could be curious freaks trying to get their dicks wet from some dark meat in a secret fantasy, then go to church the next morning with their White families to sing church hymns and talk shit about 'the ghetto Black folk' ruining the country.

These guys though did not fit those descriptions. Something about the one closest to the stage smelled off…

She could see his bright, steely blue eyes reflecting like a cat's in some dark alley, and didn't miss the bulge in his right pocket. A boiling rage burned inside of her and spread to her heart, making it thump loud and hard. She spun around and around, shimmying and shaking as A Boogie Wit da Hoodie's 'Body,' featuring Cash Cobain, blasted through the speakers.

A few big spenders approached, their fingers adorned with mammoth diamond and emerald rings, and shoved crisp money in her G-string, administering rugged caresses on her legs. Deep voices close to her ear yelled nasty shit over the music. Some though uttered kind farewells.

"Take care, baby girl! Do this last dance for big daddy!"

"Velvet, you got my heart. On soul! Ride out, queen!"

"You da baddest bitch, baby!"

"I wish I coulda fucked yo' pretty ass. I been tryin' for months! It's too late now, but I'mma send you out in style!"

The song began to fade, and she was surrounded by dense cigar smoke, dull purple lights, and her last performance high. She stood covered in cash, drowning in dinero, her bare breasts heaving as sweat collected between her cleavage. Her adrenaline pumped as she eyed the White ninja who'd skulked to the other side of the room. Turning her attention away from him, she looked into the eyes of her patrons for the final time. The DJ walked over and handed her the microphone.

"Thank y'all for lettin' me entertain you tonight, and all

the nights before now. We've shared some moments in time, and I hope that I was at least able to brighten your evening. It's been a pleasure." The mob gushed with accolades and applause. "I'm leaving, but my gang-gang still here, givin' y'all the show of a lifetime." The eruption of feminine voices commenced with happy screams and clapping hands. "Bosses and kings, make sure y'all treat these ladies standin' behind me right," she stated breathlessly. "They work hard for the money, and they deserve every dime. These are dancers. *Real* dancers. The best of the fuckin' best. We took classes for this shit. Invested in it, so that *you* could be entertained the way you deserve to be.

"We're professionals, so show my sistas some respect in the form of a smile and an open wallet." More applause broke out from some of the ladies. "Some of y'all are real stand-up dudes. And I appreciate you, more than you know. I'm gone but I could never be forgotten. Blow the whistle! Velvet has left the building!"

With that, she tossed down the mic and raised her arm, pointing to the ceiling as men jumped to their feet, tossing more money on the stage and clapping. Some of the ladies jumped on the stage with her and grabbed the cash, handing it to her or stuffing it in her boots or G-string. The DJ came with the broom, sweeping the rest of the money in a nice, neat pile. She felt glossy kisses on her face, warm hugs and yells of excitement. The feminine energy was a beautiful thing. A beautiful vibe. A beautiful night.

After a few more hugs and teary-eyed goodbyes, she went back to her dressing room with her bags of money, and quickly disrobed. Instead of taking her attire with her, she set it aside for Lydia, jotting a quick note for her:

You're a little shorter and thinner than me, baby girl, but I bet with a bit of tailoring you can wear my outfits. Some of 'em cost hundreds of dollars. I am leaving them to you. She decided to keep the one she wore this evening for herself. Sentimental reasons. *They are dry cleaned and ready for you, with the exception of the one I had on tonight. I will text you my locker combination inside of my changing room so you can get them out. I want you to enjoy them and earn even more money than I did. I don't need them anymore and soon, you won't either. Pay it forward when the time comes.*

The pulsing music soared through her veins, and her heart was still thumping. She had a sudden urge to vanish, to get out of there, and yet, she was torn. She was missing the place already, and that surprised the hell out of her. Perhaps the reason was because this had to be one of the classier joints she'd ever worked at, and it was where she'd made the most money throughout her entire dancing career.

Standing, she seized her money and locked it away. She grabbed her bath gel, towel and washcloth, as well as her jeans, purse, underwear, shirt and a few odds and ends and stuffed them all in a grocery sack, and made her way out of the dressing room when she was certain that most of the ladies were either dancing, working the floor or VIP room. She walked naked with only her slippers on as she often did, down the back hallway which resembled the posterior of a theatre with scaffolding, large lights, wires, and all, and laughed when one of the few ladies around, Sunshine, a white dancer who loved Black men, Black culture, and jet-black hair, slapped her bare ass and wished her good luck.

There were three open shower stalls in the back area and she quickly secured one, making fast work to scrub and clean all of the bad memories away. All the glitter and the gold disappeared down the drain. The water hid her happy and sad tears that trailed her face. The water hid her pain, but highlighted her rebirth. It, too, was a type of rain.

She heard a bit of muted noise, a ruckus, yelling and arguing of some sort. She couldn't make out any of the words, but this happened from time to time. Guys getting into it for whatever reason. Alcohol and pussy had a way of making men turn manic. She rinsed her hair and body, blinking to remove a bit of soap from her eyes. It proved to be rather stubborn. She kept working her eye with her finger, and in between rubs, she spotted a blurred, tall, shadowy figure some distance away.

Her heart thundered and a biliousness filled her belly, but she kept running the cloth against her skin, pretending to be oblivious. Then, the footsteps ensued, slow and leisurely, towards her open shower stall. She kept right on going over her skin with the cloth. Around and around. In circles. Slick with water. The rain was coming…

Her hearing and sense of smell became acute as she pressed her eyes shut—the man was so close that she could smell his cologne, a classic scent she couldn't quite name. She could hear his breathing over the music of the next dancer doing her thing on stage. After keeping her back to him for a second or two longer, she spun around, her burning eyes wide open, her body going hot in a flash.

She held the sopping wet cloth against her stomach with

a firm grip as her gaze landed on the resolute sapphire eyes of a demon covered in white flesh. The sinewy man in the ball cap. His eyes darkened, and his mouth bent in a slanted smile. His clean-shaven face exposed a small scar along his chin. His long neck constricted with a tight swallow, like a snake finishing the final taste of his meal.

"Well hello, Nadia." He leaned leisurely against the side of the stall, his long fingers dangling close to her. "I hope I said your name right. Wouldn't want to start off on the wrong foot." His eyes scanned her real slow. "I can see why my big cousin is so fuckin' smitten with you."

Her lips parted as she looked towards the open doorway.

"You don't want to do that. You keep quiet, like a good girl." He placed his finger to his lips. Her chest heaved, and the invisible rain seemed to be falling down harder on her head now. "If you scream, bitch, then I'll have to quiet you forever. I'd hate that for Lennox, since he likes to fuck you so much." He flashed that bump resting against his hip. A revolver.

"Who the hell are you?"

"My name is of no concern to you. All you need to know is that I mean you no harm, sweetheart," he said in a sing-song voice. "I come in peace. Just here to discuss a little somethin' is all. It won't take long. Unless you *want* it to…" The motherfucker looked her up and down once again, but this time, licked his lips as if waiting for a steak on a grill.

"Ain't shit we got to discuss."

"Well, my grandaddy thinks otherwise." His eyes landed

on her breasts, then traveled down to the dark, wet thatch of hair between her legs. She noted his nature rising from beneath his pants, which made her queasy.

"What do you want?"

"Well, I'm glad you asked. You are entangled with some property that belongs to my grandfather. It's private property, and you're tresspassin'. But instead of dragging you away by your hair, Grandpa wants to offer you a parting gift instead. The best part is that you can select between two presents. Your choice."

"Parting gifts?" She stood a bit taller, her eyes never leaving him.

"You can receive three hundred thousand dollars, cold cash, to cut Lennox Wilde loose, and all of your college tuition paid in full, school girl, but the catch is, you must tell Lennox *why*, right in front of me." He waved his phone. "And you must never, under *any* circumstances, call or contact him again after you say your farewell."

"And the second option?"

"Or, you can go down in flames with him." He shrugged.

"What about Lennox? What happens to him?"

"Lennox either does what Grandaddy says, or he faces some pretty grisly consequences. Prison. His dead mama's domestic dishonor. Maybe lose a limb or two. That wouldn't bode well for his aspirations of ownin' a gym and all. Not too many folks looking for a one-legged and one-armed personal trainer. Simple as that."

"And what specifically will happen to me if I don't want this little partin' gift?"

"I'll be frank with you. If you don't take this offer, Grandaddy may not kill you, sweetheart—he's kind of funny about knockin' off women unless it's a last resort—but by the time he's done with you, you'll wish you *were* dead. Death would be appreciated. The choice is yours."

Letting go of the washcloth, it hit the tiled shower floor in a wet thud. As soon as he looked down at it, his life was in the balance. In a split second she had Parton kissing the fucker's temple. His smirk vanished quicker than a blink of an eye.

Teeth gritted, she leaned in close to him. "You lousy ass son of a bitch... you *knew* not to approach me in that dressin' room, didn't you? Because y'all been spying on me and *know* I stay strapped. I been standin' on business before I could walk, mothafucka. You figured you had a golden opportunity to take me on right here in this shower. In my birthday suit. Probably even called your grandaddy to get the green light—couldn't believe your luck! I can hear y'all talking now, *'Where the fuck she gonna keep a gun? Up her ass?'* That's what you thought, ain't it?!" She cackled as she clicked the gun, pressing it hard against his skull.

"Now hold on, hold on!" He stumbled over his words as he waved his hands. "I'm just the messenger, okay? I'm just—"

"Don't you move a mothafuckin' muscle! I see you tryna go for that hip. You let me see that heat on you for a reason. Now it's *my* turn!"

"Sweetheart, I—"

"Shut tha fuck up! Talkin' about you come here in peace, but you about to leave here in pieces! I wrapped my gun up in that rag because *somethin'* just didn't feel right. You a flunky! An old ass evil demon's errand boy! Can't think for yourself... too afraid to be your own man, unlike your cousin Lennox. Out here takin' care of the devil's work! He'll use you up, then chew you to mush, and spit yo' silly ass out. You gotta be at least seven or eight years younger than me... talkin' to me like I'm your fuckin' child. Lost yo' damn mind."

"I promise you that I—"

"DIDN'T I TELL YOU TO SHUT THE FUCK UP?! You good at following orders. Do what you do best! I could scream right now and have three big black mothafuckas and one Latin fuckin' King gang member up in here in less than thirty seconds! All of 'em are highly trained security, they'll come in here and turn you every which way but loose! Pull yo' damn skeleton out yo' body in one yank, then mail it to yo' grandfather in a box, with a note that reads, *'HERE'S A BONE TO PICK!'* I know what you did, little boy. I heard that scuffle out there..." The man's eyes, full of fear, darted in the direction of the door. "Y'all shoulda known better. Lennox don't want no shrinkin' violet. He loves a thug just like himself... now ya know! Your friend that you dragged in withcha must've caused a distraction and forced security to act on the main floor. He started a commotion, sidetracking everyone. That was a cute little plan, but it wasn't foolproof.

"Now, here's what you're going to do. You go on back to 'Kiss Grandaddy's Ass Ranch,' and you tell that dried up, miserable, rhinestone cowboy hat-wearin' evil mothafuckin' prune juice drinkin', raisin in the sun that he got the *wrong* one this time. He thought Lennox's mama was a handful? He ain't seen *nothin'* yet… SHAKE! SHAAAAKE!" she hollered at the top of her lungs for one of the members of security. Within seconds, a loud stomping ensued.

The White man looked like he was about to piss himself now. She found it downright comical.

It wasn't long before a large, broad-shouldered, bald-headed russet-colored man approached them, jogging briskly. Shake lobbed his gaze between her and the stranger, clearly confused for half a second, then grabbed his pistol and pointed it at the bastard, too, his lips drooping like brown candle wax. She lowered her arm, resting her gun at her side, and took a deep breath.

"What's goin' on, baby girl?" Poured a low, raspy voice.

"Shake, this mothafucka got lost on his way outta here. Sure he meant no harm. Happens to the best of us. Why don't you make like Dora, and help him explore the outside?"

"You bet, Velvet."

The man stiffened as Shake snatched him by the back of his shirt and patted him down, quickly removing the revolver from his hip and slipping it into his own pocket. She turned her back and heard nothing but the young man screaming and pleading for his damn life as he was dragged away from the bathing area.

Shivering, Nadia leaned against the shower stall and closed her eyes. The red rage within her turned thick, coal black. Lennox was the best thing that had happened to her in a long while, and she wasn't sad that he was going through this. She wasn't depressed that their love was threatened. No, she was pissed.

She slowly opened her eyes back up and bit her lower lip.

Payback was something she wanted. Revenge was something she needed. Vengeance was something she was going to have. And that was a promise.

We 'bout to kill two birds with one stone, old man. I know Lennox's plan for you, he told me, and now, I'm about to add another layer to it. One thing about me that must be understood: I've been traumatized my whole damn life, and now I'm using it as a weapon, instead of an excuse.

I got that way out of survival, and you best believe, I'm the fittest. I'm no longer drowning and feelin' sorry for myself in the rain, sir. I'm my Nana's first granddaughter, and JoAnn's child, through and through! I'm on the warpath, front and center! I come from queens of the Nile and rulers of the night! Ain't not ONE weak bitch in my family tree, mothafucka! You better believe me when I tell you. We are fighters! I AM the storm clouds, the thunder, and the gotdamn lightning! God told me don't fear the rain no more, child! I built you an arc! And on that arc are my warrior ancestors, my man, and my mama and her mama, too! You can't take me down low, old man, when I've already been to hell 'nd back. A hurricane is comin' yo way, Grandpa Wilde, and ain't a life jacket, the American Cross, or a prayer from Pope Francis himself going to save you from this tempest called Nadia. ON SOUL!

This concludes <u>Part 1 of Book 1 of "The Top Dog</u>," from the Seven Deadly Kins Series. <u>Book 2, "The Top Dog – Part 2</u>," which features the conclusion of this double novel, is available **RIGHT NOW**. There is no cliffhanger! Both books were released on the same day for your reading pleasure. See you soon!

ABOUT THE AUTHOR

USA Today bestselling author Tiana Laveen writes resilient yet loving heroines and the alpha heroes that fall for them in unlikely happily-ever-afters. An author of over 80 novels to date, Tiana creates characters from all walks of life that leap straight from the pages into your heart.

Married with two children, she enjoys a fulfilling life that includes writing books, drawing, and spending quality time with loved ones.

If you wish to stay up-to-date with her releases, please join her newsletter: www.tianalaveen.com/newsletter

Follow her on social media platforms, as well as visit her website.

Tiana Laveen website:

www.tianalaveen.com